THE
SELECTED
POETRY
AND
PROSE
OF
WORDSWORTH

Steve Maguire 1997

THE SELECTED POETRY AND PROSE OF WORDSWORTH

EDITED AND WITH AN INTRODUCTION BY
GEOFFREY H. HARTMAN

A MERIDIAN BOOK

NEW AMERICAN LIBRARY

TIMES MIRROR

NEW YORK, LONDON AND SCARBOROUGH, ONTARIO

Acknowledgements

Selections from THE POETICAL WORKS OF WILLIAM WORDSWORTH, ed. Ernest
de Selincourt and Helen Darbishire 1940-49, and from THE LETTERS OF WILLIAM
AND DOROTHY WORDSWORTH, ed. Ernest de Selincourt, 2nd ed. revised by Chester
L. Shaver 1967, are reprinted by permission of the Clarendon Press, Oxford.
"*The Ruined Cottage*" is reprinted from THE MUSIC OF HUMANITY by Jona-
than Wordsworth, copyright © 1969 by Jonathan Wordsworth, by permission of
Harper & Row, Publishers, Inc., and A. D. Peters & Co.
"*The Pedlar*" is reprinted from MS D of THE EXCURSION by permission of
the Trustees of Dove Cottage, Grasmere.

The Selected Poetry and Prose of Wordsworth
was originally published in the Signet Classics Poetry
Series, under the general editorship of poet,
lecturer, and teacher John Hollander.

Library of Congress Catalog Card Number: 80-80244

SIGNET, SIGNET CLASSICS, MENTOR, PLUME, MERIDIAN and NAL BOOKS
are published *in the United States* by The New American Library, Inc.,
1633 Broadway, New York, New York 10019, *in Canada* by The New American
Library of Canada Limited, 81 Mack Avenue, Scarborough, Ontario M1L 1M8,
in the United Kingdom by The New English Library Limited,
Barnard's Inn, Holborn, London, EC1N 2JR, England.

First Meridian Printing, March, 1980

1 2 3 4 5 6 7 8 9

PRINTED IN THE UNITED STATES OF AMERICA

THE
SELECTED
POETRY
AND
PROSE
OF
WORDSWORTH

Contents

Introduction

When Wordsworth was fourteen, the ordinary sight of boughs silhouetted against a bright evening sky left so vivid an impression on his mind that it marked the beginning of his career as poet. "I recollect distinctly," he writes as a man in his seventies, "the very spot where this first struck me. It was in the way between Hawkshead and Ambleside, and gave me extreme pleasure. The moment was important in my poetical history for I date from it my consciousness of the infinite variety of natural appearances which had been unnoticed by the poets of any age or country." Such nature-consciousness, joined to an answering self-consciousness, is the "incumbent mystery" from which Wordsworth's poetry springs. He begins with the weight of sense-experience through which, as two of his characteristic metaphors put it, the "foundations" of the mind are laid, or the soul is "seeded" by feelings and images capable of sustaining it throughout life. There is no vision in his poetry that is not a vision of natural appearances pressing upon child or adult in this way. Nature—for Wordsworth chiefly rural nature, the abiding presences of mountain, lake, and field under the influence of the changing seasons—is a haunted house through which we must pass before our spirit can be independent. Those separated too soon from this troubling and sensuous contact with Nature—the strongest passages in Wordsworth's autobiographical poem, *The Prelude,* are devoted to Nature's ministry of fear rather than her ministry of beauty—may grow up with an empty, if powerful, sense of self. They have skipped a necessary stage of development; and without a filial relation to Nature, to that animate earth and heaven which plays so crucial a role in ancient myth, they become unimaginative or require increasingly personal and violent stimuli. "The sun strengthens us no more, neither does the moon" (D. H. Lawrence). The result is that revolutionary or self-alienating, rather than creative, personality in which Wordsworth saw the great temptation of his epoch, and to which he himself almost succumbed. His poetry, with its emphasis on "the infinite variety of natural appearances" and on the way the simplest event can enrich mind, sets itself against "gross and violent stimulants" in the realm of the senses or of public action.

If Wordsworth seems prophetic in his concern with the revolutionary mentality, and with our alienation from Nature, it is because he lived at the beginning of our epoch. A country boy, born and raised in the English Lake District, he found himself at nineteen years of age in the midst of two great upheavals, the Industrial Revolution and the French Revolution. Between 1790, his first visit to France and the Alps on a walking tour (on partial truancy from his studies at Cambridge, which was little more than an "inter-world" to him), and 1800, when he settled down for good in the Lake District, Wordsworth lived these events as eyewitness and participant. He lived the French Revolution, in particular, so strongly that it shook his identity as poet and Englishman. He passed through the crisis, however; and the poems that ensued, of which *Lyrical Ballads* was the first collection (1798; second edition, expanded by a new volume, 1800), are not naive nature lyrics but expressive of a mind that had returned to health after long sickness. While the response of Wordsworth's contemporaries was less than enthusiastic, later generations were struck by the prophetic and representative character of these poems. John Stuart Mill and Matthew Arnold felt that Wordsworth's sickness, or crisis, was also theirs; and they wished for his kind of strength in overcoming it. How much agony lay behind that strength was not revealed till *The Prelude* was published in 1850, the year of the poet's death.

The Industrial Revolution was, of course, only in its beginning in the 1780's and 1790's. A "lyrical ballad" has little in common with a ballad of protest like Thomas Hood's "Song of the Shirt." At first sight it appears to be

as removed from politics as Jane Austen's novels. Words-
worth could still harbor the wish of treating the disease
itself, as well as its symptoms. He diagnosed the disease
as a disturbed relation between man and his environment.
The pressures of city life were divorcing man's imagina-
tion from an organic connection to the earth even more
than poverty had done, or supernaturalistic religion. His
preface to the 1800 *Lyrical Ballads* notes a "craving
for extraordinary excitement" created by the accelerating
rhythm of modern history and by "deluges of idle and
extravagant stories in verse." To offset this tendency he
shows us men of an older and different order, touched by
the new events yet un-uprootable, like oak and rock. The
shepherd's strength of mind, in "Michael," belongs to
nature as much as to mind: it is as "indestructible" as the
"great and permanent objects that act upon it." Words-
worth knows, of course, that rural people like Michael are
types rather than ideals: he is not proposing we become
them. But through them he depicts qualities of mind that
must be carried over into modern life, and he questions
whether they can be fostered in an industrialized society.
Lyrical Ballads, though not literature of protest, is engaged
with the problems of its time: it is a reflective, not a naive,
poetry, and draws its sustenance consciously from "the
common sights of mother earth." It remains in touch with
native ground, like the English ballads edited by Bishop
Percy in the 1760's, but relies on ordinary, rather than
extraordinary, incidents.

It was, however, the French Revolution that impinged
decisively on Wordsworth's life. Wordsworth took a second
trip to France in 1791 and stayed till obliged to return to
England at the end of 1792. He spent his time in Paris,
Blois, and Orleans; and he became increasingly involved
in revolutionary circles. There was also some private tur-
moil: an affair with a French girl, Annette Vallon, which
resulted in the birth of a daughter. (This is not revealed
in *The Prelude* but was brought to light by dramatic schol-
arly sleuthing in 1916.) Yet his own inner life did not suffer
a crisis until England formally went to war against France
in 1793.

Wordsworth had considered the French Revolution an extension of British ideals of liberty and democracy. The war against France struck him, therefore, as unforgivable, a betrayal of England as well as France. No less than three times does he return in *The Prelude* to the shock he suffered in 1793. Betrayed by their own country, the whole of the younger generation seemed threatened with a deadly skepticism vis-à-vis national ideals. The deteriorating course of the Revolution itself (not only the massacre of the Girondists but also increasing French aggressiveness, which led to the Napoleonic Wars) then confirmed the young poet's conviction that the individual had henceforth to act alone. Social liberty, as he put it, had to be built on personal liberty. Without guidance except his will and individual reason, he saw himself as a man without a past, thrown entirely upon himself in the pursuit of the millennial future of which he still dreamed.

What Wordsworth suffered so acutely may lie in the destiny of all men: a betrayal into autonomy, into self-dependence. That is the story wherever the tragic sense of life is strong: in *Oedipus Rex,* in *King Lear,* in Albee's *Who's Afraid of Virginia Woolf?,* and in Wordsworth's own drama, *The Borderers* (1796–1797). The wound inflicted is that of self-consciousness: "And they knew that they were naked." It is significant, however, that in Wordsworth's case the wound seemed to be caused by political events, and that since the time of the American Revolution it is *patricide* (murder of one's father*land*) as much as *parricide* which is the great trouble in the modern consciousness. On the part of the individual there is a sense that his country has betrayed him by crushing a war of liberation which its own founding principles inspired; and on the part of society there is a fear of the alienated intellectual who is considered a potential enemy from within.

Wordsworth's inner turmoil lasted at least till 1795, the year in which he met several times with the social philosopher William Godwin. *The Prelude* does not mention Godwin by name, and it is difficult to say what part his theories of reform may have played in a mind "sick, wearied out with contrarieties" (*Prelude* XI. 304). But we do know what brought Wordsworth to his "last and lowest ebb." It was his trust in the naked individual reason which Godwin's theories may have abetted. His loss of faith in England, that "ancient tower" on which he was "fast rooted," had meant abandoning his vocation of poet— giving England up was tantamount to giving his past up, to cutting off "all the sources of my former strength." In this state of spiritual poverty nothing but "Reason's naked self" remained. But reason, Blake's "idiot questioner," questioning everything and resolving nothing, finally began to question itself.

This proved to be the turning point of the crisis. The poet saw that reason was merely another kind of passion. It was an "idealistic" disorder all the more dangerous for claiming to be above disorder. Like Nietzsche, Ibsen, and many nineteenth-century thinkers, he understood that the obsession with analysis was a modern kind of fanaticism, insidiously solipsistic under the guise of promoting social reformation. Once reason was unmasked, the way was open for other influences to reassert themselves. Wordsworth decided he could not ignore the past just because its action on him was mainly unconscious. His relation to childhood and country (a very concrete relation, as *The Prelude* would show) might not be denied any more than syllogistic reasonings might "unsoul" the "mysteries of being." He returned consciously and devotedly to Nature—to rediscovering his roots.

Wordsworth's recovery is therefore a rediscovery of inner continuities. A personal sense of destiny is reestablished, and the past reintegrated in the stream of life. He returns to "sweet counsels between head and heart," and mends all kinds of dualisms. The famous "spots of time"— early experiences that, like Proust's involuntary memories, unexpectedly affect a present moment—reveal that we are less isolated than we think. We live in a large and beneficent sphere of influences. This sphere did not open itself to the poet at once: the period of recovery stretches from his return to the English countryside in 1794 to his stay in Germany in the winter of 1798–1799. But chronology is not helpful here, and *The Prelude* avoids it: while there was one intense period of crisis there seems to have been no one intense recovery, but rather a widening consciousness of the mind's power to renew itself, and of Nature's role in this. The poems written between 1797 and 1807 reflect the triumph of an outgoing sensibility over a brooding, self-centered mind: often they are that triumph itself.

It was, indeed, a whole sphere of influences rather than one event which restored Wordsworth. There was Dorothy, his sister, reunited with him in 1794, who maintained for him, even in the depth of his dejection, "a saving intercourse with my true self." There was, too, Coleridge's almost daily company at Alfoxden, where the *Lyrical Ballads* were planned as a joint venture. And Coleridge undoubtedly brought with him certain philosophical comforts. We know the two poets talked about Spinoza, for whom every true increase of intellectual power produced not only more intellect but more love; and there was Associationism, which had played so important a role in English empirical philosophy, and which Wordsworth used in his own way. He accepts the principle that ideas get attached to ideas, and people to places, by force of association, but denies that we can, through any sort of rational or methodical procedure, reform human nature by fostering true rather than false habits of mind. The associations that matter are too deeply and variously planted in us to be influenced by logic. In this Wordsworth is "necessitarian": he insists that the origins of our development lie beyond rememberable time, and that the process of maturation which *The Prelude* traces (its subtitle is "The Growth of a Poet's Mind") is significantly open to chance and accident. A child who had held "unconscious intercourse with beauty / Old as creation" cannot be pressed into a priori educational schemes. Wordsworth's optimism concerning a person's strength to renew himself is based on his belief in this generous multiplicity of developmental influences. His *credo* is that integration—or reintegration—will triumph. In fragments of poetry associated with "The Ruined Cottage" (c. 1797), his greatest verse-story about human hopes and their defeat, Wordsworth foresees a strengthening of the heart's contact with natural influences:

All things shall live in us and we shall live
In all things that surround us. This I deem
Our tendency, and thus shall every day
Enlarge our sphere of pleasure and of pain.

The idea of such a tendency, and even of a providential "compact" between imagination and the things of this world, is strengthened in Wordsworth by Edmund Burke's view of the social principle as a "great primeval contract . . . connecting the visible and invisible world"—a view which stresses political continuity and which the younger Wordsworth had explicitly denounced in his "Letter to Bishop Landaff" (1793).

I have spoken of a *credo,* and *Lyrical Ballads* had at least this in common with a new religion, that it proved to be a stumbling block for its generation. It was not, as recent scholarship has shown, Wordsworth's humble subject matter that caused the trouble. The magazines of the time (equivalents of our *Ladies' Home Journal* and *Saturday Evening Post*) were full of Christian sentiment about Crazy Kate or the fate of the common soldier or the starving robin. They were true to their age, the age of sensibility, and reflected the taste of a growing class of bourgeois readers. What mostly scandalized the latter were Wordsworth's strange moods of exaltation: the way he inflated a trite or private happening as if it contained a truth never before perceived. He sinned against that ironclad law of literary and social decorum which limited the poet's role to putting before his public "What e'er was thought, but ne'er so well express'd." For, in Wordsworth, the novelty seemed to lie in the quality of thought rather than the quality of its expression. The expression, indeed, was obviously flat; and whereas in the ordinary run of magazine verse the manner helped to raise the matter, here was a poet who overtly disdained this yeasty virtue of style.

Anna Seward, a not unintelligent bluestocking, failed to restrain her "disgust" on reading that now harmless anthology piece on the daffodils, "I wandered lonely as a cloud." She berates Wordsworth as an "egotistic manufacturer of metaphysic importance on trivial themes." Even Coleridge accused him of "thoughts and images too great for the subject." Keats too would be disturbed by the

"egotistical sublime" in Wordsworth. We cannot dismiss
contemporary opinion out of hand, or reduce its relevance
to that part of his poetry in which an inflated common-
place expressed in a deflated style yielded a bathos easy
to parody:

> Behind a cloud his mystic sense,
> Deep hidden, who can spy?
> Bright as the night, when not a star
> Is shining in the sky.
> —Hartley Coleridge

The only way to respond to the forceful criticism of Words-
worth's time is to face the question it raised: Is there any-
thing radically new in his thinking?

Let us take the idea which dominates his poetry. His
view of Nature as "the nurse, / The guide, the guardian
of my heart, and soul / Of all my moral being" helped his
recovery and inspired his greatest decade (1797–1807).
Now this return to Nature involves a return to the idea
of a cosmos: of the world and man as interdependent
powers. Each is fitted to the other; each lives the other's
life. The *credo* already quoted, and the great "Recluse"
fragment published in 1814 as part of the preface to *The
Excursion,* are direct and eloquent statements of the idea.
Yet the shadow-side of such reciprocity, a view of Nature
as parasitic, which we find in Milton's vision of Hell, or in
the third section of Shelley's *The Sensitive Plant,* and above
all in Shakespeare's darkest moments, seems hardly to
arise. The "ennobling interchange," the "mutual domina-
tion," the "blending" of which Wordsworth speaks rhap-
sodically, is based on love rather than on need: the mind
may be insatiable, but the world is inexhaustible; they are
of matching dignity and power. If his concept of Nature,
then, has little moral complexity, it has even less originality.
The concept can be attached to pantheistic as well as
Christian thought (cf. St. Paul's vision of a divine environ-
ment "in which we live and move and have our being");
in the seventeenth and eighteenth centuries, moreover, as
J. W. Beach has shown, concepts of a "sympathetic" uni-
verse remained commonplace.

Wordsworth's originality does not lie in his ideas as such.

It has to do with the way they emerge from the depth of felt experience. They are organic thoughts: we see them growing on him, we watch him struggling with his own—often unexpected—imaginings. "A shy spirit in my heart / That comes and goes / Will sometimes leap / From hiding-places ten years deep" (*The Waggoner*). A new attitude toward consciousness—a radical consciousness of consciousness—is brought to light: Wordsworth is truly a subjective thinker. He is the first to establish a vulgate for the imagination, to use words which are our words and feelings which move in a natural rather than fictionally condensed time. Today, when every poet "walks naked" (Yeats), it may be hard to appreciate the courage Wordsworth showed and the advance in sensibility he made possible. All the more so because, having cleansed the doors of perception, and made a supremer fiction possible, he drew back from releasing his imagination toward that end. His poetry may renounce too much and be too self-involved in its struggle against fictional or visionary devices. Many of his contemporaries did not value the stripped nature of his poetry, the characteristic Wordsworthian bareness: what they saw was poverty of imagination and the scandal of subjectivity.

A *subjective thinker:* the phrase comes from Kierkegaard. But what exactly does subjectivity, that much abused word, mean? Especially when qualified by "Romantic" it conjures up a world in schism: here objects, there subjects, here idiosyncrasy (calculated oddities, unpredictable sublimities), there normative behavior. This understanding of subjectivity is in error. Subjectivity means that the starting point for authentic reflection is placed in the individual consciousness. Not, necessarily, the empirical starting point, but the ontological, or what might also be called the Archimedean, point. Archimedes said he could move the world had he a point whereon to rest his machine. "Who has not felt," Wordsworth says, alluding to the story, "the same aspiration as regards the world of his own mind?" If this Archimedean point is genuinely within the personal consciousness, dualism is overcome, for the source of inspiration (the empirical starting point) can be anything and anywhere.

The expansion of sensibility characteristic of the modern period is certainly related to this free and eccentric placement of the empirical starting point. The modern mind can start ("turn on") anywhere because it has a surer homing instinct, or because it accepts what Hölderlin called *"die ekzentrische Bahn":* the necessity of passing through self-alienation to self-fulfillment. Wordsworth finds his inspiration virtually anywhere: he recalls us to the simplest incidents, to words or events that would pass us by. "Behold," he says, as in "The Solitary Reaper," "stop here, or gently pass." Gently, because we are on mysterious ground; and if we do not wish to stop and think further, we should allow the impression to develop in its time. The horizontal extension of the scope of the poet's subject matter is only an aspect of something more important: its vertical extension, its inward resonance.

There is always a reserve in the experiences Wordsworth depicts. It may suddenly develop in the poet or profoundly displace his initial thought. "The Solitary Reaper," for instance, did not fructify in him till two years after his sister had seen an analogous sight (Wordsworth often "borrowed" her eyes and ears), and it moves in an excursive yet natural arc from the girl through reflections covering past, present, and future. In "Tintern Abbey" this remarkable turning of the mind also makes us aware of the virtues of the vernacular, which Wordsworth brings back to dignity. Only the "subtle intercourse" of spoken language, its submerged metaphors, its quietly syntactic power, can really respect this expansion of the mind beyond its first impressions.

Let us sample this open and natural style, which can be so plain as to be anti-literary. In the first two books of *The Prelude* Wordsworth describes the education—mainly by natural influences—of a young boy. From the age of about five to thirteen consciousness of self is still merged with nature-consciousness, though there are intimations of real separateness, of genuine selfhood. Wordsworth recalls an incident which helped him to see nature as Nature: not only as a part of him but also as apart from him, as a presence enjoyed consciously rather than unconsciously, and so leading to firmer self-awareness:

Our steeds remounted and the summons given,
With whip and spur we through the chauntry flew
In uncouth race, and left the cross-legged knight,
And the stone-abbot, and that single wren
Which one day sang so sweetly in the nave
Of the old church, that—though from recent showers
The earth was comfortless, and, touched by faint
Internal breezes, sobbings of the place
And respirations, from the roofless walls
The shuddering ivy dripped large drops—yet still
So sweetly 'mid the gloom the invisible bird
Sang to herself, that there I could have made
My dwelling-place, and lived for ever there
To hear such music. Through the walls we flew
And down the valley, and, a circuit made
In wantonness of heart, through rough and smooth
We scampered homewards. Oh, ye rocks and streams,
And that still spirit shed from evening air!
Even in this joyous time I sometimes felt
Your presence, when with slackened step we breathed
Along the sides of the steep hills, or when
Lighted by gleams of moonlight from the sea
We beat with thundering hoofs the level sand.

(Prelude II. 115–37)

An aspect of inner life is vividly rendered here without
the artifice of a fictional or displaced perspective: without
allegory or personification or atomism. There is complete
respect for ordinary experience as well as for its extraordi-
nary potential. The theme of the episode is the emergence
of Nature as a distinct presence, and the relation of this
to the child's growing sense of "thereness"—of real, if still
uncertain, identity. Yet a dimension is added which is hard
to define because it is not purely the illustration of that
theme. During the act of recall the poet's consciousness
becomes, to adopt words of Wallace Stevens, "part of the
res, and not about it." The memory Wordsworth set out
to record yields as if spontaneously to a second memory
(ll. 118–28) continuous with the first but more inward.
The poet's initial memory still embraces it, but he is tempted
to rest with the supervening memory as with a symbol.
When he comes on that second, more internal image (on
the "single wren," deceptively enumerated along with the

cross-legged knight and stone-abbot, though lifting the whole out of historical into human time), he is forced to stop, to enter the solitude he then intuited, the "I" rather than the "we." He dwells on that event to the point of slowing the narrative movement to a halt that parallels even now (some thirty years later) a moment in the past which prepared him for selfhood.

Wordsworth's "open" style—the displacement of a first memory by a second—shows that memory is creative rather that nostalgic: still sensitive to a past that can modify and even reverse a present state of mind. What is peculiarly Wordsworthian, however, is that the displacement of which we have spoken is continuous, that the supervening memory remains within the frame of its matrix. Belated intuitions, which arise "from the structure of [the poet's] own mind . . . without immediate external excitement" (though with the incitement, as here, of a prior, internalized image) are not allowed to break but merely to extend the matrix. Analogously, looking to Wordsworth's poetry as a whole, there are no sharp breaks or ritual passings between one state of mind and another: vision is always continuous with sensation. Even such licensed rapture as Keats's "Already with thee!" is avoided.

Wordsworth's "underconsciousness" of the past, or his sense for renovative continuities, is to be understood as aiming for greater stakes than mental health. It has a millennial as well as a therapeutic dimension. Wordsworth shares the myth of progress characteristic of the eighteenth century, though radically modifying it. Like contemporary demythologizers he believed that the mind of man could be "enlightened" or progressively purified of myth and superstition. What Shakespeare or Milton did by the liberal use of visionary devices he would do by truth to nature alone. However, instead of clearly breaking with the past, he conceives progress as the individual's greater participation in that past—his repossession of imaginative energies denied by reason but only displaced by myth and fable. The latter are imperfect expressions of that "fear and awe" (and sense of beauty) which befall us when we are nature-haunted. When myth or fable interpose too early between us and experience they alienate the growing spirit from its universal patrimony of "Nature":

> How awful is the might of souls,
> And what they do within themselves while yet
> The yoke of earth is new to them, the world
> Nothing but a wild field where they were sown.
> (*Prelude* III. 180–83)

To that ground, then, which is in the form of memory or past experience only because of a false theory of nurture that dispossesses imagination while pretending to civilize it, Wordsworth returned. The imagination which has no past can have no future. It becomes blank or black, empty or apocalyptic. The episode from *Prelude* II roots us, therefore, in the past, and moves from the feeling of personal continuity to a vision of the chain of being. The immemorial nature of the earth evoked in the lines between dashes (120–24) adds itself to the historical past suggested by the ruined chapel and completes in this way the visionary resonance of one fugitive, personal event.

It was at Grasmere, a village nestling among the lakes of northern England, that Wordsworth became fully, prophetically conscious of his special role among the great English poets. He settled there with Dorothy in the winter of 1799 after his visit to Germany. Coleridge moved to the nearby village of Keswick. In 1802 the poet married Mary Hutchinson, a childhood friend; while her sister Sara, who came to live with the Wordsworths, was intended by them for the poet's brother John after he should have made his fortune as a merchant captain.

The Wordsworth household at Grasmere—the poet, three women, and Coleridge nearby—was not just a family but a utopian community: the Susquehanna scheme revived on the banks of Windermere. It does not last long: Coleridge, ill in health and disaffected from his wife, leaves for Malta in 1804 (*The Prelude* becomes an oversize verse letter to him); John Wordsworth is drowned in 1805, a shock from which the community never recovered; and there are many financial, as well as personal, worries. But those five years, from late 1799 to 1805, were essential.

We know a great deal about them through Coleridge's recently published *Notebooks* and through Dorothy's *Journals.*

When Wordsworth said of Dorothy, "She gave me eyes, she gave me ears," it was no vain compliment. In her *Journals* we read, for example, of their meeting the poor old man who became the Leech Gatherer of "Resolution and Independence" or that description of the daffodils which Wordsworth transformed into "I wandered lonely as a cloud." The members of the community exchanged feelings and observations, noted the slightest stirrings in nature and the simplest human excitements. Wordsworth's poetry becomes, even more than at Alfoxden, a "living calendar" which records the imaginative pleasures provided by the countryside, but also some contrary "fears and fancies . . . dim sadness . . . blind thoughts" ("Resolution and Independence"). These disturbances are often caused, paradoxically, by poetry itself: by the labor of composition, which could make the poet physically ill. Wordsworth had an intense consciousness of what great poetry was before him, and a constant need to reaffirm his own genius and difference. Thus the mystery of vocation kept moving to the center and made an autobiographical poem inevitable.

Composing *The Prelude* Wordsworth discovers—not abstractly, but in the very act of reflective writing—how vulnerable the ego is, but also how many chances there are for self-renewal. Aided only by the action of the mind on itself, and the small, affectionate community he has built up, he describes the corporate nature of selfhood, the interpenetration of past and present selves, and the quiet yet infinite ties between man and man, or man and nature, without which we could not exist. Conscious of these ties, and reinforcing the most elemental as well as the most subtle of them, his poetry emanates a healing power celebrated by Victorian readers and still recognized by critics of our era from Walter Raleigh to F. R. Leavis and Lionel Trilling. In the famous preface, which was written at Grasmere, to *Lyrical Ballads,* Wordsworth announces clearly that link between poetry and the sympathetic imagination which the younger Romantics (Hazlitt, Keats, and Shelley) will espouse more militantly:

What then does the Poet? He considers man and the objects
that surround him as acting and reacting upon each other, so as
to produce an infinite complexity of pain and pleasure; he con-
siders man in his own nature and in his ordinary life as con-
templating this ... as looking upon this complex scene of ideas
and sensations, and finding everywhere objects that immedi-
ately excite in him sympathies. ... He is the rock of defence
for human nature; an upholder and preserver, carrying every-
where with him relationship and love. In spite of difference of
soil and climate, of language and manners, of laws and cus-
toms; in spite of things silently gone out of mind, and things
violently destroyed; the Poet binds together by passion and
knowledge the vast empire of human society, as it spreads over
the whole earth, and over all time.

He considers man in his own nature and in his ordinary
life. Milton did not, and Shakespeare generally did not.
Only Chaucer, perhaps, comes close to being a master of
ordinary life in poetry. But Chaucer's realism is accom-
panied, and ironically blended, with romance modes of
narration. Nothing could be more realistic than his portrait
of the Wife of Bath, or the psychology of the tale she tells,
yet this tale is full of supernatural and romance motifs.
This difference between Chaucer and Wordsworth is more
than a difference between narrative and lyrical. Words-
worth teaches imagination to rejoice in itself in a new way:
what was expressed, prior to him, in the displaced though
magnanimous form of male Vision or female Romance,
is now confronted humanely and directly:

> Not Chaos, not
> The darkest pit of lowest Erebus,
> Nor aught of blinder vacancy, scooped out
> By help of dreams—can breed such fear and awe
> As fall upon us often when we look
> Into our Minds, into the Mind of Man—
> My haunt, and the main region of my song.
>
> ("Prospectus" [written circa 1800]
> to *The Excursion* [1814])

Out of this farewell to myth contemporary poetry is
born. Although the farewell proves somewhat premature
(Wallace Stevens' "Phoebus is dead, ephebe" is still part

of it), this example of a man resisting tradition in favor of imagination, then resisting his own imagination, dominates modern poetry. Rejecting all visionary aids, and all rhetorical inflation, Wordsworth had hoped for a progress of the sympathetic imagination anticipated by this change in the form of poetry: a progress that would humanize our feelings and expand them till they sympathized even with "mute, insensate things." Yet *The Excursion,* the later sonnets, and almost all poetry written after 1806 fail to show that progress. What went wrong?

There are many theories concerning Wordsworth's decline. Before we add to them it should be said that his later poetry is not uninteresting: its individual pathos, its awkward mixture of inwardness and unction give it a character of its own. Every word is faithful to the "kindred points of heaven and home," to earth and transcendent longings. He seeks, wherever he goes, the spirit of the place (made up of natural impressions plus the legendary or historical aura) to keep his imagination anchored. "Localized Romance" is his aim, a "scale of moral music" rising like Jacob's ladder from particular spots. It is hard to imagine another poet writing those heavy odes, those crammed— and cramped—sonnets with their wish to "awe the lightness of humanity." This line stems from a poem composed in 1818: put it against that famous passage from "Tintern Abbey," written twenty years before, and celebrating the "blessed mood" in which "the burthen of the mystery . . . Is lightened," and you get a sense of development as well as change.

A falling-off is painfully obvious, however. The later poetry is without genuine form of its own, a stream of prosy reminiscence in sonnet, ode, or conversation piece. Though iconic form (the masterful impositions of a Milton or a Yeats) is not everyone's forte, poetry must lead or purify ideas in some way. In Wordsworth, however, imaginative daring alternates with recantation, flight of fancy with moral fretting. Too much "counterbalancing or tempering" inhibits the sublime conceptions which still struggle to dawn. He "shades" them like a picturesque artist, and scatters his muse. At every place visited he leaves a charitable penny in the form of commemorative verse. Poetry begins to be used purely as a defensive reaction to strange sympathies and apocalyptic stirrings. He constantly betrays something in himself, and calmly writes about it: "That glimpse of glory, why renewed?" He protests the glory, and asks his imagination to let him alone. In 1827 Crabb Robinson is so alarmed at Wordsworth's change that he foresees the remark of a future critic: "This great poet survived to the fifth decade of the nineteenth century, but he appears to have died in the year 1814 [the year of *The Excursion*] as far as life consisted in an active sympathy with the temporal welfare of his fellow creatures."

If Wordsworth, as Keats recognized, bore "the burden of the mystery" more intensely than previous poets, it is not surprising that there should have been emotional exhaustion or desire for stability. But this explanation does not fit all the facts. Miss Fenwick, a confidante of the aging poet, writes of him as he approaches seventy: "How fearfully strong are all his feelings and affections! If his intellect had been less powerful they must have destroyed him long ago." The trouble is that Wordsworth never really renounced his younger self: he secretly canonized it, and much of his later poetry is written in bad faith. For it is impossible to guess the content of *The Prelude* from reading, in a typical later sonnet,

> Earth prompts—Heaven urges; let us seek the light
> Studious of that pure intercourse begun
> When our first infant brows their lustre won.
> *(Ecclesiastical Sonnets)*

The sublime or public diction to which he returns conceals the fact that he relies for the vigor of this thought on the authority of his greatest poem, which remains unpublished, and as scripture to himself undermines the necessity of reconception. Whether publishing *The Prelude* in its time would have made a difference to his later development is impossible to say, but it would have reduced the number of poems reflecting earlier insights at second or third remove. The older Wordsworth is standing on ground already beaten; the brilliant quarry has been dislodged; the hiding places will not yield more.

Wordsworth's real danger was always the "sublime"—

the public and preacherly dimension—rather than the "egotistical." He hankers increasingly after vision old-style, after the explicit prophetic dimension of a poetry like Milton's. *The Excursion,* the only long poem published in his lifetime, is, like Cowper's *The Task,* a consciously public poem. When Matthew Arnold said that in Wordsworth "philosophy is the illusion, poetry . . . the reality," he must have meant by "philosophy" Wordsworth's desire to harmonize his experience with received ideas, and particularly with the sublime philosophy of the Anglo-Catholic Church. The *Ecclesiastical Sonnets* (1822) still describe a Progress of the Mind, but it is virtually equated with the emergence of the English Church in the Reformation.

We turn back to the young Wordsworth. His vision of that Progress was not parochial but universal. *The Prelude* implies a new and original model for human development. Its realism clarifies the mystery of identity. Like Freud, Wordsworth begins at a point far removed from the humanistic axiom, "Nothing human is alien to me." On the contrary everything human is alien to us initially. The sense for the human is achieved, painfully won, not given. The quasi-mythical scheme underlying *The Prelude's* theory of development is similar to that sketched in the "Intimations Ode": we are born as aliens into a world which is at most a foster home, or substitute heaven. Our destiny, therefore, is to accept a world which is less than our hopes conceive, though great enough. Nature, with lesser glory than the mythical heaven from which the child fell, attracts our imagination until it becomes this-worldly. It sows its images in the child's mind, it blends with our imagination: the river Derwent, Wordsworth writes, "sent a voice / That flowed along my dreams." The first two books of *The Prelude* describe this naturalization of the child, its weaning from the milk of paradise, from inchoate dreams and apocalyptic stirrings. The sentimentalists who hold that for Wordsworth childhood is all could not be further from the truth. Yes, childhood is closest to divinity, but also to narcissistic self-absorption. The question is how to humanize one's soul without losing it, how to bind the child's imagination without binding it down. A man's sense of the light that was can be his greatest obstacle. Wordsworth describes some of the trials of the soul that we undergo to become civilized persons.

If Nature fails, the child's development is arrested, and he becomes either an idiot whose "life is with God," or a premature adult, doomed to cynicism or alienation. If Nature succeeds, the child is organically ready to be humanized, and humanization is the second developmental step covered by *The Prelude*. The two steps are, of course, interrelated: and the road from "love of nature" to "love of man," even though built, in Wordsworth's case, on a strong and sensuous foundation, is so precarious that its charting occupies the greater part of his secular poem. Thus *The Prelude* is a *Bildungsroman* that takes the child from solipsism to society and from his unconsciously apocalyptic mind, dreaming of an utterly different world, to a sense of realities. It is the epic of civilization, the epic of the emergence of an individual consciousness out of a field of forces that includes imagination, nature, and society. "How then are Souls to be made?" asks Keats. "How then are these sparks which are God to have identity given them—so as ever to possess a bliss peculiar to each one's individual existence? How but by the medium of a world like this?" That, after Wordsworth, is the unforgettable theme.

Wordsworth, together with Blake, is the last of a giant race of poets to whom the moderns are as indebted as the neoclassical poets to their Renaissance predecessors. Sometimes, with the pressures of contemporary life what they are, Wordsworth's poetry may seem too reflective or low-powered. Yet we rarely cease to feel the agony or urgency from which it sprang. It mediates between the modern world and a desperate imagination, one that sees itself deprived of genuine relations with that world. The tempo of industrialization seemed to Wordsworth to encourage a rootless and abstract kind of existence, a man-made nature alienating us from Nature. Love, or the sympathetic imagination, could not flourish long in that artificial environment: imagination, indeed, could not even grow to become love in that soil. It needed a slower birth and a more generous nurture, for the imaginative spirit in us is wild, and only gradually humanized. Wordsworth's sense of apocalypse is simply his pre-vision of the failure of that process of humanization. The modern imagination, stronger than ever, but also more homeless than ever, falls back into itself, or endlessly outward. It becomes solipsistic or seeming-mad. We understand Wordsworth best when we are too near ourselves, too naked in our self-consciousness. Then his poetry, its strange spiritual calculus, its balancing of imaginative failure with elemental gratitudes, can still infuse a modest and rocky strength: "O joy! That in our embers / Is something that doth live" ("Intimations Ode").

Chronology

1770   April 7. William Wordsworth born at Cockermouth, Cumberland.
1778   Death of his mother.
1779–87   Attends grammar school at Hawkshead.
1783   Death of his father.
1787   Enters St. John's College, Cambridge.
1790   Summer walking tour through the Alps.
1791   Receives B.A. degree. Goes to France.
1792   Daughter Caroline born of Annette Vallon. Returns to England in December.
1793   *An Evening Walk* and *Descriptive Sketches*. Writes "Letter to the Bishop of Landaff."
1794   With his sister Dorothy, February–June.
1795   Meets Coleridge. In September, moves with Dorothy to Racedown, Dorset, where they live till June, 1797.
1796   A first version of *The Borderers*.
1797   July. Moves with Dorothy to Alfoxden near Nether Stowey, where Coleridge is staying.
1798   March. Completes *The Ruined Cottage*.
         October. Publishes, with Coleridge, *Lyrical Ballads*.
1798–99   Composes drafts of the first two books of *The Prelude*.
         October–April. In Germany with Dorothy. The Lucy poems.
1799   December. Moves with Dorothy to Dove Cottage, Grasmere.
1800   July. Coleridge settles at Keswick.
1801   January. Second edition of *Lyrical Ballads* (dated 1800).

1802   Spring. Period of great productivity. Begins "Intimations Ode." Trip to France during Peace of Amiens. "Calais Sonnets."

October 4. Marries Mary Hutchinson.

1804   Coleridge leaves for Malta. Intense composition on *The Prelude*.

1805   Finishes *The Prelude*.

February 5. His brother John drowns.

1807   *Poems in Two Volumes.*

1809   *Convention of Cintra; Essay on Epitaphs.*

1812   His children Catherine and Thomas die.

1813   Moves to Rydal Mount, Grasmere, his residence till death.

1814   *The Excursion.* Tours Scotland.

1815   *Collected Poems* and *The White Doe of Rylstone.*

1819   *Peter Bell.*

1820   *The River Duddon* and *Miscellaneous Poems* (four volumes). Tours Switzerland, Italy, and France.

1822   *Ecclesiastical Sketches; Memorials of a Tour on the Continent.*

1823–33   Tours in the Netherlands (1823), North Wales (1824), Rhine district with Coleridge (1828), Ireland (1829), Scotland (1831).

1835   *Yarrow Revisited and Other Poems.* After the death of Sara Hutchinson, Dorothy enters a mental and physical decline.

1842   *The Borderers.*

1843   Made Poet Laureate.

1847   Death of his daughter, Dora.

1849   Last personally revised edition of the collected poems.

1850   April 23. Dies and is buried at Grasmere.

July. *The Prelude* is published.

Selected Bibliography

Editions of the Works

The Poetical Works of William Wordsworth. Ernest de Selincourt and Helen Darbishire (eds.), 5 vols. Oxford, 1940–49.

The Prelude, or Growth of a Poet's Mind. Ernest de Selincourt (ed.). Oxford, 1926; 2nd ed., revised by Helen Darbishire, 1959.

The Prose Works of William Wordsworth. W. J. B. Owen and J. W. Smyser (eds.). 3 vols. Oxford, 1974.

The Letters of William and Dorothy Wordsworth. Ernest de Selincourt (ed.). 6 vols. Oxford, 1935–39; 2nd ed., revised by C. L. Shaver, 1967–.

Journals of Dorothy Wordsworth. E. de Selincourt (ed.). 2 vols. London, 1941.

Wordsworth, Dorothy. *Journals: The Alfoxden Journal, 1798,* and *The Grasmere Journals, 1800–1803.* Helen Darbishire (ed.). London, New York, 1958 (The World's Classics).

Wordsworth, William. *Preface to Lyrical Ballads.* W. J. B. Owen (ed.). Copenhagen, 1957.

Literary Criticism of William Wordsworth. Paul M. Zall (ed.). Lincoln, Neb., 1966.

The Cornell Wordsworth is a definitive reedition of the longer poems. The following have appeared: *The Salisbury Plain Poems,* ed. Stephen Gill. *The Prelude, 1798–1799,* ed. Stephen Parrish. *Home at Grasmere,* ed. Beth Darlington. *The Ruined Cottage,* ed. James Butler.

Biographies

Harper, George McLean. *William Wordsworth: His Life, Works, and Influence.* 2 vols. New York, 1916; revised ed., 1 vol., 1929.

Moorman, Mary. *William Wordsworth: A Biography,* 2 vols. Oxford, 1957, 1965.

Legouis, Emile. *The Early Life of William Wordsworth, 1770–1798: A Study of "The Prelude."* J. W. Matthews, trans. London, 1897.

Reed, Mark L. *Wordsworth: The Chronology of the Early Years, 1770–1799.* Cambridge, Mass., 1967.

————. *The Chronology of the Middle Years, 1800–1815.* Cambridge, Mass., 1975.

Criticism

Abrams, M. H. "The Greater Romantic Lyric" in *From Sensibility to Romanticism.* F. Hilles and H. Bloom (eds.). New York, 1965.

————. *The Mirror and the Lamp.* New York, 1963.

————. *Natural Supernaturalism.* New York, 1971.

Arnold, Matthew. "Wordsworth" in *Essays in Criticism, Second Series.* London, 1888.

Bateson, F. W. *Wordsworth: A Re-Interpretation.* London, 1956 (2nd ed.).

Beatty, Arthur. *William Wordsworth: His Doctrine and Art in Their Historical Relations.* 1922; University of Wisconsin Press, 1960 (3rd ed.).

Bloom, Harold. *The Visionary Company: A Reading of English Romantic Poetry.* Garden City, N. Y., 1961.

————. *Poetry and Repression.* New Haven, 1978.

Bradley, A. C. *Oxford Lectures on Poetry.* London, 1909.

Brisman, Leslie. *Romantic Origins.* Ithaca, 1978.

Brooks, Cleanth. *The Well Wrought Urn.* New York, 1947.

Brower, Reuben Arthur. *The Fields of Light*. New York, 1951, pp. 75–92.

Coleridge, S. T. *Biographia Literaria*. London, 1817; J. Shawcross (ed.), 2 vols., Oxford, 1907.

Cooke, M. G. *The Romantic Will*. New Haven, 1977.

Davie, Donald. *Articulate Energy: An Inquiry into the Syntax of English Poetry*. London, 1955.

Davis, Jack (ed.). *Discussions of William Wordsworth*. Boston, 1964.

de Man, Paul. "Symbolic Landscape in Wordsworth and Yeats" in *In Defense of Reading*. R. A. Brower and R. Poirier (eds.). New York, 1962.

De Quincey, Thomas. *The Lake Poets: Wordsworth* in *Collected Writings*. David Masson (ed). Edinburgh, 1889.

Dunklin, Gilbert T. (ed.). *Wordsworth Centenary Studies*. Princeton, 1951.

Ferguson, Frances. *Wordsworth: Language as Counter-Spirit*. New Haven, 1977.

Ferry, David. *The Limits of Mortality: An Essay on Wordsworth's Major Poems*. Middletown, Conn., 1959.

Frye, Northrop (ed.). *Romanticism Reconsidered*. New York, 1963.

Hartman, Geoffrey H. *The Unmediated Vision*. New Haven, 1954 & 1966.

———. "Words, Wish, Worth" in *Deconstruction and Criticism,* New York, 1979.

———. *New Perspectives on Coleridge and Wordsworth,* ed. G. H. Hartman. New York, 1972.

———. *Wordsworth's Poetry 1787–1814*. New Haven and London, 1964 & 1967.

Havens, Raymond Dexter. *The Mind of a Poet*. Baltimore, 1941.

Hazlitt, William. "Mr. Wordsworth" in *The Spirit of the Age*. London, 1825.

Hirsch, E. D. *Wordsworth and Schelling*. New Haven, 1960.

Jeffrey, Francis. *Contributions to the Edinburgh Review*. 4 vols. London, 1844, Vol. 3.

Jones, John. *The Egotistical Sublime: A History of Wordsworth's Imagination*. London, 1954.

Knight, G. Wilson. *The Starlit Dome*. New York, 1941.

Langbaum, R. *The Mysteries of Identity*. New York, 1977.
————. Onorato, Richard S. *The Character of the Poet: Wordsworth in the The Prelude*. Princeton, 1971.
————. *The Poetry of Experience*. New York, 1957
Leavis, F. R. "Wordsworth" in *Revaluation: Tradition and Development in English Poetry*. London, 1936.
Lindenberger, H. *On Wordsworth's Prelude*. Princeton, 1963.
Margoliouth, H. M. *Wordsworth and Coleridge, 1795–1834*. London, New York, Toronto, 1953.
McConnell, F. D. *The Confessional Imagination*. Baltimore, 1979.
Miles, Josephine. "Wordsworth and Glitter," *Studies in Philology*, 40 (1943), 552–59.
Murray, Roger N. *Wordsworth's Style: Figures and Themes in the Lyrical Ballads of 1800*. Lincoln, Nebr., 1967.
Parrish, Stephen Maxfield. " 'The Thorn': Wordsworth's Dramatic Monologue," *ELH*, 24 (1957), 153–63.
————. *The Art of the Lyrical Ballads*. Cambridge, Mass. 1973.
Perkins, David. *The Quest for Permanence: The Symbolism of Wordsworth, Shelley and Keats*. Cambridge, Mass., 1959.
————. *Wordsworth and the Poetry of Sincerity*. Cambridge, Mass. 1964.
Pottle, Frederick A. *The Idiom of Poetry*. New York, 1946 (rev. ed.).
————. "The Eye and the Object in the Poetry of Wordsworth" in *Wordsworth: Centenary Studies*. Gilbert T. Dunklin (ed.). Princeton, 1951, pp. 23–44.
Rader, Melvin. *Wordsworth: A Philosophical Approach*. Oxford, 1967.
————. Regueiro, Helen. *The Limits of Imagination*. Ithaca, 1976.
Sperry, Willard. *Wordsworth's Anti-Climax*. Cambridge, Mass., 1935.
Trilling, Lionel. *The Liberal Imagination*. New York, 1950, pp. 129–60.
————. Weiskel, Thomas. *The Romantic Sublime*. Baltimore, 1976.
Whitehead, Alfred North. "The Romantic Reaction" in *Science and the Modern World*. New York, 1925.

Willey, Basil. "On Wordsworth and the Locke Tradition" in *The Seventeenth Century Background: Studies in the Thought of the Age in Relation to Poetry and Religion.* London, 1934.

Woodring, Carl. *Wordsworth.* Boston, 1965.

Wordsworth, Jonathan. *The Music of Humanity.* London and New York, 1969.

I. Beginnings

DESCRIPTIVE SKETCHES°

The Gypsy
—She solitary through the desert drear
Spontaneous wanders, hand in hand with Fear.   200
A giant moan along the forest swells
Protracted, and the twilight storm foretells,
And, ruining from the cliffs their deafening load°
Tumbles, the wildering Thunder slips abroad;
On the high summits Darkness comes and goes,   205
Hiding their fiery clouds, their rocks, and snows;
The torrent, travers'd by the lustre broad,
Starts like a horse beside the flashing road;
In the roof'd bridge, at that despairing hour,
She seeks a shelter from the battering show'r.   210
—Fierce comes the river down; the crashing wood
Gives way, and half its pines torment the flood;
Fearful, beneath, the Water-spirits call,
And the bridge vibrates, tottering to its fall.

1791–92   1793

Alpine Storm°
'Tis storm; and hid in mist from hour to hour
All day the floods a deeper murmur pour,
And mournful sounds, as of a Spirit lost,
Pipe wild along the hollow-blustering coast,   835
'Till the Sun walking on his western field

0 **Descriptive Sketches** In 1793 Wordsworth published two "loco-
descriptive" poems, or travelogues in verse, one on English scenery
("An Evening Walk") and this one based on his 1790 tour of the
Alps which also became the subject of *Prelude* VI. Solitaries in the
landscape, like the gypsy woman, are set in a context of—some-
times mild, sometimes fearful—"powers and presences." 203 **ruin-
ing . . . load** A later version reads: "a deafening load."

0 **Alpine Storm** Coleridge cites this passage in Chapter IV of the
Biographia Literaria as an early, if harsh, manifestation of Words-
worth's genius.

Shakes from behind the clouds his flashing shield.
Triumphant on the bosom of the storm,
Glances the fire-clad eagle's wheeling form;
840 Eastward, in long perspective glittering, shine
The wood-crowned cliffs that o'er the lake recline;
Wide o'er the Alps a hundred streams unfold,
At once to pillars turned that flame with gold;
Behind his sail the peasant strives to shun
845 The west that burns like one dilated sun,
Where in a mighty crucible expire
The mountains, glowing hot, like coals of fire.

1791–92　　　　　　　　　　　　　　　　　　1793

THE BORDERERS°

SCENE, *the Wood on the edge of the Moor.* MARMA-
DUKE (*alone*).

　Mar. Deep, deep and vast, vast beyond human
　　　thought,
Yet calm.—I could believe that there was here
The only quiet heart on earth. In terror,
Remembered terror, there is peace and rest.

Enter OSWALD.°

　Osw. Ha! my dear Captain.
1470　*Mar.*　　　　　　　　　A later meeting, Oswald,
Would have been better timed.

0 **The Borderers,** a tragedy written between 1795 and 1797, in which
Marmaduke, leader of the "Borderers," benevolent outlaws operat-
ing in the border region between England and Scotland, is betrayed
by the Iago-like Oswald into causing the death of an innocent man.
In this scene from the third act, Oswald confronts Marmaduke just
after the crime and exults in it as a forward step in the achievement
of a morality free of pity and conventional feelings. The 1842 text,
used here, accords substantially with earlier manuscripts. 1469
Oswald, originally called Rivers, is described in the "Growth of a
Criminal's Mind," pp. 405 ff., below.

Osw.   Alone, I see;
You have done your duty. I had hopes, which now
I feel that you will justify.
  Mar.   I had fears,
From which I have freed myself—but 'tis my wish
To be alone, and therefore we must part.   *1475*
  Osw. Nay, then—I am mistaken. There's a weakness
About you still; you talk of solitude—
I am your friend.
  Mar.   What need of this assurance
At any time? and why given now?
  Osw.   Because
You are now in truth my Master; you have taught me   *1480*
What there is not another living man
Had strength to teach;—and therefore gratitude
Is bold, and would relieve itself by praise.
  Mar. Wherefore press this on me?
  Osw.   Because I feel
That you have shown, and by a signal instance,   *1485*
How they who would be just must seek the rule
By diving for it into their own bosoms.
To-day you have thrown off a tyranny
That lives but in the torpid acquiescence
Of our emasculated souls, the tyranny   *1490*
Of the world's masters,° with the musty rules
By which they uphold their craft from age to age:
You have obeyed the only law that sense
Submits to recognize; the immediate law,
From the clear light of circumstances, flashed   *1495*
Upon an independent Intellect.°
Henceforth new prospects open on your path;
Your faculties should grow with the demand;
I still will be your friend, will cleave to you
Through good and evil, obloquy and scorn,   *1500*
Oft as they dare to follow on your steps.
  Mar. I would be left alone.
  Osw. (*exultingly*).   I know your motives!

1491 **world's masters** identified in a earlier manuscript as "moralists
and saints and law givers."   1494–96 **immediate law . . . Intellect.**
Cf. *Prelude* XI. 241–44.

I am not of the world's presumptuous judges,
Who damn where they can neither see nor feel,
1505 With a hard-hearted ignorance; your struggles
I witnessed, and now hail your victory.
    Mar. Spare me awhile that greeting.
    Osw.   It may be
That some there are, squeamish half-thinking cowards,
Who will turn pale upon you, call you murderer,
1510 And you will walk in solitude among them.
A mighty evil for a strong-built mind!—
Join twenty tapers of unequal height
And light them joined, and you will see the less
How 'twill burn down the taller; and they all
1515 Shall prey upon the tallest. Solitude!—
The Eagle lives in Solitude!
    Mar.   Even so,
The Sparrow so on the house-top, and I,
The weakest of God's creatures, stand resolved
To abide the issue of my act, alone.
    Osw. Now would you? and for ever?—My young
1520   Friend,
As time advances either we become
The prey or masters of our own past deeds.
Fellowship we *must* have, willing or no;
And if good Angels fail, slack in their duty,
1525 Substitutes, turn our faces where we may,
Are still forthcoming; some which, though they bear
Ill names, can render no ill services,
In recompense for what themselves required.
So meet extremes in this mysterious world,
1530 And opposites thus melt into each other.
    Mar. Time, since Man first drew breath, has never
    moved
With such a weight upon his wings as now;
But they will soon be lightened.
    Osw.   Ay, look up—
Cast round you your mind's eye,° and you will learn
1535 Fortitude is the child of Enterprise:
Great actions move our admiration, chiefly

1516–34 **Even so . . . eye** These lines appear only in 1842.

Because they carry in themselves an earnest
That we can suffer greatly.
    Mar.   Very true.
    Osw. Action is transitory—a step, a blow,
The motion of a muscle—this way or that—   *1540*
'Tis done, and in the after-vacancy
We wonder at ourselves like men betrayed:
Suffering is permanent, obscure and dark,
And shares the nature of infinity.°
    Mar. Truth—and I feel it.
    Osw.   What! if you had bid   *1545*
Eternal farewell to unmingled joy
And the light dancing of the thoughtless heart;
It is the toy of fools, and little fit
For such a world as this. The wise abjure
All thoughts whose idle composition lives   *1550*
In the entire forgetfulness of pain.
—I see I have disturbed you.
    Mar.   By no means.
    Osw. Compassion!—pity!—pride can do without
      them;
And what if you should never know them more!—
He is a puny soul who, feeling pain,   *1555*
Finds ease because another feels it too.
If e'er I open out this heart of mine
It shall be for a nobler end—to teach
And not to purchase puling sympathy.
—Nay, you are pale.
    Mar.   It may be so.
    Osw.   Remorse—   *1560*
It cannot live with thought; think on, think on,
And it will die. What! in this universe,
Where the least things control the greatest, where
The faintest breath that breathes can move a world;
What! feel remorse, where, if a cat had sneezed,   *1565*
A leaf had fallen, the thing had never been
Whose very shadow gnaws us to the vitals.
    Mar. Now, whither are you wandering? That a man,
So used to suit his language to the time,

1539–44 Action . . . infinity These lines served as part of the epi-
graph for *The White Doe of Rylstone* (1815).

1570 Should thus so widely differ from himself—
    It is most strange.
         Osw.   Murder!—what's in the word!—
    I have no cases by me ready made
    To fit all deeds. Carry him to the Camp!—
    A shallow project;—you of late have seen
1575 More deeply, taught us that the institutes
    Of Nature, by a cunning usurpation
    Banished from human intercourse, exist
    Only in our relations to the brutes
    That make the fields their dwelling. If a snake
1580 Crawl from beneath our feet we do not ask
    A license to destroy him: our good governors
    Hedge in the life of every pest and plague
    That bears the shape of man; and for what purpose,
    But to protect themselves from extirpation?—
1585 This flimsy barrier you have overleaped.
         Mar. My Office is fulfilled—the Man° is now
    Delivered to the Judge of all things.
         Osw.   Dead!
         Mar. I have borne my burthen to its destined end.

1795–97   1842

THE RUINED COTTAGE°

First Part

'Twas Summer and the sun was mounted high.
Along the south the uplands feebly glared
Through a pale steam, and all the northern downs,
In clearer air ascending, shewed far off

1586 **the Man** Baron Herbert, who was "judged" by Marmaduke
and left to die.

0 **The Ruined Cottage** Composed in 1797–98 this "common tale . . .
of silent suffering" was expanded by Wordsworth into Book I of
The Excursion (1814). The version here printed was established by
Jonathan Wordsworth in *The Music of Humanity* (1969) and gives
the story in what was probably its earliest and sparsest form.

Their surfaces with shadows dappled o'er   *5*
Of deep embattled clouds. Far as the sight
Could reach those many shadows lay in spots
Determined and unmoved, with steady beams
Of clear and pleasant sunshine interposed—
Pleasant to him who on the soft cool moss   *10*
Extends his careless limbs beside the root
Of some huge oak whose aged branches make
A twilight of their own, a dewy shade
Where the wren warbles while the dreaming man,
Half conscious of that soothing melody,   *15*
With sidelong eye looks out upon the scene,
By those impending branches made more soft,
More soft and distant.

               Other lot was mine.
Across a bare wide Common I had toiled
With languid feet which by the slipp'ry ground   *20*
Were baffled still, and when I stretched myself
On the brown earth my limbs from very heat
Could find no rest, nor my weak arm disperse
The insect host which gathered round my face
And joined their murmurs to the tedious noise   *25*
Of seeds of bursting gorse that crackled round.
I rose and turned towards a group of trees
Which midway in that level stood alone;
And thither come at length, beneath a shade
Of clustering elms that sprang from the same root   *30*
I found a ruined house, four naked walls
That stared upon each other. I looked round
And near the door I saw an aged Man,
Alone and stretched upon the cottage bench,
An iron-pointed staff lay at his side.   *35*
With instantaneous joy I recognized
That pride of nature and of lowly life,
The venerable Armytage, a friend
As dear to me as is the setting sun.

                 Two days before   *40*
We had been fellow travelers. I knew
That he was in this neighborhood, and now

    Delighted found him here in the cool shade.
    He lay, his pack of rustic merchandise
45 Pillowing his head. I guess he had no thought
    Of his way-wandering life. His eyes were shut,
    The shadows of the breezy elms above
    Dappled his face. With thirsty heat oppressed
    At length I hailed him, glad to see his hat
50 Bedewed with waterdrops, as if the brim
    Had newly scooped a running stream. He rose
    And pointing to a sunflower, bade me climb
    The [   ] wall where that same gaudy flower
    Looked out upon the road.

                      It was a plot
55 Of garden ground now wild, its matted weeds
    Marked with the steps of those whom as they passed,
    The gooseberry trees that shot in long lank slips,
    Or currants hanging from their leafless stems
    In scanty strings, had tempted to o'erleap
60 The broken wall. Within that cheerless spot,
    Where two tall hedgerows of thick alder boughs
    Joined in a damp cold nook, I found a well
    Half covered up with willow flowers and grass.
    I slaked my thirst and to the shady bench
65 Returned, and while I stood unbonneted
    To catch the motion of the cooler air,
    The old Man said, "I see around me here
    Things which you cannot see. We die, my Friend,
    Nor we alone, but that which each man loved
70 And prized in his peculiar nook of earth
    Dies with him, or is changed, and very soon
    Even of the good is no memorial left.
    The Poets, in their elegies and songs
    Lamenting the departed, call the groves,
75 They call upon the hills and streams to mourn,
    And senseless rocks—nor idly, for they speak
    In these their invocations with a voice
    Obedient to the strong creative power
    Of human passion. Sympathies there are
80 More tranquil, yet perhaps of kindred birth,
    That steal upon the meditative mind

And grow with thought. Beside yon spring I stood,
And eyed its waters till we seemed to feel
One sadness, they and I. For them a bond
Of brotherhood is broken; time has been   *85*
When every day the touch of human hand
Disturbed their stillness, and they ministered
To human comfort. When I stooped to drink
A spider's web hung to the water's edge,
And on the wet and slimy footstone lay   *90*
The useless fragment of a wooden bowl.
It moved my very heart.

        "The day has been
When I could never pass this road but she
Who lived within these walls, when I appeared,
A daughter's welcome gave me, and I loved her   *95*
As my own child. Oh Sir, the good die first,
And they whose hearts are dry as summer dust
Burn to the socket. Many a passenger
Has blessed poor Margaret for her gentle looks
When she upheld the cool refreshment drawn   *100*
From that forsaken spring, and no one came
But he was welcome, no one went away
But that it seemed she loved him. She is dead,
The worm is on her cheek, and this poor hut,
Stripped of its outward garb of household flowers,   *105*
Of rose and sweetbriar, offers to the wind
A cold bare wall whose earthy top is tricked
With weeds and the rank spear grass. She is dead,
And nettles rot and adders sun themselves
Where we have sate together while she nursed   *110*
Her infant at her breast. The unshod colt,
The wand'ring heifer and the Potter's ass,
Find shelter now within the chimney wall
Where I have seen her evening hearthstone blaze
And through the window spread upon the road   *115*
Its cheerful light. You will forgive me, sir,
But often on this cottage do I muse
As on a picture, till my wiser mind
Sinks, yielding to the foolishness of grief.

120 "She had a husband, an industrious man,
Sober and steady. I have heard her say
That he was up and busy at his loom
In summer ere the mower's scythe had swept
The dewy grass, and in the early spring
125 Ere the last star had vanished. They who passed
At evening, from behind the garden fence
Might hear his busy spade, which he would ply
After his daily work till the daylight
Was gone, and every leaf and flower were lost
130 In the dark hedges. So they passed their days
In peace and comfort, and two pretty babes
Were their best hope next to the God in Heaven.

"You may remember, now some ten years gone,
Two blighting seasons when the fields were left
135 With half a harvest. It pleased heaven to add
A worse affliction in the plague of war,
A happy land was stricken to the heart,
'Twas a sad time of sorrow and distress.
A wanderer among the cottages,
140 I with my pack of winter raiment saw
The hardships of that season. Many rich
Sunk down as in a dream among the poor,
And of the poor did many cease to be,
And their place knew them not. Meanwhile, abridged
145 Of daily comforts, gladly reconciled
To numerous self-denials, Margaret
Went struggling on through those calamitous years
With cheerful hope. But ere the second autumn
A fever seized her husband. In disease
150 He lingered long, and when his strength returned
He found the little he had stored to meet
The hour of accident, or crippling age,
Was all consumed. As I have said, 'twas now
A time of trouble: shoals of artisans
155 Were from their daily labor turned away
To hang for bread on parish charity,
They and their wives and children, happier far
Could they have lived as do the little birds

That peck along the hedges, or the kite
That makes her dwelling in the mountain rocks.   *160*

"Ill fared it now with Robert, he who dwelt
In this poor cottage. At his door he stood
And whistled many a snatch of merry tunes
That had no mirth in them, or with his knife
Carved uncouth figures on the heads of sticks,   *165*
Then idly sought about through every nook
Of house or garden any casual task
Of use or ornament, and with a strange
Amusing but uneasy novelty
He blended where he might the various tasks   *170*
Of summer, autumn, winter, and of spring.
But this endured not, his good humor soon
Became a weight in which no pleasure was,
And poverty brought on a petted mood
And a sore temper. Day by day he drooped,   *175*
And he would leave his home, and to the town
Without an errand would he turn his steps,
Or wander here and there among the fields.
One while he would speak lightly of his babes
And with a cruel tongue, at other times   *180*
He played with them wild freaks of merriment,
And 'twas a piteous thing to see the looks
Of the poor innocent children. 'Every smile,'
Said Margaret to me here beneath these trees,
'Made my heart bleed.' "   *185*

                    At this the old Man paused,
And looking up to those enormous elms
He said, " 'Tis now the hour of deepest noon.
At this still season of repose and peace,
This hour when all things which are not at rest
Are cheerful, while this multitude of flies   *190*
Fills all the air with happy melody,
Why should a tear be in an old man's eye?
Why should we thus with an untoward mind,
And in the weakness of humanity,
From natural wisdom turn our hearts away,   *195*

To natural comfort shut our eyes and ears,
And, feeding on disquiet, thus disturb
The calm of Nature with our restless thoughts?"
END OF THE FIRST PART

Second Part

He spake with somewhat of a solemn tone,
200 But when he ended there was in his face
Such easy cheerfulness, a look so mild,
That for a little time it stole away
All recollection, and that simple tale
Passed from my mind like a forgotten sound.
205 A while on trivial things we held discourse,
To me soon tasteless. In my own despite
I thought of that poor woman as of one
Whom I had known and loved. He had rehearsed
Her homely tale with such familiar power,
210 With such an active countenance, an eye
So busy, that the things of which he spake
Seemed present, and, attention now relaxed,
There was a heartfelt chillness in my veins.
I rose, and turning from that breezy shade
215 Went out into the open air, and stood
To drink the comfort of the warmer sun.
Long time I had not stayed ere, looking round
Upon that tranquil ruin, I returned
And begged of the old man that for my sake
220 He would resume his story.

He replied,
"It were a wantonness, and would demand
Severe reproof, if we were men whose hearts
Could hold vain dalliance with the misery
Even of the dead, contented thence to draw
225 A momentary pleasure, never marked
By reason, barren of all future good.
But we have known that there is often found
In mournful thoughts, and always might be found,
A power to virtue friendly; were 't not so
230 I am a dreamer among men, indeed

An idle dreamer. 'Tis a common tale
By moving accidents uncharactered,
A tale of silent suffering, hardly clothed
In bodily form, and to the grosser sense
But ill adapted, scarcely palpable   235
To him who does not think. But at your bidding
I will proceed.

            "While thus it fared with them
To whom this cottage till that hapless year
Had been a blessed home, it was my chance
To travel in a country far remote;   240
And glad I was when, halting by yon gate
That leads from the green lane, again I saw
These lofty elm trees. Long I did not rest:
With many pleasant thoughts I cheered my way
O'er the flat common. At the door arrived,   245
I knocked, and when I entered, with the hope
Of usual greeting, Margaret looked at me
A little while, then turned her head away
Speechless, and sitting down upon a chair
Wept bitterly. I wist not what to do,   250
Or how to speak to her. Poor wretch, at last
She rose from off her seat, and then, oh Sir,
I cannot tell how she pronounced my name.
With fervent love, and with a face of grief
Unutterably helpless, and a look   255
That seemed to cling upon me, she enquired
If I had seen her husband. As she spake
A strange surprise and fear came to my heart,
Nor had I power to answer ere she told
That he had disappeared—just two months gone.   260
He left his house: two wretched days had passed,
And on the third by the first break of light,
Within her casement full in view she saw
A purse of gold.° 'I trembled at the sight,'
Said Margaret, 'for I knew it was his hand   265
That placed it there. And on that very day
By one, a stranger, from my husband sent,

264 **gold** the money her husband had received for enlisting as a
soldier.

The tidings came that he had joined a troop
Of soldiers going to a distant land.
270 He left me thus. Poor Man, he had not heart
To take farewell of me, and he feared
That I should follow with my babes, and sink
Beneath the misery of a soldier's life.'

"This tale did Margaret tell with many tears,
275 And when she ended I had little power
To give her comfort, and was glad to take
Such words of hope from her own mouth as served
To cheer us both. But long we had not talked
Ere we built up a pile of better thoughts,
280 And with a brighter eye she looked around,
As if she had been shedding tears of joy.
We parted. It was then the early spring:
I left her busy with her garden tools,
And well remember, o'er that fence she looked,
285 And, while I paced along the footway path,
Called out and sent a blessing after me,
With tender cheerfulness, and with a voice
That seemed the very sound of happy thoughts.

"I roved o'er many a hill and many a dale
290 With this my weary load, in heat and cold,
Through many a wood and many an open ground,
In sunshine or in shade, in wet or fair,
Now blithe, now drooping, as it might befall;
My best companions now the driving winds
295 And now the 'trotting brooks' and whispering trees,
And now the music of my own sad steps,
With many a short-lived thought that passed between
And disappeared.
              "I came this way again
Towards the wane of summer, when the wheat
300 Was yellow, and the soft and bladed grass
Sprang up afresh and o'er the hay field spread
Its tender green. When I had reached the door
I found that she was absent. In the shade,
Where we now sit, I waited her return.

Her cottage in its outward look appeared   *805*
As cheerful as before, in any shew
Of neatness little changed, but that I thought
The honeysuckle crowded round the door,
And from the wall hung down in heavier tufts,
And knots of worthless stonecrop started out   *810*
Along the window's edge, and grew like weeds
Against the lower panes. I turned aside
And strolled into her garden. It was changed.
The unprofitable bindweed spread his bells
From side to side, and with unwieldy wreaths   *815*
Had dragged the rose from its sustaining wall
And bent it down to earth. The border tufts,
Daisy, and thrift, and lowly camomile,
And thyme, had straggled out into the paths
Which they were used to deck.   *820*

                    "Ere this an hour
Was wasted. Back I turned my restless steps,
And as I walked before the door it chanced
A stranger passed, and guessing whom I sought,
He said that she was used to ramble far.
The sun was sinking in the west, and now   *325*
I sate with sad impatience. From within
Her solitary infant cried aloud.
The spot though fair seemed very desolate,
The longer I remained more desolate;
And looking round I saw the cornerstones,   *330*
Till then unmarked, on either side the door
With dull red stains discolored, and stuck o'er
With tufts and hairs of wool, as if the sheep
That feed upon the commons thither came
Familiarly, and found a couching place   *335*
Even at her threshold.

                "The house clock struck eight:
I turned and saw her distant a few steps.
Her face was pale and thin, her figure too
Was changed. As she unlocked the door she said,
'It grieves me you have waited here so long,   *340*
But in good truth I've wandered much of late,

And sometimes, to my shame I speak, have need
Of my best prayers to bring me back again.'
While on the board she spread our evening meal,
345 She told me she had lost her elder child,
That he for months had been a serving boy,
Apprenticed by the parish. 'I perceive
You look at me, and you have cause. Today
I have been traveling far, and many days
350 About the fields I wander, knowing this
Only, that what I seek I cannot find.
And so I waste my time: for I am changed,
And to myself,' she said, 'have done much wrong,
And to this helpless infant. I have slept
355 Weeping, and weeping I have waked. My tears
Have flowed as if my body were not such
As others are, and I could never die.
But I am now in mind and in my heart
More easy, and I hope,' she said, 'that heaven
360 Will give me patience to endure the things
Which I behold at home.'

                              "It would have grieved
Your very soul to see her. Sir, I feel
The story linger in my heart. I fear
'Tis long and tedious, but my spirit clings
365 To that poor woman. So familiarly
Do I perceive her manner and her look
And presence, and so deeply do I feel
Her goodness, that not seldom in my walks
A momentary trance comes over me,
370 And to myself I seem to muse on one
By sorrow laid asleep or borne away,
A human being destined to awake
To human life, or something very near
To human life, when he shall come again
375 For whom she suffered. Sir, it would have grieved
Your very soul to see her: evermore
Her eyelids drooped, her eyes were downward cast,
And when she at her table gave me food
She did not look at me. Her voice was low,
380 Her body was subdued. In every act

Pertaining to her house affairs appeared
The careless stillness which a thinking mind
Gives to an idle matter. Still she sighed,
But yet no motion of the breast was seen,
No heaving of the heart. While by the fire   *885*
We sate together, sighs came on my ear,
I knew not how, and hardly whence they came.
I took my staff, and when I kissed her babe
The tears stood in her eyes. I left her then
With the best hope and comfort I could give: *890*
She thanked me for my will, but for my hope
It seemed she did not thank me.

                      "I returned
And took my rounds along this road again
Ere on its sunny bank the primrose flower
Had chronicled the earliest day of spring.   *895*
I found her sad and drooping. She had learned
No tidings of her husband; if he lived,
She knew not that he lived; if he were dead,
She knew not he was dead. She seemed the same
In person or appearance, but her house   *400*
Bespoke a sleepy hand of negligence.
The floor was neither dry nor neat, the hearth
Was comfortless,
The windows too were dim, and her few books,
Which one upon the other heretofore   *405*
Had been piled up against the corner panes
In seemly order, now with straggling leaves
Lay scattered here and there, open or shut,
As they had chanced to fall. Her infant babe
Had from its mother caught the trick of grief,   *410.*
And sighed among its playthings. Once again
I turned towards the garden gate, and saw
More plainly still that poverty and grief
Were now come nearer to her. The earth was hard,
With weeds defaced and knots of withered grass;   *415*
No ridges there appeared of clear black mould,
No winter greenness. Of her herbs and flowers
It seemed the better part were gnawed away
Or trampled on the earth. A chain of straw,

420 Which had been twisted round the tender stem
Of a young apple tree, lay at its root;
The bark was nibbled round by truant sheep.
Margaret stood near, her infant in her arms,
And, seeing that my eye was on the tree,
425 She said, 'I fear it will be dead and gone
Ere Robert come again.'

                              "Towards the house
Together we returned, and she inquired
If I had any hope. But for her Babe,
And for her little friendless Boy, she said,
430 She had no wish to live—that she must die
Of sorrow. Yet I saw the idle loom
Still in its place. His Sunday garments hung
Upon the selfsame nail, his very staff
Stood undisturbed behind the door. And when
435 I passed this way beaten by Autumn winds,
She told me that her little babe was dead,
And she was left alone. That very time,
I yet remember, through the miry lane
She walked with me a mile, when the bare trees
440 Trickled with foggy damps, and in such sort
That any heart had ached to hear her, begged
That wheresoe'r I went I still would ask
For him whom she had lost. We parted then,
Our final parting; for from that time forth
445 Did many seasons pass ere I returned
Into this tract again.

                              "Five tedious years
She lingered in unquiet widowhood,
A wife and widow. Needs must it have been
A sore heart-wasting. I have heard, my friend,
450 That in that broken arbor she would sit
The idle length of half a sabbath day;
There, where you see the toadstool's lazy head;
And when a dog passed by she still would quit
The shade and look abroad. On this old Bench
455 For hours she sate, and evermore her eye

Was busy in the distance, shaping things
Which made her heart beat quick. Seest thou that
 path?—
The green sward now has broken its gray line—
There to and fro she paced through many a day
Of the warm summer, from a belt of flax   *460*
That girt her waist, spinning the long-drawn thread
With backward steps. Yet ever as there passed
A man whose garments shewed the Soldier's red,
Or crippled Mendicant in Sailor's garb,
The little child who sate to turn the wheel   *465*
Ceased from his toil, and she, with faltering voice,
Expecting still to hear her husband's fate,
Made many a fond inquiry; and when they
Whose presence gave no comfort, were gone by,
Her heart was still more said. And by yon gate, *470*
Which bars the traveler's road, she often stood,
And when a stranger horseman came, the latch
Would lift, and in his face look wistfully,
Most happy if from aught discovered there
Of tender feeling she might dare repeat   *475*
The same sad question.

     "Meanwhile her poor hut
Sunk to decay; for he was gone, whose hand
At the first nippings of October frost
Closed up each chink, and with fresh bands of straw
Chequered the green-grown thatch. And so she lived *480*
Through the long winter, reckless and alone,
Till this reft house, by frost, and thaw, and rain,
Was sapped; and when she slept, the nightly damps
Did chill her breast, and in the stormy day
Her tattered clothes were ruffled by the wind *485*
Even at the side of her own fire. Yet still
She loved this wretched spot, nor would for worlds
Have parted hence; and still that length of road,
And this rude bench, one torturing hope endeared,
Fast rooted at her heart. And here, my friend, *490*
In sickness she remained; and here she died,
Last human tenant of these ruined walls."

The old Man ceased: he saw that I was moved.
From that low bench rising instinctively,
495 I turned aside in weakness, nor had power
To thank him for the tale which he had told.
I stood, and leaning o'er the garden gate
Reviewed that Woman's sufferings; and it seemed
To comfort me while with a brother's love
500 I blessed her in the impotence of grief.
At length towards the cottage I returned
Fondly, and traced with milder interest,
That secret spirit of humanity
Which, 'mid the calm oblivious tendencies
505 Of nature, 'mid her plants, her weeds and flowers,
And silent overgrowings, still survived.
The old man seeing this resumed, and said,
"My friend, enough to sorrow have you given,
The purposes of wisdom ask no more:
510 Be wise and cheerful, and no longer read
The forms of things with an unworthy eye.
She sleeps in the calm earth, and peace is here.
I well remember that those very plumes,
Those weeds, and the high spear grass on that wall,
515 By mist and silent raindrops silvered o'er,
As once I passed, did to my mind convey
So still an image of tranquillity,
So calm and still, and looked so beautiful
Amid the uneasy thoughts which filled my mind,
520 That what we feel of sorrow and despair
From ruin and from change, and all the grief
The passing shews of being leave behind,
Appeared an idle dream that could not live
Where meditation was. I turned away,
525 And walked along my road in happiness."

He ceased. By this the sun declining shot
A slant and mellow radiance, which began
To fall upon us where beneath the trees
We sate on that low bench. And now we felt,
530 Admonished thus, the sweet hour coming on:
A linnet warbled from those lofty elms,
A thrush sang loud, and other melodies

At distance heard, peopled the milder air.
The old man rose and hoisted up his load.
Together casting then a farewell look   535
Upon those silent walls, we left the shade;
And, ere the stars were visible, attained
A rustic inn, our evening resting place.

1797–1799   1969

THE PEDLAR°

... His eyes were turned
Towards the setting sun, while, with that staff
Behind him fixed, he propped a long white pack   5
Which crossed his shoulders: wares for maids who live
In lonely villages or straggling huts.
I knew him—he was born of lowly race
On Cumbrian° hills, and I have seen the tear
Stand in his luminous eye when he described   10
The house in which his early youth was passed
And found I was no stranger to the spot.
I loved to hear him talk of former days
And tell how when a child, ere yet of age
To be a shepherd, he had learned to read   15
His bible in a school that stood alone,
Sole building on a mountain's dreary edge,
Far from the sight of city spire, or sound

0 **The Pedlar** Early in 1798 Wordsworth expands the story of Margaret by introducing a significant point of view, that of the Pedlar. As in later (and shorter) lyrical ballads, this partially shifts the focus from story to storyteller, from the incidents to the imaginative and moral character of the narrator. In the Pedlar Wordsworth creates his first fully developed Solitary and anticipates the *Prelude's* interest in the natural history of the imagination. The excerpts here printed are from MS D of *The Excursion*, first used integrally by Jonathan Wordsworth in *The Music of Humanity* (1969). 9 **Cumbrian** from Cumberland, in the Lake District.

Of Minster° Clock. From that bleak tenement
20 He many an evening to his distant home
In solitude returning saw the hills
Grow larger in the darkness, all alone
Beheld the stars come out above his head,
And travelled through the wood, no comrade near,
25 To whom he might confess the things he saw.

So the foundations of his mind were laid.
In such communion, not from terror free,
While yet a child and long before his time,
He had perceived the presence and the power
30 Of greatness, and deep feelings had impressed
Great objects on his mind with portraiture
And colour so distinct that on his mind
They lay like substances, and almost seemed
To haunt the bodily sense. He had received
35 A precious gift, for as he grew in years
With these impressions would he still compare
All his ideal stores, his shapes and forms,
And being still unsatisfied with aught
Of dimmer character, he thence attained
40 An *active* power to fasten images
Upon his brain, and on their pictured lines
Intensely brooded, even till they acquired
The liveliness of dreams. Nor did he fail,
While yet a child, with a child's eagerness
45 Incessantly to turn his ear and eye
On all things which the rolling seasons brought
To feed such appetite. Nor this alone
Appeased his yearning. In the after day
Of boyhood, many an hour in caves forlorn
50 And in the hollow depths of naked crags
He sate, and even in their fixed lineaments,
Or from the power of a peculiar eye,
Or by creative feeling overborne,
Or by predominance of thought oppressed,
55 Even in their fixed and steady lineaments
He traced an ebbing and a flowing mind,
Expression ever varying.

19 **Minister** church.

Thus informed,
He had small need of books; for many a tale
Traditionary round the mountains hung,
And many a legend peopling the dark woods   *60*
Nourished Imagination in her growth
And gave the mind that apprehensive power°
By which she is made quick to recognize
The moral properties and scope of things.
But greedily he read and read again   *65*
Whate'er the rustic Vicar's shelf supplied:
The life and death of martyrs who sustained
Intolerable pangs, and here and there
A straggling volume, torn and incomplete,
Which left half-told the preternatural tale,   *70*
Romance of giants, chronicle of fiends,
Profuse in garniture of wooden cuts°
Strange and uncouth, dire faces, figures dire
Sharp-kneed, sharp-elbowed, and lean-ankled too,
With long and ghostly shanks, forms which once seen   *75*
Could never be forgotten—things though low,
Though low and humble, not to be despised
By such as have observed the curious links
With which the perishable hours of life
Are bound together, and the world of thought   *80*
Exists and is sustained.
                              Within his heart
Love was not yet, nor the pure joy of love,
By sound diffused, or by the breathing air,
Or by the silent looks of happy things,
Or flowing from the universal face   *85*
Of earth and sky. But he had felt the power
Of nature, and already was prepared
By his intense conceptions to receive
Deeply the lesson deep of love, which he
Whom Nature, by whatever means, has taught   *90*
To feel intensely, cannot but receive.

Ere his ninth year he had been sent abroad

---

62 **apprehensive power** apprehension, perception (here sharpened by imaginative fears).   72 **Profuse . . . cuts** profusely illustrated.

To tend his father's sheep: such was his task
Henceforward till the later day of youth.
95 Oh then what soul was his, when on the tops
Of the high mountains he beheld the sun
Rise up and bathe the world in light. He looked,
The ocean and the earth beneath him lay
In gladness and deep joy. The clouds were touched,
100 And in their silent faces did he read
Unutterable love. Sound needed none,
Nor any voice of joy: his spirit drank
The spectacle. Sensation, soul and form
All melted into him. They swallowed up
105 His animal being. In them did he live,
And by them did he live. They were his life.
In such access of mind, in such high hour
Of visitation from the living God,
He did not feel the God, he felt his works.
110 Thought was not: in enjoyment it expired.
Such hour by prayer or praise was unprofaned;
He neither prayed, nor offered thanks or praise;
His mind was a thanksgiving to the power
That made him. It was blessedness and love.

115   A Shepherd on the lonely mountain-tops
Such intercourse was his, and in this sort
Was his existence oftentimes possessed.
Oh *then* how beautiful, how bright, appeared
The written promise.° He had early learned
120 To reverence the volume which displays
The mystery, the life which cannot die,
But in the mountains did he FEEL his faith,
There did he see the writing. All things there
Breathed immortality, revolving life,
125 And greatness still revolving, infinite.
There littleness was not, the least of things
Seemed infinite, and there his spirit shaped
Her prospects, nor did he *believe*—he saw.

          *   *   *   *

185   ... Before his twentieth year was passed,
119 **the written promise** Scripture.

Accumulated feelings pressed his heart
With an encreasing weight; he was o'erpowered
By nature, and his spirit was on fire
With restless thoughts. His eye became disturbed,
And many a time he wished the winds might rage   190
When they were silent. Far more fondly now
Than in his earlier season did he love
Tempestuous nights, the uproar and the sounds
That live in darkness. From his intellect,
And from the stillness of abstracted thought,   195
He sought repose in vain. I have heard him say
That at this time he scanned the laws of light
Amid the roar of torrents, where they send
From hollow clefts up to the clearer air
A cloud of mist, which in the shining sun   200
Varies its rainbow hues. But vainly thus,
And vainly by all other means he strove
To mitigate the fever of his heart.

*   *   *   *

These things he had sustained in solitude
Even till his bodily strength began to yield
Beneath their weight. The mind within him burnt,   225
And he resolved to quit his native hills.

*   *   *   *

                              Among the woods
A lone enthusiast, and among the hills,
Itinerant in this labour° he had passed
The better portion of his time, and there
From day to day had his affections breathed
The wholesome air of nature; there he kept   265
In solitude and solitary thought,
So pleasant were those comprehensive views,
His mind in a just equipoise of love.
Serene it was, unclouded by the cares
Of ordinary life; unvexed, unwarped   270
By partial bondage. In his steady course

262 this labour peddling.

No piteous revolutions° had he felt,
No wild varieties of joy or grief.
Unoccupied by sorrow of its own,
275 His heart lay open; and, by nature tuned
And constant disposition of his thoughts
To sympathy with man, he was alive
To all that was enjoyed where'er he went,
And all that was endured; and in himself
280 Happy, and quiet in his cheerfulness,
He had no painful pressure from within
Which made him turn aside from wretchedness
With coward fears. He could afford to suffer
With those whom he saw suffer. . . .
315   Many a time
He made a holiday and left his pack
Behind, and we two wandered through the hills
A pair of random travellers. His eye
Flashing poetic fire he would repeat
320 The songs of Burns, or many a ditty wild
Which he had fitted to the moorland harp,
His own sweet verse, and as we trudged along
Together did we make the hollow grove
Ring with our transports.°
                         Though he was untaught,
325 In the dead lore of schools undisciplined,
Why should he grieve? He was a chosen son.°
He yet retained an ear which deeply felt
The voice of Nature in the obscure wind,
The sounding mountain, and the running stream.
330 From deep analogies by thought supplied,
Or consciousnesses not to be subdued,
To every natural form, rock, fruit, and flower,
Even the loose stones that cover the highway,
He gave a moral life; he saw them feel,
335 Or linked them to some feeling. In all shapes
He found a secret and mysterious soul,

272 **piteous revolutions** emotional upheavals.   324 **transports** enthu-
siasms.   326 That lines 326–355 (the end of the poem) are, like so
much in *The Pedlar,* disguised autobiography is shown by their
development as *Prelude* (1805) III. 82–167 and *Prelude* (1850) III.
82–169

A fragrance and a Spirit of strange meaning.
Though poor in outward shew, he was most rich:
He had a world about him—'twas his own,
He made it—for it only lived to him,   *840*
And to the God who looked into his mind.

*   *   *   *

II. Lyrical Ballads 1798-1800

ADVERTISEMENT°

It is the honourable characteristic of Poetry that its materials are to be found in every subject which can interest the human mind. The evidence of this fact is to be sought, not in the writings of Critics, but in those of Poets themselves.

The majority of the following poems are to be considered as experiments. They were written chiefly with a view to ascertain how far the language of conversation in the middle and lower classes of society is adapted to the purposes of poetic pleasure. Readers accustomed to the gaudiness and inane phraseology of many modern writers, if they persist in reading this book to its conclusion, will perhaps frequently have to struggle with feelings of strangeness and awkwardness: they will look round for poetry, and will be induced to enquire by what species of courtesy these attempts can be permitted to assume that title. It is desirable that such readers, for their own sakes, should not suffer the solitary word Poetry, a word of very disputed meaning, to stand in the way of their gratification; but that, while they are perusing this book, they should ask themselves if it contains a natural delineation of human passions, human characters, and human incidents; and if the answer be favorable to the author's wishes, that they should consent to be pleased in spite of that most dreadful enemy to our pleasures, our own pre-established codes of decision.

LINES

Left upon a Seat in a Yew-tree, which stands near the lake of Esthwaite, on a desolate part of the shore, commanding a beautiful prospect.

Nay, Traveller! rest. This lonely Yew-tree stands
Far from all human dwelling: what if here

0 **Advertisement** From the "Advertisement" to *Lyrical Ballads* of 1798. The famous Preface was not added till the second edition (1800).

No sparkling rivulet spread the verdant herb?
What if the bee love not these barren boughs?
5   Yet, if the wind breathe soft, the curling waves,
That break against the shore, shall lull thy mind
By one soft impulse saved from vacancy.
                  Who he was
That piled these stones and with the mossy sod
10 First covered, and here taught this agèd Tree
With its dark arms to form a circling bower,
I well remember.——He was one who owned
No common soul. In youth by science nursed,
And led by nature into a wild scene
15 Of lofty hopes, he to the world went forth
A favoured Being, knowing no desire
Which genius did not hallow; 'gainst the taint
Of dissolute tongues, and jealousy, and hate,
And scorn,——against all enemies prepared,
20 All but neglect. The world, for so it thought,
Owed him no service; wherefore he at once
With indignation turned himself away,
And with the food of pride sustained his soul
In solitude.——Stranger! these gloomy boughs
25 Had charms for him; and here he loved to sit,
His only visitants a straggling sheep,
The stone-chat, or the glancing sand-piper:
And on these barren rocks, with fern and heath,
And juniper and thistle, sprinkled o'er,
30 Fixing his downcast eye, he many an hour
A morbid pleasure nourished, tracing here
An emblem of his own unfruitful life:
And, lifting up his head, he then would gaze
On the more distant scene,——how lovely 'tis
35 Thou seest,——and he would gaze till it became
Far lovelier, and his heart could not sustain
The beauty, still more beauteous! Nor, that time,
When nature had subdued him to herself,
Would he forget those Beings to whose minds
40 Warm from the labours of benevolence
The world, and human life, appeared a scene
Of kindred loveliness: then he would sigh,
Inly disturbed, to think that others felt

What he must never feel: and so, lost Man!
On visionary views would fancy feed, *45*

Till his eye streamed with tears. In this deep vale
He died,—this seat his only monument.

 If Thou be one whose heart the holy forms
Of young imagination have kept pure,
Stranger! henceforth be warned; and know that pride, *50*
Howe'er disguised in its own majesty,
Is littleness; that he who feels contempt
For any living thing, hath faculties
Which he has never used; that thought with him
Is in its infancy. The man whose eye *55*
Is ever on himself doth look on one,
The least of Nature's works, one who might move
The wise man to that scorn which wisdom holds
Unlawful, ever. O be wiser, Thou!
Instructed that true knowledge leads to love; *60*
True dignity abides with him alone
Who, in the silent hour of inward thought,
Can still suspect, and still revere himself,
In lowliness of heart.

1795   1798

TO MY SISTER

It is the first mild day of March:
Each minute sweeter than before,
The redbreast sings from the tall larch
That stands beside our door.

There is a blessing in the air, *5*
Which seems a sense of joy to yield
To the bare trees, and mountains bare,
And grass in the green field.

My sister! ('tis a wish of mine)
10 Now that our morning meal is done,
Make haste, your morning task resign;
Come forth and feel the sun.

Edward will come with you;—and, pray,
Put on with speed your woodland dress;
15 And bring no book: for this one day
We'll give to idleness.

No joyless forms shall regulate
Our living calendar:
We from to-day, my Friend, will date
20 The opening of the year.

Love, now a universal birth,
From heart to heart is stealing.
From earth to man, from man to earth:
—It is the hour of feeling.

25 One moment now may give us more
Than years of toiling reason:
Our minds shall drink at every pore
The spirit of the season.

Some silent laws our hearts will make,
30 Which they shall long obey:
We for the year to come may take
Our temper from to-day.

And from the blessed power that rolls
About, below, above,
35 We'll frame the measure of our souls:
They shall be tuned to love.

Then come, my Sister! come, I pray,
With speed put on your woodland dress;
And bring no book: for this one day
40 We'll give to idleness.

1798   1798

SIMON LEE

The Old Huntsman;
With an Incident in Which He Was Concerned

In the sweet shire of Cardigan,
Not far from pleasant Ivor-hall,
An old Man dwells, a little man,—
'Tis said he once was tall.
Full five-and-thirty years he lived   *5*
A running huntsman merry;
And still the centre of his cheek
Is red as a ripe cherry.

No man like him the horn could sound,
And hill and valley rang with glee   *10*
When Echo bandied, round and round,
The halloo of Simon Lee.
In those proud days, he little cared
For husbandry or tillage;
To blither tasks did Simon rouse   *15*
The sleepers of the village.

He all the country could outrun,
Could leave both man and horse behind;
And often, ere the chase was done,
He reeled, and was stone-blind.   *20*
And still there's something in the world
At which his heart rejoices;
For when the chiming hounds are out,
He dearly loves their voices!

But, oh the heavy change!—bereft   *25*
Of health, strength, friends, and kindred, see!
Old Simon to the world is left
In liveried poverty.
His Master's dead,—and no one now
Dwells in the Hall of Ivor;   *30*
Men, dogs, and horses, all are dead;
He is the sole survivor.

And he is lean and he is sick;
His body, dwindled and awry,
35 Rests upon ankles swoln and thick;
His legs are thin and dry.
One prop he has, and only one,
His wife, an agèd woman,
Lives with him, near the waterfall,
40 Upon the village Common.

Beside their moss-grown hut of clay,
Not twenty paces from the door,
A scrap of land they have, but they
Are poorest of the poor.
45 This scrap of land he from the heath
Enclosed when he was stronger;
But what to them avails the land
Which he can till no longer? '

Oft, working by her Husband's side,
50 Ruth does what Simon cannot do;
For she, with scanty cause for pride,
Is stouter of the two.
And, though you with your utmost skill
From labour could not wean them,
55 'Tis little, very little—all
That they can do between them.

Few months of life has he in store
As he to you will tell,
For still, the more he works, the more
60 Do his weak ankles swell.
My gentle Reader, I perceive
How patiently you've waited,
And now I fear that you expect
Some tale will be related.

65 O Reader! had you in your mind
Such stores as silent thought can bring,
O gentle Reader! you would find
A tale in every thing.
What more I have to say is short,
70 And you must kindly take it:

It is no tale; but, should you think,
Perhaps a tale you'll make it.

One summer-day I chanced to see
This old Man doing all he could
To unearth the root of an old tree,   75
A stump of rotten wood.
The mattock tottered in his hand;
So vain was his endeavour,
That at the root of the old tree
He might have worked for ever.   80

"You're overtasked, good Simon Lee,
Give me your tool," to him I said;
And at the word right gladly he
Received my proffered aid.
I struck, and with a single blow   85
The tangled root I severed,
At which the poor old Man so long
And vainly had endeavoured.

The tears into his eyes were brought,
And thanks and praises seemed to run   90
So fast out of his heart, I thought
They never would have done.
—I've heard of hearts unkind, kind deeds
With coldness still returning;
Alas! the gratitude of men   95
Hath oftener left me mourning.

1798   1798

ANECDOTE FOR FATHERS

"Retine vim istam, falsa enim dicam, si coges."°
                                        EUSEBIUS

I have a boy of five years old;
His face is fair and fresh to see;

0 **Retine . . . coges** "Restrain that force of yours, for I shall tell lies
if you press me."

His limbs are cast in beauty's mould,
And dearly he loves me.

5   One morn we strolled on our dry walk,
Our quiet home all full in view,
And held such intermitted talk
As we are wont to do.

My thoughts on former pleasures ran;
10   I thought of Kilve's delightful shore,
Our pleasant home when spring began,
A long, long year before.

A day it was when I could bear
Some fond regrets to entertain;
15   With so much happiness to spare,
I could not feel a pain.

The green earth echoed to the feet
Of lambs that bounded through the glade,
From shade to sunshine, and as fleet
20   From sunshine back to shade.

Birds warbled round me—and each trace
Of inward sadness had its charm;
Kilve, thought I, was a favoured place,
And so is Liswyn farm.

25   My boy beside me tripped, so slim
And graceful in his rustic dress!
And, as he talked, I questioned him,
In very idleness.

"Now tell me, had you rather be,"
30   I said, and took him by the arm,
"On Kilve's smooth shore, by the green sea,
Or here at Liswyn farm?"

In careless mood he looked at me,
While still I held him by the arm,
35   And said, "At Kilve I'd rather be
Than here at Liswyn farm."

"Now, little Edward, say why so:
My little Edward, tell me why."—
"I cannot tell, I do not know."—
"Why, this is strange," said I;   *40*

"For here are woods, hills smooth and warm:
There surely must some reason be
Why you would change sweet Liswyn farm
For Kilve by the green sea."

At this my boy hung down his head,   *45*
He blushed with shame, nor made reply;
And three times to the child I said,
"Why, Edward, tell me why?"

His head he raised—there was in sight,
It caught his eye, he saw it plain—   *50*
Upon the house-top, glittering bright,
A broad and gilded vane.

Then did the boy his tongue unlock,
And eased his mind with this reply:
"At Kilve there was no weather-cock;   *55*
And that's the reason why."

O dearest, dearest boy! my heart
For better lore would seldom yearn,
Could I but teach the hundredth part
Of what from thee I learn.   *60*

1798   1798

WE ARE SEVEN

—A simple Child,
That lightly draws its breath,
And feels its life in every limb,
What should it know of death?

5   I met a little cottage Girl:
She was eight years old, she said;
Her hair was thick with many a curl
That clustered round her head.

She had a rustic, woodland air,
10 And she was wildly clad:
Her eyes were fair, and very fair;
—Her beauty made me glad.

"Sisters and brothers, little maid,
How many may you be?"
15 "How many? Seven in all," she said,
And wondering looked at me.

"And where are they? I pray you tell."
She answered, "Seven are we;
And two of us at Conway dwell,
20 And two are gone to sea.

"Two of us in the church-yard lie,
My sister and my brother;
And, in the church-yard cottage, I
Dwell near them with my mother."

25 "You say that two at Conway dwell,
And two are gone to sea,
Yet ye are seven! I pray you tell,
Sweet Maid, how this may be."

Then did the little Maid reply,
30 "Seven boys and girls are we;
Two of us in the church-yard lie,
Beneath the church-yard tree."

"You run about, my little Maid,
Your limbs they are alive;
35 If two are in the church-yard laid,
Then ye are only five."

"Their graves are green, they may be seen,"
The little Maid replied,
"Twelve steps or more from my mother's door,
And they are side by side. 40

"My stockings there I often knit,
My kerchief there I hem;
And there upon the ground I sit,
And sing a song to them.

"And often after sun-set, Sir, 45
When it is light and fair,
I take my little porringer,
And eat my supper there.

"The first that died was sister Jane;
In bed she moaning lay, 50
Till God released her of her pain;
And then she went away.

"So in the church-yard she was laid;
And, when the grass was dry,
Together round her grave we played, 55
My brother John and I.

"And when the ground was white with snow,
And I could run and slide,
My brother John was forced to go,
And he lies by her side." 60

"How many are you, then," said I,
"If they two are in heaven?"
Quick was the little Maid's reply,
"O Master! we are seven."

"But they are dead; those two are dead! 65
Their spirits are in heaven!"
'Twas throwing words away; for still

The little Maid would have her will,
And said, "Nay, we are seven!"

1798   1798

LINES WRITTEN IN EARLY SPRING

I heard a thousand blended notes,
While in a grove I sate reclined,
In that sweet mood when pleasant thoughts
Bring sad thoughts to the mind.

5 To her fair works did Nature link
The human soul that through me ran;
And much it grieved my heart to think
What man has made of man.

Through primrose tufts, in that green bower,
10 The periwinkle trailed its wreaths;
And 'tis my faith that every flower
Enjoys the air it breathes.

The birds around me hopped and played,
Their thoughts I cannot measure:—
15 But the least motion which they made,
It seemed a thrill of pleasure.

The budding twigs spread out their fan,
To catch the breezy air;
And I must think, do all I can,
20 That there was pleasure there.

If this belief from heaven be sent,
If such be Nature's holy plan,
Have I not reason to lament
What man has made of man?

1798   1798

THE THORN°

I

"There is a Thorn—it looks so old,
In truth, you'd find it hard to say
How it could ever have been young,
It looks so old and grey.
Not higher than a two years' child   5
It stands erect, this aged Thorn;
No leaves it has, no prickly points;
It is a mass of knotted joints,
A wretched thing forlorn.
It stands erect, and like a stone   10
With lichens is it overgrown.

II

"Like rock or stone, it is o'ergrown,
With lichens to the very top,
And hung with heavy tufts of moss,
A melancholy crop: 15
Up from the earth these mosses creep,
And this poor Thorn they clasp it round
So close, you'd say that they are bent
With plain and manifest intent
To drag it to the ground;   20
And all have joined in one endeavour
To bury this poor Thorn for ever.

III

"High on a mountain's highest ridge,
Where oft the stormy winter gale
Cuts like a scythe, while through the clouds   25
It sweeps from vale to vale;

0 **The Thorn** In 1800 Wordsworth appended a note emphasizing
the poem as a psychological study. "Superstitious men are almost
always men of slow faculties and deep feelings; their minds are not
loose but adhesive. . . . It was my wish in this poem to show the
manner in which such men cleave to the same ideas; and to follow
the turns of passion, always different, yet not palpably different, by
which their conversation is swayed."

Not five yards from the mountain path,
This Thorn you on your left espy;
And to the left, three yards beyond,
30 You see a little muddy pond
Of water—never dry,
Though but of compass small, and bare
To thirsty suns and parching air.

IV

"And, close beside this agèd Thorn,
35 There is a fresh and lovely sight,
A beauteous heap, a hill of moss,
Just half a foot in height.
All lovely colours there you see,
All colours that were ever seen;
40 And mossy network too is there,
As if by hand of lady fair
The work had woven been;
And cups, the darlings of the eye,
So deep is their vermilion dye.

V

45 "Ah me! what lovely tints are there
Of olive green and scarlet bright,
In spikes, in branches, and in stars,
Green, red, and pearly white!
This heap of earth o'ergrown with moss,
50 Which close beside the Thorn you see,
So fresh in all its beauteous dyes,
Is like an infant's grave in size,
As like as like can be:
But never, never any where,
55 An infant's grave was half so fair.

VI

"Now would you see this agèd Thorn,
This pond, and beauteous hill of moss,
You must take care and choose your time
The mountain when to cross.
60 For oft there sits between the heap,
So like an infant's grave in size,

And that same pond of which I spoke,
A Woman in a scarlet cloak,
And to herself she cries,
'Oh misery! oh misery!   *65*
Oh woe is me! oh misery!'

VII
"At all times of the day and night
This wretched Woman thither goes;
And she is known to every star,
And every wind that blows;   *70*
And there, beside the Thorn, she sits
When the blue daylight's in the skies,
And when the whirlwind's on the hill,
Or frosty air is keen and still,
And to herself she cries,   *75*
'O misery! oh misery!
Oh woe is me! oh misery!' "

VIII°
"Now wherefore, thus, by day and night,
In rain, in tempest, and in snow,
Thus to the dreary mountain-top   *80*
Does this poor Woman go?
And why sits she beside the Thorn
When the blue daylight's in the sky
Or when the whirlwind's on the hill,
Or frosty air is keen and still,   *85*
And wherefore does she cry?—
O wherefore? wherefore? tell me why
Does she repeat that doleful cry?"

IX
"I cannot tell; I wish I could;
For the true reason no one knows: *90*
But would you gladly view the spot,
The spot to which she goes;
The hillock like an infant's grave,
The pond—and Thorn, so old and grey;

VIII The eighth stanza and the first four lines of the nineteenth are
spoken by an anonymous interlocutor.

95 Pass by her door—'tis seldom shut—
    And if you see her in her hut—
    Then to the spot away!
    I never heard of such as dare
    Approach the spot when she is there."

                    X
100 "But wherefore to the mountain-top
     Can this unhappy Woman go,
     Whatever star is in the skies,
     Whatever wind may blow?"
     "Full twenty years are past and gone
105 Since she (her name is Martha Ray)
     Gave with a maiden's true good-will
     Her company to Stephen Hill;
     And she was blithe and gay,
     While friends and kindred all approved
110 Of him whom tenderly she loved.

                    XI
     "And they had fixed the wedding day,
     The morning that must wed them both
     But Stephen to another Maid
     Had sworn another oath;
115 And, with this other Maid, to church
     Unthinking Stephen went—
     Poor Martha! on that woeful day
     A pang of pitiless dismay
     Into her soul was sent;
120 A fire was kindled in her breast,
     Which might not burn itself to rest.

                    XII
     "They say, full six months after this,
     While yet the summer leaves were green,
     She to the mountain-top would go,
125 And there was often seen.
     What could she seek?—or wish to hide?
     Her state to any eye was plain;
     She was with child, and she was mad;
     Yet often was she sober sad

From her exceeding pain.   *130*
O guilty Father—would that death
Had saved him from that breach of faith!

XIII

"Sad case for such a brain to hold
Communion with a stirring child!
Sad case, as you may think, for one   *135*
Who had a brain so wild!
Last Christmas-eve we talked of this,
And grey-haired Wilfred of the glen
Held that the unborn infant wrought
About its mother's heart, and brought   *140*
Her senses back again:
And, when at last her time drew near,
Her looks were calm, her senses clear.

XIV

"More know I not, I wish I did,
And it should all be told to you;   *145*
For what became of this poor child
No mortal ever knew;
Nay—if a child to her was born
No earthly tongue could ever tell;
And if 'twas born alive or dead,   *150*
Far less could this with proof be said;
But some remember well
That Martha Ray about this time
Would up the mountain often climb.

XV

"And all that winter, when at night   *155*
The wind blew from the mountain-peak,
'Twas worth your while, though in the dark,
The churchyard path to seek:
For many a time and oft were heard
Cries coming from the mountain head: *160*
Some plainly living voices were;
And others, I've heard many swear,
Were voices of the dead:

I cannot think, whate'er they say,
165　They had to do with Martha Ray.

XVI

"But that she goes to this old Thorn,
The Thorn which I described to you,
And there sits in a scarlet cloak,
I will be sworn is true.
170　For one day with my telescope,
To view the ocean wide and bright,
When to this country first I came,
Ere I had heard of Martha's name,
I climbed the mountain's height:—
175　A storm came on, and I could see
No object higher than my knee.

XVII

" 'Twas mist and rain, and storm and rain:
No screen, no fence could I discover;
And then the wind! in sooth, it was
180　A wind full ten times over.
I looked around, I thought I saw
A jutting crag,—and off I ran,
Head-foremost, through the driving rain,
The shelter of the crag to gain;
185　And, as I am a man,
Instead of jutting crag I found
A Woman seated on the ground.

XVIII

"I did not speak—I saw her face;
Her face!—it was enough for me;
190　I turned about and heard her cry,
'Oh misery! oh misery!'
And there she sits, until the moon
Through half the clear blue sky will go;
And, when the little breezes make
195　The waters of the pond to shake,
As all the country know,
She shudders, and you hear her cry,
'Oh misery! oh misery!' "

XIX

"But what's the Thorn? and what the pond?
And what the hill of moss to her?   *200*
And what the creeping breeze that comes
The little pond to stir?"
"I cannot tell; but some will say
She hanged her baby on the tree;
Some say she drowned it in the pond,   *205*
Which is a little step beyond:
But all and each agree,
The little Babe was buried there,
Beneath that hill of moss so fair.

XX

"I've heard, the moss is spotted red   *210*
With drops of that poor infant's blood;
But kill a new-born infant thus,
I do not think she could!
Some say if to the pond you go,
And fix on it a steady view,   *215*
The shadow of a babe you trace,
A baby and a baby's face,
And that it looks at you;
Whene'er you look on it, 'tis plain
The baby looks at you again.   *220*

XXI

"And some had sworn an oath that she
Should be to public justice brought;
And for the little infant's bones
With spades they would have sought.
But instantly the hill of moss   *225*
Before their eyes began to stir!
And, for full fifty yards around,
The grass—it shook upon the ground!
Yet all do still aver
The little Babe lies buried there,   *230*
Beneath that hill of moss so fair.

XXII

"I cannot tell how this may be,
But plain it is the Thorn is bound

With heavy tufts of moss that strive
235 To drag it to the ground;
And this I know, full many a time,
When she was on the mountain high,
By day, and in the silent night,
When all the stars shone clear and bright,
240 That I have heard her cry,
'Oh misery! oh misery!
Oh woe is me! oh misery!' "

1798   1798

THE LAST OF THE FLOCK

I

In distant countries have I been,
And yet I have not often seen
A healthy man, a man full grown,
Weep in the public roads, alone.
5 But such a one, on English ground,
And in the broad highway, I met;
Along the broad highway he came,
His cheeks with tears were wet:
Sturdy he seemed, though he was sad;
10 And in his arms a Lamb he had.

II

He saw me, and he turned aside,
As if he wished himself to hide:
And with his coat did then essay
To wipe those briny tears away.
15 I followed him, and said, "My friend,
What ails you? wherefore weep you so?"
—"Shame on me, Sir! this lusty Lamb,
He makes my tears to flow.
To-day I fetched him from the rock;
20 He is the last of all my flock.

III

"When I was young, a single man,
And after youthful follies ran,
Though little given to care and thought,
Yet, so it was, an ewe I bought;
And other sheep from her I raised,   25
As healthy sheep as you might see;
And then I married, and was rich
As I could wish to be;
Of sheep I numbered a full score,
And every year increased my store.   30

IV

"Year after year my stock it grew;
And from this one, this single ewe,
Full fifty comely sheep I raised,
As fine a flock as ever grazed!
Upon the Quantock hills they fed;   35
They throve, and we at home did thrive:
—This lusty Lamb of all my store
Is all that is alive;
And now I care not if we die,
And perish all of poverty.   40

V

"Six Children, Sir! had I to feed;
Hard labour in a time of need!
My pride was tamed, and in our grief
I of the Parish asked relief.
They said, I was a wealthy man;   45
My sheep upon the uplands fed,
And it was fit that thence I took
Whereof to buy us bread.
'Do this: how can we give to you,'
They cried, 'what to the poor is due?'   50

VI

"I sold a sheep, as they had said,
And bought my little children bread,
And they were healthy with their food;
For me—it never did me good.

55 A woeful time it was for me,
To see the end of all my gains,
The pretty flock which I had reared
With all my care and pains,
To see it melt like snow away—
60 For me it was a woeful day.

VII
"Another still! and still another
A little lamb, and then its mother!
It was a vein that never stopped—
Like blood-drops from my heart they
dropped.
65 Till thirty were not left alive
They dwindled, dwindled, one by one;
And I may say, that many a time
I wished they all were gone—
Reckless of what might come at last
70 Were but the bitter struggle past.

VIII
"To wicked deeds I was inclined,
And wicked fancies crossed my mind;
And every man I chanced to see,
I thought he knew some ill of me:
75 No peace, no comfort could I find,
No ease, within doors or without;
And crazily and wearily
I went my work about;
And oft was moved to flee from home,
And hide my head where wild beasts
80   roam.

IX
"Sir! 'twas a precious flock to me,
As dear as my own children be;
For daily with my growing store
I loved my children more and more.
85 Alas! it was an evil time;
God cursed me in my sore distress;
I prayed, yet every day I thought

I loved my children less;
And every week, and every day,
My flock it seemed to melt away. 90

X
"They dwindled, Sir, sad sight to see!
From ten to five, from five to three,
A lamb, a wether, and a ewe;—
And then at last from three to two;
And, of my fifty, yesterday 95
I had but only one:
And here it lies upon my arm,
Alas! and I have none;—
To-day I fetched it from the rock;
It is the last of all my flock." 100

1798 1798

HER EYES ARE WILD

I
Her eyes are wild, her head is bare,
The sun has burnt her coal-black hair;
Her eyebrows have a rusty stain,
And she came far from over the main.
She has a baby on her arm, 5
Or else she were alone:
And underneath the hay-stack warm,
And on the greenwood stone,
She talked and sung the woods among,
And it was in the English tongue. 10

II
"Sweet babe! they say that I am mad,
But nay, my heart is far too glad;
And I am happy when I sing
Full many a sad and doleful thing:
Then, lovely baby, do not fear! 15

I pray thee have no fear of me;
But safe as in a cradle, here
My lovely baby! thou shalt be:
To thee I know too much I owe;
20 I cannot work thee any woe.

III

"A fire was once within my brain;
And in my head a dull, dull pain;
And fiendish faces, one, two, three,
Hung at my breast, and pulled at me;
25 But then there came a sight of joy;
It came at once to do me good;
I waked, and saw my little boy,
My little boy of flesh and blood;
Oh joy for me that sight to see!
30 For he was here, and only he.

IV

"Suck, little babe, oh suck again!
It cools my blood; it cools my brain;
Thy lips I feel them, baby! they
Draw from my heart the pain away.
35 Oh! press me with thy little hand;
It loosens something at my chest;
About that tight and deadly band
I feel thy little fingers prest.
The breeze I see is in the tree:
40 It comes to cool my babe and me.

V

"Oh! love me, love me, little boy!
Thou art thy mother's only joy;
And do not dread the waves below,
When o'er the sea-rock's edge we go;
45 The high crag cannot work me harm,
Nor leaping torrents when they howl;
The babe I carry on my arm,
He saves for me my precious soul;
Then happy lie; for blest am I;
50 Without me my sweet babe would die.

VI

"Then do not fear, my boy! for thee
Bold as a lion will I be;
And I will always be thy guide,
Through hollow snows and rivers wide.
I'll build an Indian bower; I know   *55*
The leaves that make the softest bed:
And, if from me thou wilt not go,
But still be true till I am dead,
My pretty thing! then thou shalt sing
As merry as the birds in spring.   *60*

VII

"Thy father cares not for my breast,
'Tis thine, sweet baby, there to rest;
'Tis all thine own!—and, if its hue
Be changed, that was so fair to view,
'Tis fair enough for thee, my dove!   *65*
My beauty, little child, is flown,
But thou wilt live with me in love;
And what if my poor cheek be brown?
'Tis well for me, thou canst not see
How pale and wan it else would be.   *70*

VIII

"Dread not their taunts, my little Life;
I am thy father's wedded wife;
And underneath the spreading tree
We two will live in honesty.
If his sweet boy he could forsake,   *75*
With me he never would have stayed:
From him no harm my babe can take;
But he, poor man! is wretched made;
And every day we two will pray
For him that's gone and far away.   *80*

IX

"I'll teach my boy the sweetest things:
I'll teach him how the owlet sings.
My little babe! thy lips are still,
And thou hast almost sucked thy fill.

85   —Where art thou gone, my own dear child?
      What wicked looks are those I see?
      Alas! alas! that look so wild,
      It never, never came from me:
      If thou art mad, my pretty lad,
90   Then I must be for ever sad.

X

      "Oh! smile on me, my little lamb!
      For I thy own dear mother am:
      My love for thee has well been tried:
      I've sought thy father far and wide.
95   I know the poisons of the shade;
      I know the earth-nuts fit for food:
      Then, pretty dear, be not afraid:
      We'll find thy father in the wood.
      Now laugh and be gay, to the woods away!
100   And there, my babe, we'll live for aye."

1798   1798

EXPOSTULATION AND REPLY

      "Why, William, on that old grey stone,
      Thus for the length of half a day,
      Why, William, sit you thus alone,
      And dream your time away?

5   "Where are your books?—that light bequeathed
      To Beings else forlorn and blind!
      Up! up! and drink the spirit breathed
      From dead men to their kind.

      "You look round on your Mother Earth,
10   As if she for no purpose bore you;
      As if you were her first-born birth,
      And none had lived before you!"

One morning thus, by Esthwaite lake,
When life was sweet, I knew not why,
To me my good friend Matthew° spake,   *15*
And thus I made reply:

"The eye—it cannot choose but see;
We cannot bid the ear be still;
Our bodies feel, where'er they be,
Against or with our will.   *20*

"Nor less I deem that there are Powers
Which of themselves our minds impress;
That we can feed this mind of ours
In a wise passiveness.

"Think you, 'mid all this mighty sum   *25*
Of things for ever speaking,
That nothing of itself will come,
But we must still be seeking?

"—Then ask not wherefore, here, alone,
Conversing as I may,   *30*
I sit upon this old grey stone,
And dream my time away."

1798   1798

THE TABLES TURNED

An Evening Scene on the Same Subject

Up! up! my Friend, and quit your books;
Or surely you'll grow double:

15 **Matthew** a schoolmaster; see also "The Two April Mornings"
and "The Fountain."

Up! up! my Friend, and clear your looks;
Why all this toil and trouble?

5   The sun, above the mountain's head,
A freshening lustre mellow
Through all the long green fields has spread,
His first sweet evening yellow.

Books! 'tis a dull and endless strife:
10   Come, hear the woodland linnet,
How sweet his music! on my life,
There's more of wisdom in it.

And hark! how blithe the throstle sings!
He, too, is no mean preacher:
15   Come forth into the light of things,
Let Nature be your Teacher.

She has a world of ready wealth,
Our minds and hearts to bless—
Spontaneous wisdom breathed by health,
20   Truth breathed by cheerfulness.

One impulse from a vernal wood
May teach you more of man,
Of moral evil and of good,
Than all the sages can.

25   Sweet is the lore which Nature brings;
Our meddling intellect
Mis-shapes the beauteous forms of things:—
We murder to dissect.

Enough of Science and of Art;
30   Close up those barren leaves;
Come forth, and bring with you a heart
That watches and receives.

1798   1798

OLD MAN TRAVELLING°

Animal Tranquillity and Decay,
A Sketch

           The little hedge-row birds,
That peck along the road, regard him not.
He travels on, and in his face, his step,
His gait, is one expression; every limb,
His look and bending figure, all bespeak   *5*
A man who does not move with pain, but moves
With thought—He is insensibly subdued
To settled quiet; he is one by whom
All effort seems forgotten, one to whom
Long patience has such mild composure given,   *10*
That patience now doth seem a thing, of which
He hath no need. He is by nature led
To peace so perfect, that the young behold
With envy, what the old man hardly feels.
—I asked him whither he was bound, and what   *15*
The object of his journey; he replied
"Sir! I am going many miles to take
A last leave of my son, a mariner,
Who from a sea-fight has been brought to Falmouth,
And there is dying in an hospital."   *20*

1797   1798

LINES

Composed a few miles above Tintern Abbey, on revisit-
ing the banks of the Wye during a tour. July 13, 1798.

Five years have past; five summers, with the length
Of five long winters! and again I hear

0 **Old Man Travelling** The political context is the war between En-
gland and France, which had begun in 1793.

These waters, rolling from their mountain-springs
With a soft inland murmur.——Once again
5 Do I behold these steep and lofty cliffs,
That on a wild secluded scene impress
Thoughts of more deep seclusion; and connect
The landscape with the quiet of the sky.
The day is come when I again repose
10 Here, under this dark sycamore, and view
These plots of cottage-ground, these orchard-tufts,
Which at this season, with their unripe fruits,
Are clad in one green hue, and lose themselves
'Mid groves and copses. Once again I see
15 These hedge-rows, hardly hedge-rows, little lines
Of sportive wood run wild: these pastoral farms,
Green to the very door; and wreaths of smoke
Sent up, in silence, from among the trees!
With some uncertain notice, as might seem
20 Of vagrant dwellers in the houseless woods,
Or of some Hermit's cave, where by his fire
The Hermit sits alone.

                     These beauteous forms,
Through a long absence, have not been to me
As is a landscape to a blind man's eye:
25 But oft, in lonely rooms, and 'mid the din
Of towns and cities, I have owed to them,
In hours of weariness, sensations sweet,
Felt in the blood, and felt along the heart;
And passing even into my purer mind,
30 With tranquil restoration:——feelings too
Of unremembered pleasure: such, perhaps,
As have no slight or trivial influence
On that best portion of a good man's life,
His little, nameless, unremembered, acts
35 Of kindness and of love. Nor less, I trust,
To them I may have owed another gift,
Of aspect more sublime; that blessed mood,
In which the burthen of the mystery,
In which the heavy and the weary weight
40 Of all this unintelligible world,
Is lightened:——that serene and blessèd mood,

In which the affections gently lead us on,—
Until, the breath of this corporeal frame
And even the motion of our human blood
Almost suspended, we are laid asleep   *45*
In body, and become a living soul:
While with an eye made quiet by the power
Of harmony, and the deep power of joy,
We see into the life of things.

                If this
Be but a vain belief, yet, oh! how oft—   *50*
In darkness and amid the many shapes
Of joyless daylight; when the fretful stir
Unprofitable, and the fever of the world,
Have hung upon the beatings of my heart—
How oft, in spirit, have I turned to thee,   *55*
O sylvan Wye! thou wanderer thro' the woods,
How often has my spirit turned to thee!

    And now, with gleams of half-extinguished thought,
With many recognitions dim and faint,
And somewhat of a sad perplexity,   *60*
The picture of the mind revives again:
While here I stand, not only with the sense
Of present pleasure, but with pleasing thoughts
That in this moment there is life and food
For future years. And so I dare to hope,   *65*
Though changed, no doubt, from what I was when first
I came among these hills;° when like a roe
I bounded o'er the mountains, by the sides
Of the deep rivers, and the lonely streams,
Wherever nature led: more like a man   *70*
Flying from something that he dreads, than one
Who sought the thing he loved. For nature then
(The coarser pleasures of my boyish days,
And their glad animal movements all gone by)
To me was all in all.—I cannot paint   *75*
What then I was. The sounding cataract
Haunted me like a passion: the tall rock,

66–67 first . . . hills referring to his previous visit in 1793 when he was twenty-three, or to an even earlier time.

The mountain, and the deep and gloomy wood,
Their colours and their forms, were then to me
80 An appetite; a feeling and a love,
That had no need for a remoter charm,
By thought supplied, nor any interest
Unborrowed from the eye.—That time is past,
And all its aching joys are now no more,
85 And all its dizzy raptures. Not for this
Faint° I, nor mourn nor murmur; other gifts
Have followed; for such loss, I would believe,
Abundant recompense. For I have learned
To look on nature, not as in the hour
90 Of thoughtless youth; but hearing oftentimes
The still, sad music of humanity,
Nor harsh nor grating, though of ample power
To chasten and subdue. And I have felt
A presence that disturbs me with the joy
95 Of elevated thoughts; a sense sublime
Of something far more deeply interfused,
Whose dwelling is the light of setting suns,
And the round ocean and the living air,
And the blue sky, and in the mind of man:
100 A motion and a spirit, that impels
All thinking things, all objects of all thought,
And rolls through all things. Therefore am I still
A lover of the meadows and the woods,
And mountains; and of all that we behold
105 From this green earth; of all the mighty world
Of eye, and ear,—both what they half create,
And what perceive; well pleased to recognise
In nature and the language of the sense
The anchor of my purest thoughts, the nurse,
110 The guide, the guardian of my heart, and soul
Of all my moral being.

              Nor perchance,
If I were not thus taught, should I the more
Suffer my genial spirits° to decay:
For thou art with me here upon the banks

86 **Faint** become faint-hearted. 113 **genial spirits** natural zest, inborn poetic powers.

Of this fair river; thou my dearest Friend, *115*
My dear, dear Friend; and in thy voice I catch
The language of my former heart, and read
My former pleasures in the shooting lights
Of thy wild eyes. Oh! yet a little while
May I behold in thee what I was once, *120*
My dear, dear Sister! and this prayer I make,
Knowing that Nature never did betray
The heart that loved her; 'tis her privilege,
Through all the years of this our life, to lead
From joy to joy: for she can so inform *125*
The mind that is within us, so impress
With quietness and beauty, and so feed
With lofty thoughts, that neither evil tongues,
Rash judgments, nor the sneers of selfish men,
Nor greetings where no kindness is, nor all *130*
The dreary intercourse of daily life,
Shall e'er prevail against us, or disturb
Our cheerful faith, that all which we behold
Is full of blessings. Therefore let the moon
Shine on thee in thy solitary walk; *135*
And let the misty mountain-winds be free
To blow against thee: and, in after years,
When these wild ecstasies shall be matured
Into a sober pleasure; when thy mind
Shall be a mansion for all lovely forms, *140*
Thy memory be as a dwelling-place
For all sweet sounds and harmonies; oh! then,
If solitude, or fear, or pain, or grief,
Should be thy portion, with what healing thoughts
Of tender joy wilt thou remember me, *145*
And these my exhortations! Nor, perchance—
If I should be where I no more can hear
Thy voice, nor catch from thy wild eyes these gleams
Of past existence—wilt thou then forget
That on the banks of this delightful stream *150*
We stood together; and that I, so long
A worshipper of Nature, hither came
Unwearied in that service: rather say
With warmer love—oh! with far deeper zeal
Of holier love. Nor wilt thou then forget *155*

That after many wanderings, many years
Of absence, these steep woods and lofty cliffs,
And this green pastoral landscape, were to me
More dear, both for themselves and for thy sake!

1798   1798

A NIGHT-PIECE°

                                 —The sky is overcast
With a continuous cloud of texture close,
Heavy and wan, all whitened by the Moon,
Which through that veil is indistinctly seen,
5   A dull, contracted circle, yielding light
So feebly spread, that not a shadow falls,
Chequering the ground—from rock, plant, tree, or tower.
At length a pleasant instantaneous gleam
Startles the pensive traveller while he treads
10   His lonesome path, with unobserving eye
Bent earthwards; he looks up—the clouds are split
Asunder,—and above his head he sees
The clear Moon, and the glory of the heavens.
There, in a black-blue vault she sails along,
15   Followed by multitudes of stars, that, small
And sharp, and bright, along the dark abyss
Drive as she drives: how fast they wheel away,
Yet vanish not!—the wind is in the tree,
But they are silent;—still they roll along
20   Immeasurably distant; and the vault,
Built round by those white clouds, enormous clouds,
Still deepens its unfathomable depth.
At length the Vision closes; and the mind,
Not undisturbed by the delight it feels,
25   Which slowly settles into peaceful calm,
Is left to muse upon the solemn scene.

1798   1815

0 **A Night-Piece** Not published in *Lyrical Ballads* but from the
period.

NUTTING

It seems a day
(I speak of one from many singled out)
One of those heavenly days that cannot die;
When, in the eagerness of boyish hope,
I left our cottage-threshold, sallying forth   5
With a huge wallet o'er my shoulders slung,
A nutting-crook in hand; and turned my steps
Tow'rd some far-distant wood, a Figure quaint,
Tricked out in proud disguise of cast-off weeds
Which for that service had been husbanded,   10
By exhortation of my frugal Dame—
Motley accoutrement, of power to smile
At thorns, and brakes, and brambles,—and, in truth,
More ragged than need was! O'er pathless rocks,
Through beds of matted fern, and tangled thickets, 15
Forcing my way, I came to one dear nook
Unvisited, where not a broken bough
Drooped with its withered leaves, ungracious sign
Of devastation; but the hazels rose
Tall and erect, with tempting clusters hung,   20
A virgin scene!—A little while I stood,
Breathing with such suppression of the heart
As joy delights in; and, with wise restraint
Voluptuous, fearless of a rival, eyed
The banquet;—or beneath the trees I sate   25
Among the flowers, and with the flowers I played;
A temper known to those, who, after long
And weary expectation, have been blest
With sudden happiness beyond all hope.
Perhaps it was a bower beneath whose leaves   30
The violets of five seasons re-appear
And fade, unseen by any human eye;
Where fairy water-breaks do murmur on
For ever; and I saw the sparkling foam,
And—with my cheek on one of those green stones   35
That, fleeced with moss, under the shady trees,
Lay round me, scattered like a flock of sheep—
I heard the murmur and the murmuring sound,

In that sweet mood when pleasure loves to pay
40 Tribute to ease; and, of its joy secure,
The heart luxuriates with indifferent things,
Wasting its kindliness on stocks and stones,
And on the vacant air. Then up I rose,
And dragged to earth both branch and bough, with crash
45 And merciless ravage: and the shady nook
Of hazels, and the green and mossy bower,
Deformed and sullied, patiently gave up
Their quiet being: and, unless I now
Confound my present feelings with the past;
50 Ere from the mutilated bower I turned
Exulting, rich beyond the wealth of kings,
I felt a sense of pain when I beheld
The silent trees, and saw the intruding sky.—
Then, dearest Maiden, move along these shades
55 In gentleness of heart; with gentle hand
Touch—for there is a spirit in the woods.

1798–99   1800

THE TWO APRIL MORNINGS

We walked along, while bright and red
Uprose the morning sun;
And Matthew stopped, he looked, and said,
"The will of God be done!"

5 A village schoolmaster was he,
With hair of glittering grey;
As blithe a man as you could see
On a spring holiday.

And on that morning, through the grass,
10 And by the steaming rills,
We travelled merrily, to pass
A day among the hills.

"Our work," said I, "was well begun,
Then, from thy breast what thought,
Beneath so beautiful a sun,   *15*
So sad a sigh has brought?"

A second time did Matthew stop;
And fixing still his eye
Upon the eastern mountain-top,
To me he made reply: *20*

"Yon cloud with that long purple cleft
Brings fresh into my mind
A day like this which I have left
Full thirty years behind.

"And just above yon slope of corn   *25*
Such colours, and no other,
Were in the sky, that April morn,
Of this the very brother.

"With rod and line I sued the sport
Which that sweet season gave,   *30*
And, to the church-yard come, stopped short
Beside my daughter's grave.

"Nine summers had she scarcely seen,
The pride of all the vale;
And then she sang;—she would have been   *35*
A very nightingale.

"Six feet in earth my Emma lay;
And yet I loved her more,
For so it seemed, than till that day
I e'er had loved before.   *40*

"And, turning from her grave, I met,
Beside the churchyard yew,
A blooming Girl, whose hair was wet
With points of morning dew.

45 "A basket on her head she bare;
 Her brow was smooth and white:
 To see a child so very fair,
 It was a pure delight!

 "No fountain from its rocky cave
50 E'er tripped with foot so free;
 She seemed as happy as a wave
 That dances on the sea.

 "There came from me a sigh of pain
 Which I could ill confine;
55 I looked at her, and looked again:
 And did not wish her mine!"

 Matthew is in his grave, yet now,
 Methinks, I see him stand,
 As at that moment, with a bough
60 Of wilding in his hand.

1799   1800

THE FOUNTAIN

A Conversation

 We talked with open heart, and tongue
 Affectionate and true,
 A pair of friends, though I was young,
 And Matthew seventy-two.

5 We lay beneath a spreading oak,
 Beside a mossy seat;
 And from the turf a fountain broke,
 And gurgled at our feet.

"Now, Matthew!" said I, "let us match
This water's pleasant tune   10
With some old border-song, or catch
That suits a summer's noon;

"Or of the church-clock and the chimes
Sing here beneath the shade,
That half-mad thing of witty rhymes   15
Which you last April made!"

In silence Matthew lay, and eyed
The spring beneath the tree;
And thus the dear old Man replied,
The grey-haired man of glee: 20

"No check, no stay, this Streamlet fears;
How merrily it goes!
'Twill murmur on a thousand years,
And flow as now it flows.

"And here, on this delightful day,   25
I cannot choose but think
How oft, a vigorous man, I lay
Beside this fountain's brink.

"My eyes are dim with childish tears,
My heart is idly stirred,   30
For the same sound is in my ears
Which in those days I heard.

"Thus fares it still in our decay:
And yet the wiser mind
Mourns less for what age takes away   35
Than what it leaves behind.

"The blackbird amid leafy trees,
The lark above the hill,
Let loose their carols when they please,
Are quiet when they will.   40

"With Nature never do *they* wage
A foolish strife; they see
A happy youth, and their old age
Is beautiful and free:

45   "But we are pressed by heavy laws;
And often, glad no more,
We wear a face of joy, because
We have been glad of yore.

. "If there be one who need bemoan
50   His kindred laid in earth,
The household hearts that were his own;
It is the man of mirth.

"My days, my Friend, are almost gone,
My life has been approved,
55   And many love me; but by none
Am I enough beloved."

"Now both himself and me he wrongs,
The man who thus complains!
I live and sing my idle songs
60   Upon these happy plains;

"And, Matthew, for thy children dead
I'll be a son to thee!"
At this he grasped my hand, and said,
"Alas! that cannot be."

65   We rose up from the fountain-side;
And down the smooth descent
Of the green sheep-track did we glide;
And through the wood we went;

And, ere we came to Leonard's rock,
70   He sang those witty rhymes
About the crazy old church-clock,
And the bewildered chimes.

THE REVERIE OF POOR SUSAN

At the corner of Wood Street,° when daylight appears,
Hangs a Thrush that sings loud, it has sung for three
     years:
Poor Susan has passed by the spot, and has heard
In the silence of morning the song of the Bird.

'Tis a note of enchantment; what ails her? She sees   *5*
A mountain ascending, a vision of trees;
Bright volumes of vapour through Lothbury glide,
And a river flows on through the vale of Cheapside.

Green pastures she views in the midst of the dale,
Down which she so often has tripped with her pail;   *10*
And a single small cottage, a nest like a dove's,
The one only dwelling on earth that she loves.

She looks, and her heart is in heaven: but they fade,
The mist and the river, the hill and the shade:
The stream will not flow, and the hill will not rise,   *15*
And the colours have all passed away from her eyes!

1797   **1800**

THE SAILOR'S MOTHER°

One morning (raw it was and wet,
A foggy day in winter time)
A Woman in the road I met,

---

1 **Wood Street** in London, like Lothbury (line 7) and Cheapside (8).
"This [poem] arose out of my observation of the affecting music of
these birds hanging in this way [caged] in the London streets during
the freshness and stillness of the Spring morning" (Wordsworth).

0 **The Sailor's Mother** included here as a "lyrical ballad" though
composed somewhat later.

Not old, though something past her prime:
5   Majestic in her person, tall and straight;
And like a Roman matron's was her mien and gait.

The ancient Spirit is not dead;
Old times, thought I, are breathing there;
Proud was I that my country bred
10   Such strength, a dignity so fair:
She begged an alms, like one in poor estate;
I looked at her again, nor did my pride abate.

When from these lofty thoughts I woke,
With the first word I had to spare
15   I said to her, "Beneath your Cloak
What's that which on your arm you bear?"
She answered soon as she the question heard,
"A simple burthen, Sir, a little Singing-bird."

And, thus continuing, she said,
20   "I had a Son, who many a day
Sailed on the seas; but he is dead;
In Denmark he was cast away;
And I have been as far as Hull, to see
What clothes he might have left, or other property.

25   The Bird and Cage they both were his;
'Twas my Son's Bird; and neat and trim
He kept it: many voyages
This Singing-bird hath gone with him;
When last he sailed he left the Bird behind;
30   As it might be, perhaps, from bodings of his mind.

He to a Fellow-lodger's care
Had left it, to be watched and fed,
Till he came back again; and there
I found it when my Son was dead;
35   And now, God help me for my little wit!
I trail it with me, Sir! he took so much delight in it."

1802
                                              1807

THE OLD CUMBERLAND BEGGAR

I saw an agèd Beggar in my walk;
And he was seated, by the highway side,
On a low structure of rude masonry
Built at the foot of a huge hill, that they
Who lead their horses down the steep rough road   5
May thence remount at ease. The agèd Man
Had placed his staff across the broad smooth stone
That overlays the pile; and, from a bag
All white with flour, the dole of village dames,
He drew his scraps and fragments, one by one;   10
And scanned them with a fixed and serious look
Of idle computation. In the sun,
Upon the second step of that small pile,
Surrounded by those wild unpeopled hills,
He sat, and ate his food in solitude: 15
And ever, scattered from his palsied hand,
That, still attempting to prevent the waste,
Was baffled still, the crumbs in little showers
Fell on the ground; and the small mountain birds,
Not venturing yet to peck their destined meal,   20
Approached within the length of half his staff.

Him from my childhood have I known; and then
He was so old, he seems not older now;
He travels on, a solitary Man,
So helpless in appearance, that for him   25
The sauntering Horseman throws not with a slack
And careless hand his alms upon the ground,
But stops,—that he may safely lodge the coin
Within the old Man's hat; nor quits him so,
But still, when he has given his horse the rein,   30
Watches the agèd Beggar with a look
Sidelong, and half-reverted. She who tends
The toll-gate, when in summer at her door
She turns her wheel,° if on the road she sees
The agèd Beggar coming, quits her work,   35
And lifts the latch for him that he may pass.

34 wheel spinning wheel.

The post-boy, when his rattling wheels o'ertake
The agèd Beggar in the woody lane,
Shouts to him from behind; and, if thus warned
40 The old man does not change his course, the boy
Turns with less noisy wheels to the roadside,
And passes gently by, without a curse
Upon his lips or anger at his heart.

He travels on, a solitary Man;
45 His age has no companion. On the ground
His eyes are turned, and, as he moves along,
They move along the ground; and, evermore,
Instead of common and habitual sight
Of fields with rural works, of hill and dale,
50 And the blue sky, one little span of earth
Is all his prospect. Thus, from day to day,
Bow-bent, his eyes for ever on the ground,
He plies his weary journey; seeing still,
And seldom knowing that he sees, some straw,
55 Some scattered leaf, or marks which, in one track,
The nails of cart or chariot-wheel have left
Impressed on the white road,—in the same line,
At distance still the same. Poor Traveller!
His staff trails with him; scarcely do his feet
60 Disturb the summer dust; he is so still
In look and motion, that the cottage curs,
Ere he has passed the door, will turn away,
Weary of barking at him. Boys and girls,
The vacant and the busy, maids and youths,
65 And urchins newly breeched—all pass him by:
Him even the slow-paced waggon leaves behind.

But deem not this Man useless.—Statesmen! ye
Who are so restless in your wisdom, ye
Who have a broom still ready in your hands
70 To rid the world of nuisances; ye proud,
Heart-swoln, while in your pride ye contemplate
Your talents, power, or wisdom, deem him not
A burthen of the earth! 'Tis Nature's law
That none, the meanest of created things,
75 Of forms created the most vile and brute,

The dullest or most noxious, should exist
Divorced from good—a spirit and pulse of good,
A life and soul, to every mode of being
Inseparably linked. Then be assured
That least of all can aught—that ever owned   80
The heaven-regarding eye and front sublime
Which man is born to—sink, howe'er depressed,
So low as to be scorned without a sin;
Without offence to God cast out of view;
Like the dry remnant of a garden-flower   85
Whose seeds are shed, or as an implement
Worn out and worthless. While from door to door,
This old Man creeps, the villagers in him
Behold a record which together binds
Past deeds and offices of charity,   90
Else unremembered, and so keeps alive
The kindly mood in hearts which lapse of years,
And that half-wisdom half-experience gives,
Make slow to feel, and by sure steps resign
To selfishness and cold oblivious cares.   95
Among the farms and solitary huts,
Hamlets and thinly-scattered villages,
Where'er the agèd Beggar takes his rounds,
The mild necessity of use° compels
To acts of love; and habit does the work   100
Of reason; yet prepares that after-joy
Which reason cherishes. And thus the soul,
By that sweet taste of pleasure unpursued,
Doth find herself insensibly disposed
To virtue and true goodness.   105

                Some there are,
By their good works exalted, lofty minds
And meditative, authors of delight
And happiness, which to the end of time
Will live, and spread, and kindle: even such minds
In childhood, from this solitary Being,   110
Or from like wanderer, haply have received

99 **mild necessity of use** This difficult phrase introduces an attack
on "moral philosophy" and "cold reason" as the prerequisites for
charitable acts. The effect of charity, both on giver and receiver, is
greatest when spontaneous or induced by habit ("use").

(A thing more precious far than all that books
Or the solicitudes of love can do!)
That first mild touch of sympathy and thought,
115 In which they found their kindred with a world
Where want and sorrow were. The easy man
Who sits at his own door,—and, like the pear
That overhangs his head from the green wall,
Feeds in the sunshine; the robust and young,
120 The prosperous and unthinking, they who live
Sheltered, and flourish in a little grove
Of their own kindred;—all behold in him
A silent monitor, which on their minds
Must needs impress a transitory thought
125 Of self-congratulation, to the heart
Of each recalling his peculiar boons,
His charters and exemptions; and, perchance,
Though he to no one give the fortitude
And circumspection needful to preserve
130 His present blessings, and to husband up
The respite of the season, he, at least,
And 'tis no vulgar service, makes them felt.

　　Yet further.—Many, I believe, there are
Who live a life of virtuous decency,
135 Men who can hear the Decalogue and feel
No self-reproach; who of the moral law
Established in the land where they abide
Are strict observers; and not negligent
In acts of love to those with whom they dwell,
140 Their kindred, and the children of their blood.
Praise be to such, and to their slumbers peace!
—But of the poor man ask, the abject poor;
Go, and demand of him, if there be here
In this cold abstinence from evil deeds,
145 And these inevitable charities,
Wherewith to satisfy the human soul?
No—man is dear to man; the poorest poor
Long for some moments in a weary life
When they can know and feel that they have been,
150 Themselves, the fathers and the dealers-out
Of some small blessings; have been kind to such
As needed kindness, for this single cause,

That we have all of us one human heart.
—Such pleasure is to one kind Being known,
My neighbour, when with punctual care, each week   *155*
Duly as Friday comes, though pressed herself
By her own wants, she from her store of meal
Takes one unsparing handful for the scrip
Of this old Mendicant, and, from her door
Returning with exhilarated heart,   *160*
Sits by her fire, and builds her hope in heaven.

Then let him pass, a blessing on his head!
And while in that vast solitude to which
The tide of things has borne him, he appears
To breathe and live but for himself alone,   *165*
Unblamed, uninjured, let him bear about
The good which the benignant law of Heaven
Has hung around him: and, while life is his,
Still let him prompt the unlettered villagers
To tender offices and pensive thoughts.   *170*
—Then let him pass, a blessing on his head!
And, long as he can wander, let him breathe
The freshness of the valleys; let his blood
Struggle with frosty air and winter snows;
And let the chartered wind that sweeps the heath   *175*
Beat his grey locks against his withered face.
Reverence the hope whose vital anxiousness
Gives the last human interest to his heart.
May never HOUSE, misnamed of INDUSTRY,°
Make him a captive!—for that pent-up din,   *180*
Those life-consuming sounds that clog the air,
Be his the natural silence of old age!
Let him be free of mountain solitudes;
And have around him, whether heard or not,
The pleasant melody of woodland birds.   *185*
Few are his pleasures: if his eyes have now
Been doomed so long to settle upon earth
That not without some effort they behold
The countenance of the horizontal sun,
Rising or setting, let the light at least   *190*

179 **House . . . Industry** For Wordsworth's attack on these institutions, see his letter to Charles James Fox (January 14, 1801).

Find a free entrance to their languid orbs,
And let him, *where* and *when* he will, sit down
Beneath the trees, or on a grassy bank
Of highway side, and with the little birds
195 Share his chance-gathered meal; and, finally,
As in the eye of Nature he has lived,
So in the eye of Nature let him die!

1797

1800

PETER BELL°

*   *   *   *

"He roved among the vales and streams,
In the green wood and hollow dell;
They were his dwellings night and day,—
But nature ne'er could find the way
245 Into the heart of Peter Bell.

"In vain, through every changeful year,
Did Nature lead him as before;
A primrose by a river's brim
A yellow primrose was to him,
250 And it was nothing more.

"Small change it made in Peter's heart
To see his gentle panniered train
With more than vernal pleasure feeding,
Where'er the tender grass was leading
255 Its earliest green along the lane.

0 **Peter Bell,** written in 1798 but not published until 1819, is the
tale of a ruffian converted to kindness. This extract evokes his first
awakening to true feelings for Nature.

"In vain, through water, earth, and air,
The soul of happy sound was spread,
When Peter on some April morn,
Beneath the broom or budding thorn,
Made the warm earth his lazy bed.   260

"At noon, when, by the forest's edge
He lay beneath the branches high,
The soft blue sky did never melt
Into his heart; he never felt
The witchery of the soft blue sky!   265

"On a fair prospect some have looked
And felt, as I have heard them say,
As if the moving time had been
A thing as steadfast as the scene
On which they gazed themselves away.   270

"Within the breast of Peter Bell
These silent raptures found no place;
He was a Carl° as wild and rude
As ever hue-and-cry pursued,
As ever ran a felon's race.   275

"Of all that lead a lawless life,
Of all that love their lawless lives,
In city or in village small,
He was the wildest far of all;—
He had a dozen wedded wives.   280

"Nay, start not!—wedded wives—and twelve!
But how one wife could e'er come near him,
In simple truth I cannot tell;
For, be it said of Peter Bell,
To see him was to fear him.   285

"Though Nature could not touch his heart
By lovely forms, and silent weather,
And tender sounds, yet you might see
At once that Peter Bell and she
Had often been together.   290

273 **Carl** churl.

"A savage wildness round him hung
As of a dweller out of doors;
In his whole figure and his mien
A savage character was seen
295 Of mountains and of dreary moors.

"To all the unshaped half-human thoughts
Which solitary Nature feeds
'Mid summer storms or winter's ice,
Had Peter joined whatever vice
300 The cruel city breeds.

"His face was keen as is the wind
That cuts along the hawthorn-fence;
Of courage you saw little there,
But, in its stead, a medley air
305 Of cunning and of impudence.

"He had a dark and sidelong walk,
And long and slouching was his gait;
Beneath his looks so bare and bold,
You might perceive, his spirit cold
310 Was playing with some inward bait.

"His forehead wrinkled was and furred;
A work, one half of which was done
By thinking of his *'whens'* and *'hows';*
And half, by knitting of his brows
315 Beneath the glaring sun.

"There was a hardness in his cheek,
There was a hardness in his eye,
As if the man had fixed his face,
In many a solitary place,
320 Against the wind and open sky!"

  *   *   *   *

Across the deep and quiet spot
Is Peter driving through the grass—
And now has reached the skirting trees;
When, turning round his head, he see-
385 A solitary Ass.

"A prize!" cries Peter—but he first
Must spy about him far and near:
There's not a single house in sight,
No woodman's hut, no cottage light—
Peter, you need not fear!   *890*

There's nothing to be seen but woods,
And rocks that spread a hoary gleam,
And this one Beast, that from the bed
Of the green meadow hangs his head
Over the silent stream.   *895*

His head is with a halter bound;
The halter seizing, Peter leapt
Upon the Creature's back, and plied
With ready heels his shaggy side;
But still the Ass his station kept.   *400*

Then Peter gave a sudden jerk,
A jerk that from a dungeon-floor
Would have pulled up an iron ring;
But still the heavy-headed Thing
Stood just as he had stood before!   *405*

Quoth Peter, leaping from his seat,
"There is some plot against me laid;"
Once more the little meadow-ground
And all the hoary cliffs around
He cautiously surveyed.   *410*

All, all is silent—rocks and woods,
All still and silent—far and near!
Only the Ass, with motion dull,
Upon the pivot of his skull
Turns round his long left ear.   *415*

Thought Peter, What can mean all this?
Some ugly witchcraft must be here!
—Once more the Ass, with motion dull,
Upon the pivot of his skull
Turned round his long left ear.   *420*

Suspicion ripened into dread;
Yet with deliberate action slow,
His staff high-raising, in the pride
Of skill, upon the sounding hide
425 He dealt a sturdy blow.

The poor Ass staggered with the shock;
And then, as if to take his ease,
In quiet uncomplaining mood,
Upon the spot where he had stood,
430 Dropped gently down upon his knees;

As gently on his side he fell;
And by the river's brink did lie;
And, while he lay like one that mourned,
The patient Beast on Peter turned
435 His shining hazel eye.

'Twas but one mild, reproachful look,
A look more tender than severe;
And straight in sorrow, not in dread,
He turned the eye-ball in his head
440 Towards the smooth river deep and clear.

Upon the Beast the sapling rings;
His lank sides heaved, his limbs they stirred;
He gave a groan, and then another,
Of that which went before the brother,
445 And then he gave a third.

All by the moonlight river side
He gave three miserable groans;
And not till now hath Peter seen
How gaunt the Creature is,—how lean
450 And sharp his staring bones!

With legs stretched out and stiff he lay:—
No word of kind commiseration
Fell at the sight from Peter's tongue;
With hard contempt his heart was wrung,
455 With hatred and vexation.

The meagre beast lay still as death;
And Peter's lips with fury quiver;
Quoth he, "You little mulish dog,
I'll fling your carcass like a log
Head-foremost down the river!"   460

An impious oath confirmed the threat—
Whereat from the earth on which he lay
To all the echoes, south and north,
And east and west, the Ass sent forth
A long and clamorous bray!   465

This outcry, on the heart of Peter,
Seems like a note of joy to strike,—
Joy at the heart of Peter knocks;
But in the echo of the rocks
Was something Peter did not like.   470

Whether to cheer his coward breast,
Or that he could not break the chain,
In this serene and solemn hour,
Twined round him by demoniac power,
To the blind work he turned again.   475

Among the rocks and winding crags;
Among the mountains far away;
Once more the Ass did lengthen out
More ruefully a deep-drawn shout,
The hard dry see-saw of his horrible bray!   480

What is there now in Peter's heart?
Or whence the might of this strange sound?
The moon uneasy looked and dimmer,
The broad blue heavens appeared to glimmer,
And the rocks staggered all around—   485

         *   *   *   *

1798   1819

STRANGE FITS OF PASSION
HAVE I KNOWN°

Strange fits of passion have I known:
And I will dare to tell,
But in the Lover's ear alone,
What once to me befel.

5   When she I loved looked every day
Fresh as a rose in June,
I to her cottage bent my way,
Beneath an evening-moon.

Upon the moon I fixed my eye,
10   All over the wide lea;
With quickening pace my horse drew nigh
Those paths so dear to me.

And now we reached the orchard-plot;
And, as we climbed the hill,
15   The sinking moon to Lucy's cot
Came near, and nearer still.

In one of those sweet dreams I slept,
Kind Nature's gentlest boon!
And all the while my eyes I kept
20   On the descending moon.

My horse moved on; hoof after hoof
He raised, and never stopped:
When down behind the cottage roof,
At once, the bright moon dropped.

25   What fond and wayward thoughts° will slide
Into a Lover's head!
"O mercy!" to myself I cried,
"If Lucy should be dead!"

1799

1800

0 **Strange . . . Known** This and the four poems that follow are
known as "the Lucy poems." 25 **fond . . . thoughts** foolish yet
engaging thoughts.

SHE DWELT AMONG THE
UNTRODDEN WAYS

She dwelt among the untrodden ways
    Beside the springs of Dove,
A Maid whom there were none to praise
    And very few to love:

A violet by a mossy stone   *5*
    Half hidden from the eye!
—Fair as a star, when only one
    Is shining in the sky.

She lived unknown, and few could know
    When Lucy ceased to be;   *10*
But she is in her grave, and, oh,
    The difference to me!

1799   1800

THREE YEARS SHE GREW IN
SUN AND SHOWER

Three years she grew in sun and shower,
Then Nature said, "A lovelier flower
On earth was never sown;
This Child I to myself will take;
She shall be mine, and I will make   *5*
A Lady of my own.

"Myself will to my darling be
Both law and impulse: and with me
The Girl, in rock and plain,

10   In earth and heaven, in glade and bower,
      Shall feel an overseeing power
      To kindle or restrain.

      "She shall be sportive as the fawn
      That wild with glee across the lawn
15   Or up the mountain springs;
      And hers shall be the breathing balm,
      And hers the silence and the calm
      Of mute insensate things.

      "The floating clouds their state shall lend
20   To her; for her the willow bend;
      Nor shall she fail to see
      Even in the motions of the Storm
      Grace that shall mould the Maiden's form
      By silent sympathy.

25   "The stars of midnight shall be dear
      To her; and she shall lean her ear
      In many a secret place
      Where rivulets dance their wayward round,
      And beauty born of murmuring sound
30   Shall pass into her face.

      "And vital feelings of delight
      Shall rear her form to stately height,
      Her virgin bosom swell;
      Such thoughts to Lucy I will give
85   While she and I together live
      Here in this happy dell."

      Thus Nature spake—The work was done—
      How soon my Lucy's race was run!
      She died, and left to me
40   This heath, this calm, and quiet scene;
      The memory of what has been,
      And never more will be.

1799   1800

A SLUMBER DID MY SPIRIT SEAL

A slumber did my spirit seal;
   I had no human fears:
She seemed a thing that could not feel
   The touch of earthly years.

No motion has she now, no force;   *5*
   She neither hears nor sees;
Rolled round in earth's diurnal course,
   With rocks, and stones, and trees.

1799   1800

I TRAVELLED AMONG UNKNOWN MEN

I travelled among unknown men,
   In lands beyond the sea;
Nor, England! did I know till then
   What love I bore to thee.

'Tis past, that melancholy dream!   *5*
   Nor will I quit thy shore
A second time; for still I seem
   To love thee more and more.

Among thy mountains did I feel
   The joy of my desire;   *10*
And she I cherished turned her wheel
   Beside an English fire.

Thy mornings showed, thy nights concealed,
   The bowers where Lucy played;
And thine too is the last green field   *15*
   That Lucy's eyes surveyed.

1801   1807

LUCY GRAY

or, Solitude

Oft I had heard of Lucy Gray:
And, when I crossed the wild,
I chanced to see at break of day
The solitary child.

5   No mate, no comrade Lucy knew;
She dwelt on a wide moor,
—The sweetest thing that ever grew
Beside a human door!

You yet may spy the fawn at play,
10   The hare upon the green;
But the sweet face of Lucy Gray
Will never more be seen.

"To-night will be a stormy night—
You to the town must go;
15   And take a lantern, Child, to light
Your mother through the snow."

"That, Father! will I gladly do:
'Tis scarcely afternoon—
The minster-clock has just struck two,
20   And yonder is the moon!"

At this the Father raised his hook,
And snapped a faggot-band;
He plied his work;—and Lucy took
The lantern in her hand.

25   Not blither is the mountain roe:
With many a wanton stroke
Her feet disperse the powdery snow,
That rises up like smoke.

The storm came on before its time:
30   She wandered up and down;
And many a hill did Lucy climb:
But never reached the town.

The wretched parents all that night
Went shouting far and wide;
But there was neither sound nor sight   *35*
To serve them for a guide.

At day-break on a hill they stood
That overlooked the moor;
And thence they saw the bridge of wood,
A furlong from their door.   *40*

They wept—and, turning homeward, cried,
"In heaven we all shall meet;"
—When in the snow the mother spied
The print of Lucy's feet.

Then downwards from the steep hill's edge   *45*
They tracked the footmarks small;
And through the broken hawthorn hedge,
And by the long stone-wall;

And then an open field they crossed:
The marks were still the same;   *50*
They tracked them on, nor ever lost;
And to the bridge they came.

They followed from the snowy bank
Those footmarks, one by one,
Into the middle of the plank;   *55*
And further there were none!

—Yet some maintain that to this day
She is a living child;
That you may see sweet Lucy Gray
Upon the lonesome wild.   *60*

O'er rough and smooth she trips along,
And never looks behind;
And sings a solitary song
That whistles in the wind.

1799   **1800**

TO M. H.°

Our walk was far among the ancient trees:
There was no road, nor any woodman's path;
But a thick umbrage—checking the wild growth
Of weed and sapling, along soft green turf
5 Beneath the branches—of itself had made
A track, that brought us to a slip of lawn,
And a small bed of water in the woods.
All round this pool both flocks and herds might drink
On its firm margin, even as from a well,
10 Or some stone-basin which the herdsman's hand
Had shaped for their refreshment; nor did sun,
Or wind from any quarter, ever come,
But as a blessing to this calm recess,
This glade of water and this one green field.
15 The spot was made by Nature for herself;
The travellers know it not, and 'twill remain
Unknown to them; but it is beautiful;
And if a man should plant his cottage near,
Should sleep beneath the shelter of its trees,
20 And blend its waters with his daily meal,
He would so love it, that in his death-hour
Its image would survive among his thoughts:
And therefore, my sweet Mary, this still Nook,
With all its beeches, we have named from You!

1799

1800

HART-LEAP WELL

Hart-Leap Well is a small spring of water, about five miles
from Richmond in Yorkshire, and near the side of the road
that leads from Richmond to Askrigg. Its name is derived

0 **M. H.** Mary Hutchinson, his future wife. The poem belongs to a
series on the "Naming of Places."

from a remarkable Chase, the memory of which is pre-
served by the monuments spoken of in the second Part of
the following Poem, which monuments do now exist as I
have there described them.

Part First

The Knight had ridden down from Wensley Moor
With the slow motion of a summer's cloud,
And now, as he approached a vassal's door,
"Bring forth another horse!" he cried aloud.

"Another horse!"—That shout the vassal heard   *5*
And saddled his best Steed, a comely grey;
Sir Walter mounted him; he was the third
Which he had mounted on that glorious day.

Joy sparkled in the prancing courser's eyes;
The horse and horseman are a happy pair;   *10*
But, though Sir Walter like a falcon flies,
There is a doleful silence in the air.

A rout this morning left Sir Walter's Hall,
That as they galloped made the echoes roar;
But horse and man are vanished, one and all;   *15*
Such race, I think, was never seen before.

Sir Walter, restless as a veering wind,
Calls to the few tired dogs that yet remain:
Blanch, Swift, and Music, noblest of their kind,
Follow, and up the weary mountain strain.   *20*

The Knight hallooed, he cheered and chid them on
With suppliant gestures and upbraidings stern;
But breath and eyesight fail; and, one by one,
The dogs are stretched among the mountain fern.

Where is the throng, the tumult of the race?   *25*
The bugles that so joyfully were blown?
—This chase it looks not like an earthly chase;
Sir Walter and the Hart are left alone.

The poor Hart toils along the mountain-side;
30 I will not stop to tell how far he fled,
Nor will I mention by what death he died;
But now the Knight beholds him lying dead.

Dismounting, then, he leaned against a thorn;
He had no follower, dog, nor man, nor boy:
35 He neither cracked his whip, nor blew his horn,
But gazed upon the spoil with silent joy.

Close to the thorn on which Sir Walter leaned,
Stood his dumb partner in this glorious feat;
Weak as a lamb the hour that it is yeaned;
40 And white with foam as if with cleaving sleet.

Upon his side the Hart was lying stretched:
His nostril touched a spring beneath a hill,
And with the last deep groan his breath had fetched
The waters of the spring were trembling still.

45 And now, too happy for repose or rest,
(Never had living man such joyful lot!)
Sir Walter walked all round, north, south, and west,
And gazed and gazed upon that darling spot.

And climbing up the hill—(it was at least
50 Four roods of sheer ascent) Sir Walter found
Three several hoof-marks which the hunted Beast
Had left imprinted on the grassy ground.

Sir Walter wiped his face, and cried, "Till now
Such sight was never seen by human eyes:
55 Three leaps have borne him from this lofty brow,
Down to the very fountain where he lies.

"I'll build a pleasure-house upon this spot,
And a small arbour, made for rural joy;
'Twill be the traveller's shed, the pilgrim's cot,
60 A place of love for damsels that are coy.

"A cunning artist will I have to frame
A basin for that fountain in the dell!
And they who do make mention of the same,
From this day forth, shall call it HART-LEAP WELL.

"And, gallant Stag! to make thy praises known,   65
Another monument shall here be raised;
Three several pillars, each a rough-hewn stone,
And planted where thy hoofs the turf have grazed.

"And, in the summer-time when days are long,
I will come hither with my Paramour;   70
And with the dancers and the minstrel's song
We will make merry in that pleasant bower.

"Till the foundations of the mountains fail
My mansion with its arbour shall endure;—
The joy of them who till the fields of Swale,   75
And them who dwell among the woods of Ure!"

Then home he went, and left the Hart, stone-dead,
With breathless nostrils stretched above the spring.
—Soon did the Knight perform what he had said;
And far and wide the fame thereof did ring.   80

Ere thrice the Moon into her port had steered,
A cup of stone received the living well;
Three pillars of rude stone Sir Walter reared,
And built a house of pleasure in the dell.

And near the fountain, flowers of stature tall   85
With trailing plants and trees were intertwined,—
Which soon composed a little sylvan hall,
A leafy shelter from the sun and wind.

And thither, when the summer days were long,
Sir Walter led his wondering Paramour;   90
And with the dancers and the minstrel's song
Made merriment within that pleasant bower.

The Knight, Sir Walter, died in course of time,
And his bones lie in his paternal vale.—
95 But there is matter for a second rhyme,
And I to this would add another tale.

Part Second

The moving accident is not my trade;
To freeze the blood I have no ready arts:
'Tis my delight, alone in summer shade,
100 To pipe a simple song for thinking hearts.

As I from Hawes to Richmond did repair,
It chanced that I saw standing in a dell
Three aspens at three corners of a square;
And one, not four yards distant, near a well.

105 What this imported I could ill divine:
And, pulling now the rein my horse to stop,
I saw three pillars standing in a line,—
The last stone-pillar on a dark hill-top.

The trees were grey, with neither arms nor head;
110 Half wasted the square mound of tawny green;
So that you just might say, as then I said,
"Here in old time the hand of man hath been."

I looked upon the hill both far and near,
More doleful place did never eye survey;
115 It seemed as if the spring-time came not here,
And Nature here were willing to decay.

I stood in various thoughts and fancies lost,
When one, who was in shepherd's garb attired,
Came up the hollow:—him did I accost,
120 And what this place might be I then inquired.

The Shepherd stopped, and that same story told
Which in my former rhyme I have rehearsed.
"A jolly place," said he, "in times of old!
But something ails it now: the spot is curst.

"You see these lifeless stumps of aspen wood—   125
Some say that they are beeches, others elms—
These were the bower; and here a mansion stood,
The finest palace of a hundred realms!

"The arbour does its own condition tell;
You see the stones, the fountain, and the stream;   130
But as to the great Lodge! you might as well
Hunt half a day for a forgotten dream.

"There's neither dog nor heifer, horse nor sheep,
Will wet his lips within that cup of stone;
And oftentimes, when all are fast asleep,   135
This water doth send forth a dolorous groan.

"Some say that here a murder has been done,
And blood cries out for blood: but, for my part,
I've guessed, when I've been sitting in the sun,
That it was all for that unhappy Hart.   140

"What thoughts must through the creature's brain have past!
Even from the topmost stone, upon the steep,
Are but three bounds—and look, Sir, at this last—
O Master! it has been a cruel leap.

"For thirteen hours he ran a desperate race;   145
And in my simple mind we cannot tell
What cause the Hart might have to love this place,
And come and make his death-bed near the well.

"Here on the grass perhaps asleep he sank,
Lulled by the fountain in the summer-tide;   150
This water was perhaps the first he drank
When he had wandered from his mother's side.

"In April here beneath the flowering thorn
He heard the birds their morning carols sing;
And he, perhaps, for aught we know, was born   155
Not half a furlong from that self-same spring.

"Now, here is neither grass nor pleasant shade;
The sun on drearier hollow never shone;
So will it be, as I have often said,
160 Till trees, and stones, and fountain, all are gone."

"Grey-headed Shepherd, thou hast spoken well;
Small difference lies between thy creed and mine:
This Beast not unobserved by Nature fell;
His death was mourned by sympathy divine.

165 "The Being, that is in the clouds and air,
That is in the green leaves among the groves,
Maintains a deep and reverential care
For the unoffending creatures whom he loves.

"The pleasure-house is dust:——behind, before,
170 This is no common waste, no common gloom;
But Nature, in due course of time, once more
Shall here put on her beauty and her bloom.

"She leaves these objects to a slow decay,
That what we are, and have been, may be known;
175 But at the coming of the milder day,
These monuments shall all be overgrown.

"One lesson, Shepherd, let us two divide,
Taught both by what she shows, and what conceals;
Never to blend our pleasure or our pride
180 With sorrow of the meanest thing that feels."

1800   1800

IT WAS AN APRIL MORNING

It was an April morning: fresh and clear
The Rivulet, delighting in its strength,
Ran with a young man's speed; and yet the voice

Of waters which the winter had supplied
Was softened down into a vernal tone.   *5*
The spirit of enjoyment and desire,
And hopes and wishes, from all living things
Went circling, like a multitude of sounds.
The budding groves seemed eager to urge on
The steps of June; as if their various hues   *10*
Were only hindrances that stood between
Them and their object: but, meanwhile, prevailed
Such an entire contentment in the air
That every naked ash, and tardy tree
Yet leafless, showed as if the countenance   *15*
With which it looked on this delightful day
Were native to the summer.—Up the brook
I roamed in the confusion of my heart,
Alive to all things and forgetting all.
At length I to a sudden turning came   *20*
In this continuous glen, where down a rock
The Stream, so ardent in its course before,
Sent forth such sallies of glad sound, that all
Which I till then had heard, appeared the voice
Of common pleasure: beast and bird, the lamb,   *25*
The shepherd's dog, the linnet and the thrush
Vied with this waterfall, and made a song,
Which, while I listened, seemed like the wild growth
Or like some natural produce of the air,
That could not cease to be. Green leaves were here;   *30*
But 'twas the foliage of the rocks—the birch,
The yew, the holly, and the bright green thorn,
With hanging islands of resplendent furze:
And, on a summit, distant a short space,
By any who should look beyond the dell,   *35*
A single mountain-cottage might be seen.
I gazed and gazed, and to myself I said,
"Our thoughts at least are ours; and this wild nook,
My EMMA,° I will dedicate to thee."
—Soon did the spot become my other home,   *40*
My dwelling, and my out-of-doors abode.
And, of the Shepherds who have seen me there,

39 **Emma** In several poems Wordsworth so names his sister Dorothy.

To whom I sometimes in our idle talk
Have told this fancy, two or three, perhaps,
45   Years after we are gone and in our graves,
When they have cause to speak of this wild place,
May call it by the name of Emma's Dell.

1800   1800

MICHAEL°

A Pastoral Poem

If from the public way you turn your steps
Up the tumultuous brook of Green-head Ghyll,
You will suppose that with an upright path
Your feet must struggle; in such bold ascent
5   The pastoral mountains front you, face to face.
But, courage! for around that boisterous brook
The mountains have all opened out themselves,
And made a hidden valley of their own.
No habitation can be seen; but they
10   Who journey thither find themselves alone
With a few sheep, with rocks and stones, and kites
That overhead are sailing in the sky.
It is in truth an utter solitude;
Nor should I have made mention of this Dell
15   But for one object which you might pass by,
Might see and notice not. Beside the brook
Appears a straggling heap of unhewn stones!
And to that simple object appertains

0 **Michael** depicts a man moved by emotions Wordsworth consid-
ered basic: "the parental affection, and the love of property, *landed*
property, including the feeling of inheritance, home, and personal
and family independence" (letter to Thomas Poole, April, 1801).
The poet had seen wartime inflation and the growth of factories
break up small estates and their families, and he feared (as in "The
Last of the Flock") that the class of men represented by Michael—
of independent, almost patriarchal imagination—would disappear.

A story—unenriched with strange events,
Yet not unfit, I deem, for the fireside,   *20*
Or for the summer shade. It was the first
Of those domestic tales that spake to me
Of Shepherds, dwellers in the valleys, men
Whom I already loved;—not verily
For their own sakes, but for the fields and hills   *25*
Where was their occupation and abode.
And hence this Tale, while I was yet a Boy
Careless of books, yet having felt the power
Of Nature, by the gentle agency
Of natural objects, led me on to feel   *30*
For passions that were not my own, and think
(At random and imperfectly indeed)
On man, the heart of man, and human life.°
Therefore, although it be a history
Homely and rude, I will relate the same   *35*
For the delight of a few natural hearts;
And, with yet fonder feeling, for the sake
Of youthful Poets, who among these hills
Will be my second self when I am gone.

   Upon the forest-side in Grasmere Vale   *40*
There dwelt a Shepherd, Michael was his name;
An old man, stout of heart, and strong of limb.
His bodily frame had been from youth to age
Of an unusual strength: his mind was keen,
Intense, and frugal, apt for all affairs,   *45*
And in his shepherd's calling he was prompt
And watchful more than ordinary men.
Hence had he learned the meaning of all winds,
Of blasts of every tone; and, oftentimes,
When others heeded not, he heard the South   *50*
Make subterraneous music, like the noise
Of bagpipers on distant Highland hills.
The Shepherd, at such warning, of his flock
Bethought him, and he to himself would say,
"The winds are now devising work for me!"   *55*
And, truly, at all times, the storm, that drives
The traveller to a shelter, summoned him

33 **On man . . . life** Cf. "Home at Grasmere," line 754.

Up to the mountains: he had been alone
Amid the heart of many thousand mists,
60 That came to him, and left him, on the heights.
So lived he till his eightieth year was past.
And grossly that man errs, who should suppose
That the green valleys, and the streams and rocks,
Were things indifferent to the Shepherd's thoughts.
65 Fields, where with cheerful spirits he had breathed
The common air; hills, which with vigorous step
He had so often climbed; which had impressed
So many incidents upon his mind
Of hardship, skill or courage, joy or fear;
70 Which, like a book, preserved the memory
Of the dumb animals, whom he had saved,
Had fed or sheltered, linking to such acts
The certainty of honourable gain;
Those fields, those hills—what could they less? had
    laid
75 Strong hold on his affections, were to him
A pleasurable feeling of blind love,
The pleasure which there is in life itself.

His days had not been passed in singleness.
His Helpmate was a comely matron, old—
80 Though younger than himself full twenty years.
She was a woman of a stirring life,
Whose heart was in her house: two wheels she had
Of antique form; this large, for spinning wool;
That small, for flax; and if one wheel had rest,
85 It was because the other was at work.
The Pair had but one inmate in their house,
An only Child, who had been born to them
When Michael, telling o'er his years, began
To deem that he was old,—in shepherd's phrase,
90 With one foot in the grave. This only Son,
With two brave sheep-dogs tried in many a storm,
The one of an inestimable worth,
Made all their household. I may truly say,
That they were as a proverb in the vale
95 For endless industry. When day was gone,
And from their occupations out of doors

The Son and Father were come home, even then,
Their labour did not cease; unless when all
Turned to the cleanly supper-board, and there,
Each with a mess of pottage and skimmed milk,   *100*
Sat round the basket piled with oaten cakes,
And their plain home-made cheese. Yet when the meal
Was ended, Luke (for so the Son was named)
And his old Father both betook themselves
To such convenient work as might employ   *105*
Their hands by the fire-side; perhaps to card
Wool for the Housewife's spindle, or repair
Some injury done to sickle, flail, or scythe,
Or other implement of house or field.

   Down from the ceiling, by the chimney's edge,   *110*
That in our ancient uncouth country style
With huge and black projection overbrowed
Large space beneath, as duly as the light
Of day grew dim the Housewife hung a lamp;
An agèd utensil, which had performed   *115*
Service beyond all others of its kind.
Early at evening did it burn—and late,
Surviving comrade of uncounted hours,
Which, going by from year to year, had found,
And left, the couple neither gay perhaps   *120*
Nor cheerful, yet with objects and with hopes,
Living a life of eager industry.
And now, when Luke had reached his eighteenth year,
There by the light of this old lamp they sate,
Father and Son, while far into the night   *125*
The Housewife plied her own peculiar work,
Making the cottage through the silent hours
Murmur as with the sound of summer flies.
This light was famous in its neighbourhood,
And was a public symbol of the life   *130*
That thrifty Pair had lived. For, as it chanced,
Their cottage on a plot of rising ground
Stood single, with large prospect, north and south,
High into Easedale, up to Dunmail-Raise,
And westward to the village near the lake;   *135*
And from this constant light, so regular

And so far seen, the House itself, by all
Who dwelt within the limits of the vale,
Both old and young, was named THE EVENING STAR.

140   Thus living on through such a length of years,
The Shepherd, if he loved himself, must needs
Have loved his Helpmate; but to Michael's heart
This son of his old age was yet more dear—
Less from instinctive tenderness, the same
145 Fond spirit that blindly works in the blood of all—
Than that a child, more than all other gifts
That earth can offer to declining man,
Brings hope with it, and forward-looking thoughts,
And stirrings of inquietude, when they
150 By tendency of nature needs must fail.
Exceeding was the love he bare to him,
His heart and his heart's joy! For oftentimes
Old Michael, while he was a babe in arms,
Had done him female service, not alone
155 For pastime and delight, as is the use
Of fathers, but with patient mind enforced
To acts of tenderness; and he had rocked
His cradle, as with a woman's gentle hand.

    And, in a later time, ere yet the Boy
160 Had put on boy's attire, did Michael love,
Albeit of a stern unbending mind,
To have the Young-one in his sight, when he
Wrought in the field, or on his shepherd's stool
Sate with a fettered sheep before him stretched
165 Under the large old oak, that near his door
Stood single, and, from matchless depth of shade,
Chosen for the Shearer's covert from the sun,
Thence in our rustic dialect was called
The CLIPPING TREE, a name which yet it bears.
170 There, while they two were sitting in the shade,
With others round them, earnest all and blithe,
Would Michael exercise his heart with looks
Of fond correction and reproof bestowed
Upon the Child, if he disturbed the sheep
175 By catching at their legs, or with his shouts
Scared them, while they lay still beneath the shears.

And when by Heaven's good grace the boy grew up
A healthy Lad, and carried in his cheek
Two steady roses that were five years old;
Then Michael from a winter coppice° cut   *180*
With his own hand a sapling, which he hooped
With iron, making it throughout in all
Due requisites a perfect shepherd's staff,
And gave it to the Boy; wherewith equipt
He as a watchman oftentimes was placed   *185*
At gate or gap, to stem or turn the flock;
And, to his office prematurely called,
There stood the urchin, as you will divine,
Something between a hindrance and a help;
And for this cause not always, I believe,   *190*
Receiving from his Father hire of praise;
Though nought was left undone which staff, or voice,
Or looks, or threatening gestures, could perform.

But soon as Luke, full ten years old, could stand
Against the mountain blasts; and to the heights,   *195*
Not fearing toil, nor length of weary ways,
He with his Father daily went, and they
Were as companions, why should I relate
That objects which the Shepherd loved before
Were dearer now? that from the Boy there came   *200*
Feelings and emanations—things which were
Light to the sun and music to the wind;
And that the old Man's heart seemed born again?

Thus in his Father's sight the Boy grew up:
And now, when he had reached his eighteenth year,   *205*
He was his comfort and his daily hope.

While in this sort the simple household lived
From day to day, to Michael's ear there came
Distressful tidings. Long before the time
Of which I speak, the Shepherd had been bound   *210*
In surety for his brother's son, a man
Of an industrious life, and ample means;
But unforeseen misfortunes suddenly

180 **coppice** copse.

Had prest upon him; and old Michael now
215 Was summoned to discharge the forfeiture,
A grievous penalty, but little less
Than half his substance. This unlooked-for claim,
At the first hearing, for a moment took
More hope out of his life than he supposed
220 That any old man ever could have lost.
As soon as he had armed himself with strength
To look his trouble in the face, it seemed
The Shepherd's sole resource to sell at once
A portion of his patrimonial fields.
225 Such was his first resolve; he thought again,
And his heart failed him. "Isabel," said he,
Two evenings after he had heard the news,
"I have been toiling more than seventy years,
And in the open sunshine of God's love
230 Have we all lived; yet, if these fields of ours
Should pass into a stranger's hand, I think
That I could not lie quiet in my grave.
Our lot is a hard lot; the sun himself
Has scarcely been more diligent than I;
235 And I have lived to be a fool at last
To my own family. An evil man
That was, and made an evil choice, if he
Were false to us; and, if he were not false,
There are ten thousand to whom loss like this
240 Had been no sorrow. I forgive him;—but
'Twere better to be dumb than to talk thus.

"When I began, my purpose was to speak
Of remedies and of a cheerful hope.
Our Luke shall leave us, Isabel; the land
245 Shall not go from us, and it shall be free;
He shall possess it, free as is the wind
That passes over it. We have, thou know'st,
Another kinsman—he will be our friend
In this distress. He is a prosperous man,
250 Thriving in trade—and Luke to him shall go,
And with his kinsman's help and his own thrift
He quickly will repair this loss, and then
He may return to us. If here he stay,

What can be done? Where every one is poor,
What can be gained?"
              At this the old Man paused,   255
And Isabel sat silent, for her mind
Was busy, looking back into past times.
There's Richard Bateman, thought she to herself,
He was a parish-boy—at the church-door
They made a gathering for him, shillings, pence,   260
And halfpennies, wherewith the neighbours bought
A basket, which they filled with pedlar's wares;
And, with this basket on his arm, the lad
Went up to London, found a master there,
Who, out of many, chose the trusty boy   265
To go and overlook his merchandise
Beyond the seas; where he grew wondrous rich,
And left estates and monies to the poor,
And, at his birth-place, built a chapel floored
With marble, which he sent from foreign lands.   270
These thoughts, and many others of like sort,
Passed quickly through the mind of Isabel,
And her face brightened. The old Man was glad,
And thus resumed:—"Well, Isabel! this scheme
These two days has been meat and drink to me.   275
Far more than we have lost is left us yet.
—We have enough—I wish indeed that I
Were younger;—but this hope is a good hope.
Make ready Luke's best garments, of the best
Buy for him more, and let us send him forth   280
To-morrow, or the next day, or to-night:
—If he *could* go, the Boy should go to-night."

    Here Michael ceased, and to the fields went forth
With a light heart. The Housewife for five days
Was restless morn and night, and all day long   285
Wrought on with her best fingers to prepare
Things needful for the journey of her son.
But Isabel was glad when Sunday came
To stop her in her work: for, when she lay
By Michael's side, she through the last two nights   290
Heard him, how he was troubled in his sleep:
And when they rose at morning she could see

That all his hopes were gone. That day at noon
She said to Luke, while they two by themselves
295 Were sitting at the door, "Thou must not go:
We have no other Child but thee to lose,
None to remember—do not go away,
For if thou leave thy Father he will die."
The Youth made answer with a jocund voice;
300 And Isabel, when she had told her fears,
Recovered heart. That evening her best fare
Did she bring forth, and all together sat
Like happy people round a Christmas fire.

With daylight Isabel resumed her work;
305 And all the ensuing week the house appeared
As cheerful as a grove in Spring: at length
The expected letter from their kinsman came,
With kind assurances that he would do
His utmost for the welfare of the Boy;
310 To which, requests were added, that forthwith
He might be sent to him. Ten times or more
The letter was read over; Isabel
Went forth to show it to the neighbours round;
Nor was there at that time on English land
315 A prouder heart than Luke's. When Isabel
Had to her house returned, the old Man said,
"He shall depart to-morrow." To this word
The Housewife answered, talking much of things
Which, if at such short notice he should go,
320 Would surely be forgotten. But at length
She gave consent, and Michael was at ease.

Near the tumultuous brook of Green-head Ghyll,
In that deep valley, Michael had designed
To build a Sheep-fold; and, before he heard
325 The tidings of his melancholy loss,
For this same purpose he had gathered up
A heap of stones, which by the streamlet's edge
Lay thrown together, ready for the work.
With Luke that evening thitherward he walked;
330 And soon as they had reached the place he stopped,
And thus the old Man spake to him:—"My son,

To-morrow thou wilt leave me: with full heart
I look upon thee, for thou art the same
That wert a promise to me ere thy birth,
And all thy life hast been my daily joy. 835
I will relate to thee some little part
Of our two histories; 'twill do thee good
When thou art from me, even if I should touch
On things thou canst not know of.—After thou
First cam'st into the world—as oft befals 840
To new-born infants—thou didst sleep away
Two days, and blessings from thy Father's tongue
Then fell upon thee. Day by day passed on,
And still I loved thee with increasing love.
Never to living ear came sweeter sounds 845
Than when I heard thee by our own fire-side
First uttering, without words, a natural tune;
While thou, a feeding babe, didst in thy joy
Sing at thy Mother's breast. Month followed month,
And in the open fields my life was passed 850
And on the mountains; else I think that thou
Hadst been brought up upon thy Father's knees.
But we were playmates, Luke: among these hills,
As well thou knowest, in us the old and young
Have played together, nor with me didst thou 855
Lack any pleasure which a boy can know."
Luke had a manly heart; but at these words
He sobbed aloud. The old Man grasped his hand,
And said, "Nay, do not take it so—I see
That these are things of which I need not speak. 860
—Even to the utmost I have been to thee
A kind and a good Father: and herein
I but repay a gift which I myself
Received at others' hands; for, though now old
Beyond the common life of man, I still 865
Remember them who loved me in my youth.
Both of them sleep together: here they lived,
As all their Forefathers had done; and when
At length their time was come, they were not loth
To give their bodies to the family mould. 870
I wished that thou should'st live the life they lived:
But 'tis a long time to look back, my Son,

And see so little gain from threescore years.
These fields were burthened° when they came to me;
375 Till I was forty years of age, not more
Than half of my inheritance was mine.
I toiled and toiled; God blessed me in my work,
And till these three weeks past the land was free.
—It looks as if it never could endure
380 Another Master. Heaven forgive me, Luke,
If I judge ill for thee, but it seems good
That thou shouldst go."
                                    At this the old Man paused;
Then, pointing to the stones near which they stood,
Thus, after a short silence, he resumed:
385 "This was a work for us; and now, my Son,
It is a work for me. But, lay one stone—
Here, lay it for me, Luke, with thine own hands.
Nay, Boy, be of good hope;—we both may live
To see a better day. At eighty-four
390 I still am strong and hale;—do thou thy part;
I will do mine.—I will begin again
With many tasks that were resigned to thee:
Up to the heights, and in among the storms,
Will I without thee go again, and do
395 All works which I was wont to do alone,
Before I knew thy face.—Heaven bless thee, Boy!
Thy heart these two weeks has been beating fast
With many hopes; it should be so—yes—yes—
I knew that thou couldst never have a wish
400 To leave me, Luke: thou hast been bound to me
Only by links of love: when thou art gone,
What will be left to us!—But I forget
My purposes. Lay now the corner-stone,
As I requested; and hereafter, Luke,
405 When thou art gone away, should evil men
Be thy companions, think of me, my Son,
And of this moment; hither turn thy thoughts,
And God will strengthen thee: amid all fear
And all temptation, Luke, I pray that thou
410 May'st bear in mind the life thy Fathers lived,
Who, being innocent, did for that cause

374 **burthened** mortgaged.

Bestir them in good deeds. Now, fare thee well—
When thou return'st, thou in this place wilt see
A work which is not here: a covenant
'Twill be between us; but, whatever fate   *415*
Befal thee, I shall love thee to the last,
And bear thy memory with me to the grave."

    The Shepherd ended here; and Luke stooped down,
And, as his Father had requested, laid
The first stone of the Sheep-fold. At the sight   *420*
The old Man's grief broke from him; to his heart
He pressed his Son, he kissèd him and wept;
And to the house together they returned.
—Hushed was that House in peace, or seeming peace
Ere the night fell:—with morrow's dawr the Boy   *425*
Began his journey, and, when he had reached
The public way, he put on a bold face;
And all the neighbours, as he passed their doors,
Came forth with wishes and with farewell prayers,
That followed him till he was out of sight.   *430*

    A good report did from their Kinsman come,
Of Luke and his well-doing: and the Boy
Wrote loving letters, full of wondrous news,
Which, as the Housewife phrased it, were throughout
"The prettiest letters that were ever seen."   *435*
Both parents read them with rejoicing hearts.
So, many months passed on: and once again
The Shepherd went about his daily work
With confident and cheerful thoughts; and now
Sometimes when he could find a leisure hour   *440*
He to that valley took his way, and there
Wrought at the Sheep-fold. Meantime Luke began
To slacken in his duty; and, at length,
He in the dissolute city gave himself
To evil courses: ignominy and shame   *445*
Fell on him, so that he was driven at last
To seek a hiding-place beyond the seas.

    There is a comfort in the strength of love;
'Twill make a thing endurable, which else

450 Would overset the brain, or break the heart:
I have conversed with more than one who well
Remember the old Man, and what he was
Years after he had heard this heavy news.
His bodily frame had been from youth to age
455 Of an unusual strength. Among the rocks
He went, and still looked up to sun and cloud,
And listened to the wind; and, as before,
Performed all kinds of labour for his sheep,
And for the land, his small inheritance.
460 And to that hollow dell from time to time
Did he repair, to build the Fold of which
His flock had need. 'Tis not forgotten yet
The pity which was then in every heart
For the old Man—and 'tis believed by all
465 That many and many a day he thither went,
And never lifted up a single stone.

There, by the Sheep-fold, sometimes was he seen
Sitting alone, or with his faithful Dog,
Then old, beside him, lying at his feet.
470 The length of full seven years, from time to time,
He at the building of this Sheep-fold wrought,
And left the work unfinished when he died.
Three years, or little more, did Isabel
Survive her Husband: at her death the estate
475 Was sold, and went into a stranger's hand.
The Cottage which was named the Evening Star
Is gone—the ploughshare has been through the ground
On which it stood; great changes have been wrought
In all the neighbourhood:—yet the oak is left
480 That grew beside their door; and the remains
Of the unfinished Sheep-fold may be seen
Beside the boisterous brook of Green-head Ghyll.

1800   1800

III. Poems 1801-1815

LYRICS

WRITTEN IN MARCH

While Resting on the Bridge at the Foot of Brother's Water

The Cock is crowing,
The stream is flowing,
The small birds twitter,
The lake doth glitter,
The green field sleeps in the sun;   *5*
 The oldest and youngest
 Are at work with the strongest;
 The cattle are grazing,
 Their heads never raising;
There are forty feeding like one!   *10*

Like an army defeated
The snow hath retreated,
And now doth fare ill
On the top of the bare hill;
The Ploughboy is whooping—anon—anon: *15*
 There's joy in the mountains;
 There's life in the fountains;
 Small clouds are sailing,
 Blue sky prevailing;
The rain is over and gone!   *20*

1802   1807

TO THE CUCKOO

O blithe New-comer! I have heard,
I hear thee and rejoice.
O Cuckoo! shall I call thee Bird,
Or but a wandering Voice?

5 While I am lying on the grass
Thy twofold shout I hear,
From hill to hill it seems to pass
At once far off, and near.

Though babbling only to the Vale,
10 Of sunshine and of flowers,
Thou bringest unto me a tale
Of visionary hours.

Thrice welcome, darling of the Spring!
Even yet thou art to me
15 No bird, but an invisible thing,
A voice, a mystery;

The same whom in my school-boy days
I listened to; that Cry
Which made me look a thousand ways
20 In bush, and tree, and sky.

To seek thee did I often rove
Through woods and on the green;
And thou wert still a hope, a love;
Still longed for, never seen.

25 And I can listen to thee yet;
Can lie upon the plain
And listen, till I do beget
That golden time again.

O blessèd Bird! the earth we pace
30 Again appears to be
An unsubstantial, faery place;
That is fit home for Thee!

1802   1807

MY HEART LEAPS UP

My heart leaps up when I behold
   A rainbow in the sky:
So was it when my life began;
So is it now I am a man;
So be it when I shall grow old,   5
   Or let me die!
The Child is Father of the Man;
And I could wish my days to be
Bound each to each by natural piety.

1802   1807

I WANDERED LONELY AS A CLOUD°

I wandered lonely as a cloud
That floats on high o'er vales and hills,
When all at once I saw a crowd,
A host, of golden daffodils;
Beside the lake, beneath the trees,   5
Fluttering and dancing in the breeze.

Continuous as the stars that shine
And twinkle on the milky way,
They stretched in never-ending line
Along the margin of a bay: 10
Ten thousand saw I at a glance,
Tossing their heads in sprightly dance.

The waves beside them danced; but they
Out-did the sparkling waves in glee:
A poet could not but be gay,   15
In such a jocund company:
I gazed—and gazed—but little thought
What wealth the show to me had brought:

0 **I Wandered ... Cloud** See Appendix, p 448. The second stanza
was added in 1815.

For oft, when on my couch I lie
20 In vacant or in pensive mood,
They flash upon that inward eye
Which is the bliss of solitude;
And then my heart with pleasure fills,
And dances with the daffodils.

1804   1807

THE SOLITARY REAPER

Behold her, single in the field,
Yon solitary Highland Lass!
Reaping and singing by herself;
Stop here, or gently pass!
5 Alone she cuts and binds the grain,
And sings a melancholy strain;
O listen! for the Vale profound
Is overflowing with the sound.

No Nightingale did ever chaunt
10 More welcome notes to weary bands
Of travellers in some shady haunt,
Among Arabian sands:
A voice so thrilling ne'er was heard
In spring-time from the Cuckoo-bird,
15 Breaking the silence of the seas
Among the farthest Hebrides.

Will no one tell me what she sings?°—
Perhaps the plaintive numbers flow
For old, unhappy, far-off things,
20 And battles long ago:
Or is it some more humble lay,
Familiar matter of to-day?
Some natural sorrow, loss, or pain,
That has been, and may be again?

17 what she sings? The literal reason for this question is that the girl sings in Erse.

Whate'er the theme, the Maiden sang   25
As if her song could have no ending;
I saw her singing at her work,
And o'er the sickle bending:—
I listened, motionless and still;
And, as I mounted up the hill,   30
The music in my heart I bore,
Long after it was heard no more.

1805   1807

STEPPING WESTWARD

While my Fellow-traveller and I were walking by the side
of Loch Ketterine [Scotland], one fine evening after sunset,
in our road to a Hut where, in the course of our Tour, we
had been hospitably entertained some weeks before, we
met, in one of the loneliest parts of that solitary region, two
well-dressed Women, one of whom said to us, by way of
greeting, "What, you are stepping westward?"

"What, you are stepping westward?"—"Yea."
—'Twould be a *wildish* destiny,
If we, who thus together roam
In a strange Land, and far from home,
Were in this place the guests of Chance: 5
Yet who would stop, or fear to advance,
Though home or shelter he had none,
With such a sky to lead him on?

The dewy ground was dark and cold;
Behind, all gloomy to behold;   10
And stepping westward seemed to be
A kind of *heavenly* destiny:
I liked the greeting; 'twas a sound
Of something without place or bound;
And seemed to give me spiritual right   15
To travel through that region bright.

The voice was soft, and she who spake
Was walking by her native lake:
The salutation had to me
20 The very sound of courtesy:
Its power was felt; and while my eye
Was fixed upon the glowing Sky,
The echo of the voice enwrought
A human sweetness with the thought
25 Of travelling through the world that lay
Before me in my endless way.

1805   1807

YARROW VISITED

September, 1814

And is this—Yarrow?—*This* the Stream
Of which my fancy cherished,
So faithfully, a waking dream?
An image that hath perished!
5 O that some Minstrel's harp were near,
To utter notes of gladness,
And chase this silence from the air,
That fills my heart with sadness!

Yet why?—a silvery current flows
10 With uncontrolled meanderings;
Nor have these eyes by greener hills
Been soothed, in all my wanderings.
And, through her depths, Saint Mary's Lake
Is visibly delighted;
15 For not a feature of those hills
Is in the mirror slighted.

A blue sky bends o'er Yarrow vale,
Save where that pearly whiteness
Is round the rising sun diffused,
A tender hazy brightness; 20
Mild dawn of promise! that excludes
All profitless dejection;
Though not unwilling here to admit
A pensive recollection.

Where was it that the famous Flower° 25
Of Yarrow Vale lay bleeding?
His bed perchance was yon smooth mound
On which the herd is feeding:
And haply from this crystal pool,
Now peaceful as the morning, 30
The Water-wraith ascended thrice—
And gave his doleful warning.

Delicious is the Lay that sings
The haunts of happy Lovers,
The path that leads them to the grove, 35
The leafy grove that covers:
And Pity sanctifies the Verse
That paints, by strength of sorrow,
The unconquerable strength of love;
Bear witness, rueful Yarrow! 40

But thou, that didst appear so fair
To fond imagination,
Dost rival in the light of day
Her delicate creation:
Meek loveliness is round thee spread, 45
A softness still and holy;
The grace of forest charms decayed,
And pastoral melancholy.

That region left, the vale unfolds
Rich groves of lofty stature, 50
With Yarrow winding through the pomp
Of cultivated nature;
And, rising from those lofty groves,

25 **famous Flower** the slain lover lamented in ballads that deal with
Yarrow.

Behold a Ruin hoary!
55   The shattered front of Newark's Towers,
Renowned in Border story.°

Fair scenes for childhood's opening bloom,
For sportive youth to stray in;
For manhood to enjoy his strength;
60   And age to wear away in!
Yon cottage seems a bower of bliss,
A covert for protection
Of tender thoughts, that nestle there—
The brood of chaste affection.

65   How sweet, on this autumnal day,
The wild-wood fruits to gather,
And on my True-love's forehead plant
A crest of blooming heather!
And what if I enwreathed my own!
70   'Twere no offence to reason;
The sober Hills thus deck their brows
To meet the wintry season.

I see—but not by sight alone,
Loved Yarrow, have I won thee;
75   A ray of fancy still survives—
Her sunshine plays upon thee!
Thy ever-youthful waters keep
A course of lively pleasure;
And gladsome notes my lips can breathe,
80   Accordant to the measure.

The vapours linger round the Heights,
They melt, and soon must vanish;
One hour is theirs, nor more is mine—
Sad thought, which I would banish,
85   But that I know, where'er I go,
Thy genuine image, Yarrow!
Will dwell with me—to heighten joy,
And cheer my mind in sorrow.

1814   **1815**

56 **Border story** concerning the "Border" region, a wild stretch
dividing England and Scotland. Newark's Towers are the setting of
Scott's *Lay of the Last Minstrel*.

ODE
INTIMATIONS OF IMMORTALITY FROM
RECOLLECTIONS OF EARLY CHILDHOOD

The Child is Father of the Man;
And I could wish my days to be
Bound each to each by natural piety.

I

There was a time when meadow, grove, and stream,
The earth, and every common sight,
    To me did seem
    Apparelled in celestial light,
The glory and the freshness of a dream.   *5*
It is not now as it hath been of yore;—
    Turn whereso'er I may,
    By night or day,
The things which I have seen I now can see no more.

II

    The Rainbow comes and goes,   *10*
    And lovely is the Rose,
    The Moon doth with delight
Look round her when the heavens are bare,
    Waters on a starry night
    Are beautiful and fair;   *15*
  The sunshine is a glorious birth;
  But yet I know, where'er I go,
That there hath past away a glory from the earth.

III

Now, while the birds thus sing a joyous song,
    And while the young lambs bound   *20*
    As to the tabor's sound,
To me alone there came a thought of grief:
A timely utterance gave that thought relief,
    And I again am strong:
The cataracts blow their trumpets from the steep;   *25*
No more shall grief of mine the season wrong;

I hear the Echoes through the mountains throng,
The Winds come to me from the fields of sleep,
  And all the earth is gay;
80   Land and sea
  Give themselves up to jollity,
   And with the heart of May
  Doth every Beast keep holiday;—
   Thou Child of Joy,
Shout round me, let me hear thy shouts, thou happy
85   Shepherd-boy!

IV

Ye blessèd Creatures, I have heard the call
 Ye to each other make; I see
The heavens laugh with you in your jubilee;
 My heart is at your festival,
40 My head hath its coronal,°
The fulness of your bliss, I feel—I feel it all.
  Oh evil day! if I were sullen
  While Earth herself is adorning,
   This sweet May-morning,
45 And the Children are culling
   On every side,
  In a thousand valleys far and wide,
  Fresh flowers; while the sun shines warm,
And the Babe leaps up on his Mother's arm:—
50 I hear, I hear, with joy I hear!
  —But there's a Tree, of many, one,
A single Field which I have looked upon,
Both of them speak of something that is gone:
  The Pansy at my feet
55 Doth the same tale repeat:
Whither is fled the visionary gleam?
Where is it now, the glory and the dream?

V

Our birth is but a sleep and a forgetting:
The Soul that rises with us, our life's Star,
60 Hath had elsewhere its setting,

---

40 coronal small crown (of flowers).

And cometh from afar:°
Not in entire forgetfulness,
And not in utter nakedness,
But trailing clouds of glory do we come
    From God, who is our home: *65*
Heaven lies about us in our infancy!
Shades of the prison-house begin to close
    Upon the growing Boy,
But He beholds the light, and whence it flows,
    He sees it in his joy;   *70*
The Youth, who daily farther from the east
    Must travel, still is Nature's Priest,
    And by the vision splendid
    Is on his way attended;
At length the Man perceives it die away,   *75*
And fade into the light of common day.

VI

Earth fills her lap with pleasures of her own;
Yearnings she hath in her own natural kind,
And, even with something of a Mother's mind,
    And no unworthy aim,   *80*
    The homely Nurse doth all she can
To make her Foster-child, her Inmate Man,
    Forget the glories he hath known,
And that imperial palace whence he came.

VII

Behold the Child among his new-born blisses,   *85*
A six years' Darling of a pigmy size!
See, where 'mid work of his own hand he lies,
Fretted by sallies of his mother's kisses,
With light upon him from his father's eyes!
See, at his feet, some little plan or chart,   *90*
Some fragment from his dream of human life,
Shaped by himself with newly-learned art;
    A wedding or a festival,

58–61 **Our birth . . . afar** Wordsworth alludes to Plato's doctrine
that the soul has a prior existence which is forgotten when it is born
into this world. See *Phaedo*, 73–77.

A mourning or a funeral;
95   And this hath now his heart,
And unto this he frames his song:
          Then will he fit his tongue
To dialogues of business, love, or strife;
          But it will not be long
100   Ere this be thrown aside,
          And with new joy and pride
The little Actor cons another part;
Filling from time to time his "humorous stage"°
With all the Persons, down to palsied Age,
105 That Life brings with her in her equipage;
          As if his whole vocation
          Were endless imitation.

VIII

Thou, whose exterior semblance doth belie
          Thy Soul's immensity;
110 Thou best Philosopher, who yet dost keep
Thy heritage, thou Eye among the blind,
That, deaf and silent, read'st the eternal deep,
Haunted for ever by the eternal mind,—
          Mighty Prophet! Seer blest!
115   On whom those truths do rest,
Which we are toiling all our lives to find,
In darkness lost, the darkness of the grave;
Thou, over whom thy Immortality
Broods like the Day, a Master o'er a Slave,
120 A Presence which is not to be put by;
Thou little Child, yet glorious in the might
Of heaven-born freedom on thy Being's height,
Why with such earnest pains dost thou provoke
The years to bring the inevitable yoke,
125 Thus blindly with thy blessedness at strife?
Full soon thy Soul shall have her earthly freight,
And custom lie upon thee with a weight,
Heavy as frost, and deep almost as life!

103 **Filling . . . stage** Imitating various humors or passions. Quoted
from Samuel Daniel's *Musophilus.*

IX

O joy! that in our embers
Is something that doth live,   *130*
That nature yet remembers
What was so fugitive!
The thought of our past years in me doth breed
Perpetual benediction: not indeed
For that which is most worthy to be blest;   *135*
Delight and liberty, the simple creed
Of Childhood, whether busy or at rest,
With new-fledged hope still fluttering in his breast:—
Not for these I raise
The song of thanks and praise;   *140*
But for those obstinate questionings
Of sense and outward things,
Fallings from us, vanishings;
Blank misgivings of a Creature
Moving about in worlds not realised,°   *145*
High instincts before which our mortal Nature
Did tremble like a guilty Thing surprised:
But for those first affections,
Those shadowy recollections,
Which, be they what they may,   *150*
Are yet the fountain-light of all our day,
Are yet a master-light of all our seeing;
Uphold us, cherish, and have power to make
Our noisy years seem moments in the being
Of the eternal Silence: truths that wake,   *155*
To perish never:
Which neither listlessness, nor mad endeavour,
Nor Man nor Boy,
Nor all that is an enmity with joy,
Can utterly abolish or destroy!   *160*
Hence in a season of calm weather
Though inland far we be,
Our Souls have sight of that immortal sea
Which brought us hither,
Can in a moment travel thither,   *165*
And see the Children sport upon the shore,
And hear the mighty waters rolling evermore.

145 not realised appearing unreal.

X

Then sing, ye Birds, sing, sing a joyous song!
    And let the young Lambs bound
170   As to the tabor's sound!
We in thought will join your throng,
      Ye that pipe and ye that play,
      Ye that through your hearts to-day
      Feel the gladness of the May!
175 What though the radiance which was once so bright
Be now for ever taken from my sight,
    Though nothing can bring back the hour
Of splendour in the grass, of glory in the flower;
      We will grieve not, rather find
180   Strength in what remains behind;
      In the primal sympathy
      Which having been must ever be;
      In the soothing thoughts that spring
      Out of human suffering;
185   In the faith that looks through death,
In years that bring the philosophic mind.

XI

And O, ye Fountains, Meadows, Hills, and Groves,
Forebode not any severing of our loves!
Yet in my heart of hearts I feel your might;
190 I only have relinquished one delight
To live beneath your more habitual sway.
I love the Brooks which down their channels fret,
Even more than when I tripped lightly as they;
The innocent brightness of a new-born Day
195   Is lovely yet;
The Clouds that gather round the setting sun
Do take a sober colouring from an eye
That hath kept watch o'er man's mortality;
Another race hath been, and other palms are won.
200 Thanks to the human heart by which we live,
Thanks to its tenderness, its joys, and fears,
To me the meanest flower that blows can give
Thoughts that do often lie too deep for tears.

1802–1804   1807

NUNS FRET NOT AT THEIR CONVENT'S NARROW ROOM

Nuns fret not at their convent's narrow room;
And hermits are contented with their cells;
And students with their pensive citadels;
Maids at the wheel, the weaver at his loom,
Sit blithe and happy; bees that soar for bloom,   5
High as the highest Peak of Furness-fells,
Will murmur by the hour in foxglove bells:
In truth the prison, unto which we doom
Ourselves, no prison is: and hence for me,
In sundry moods, 'twas pastime to be bound   10
Within the Sonnet's scanty plot of ground;
Pleased if some Souls (for such there needs must be)
Who have felt the weight of too much liberty,
Should find brief solace there, as I have found.

1802–1804   1807

METHOUGHT I SAW THE FOOTSTEPS OF A THRONE

Methought I saw the footsteps of a throne
Which mists and vapours from mine eyes did shroud—
Nor view of who might sit thereon allowed;
But all the steps and ground about were strown
With sights the ruefullest that flesh and bone   5
Ever put on; a miserable crowd,
Sick, hale, old, young, who cried before that cloud,
"Thou art our king, O Death! to thee we groan."
Those steps I clomb; the mists before me gave
Smooth way; and I beheld the face of one   10
Sleeping alone within a mossy cave,
With her face up to heaven; that seemed to have
Pleasing remembrance of a thought foregone;
A lovely Beauty in a summer grave!

1804(?)   1807

IT IS A BEAUTEOUS EVENING, CALM AND FREE

It is a beauteous evening, calm and free,
The holy time is quiet as a Nun
Breathless with adoration; the broad sun
Is sinking down in its tranquillity;
5   The gentleness of heaven broods o'er the Sea:
Listen! the mighty Being is awake,
And doth with his eternal motion make
A sound like thunder—everlastingly.
Dear Child!° dear Girl! that walkest with me here,
10 If thou appear untouched by solemn thought,
Thy nature is not therefore less divine:
Thou liest in Abraham's bosom° all the year;
And worshipp'st at the Temple's inner shrine,
God being with thee when we know it not.

1802   1807

CHARACTERISTICS OF A CHILD THREE YEARS OLD

Loving she° is, and tractable, though wild;
And Innocence hath privilege in her
To dignify arch looks and laughing eyes;
And feats of cunning; and the pretty round
5   Of trespasses, affected to provoke
Mock-chastisement and partnership in play.
And, as a faggot sparkles on the hearth,
Not less if unattended and alone
Than when both young and old sit gathered round

9 **Dear Child** Caroline, daughter of the poet and Annette Vallon.
12 **Abraham's bosom** the repose of the righteous after death. Luke 16:22.
1 **she** Wordsworth's daughter Catherine, born in 1808.

And take delight in its activity;   10
Even so this happy Creature of herself
Is all-sufficient; solitude to her
Is blithe society, who fills the air
With gladness and involuntary songs.
Light are her sallies as the tripping fawn's   15
Forth-startled from the fern where she lay couched;
Unthought-of, unexpected, as the stir
Of the soft breeze ruffling the meadow-flowers,
Or from before it chasing wantonly
The many-coloured images imprest   20
Upon the bosom of a placid lake.

1811   1815

SURPRISED BY JOY—IMPATIENT
AS THE WIND

Surprised by joy—impatient as the Wind
I turned to share the transport—Oh! with whom
But Thee,° deep buried in the silent tomb,
That spot which no vicissitude° can find?
Love, faithful love, recalled thee to my mind—   5
But how could I forget thee? Through what power,
Even for the least division of an hour,
Have I been so beguiled as to be blind
To my most grievous loss!—That thought's return
Was the worst pang that sorrow ever bore,   10
Save one, one only, when I stood forlorn,
Knowing my heart's best treasure was no more;
That neither present time, nor years unborn
Could to my sight that heavenly face restore.

1812   1815

3 **Thee** Wordsworth's daughter Catherine died in 1812 at the age
of four.   4 **vicissitude** turn of fortune.

COMPOSED UPON WESTMINSTER BRIDGE

September 3, 1802

Earth has not anything to show more fair:
Dull would he be of soul who could pass by
A sight so touching in its majesty:
This City now doth, like a garment, wear
5 The beauty of the morning; silent, bare,
Ships, towers, domes, theatres, and temples lie
Open unto the fields, and to the sky;
All bright and glittering in the smokeless air.
Never did sun more beautifully steep
10 In his first splendour, valley, rock, or hill;
Ne'er saw I, never felt, a calm so deep!
The river glideth at his own sweet will:
Dear God! the very houses seem asleep;
And all that mighty heart is lying still!

1802   1807

THE WORLD IS TOO MUCH WITH US

The world is too much with us; late and soon,
Getting and spending, we lay waste our powers:
Little we see in Nature that is ours;
We have given our hearts away, a sordid boon!
5 This Sea that bares her bosom to the moon;
The winds that will be howling at all hours,
And are up-gathered now like sleeping flowers;
For this, for every thing, we are out of tune;
It moves us not.—Great God! I'd rather be
10 A Pagan suckled in a creed outworn;
So might I, standing on this pleasant lea,
Have glimpses that would make me less forlorn;
Have sight of Proteus rising from the sea;
Or hear old Triton blow his wreathèd horn.

1802–1804   1807

SHE WAS A PHANTOM OF DELIGHT°

She was a Phantom of delight
When first she gleamed upon my sight;
A lovely Apparition, sent
To be a moment's ornament;
Her eyes as stars of Twilight fair;   *5*
Like Twilight's, too, her dusky hair;
But all things else about her drawn
From May-time and the cheerful Dawn;
A dancing Shape, an Image gay,
To haunt, to startle, and way-lay.   *10*

I saw her upon nearer view,
A Spirit, yet a Woman too!
Her household motions light and free,
And steps of virgin-liberty;
A countenance in which did meet   *15*
Sweet records, promises as sweet;
A Creature not too bright or good
For human nature's daily food;
For transient sorrows, simple wiles,
Praise, blame, love, kisses, tears, and smiles.   *20*

And now I see with eye serene
The very pulse of the machine;
A Being breathing thoughtful breath,
A Traveller between life and death;
The reason firm, the temperate will,   *25*
Endurance, foresight, strength, and skill;
A perfect Woman, nobly planned,
To warn, to comfort, and command;
And yet a Spirit still, and bright
With something of angelic light.   *30*

1804   1807

0 **She Was ... Delight** addressed to the poet's wife.

YEW-TREES°

There is a Yew-tree, pride of Lorton Vale,
Which to this day stands single, in the midst
Of its own darkness, as it stood of yore:
Not loth to furnish weapons for the bands
5 Of Umfraville or Percy ere they marched
To Scotland's heaths; or those that crossed the sea
And drew their sounding bows at Azincour,
Perhaps at earlier Crecy, or Poictiers.
Of vast circumference and gloom profound
10 This solitary Tree! a living thing
Produced too slowly ever to decay;
Of form and aspect too magnificent
To be destroyed. But worthier still of note
Are those fraternal Four of Borrowdale,
15 Joined in one solemn and capacious grove;
Huge trunks! and each particular trunk a growth
Of interwisted fibres serpentine
Up-coiling, and inveterately convolved;
Nor uninformed with Phantasy, and looks
20 That threaten the profane;—a pillared shade,
Upon whose grassless floor of red-brown hue,
By sheddings from the pining umbrage tinged
Perennially—beneath whose sable roof
Of boughs, as if for festal purpose, decked
25 With unrejoicing berries—ghostly Shapes
May meet at noontide; Fear and trembling Hope,
Silence and Foresight; Death the Skeleton
And Time the Shadow;—there to celebrate,
As in a natural temple scattered o'er
30 With altars undisturbed of mossy stone,
United worship; or in mute repose
To lie, and listen to the mountain flood
Murmuring from Glaramara's inmost caves.

1803   1815

0 **Yew-Trees** These evergreens, growing in the Lake District (Lorton
Vale, Borrowdale, Glaramara), provided bows for English armies
fighting in the fourteenth and fifteenth centuries against Scots and
French.

STANZAS WRITTEN IN MY POCKET-COPY
OF THOMSON'S *CASTLE OF INDOLENCE*°

Within our happy Castle there dwelt One°
Whom without blame I may not overlook;
For never sun on living creature shone
Who more devout enjoyment with us took:
Here on his hours he hung as on a book,   5
On his own time here would he float away,
As doth a fly upon a summer brook;
But go to-morrow, or belike to-day,
Seek for him,—he is fled; and whither none can say.

Thus often would he leave our peaceful home,   10
And find elsewhere his business or delight;
Out of our Valley's limits did he roam:
Full many a time, upon a stormy night,
His voice came to us from the neighbouring height:
Oft could we see him driving full in view   15
At mid-day when the sun was shining bright;
What ill was on him, what he had to do,
A mighty wonder bred among our quiet crew.

Ah! piteous sight it was to see this Man
When he came back to us, a withered flower,—   20
Or like a sinful creature, pale and wan.
Down would he sit; and without strength or power
Look at the common grass from hour to hour:
And oftentimes, how long I fear to say,
Where apple-trees in blossom made a bower,   25
Retired in that sunshiny shade he lay;
And, like a naked Indian, slept himself away.

Great wonder to our gentle tribe it was
Whenever from our Valley he withdrew;
For happier soul no living creature has   80
Than he had, being here the long day through.

0 **Stanzas . . . Indolence** Following the example of James Thomson
(1700–1748), Wordsworth uses Spenserian allegory for psychologi-
cal portraiture. **1 One** Wordsworth.

Some thought he was a lover, and did woo:
Some thought far worse of him, and judged him wrong;
But verse was what he had been wedded to;
35 And his own mind did like a tempest strong
Come to him thus, and drove the weary Wight along.

With him there often walked in friendly guise,
Or lay upon the moss by brook or tree,
A noticeable Man° with large grey eyes,
40 And a pale face that seemed undoubtedly
As if a blooming face it ought to be;
Heavy his low-hung lip did oft appear,
Deprest by weight of musing Phantasy;
Profound his forehead was, though not severe;
45 Yet some did think that he had little business here:

Sweet heaven forefend! his was a lawful right;
Noisy he was, and gamesome as a boy;
His limbs would toss about him with delight
Like branches when strong winds the trees annoy.
50 Nor lacked his calmer hours device or toy
To banish listlessness and irksome care;
He would have taught you how you might employ
Yourself; and many did to him repair,—
And certes not in vain; he had inventions rare.

55 Expedients, too, of simplest sort he tried:
Long blades of grass, plucked round him as he lay,
Made, to his ear attentively applied,
A pipe on which the wind would deftly play;
Glasses he had, that little things display,
60 The beetle panoplied in gems and gold,
A mailèd angel on a battle-day;
The mysteries that cups of flowers enfold,
And all the gorgeous sights which fairies do behold.

He would entice that other Man to hear
65 His music, and to view his imagery:
And, sooth, these two were each to the other dear:
No livelier love in such a place could be:

39 **Man** Coleridge.

There did they dwell—from earthly labour free,
As happy spirits as were ever seen;
If but a bird, to keep them company,   *70*
Or butterfly sate down, they were, I ween,
As pleased as if the same had been a Maiden-queen.

1802   1815

RESOLUTION AND INDEPENDENCE°

I

There was a roaring in the wind all night;
The rain came heavily and fell in floods;
But now the sun is rising calm and bright;
The birds are singing in the distant woods;
Over his own sweet voice the Stock-dove broods;   *5*
The Jay makes answer as the Magpie chatters;
And all the air is filled with pleasant noise of waters.

II

All things that love the sun are out of doors;
The sky rejoices in the morning's birth;
The grass is bright with rain-drops;—on the moors   *10*
The hare is running races in her mirth;
And with her feet she from the plashy earth
Raises a mist; that, glittering in the sun,
Runs with her all the way, wherever she doth run.

III

I was a Traveller then upon the moor;   *15*
I saw the hare that raced about with joy;
I heard the woods and distant waters roar;
Or heard them not, as happy as a boy:
The pleasant season did my heart employ:
My old remembrances went from me wholly;   *20*
And all the ways of men, so vain and melancholy.

0 **Resolution and Independence** Concerning the genesis of this
poem, see Appendix, p. 446.

IV

But, as it sometimes chanceth, from the might
Of joy in minds that can no further go,
As high as we have mounted in delight
25 In our dejection do we sink as low;
To me that morning did it happen so;
And fears and fancies thick upon me came;
Dim sadness—and blind thoughts, I knew not, nor
    could name.

V

I heard the sky-lark warbling in the sky;
30 And I bethought me of the playful hare:
Even such a happy Child of earth am I;
Even as these blissful creatures do I fare;
Far from the world I walk, and from all care;
But there may come another day to me—
35 Solitude, pain of heart, distress, and poverty.

VI

My whole life I have lived in pleasant thought,
As if life's business were a summer mood;
As if all needful things would come unsought
To genial faith, still rich in genial good;
40 But how can He expect that others should
Build for him, sow for him, and at his call
Love him, who for himself will take no heed at all?

VII

I thought of Chatterton,° the marvellous Boy,
The sleepless Soul that perished in his pride;
45 Of Him° who walked in glory and in joy
Following his plough, along the mountain-side:
By our own spirits are we deified:
We Poets in our youth begin in gladness;
But thereof come in the end despondency and madness.

43 **Chatterton** Thomas Chatterton (1752–70), a young poet who
committed suicide because of poverty and lack of recognition.
45 **Him** Robert Burns (1759–96).

VIII

Now, whether it were by peculiar grace,   *50*
A leading from above, a something given,
Yet it befel, that, in this lonely place,
When I with these untoward thoughts had striven,
Beside a pool bare to the eye of heaven
I saw a Man before me unawares: *55*
The oldest man he seemed that ever wore grey hairs.

IX

As a huge stone is sometimes seen to lie
Couched on the bald top of an eminence;
Wonder to all who do the same espy,
By what means it could thither come, and whence;   *60*
So that it seems a thing endued with sense:
Like a sea-beast crawled forth, that on a shelf
Of rock or sand reposeth, there to sun itself;

X

Such seemed this Man, not all alive nor dead,
Nor all asleep—in his extreme old age: *65*
His body was bent double, feet and head
Coming together in life's pilgrimage;
As if some dire constraint of pain, or rage
Of sickness felt by him in times long past,
A more than human weight upon his frame had cast.   *70*

XI

Himself he propped, limbs, body, and pale face,
Upon a long grey staff of shaven wood:
And, still as I drew near with gentle pace,
Upon the margin of that moorish flood
Motionless as a cloud the old Man stood,   *75*
That heareth not the loud winds when they call;
And moveth all together, if it move at all.

XII

At length, himself unsettling, he the pond
Stirred with his staff, and fixedly did look
Upon the muddy water, which he conned,   *80*
As if he had been reading in a book:

And now a stranger's privilege I took;
And, drawing to his side, to him did say,
"This morning gives us promise of a glorious day."

XIII

85 A gentle answer did the old Man make,
In courteous speech which forth he slowly drew:
And him with further words I thus bespake,
"What occupation do you there pursue?
This is a lonesome place for one like you."
90 Ere he replied, a flash of mild surprise
Broke from the sable orbs of his yet-vivid eyes.

XIV

His words came feebly, from a feeble chest,
But each in solemn order followed each,
With something of a lofty utterance drest—
95 Choice word and measured phrase, above the reach
Of ordinary men; a stately speech;
Such as grave Livers° do in Scotland use,
Religious men, who give to God and man their dues.

XV

He told, that to these waters he had come
100 To gather leeches, being old and poor:
Employment hazardous and wearisome!
And he had many hardships to endure:
From pond to pond he roamed, from moor to moor;
Housing, with God's good help, by choice or chance;
105 And in this way he gained an honest maintenance.

XVI

The old Man still stood talking by my side;
But now his voice to me was like a stream
Scarce heard; nor word from word could I divide;
And the whole body of the Man did seem
110 Like one whom I had met with in a dream;
Or like a man from some far region sent,
To give me human strength, by apt admonishment.

97 **grave Livers** members of a sect who live soberly, gravely.

XVII

My former thoughts returned: the fear that kills;
And hope that is unwilling to be fed;
Cold, pain, and labour, and all fleshly ills;   *115*
And mighty Poets in their misery dead.
—Perplexed, and longing to be comforted,
My question eagerly did I renew,
"How is it that you live, and what is it you do?"

XVIII

He with a smile did then his words repeat;   *120*
And said, that, gathering leeches, far and wide
He travelled; stirring thus about his feet
The waters of the pools where they abide.
"Once I could meet with them on every side;
But they have dwindled long by slow decay;   *125*
Yet still I persevere, and find them where I may."

XIX

While he was talking thus, the lonely place,
The old Man's shape, and speech—all troubled me:
In my mind's eye I seemed to see him pace
About the weary moors continually,   *130*
Wandering about alone and silently.
While I these thoughts within myself pursued,
He, having made a pause, the same discourse renewed.

XX

And soon with this he other matter blended,
Cheerfully uttered, with demeanour kind,   *135*
But stately in the main; and, when he ended,
I could have laughed myself to scorn to find
In that decrepit Man so firm a mind.
"God," said I, "be my help and stay° secure;
I'll think of the Leech-gatherer on the lonely moor!"   *140*

1802   1807

139 stay (a noun).

ODE TO DUTY

*"Jam non consilio bonus, sed more eò perductus, ut
non tantum rectè facere possim, sed nisi rectè facere
non possim."*°

Stern Daughter of the Voice of God!°
O Duty! if that name thou love
Who art a light to guide, a rod
To check the erring, and reprove;
5 Thou, who art victory and law
When empty terrors overawe;
From vain temptations dost set free;
And calm'st the weary strife of frail humanity!

There are who ask not if thine eye
10 Be on them; who, in love and truth,
Where no misgiving is, rely
Upon the genial sense of youth:
Glad Hearts! without reproach or blot;
Who do thy work, and know it not:
15 Oh! if through confidence misplaced
They fail, thy saving arms, dread Power! around them
     cast.

Serene will be our days and bright,
And happy will our nature be,
When love is an unerring light,
20 And joy its own security.
And they a blissful course may hold
Even now, who, not unwisely bold,
Live in the spirit of this creed;
Yet seek thy firm support, according to their need.

0 **"Jam . . . possim."** "Not self-consciously good, but so led by
habit that not only do I act rightly, I cannot but act rightly."
Adapted from Seneca, *Moral Epistles* CXX. 10.   1 **Daughter . . .
God** See *Paradise Lost* IX. 652. A second significant allusion to
Milton comes with "lowly wise" (line 53) which recalls *Paradise
Lost* VIII. 172–74.

I, loving freedom, and untried; 25
No sport of every random gust,
Yet being to myself a guide,
Too blindly have reposed my trust:
And oft, when in my heart was heard
Thy timely mandate, I deferred 30
The task, in smoother walks to stray;
But thee I now would serve more strictly, if I may.

Through no disturbance of my soul,
Or strong compunction in me wrought,
I supplicate for thy control; 35
But in the quietness of thought:
Me this unchartered freedom tires;
I feel the weight of chance-desires:
My hopes no more must change their name,
I long for a repose that ever is the same. 40

Stern Lawgiver! yet thou dost wear
The Godhead's most benignant grace;
Nor know we anything so fair
As is the smile upon thy face:
Flowers laugh before thee on their beds 45
And fragrance in thy footing treads;
Thou dost preserve the stars from wrong;
And the most ancient heavens, through Thee, are fresh
        and strong.

To humbler functions, awful Power!
I call thee: I myself commend 50
Unto thy guidance from this hour;
Oh, let my weakness have an end!
Give unto me, made lowly wise,
The spirit of self-sacrifice;
The confidence of reason give; 55
And in the light of truth thy Bondman let me live!

1804   1807

ELEGIAC STANZAS

*Suggested by a picture of Peele Castle, in a storm,
painted by Sir George Beaumont*

I was thy neighbour once, thou rugged Pile!
Four summer weeks I dwelt in sight of thee:
I saw thee every day; and all the while
Thy Form was sleeping on a glassy sea.

5   So pure the sky, so quiet was the air!
So like, so very like, was day to day!
Whene'er I looked, thy Image still was there;
It trembled, but it never passed away.

How perfect was the calm! it seemed no sleep;
10 No mood, which season takes away, or brings:
I could have fancied that the mighty Deep
Was even the gentlest of all gentle Things.

Ah! THEN, if mine had been the Painter's hand,
To express what then I saw; and add the gleam,
15 The light that never was, on sea or land,
The consecration, and the Poet's dream;

I would have planted thee, thou hoary Pile
Amid a world how different from this!
Beside a sea that could not cease to smile;
20 On tranquil land, beneath a sky of bliss.

Thou shouldst have seemed a treasure-house divine
Of peaceful years; a chronicle of heaven;—
Of all the sunbeams that did ever shine
The very sweetest had to thee been given.

25 A Picture had it been of lasting ease,
Elysian quiet, without toil or strife;
No motion but the moving tide, a breeze,
Or merely silent Nature's breathing life.

Such, in the fond illusion of my heart,
Such Picture would I at that time have made: *30*
And seen the soul of truth in every part,
A stedfast peace that might not be betrayed.

So once it would have been,—'tis so no more;
I have submitted to a new control:
A power is gone, which nothing can restore;   *35*
A deep distress° hath humanised my Soul.

Not for a moment could I now behold
A smiling sea, and be what I have been:
The feeling of my loss will ne'er be old;
This, which I know, I speak with mind serene.   *40*

Then, Beaumont, Friend! who would have been the
    Friend,
If he had lived, of Him whom I deplore,
This work of thine I blame not, but commend;
This sea in anger, and that dismal shore.

O 'tis a passionate Work!—yet wise and well,   *45*
Well chosen is the spirit that is here;
That Hulk which labours in the deadly swell,
This rueful sky, this pageantry of fear!

And this huge Castle, standing here sublime,
I love to see the look with which it braves,   *50*
Cased in the unfeeling armour of old time,
The lightning, the fierce wind, and trampling waves.

Farewell, farewell the heart that lives alone,
Housed in a dream, at distance from the Kind!°
Such happiness, wherever it be known,   *55*
Is to be pitied; for 'tis surely blind.

But welcome fortitude, and patient cheer,
And frequent sights of what is to be borne!
Such sights, or worse, as are before me here.—
Not without hope we suffer and we mourn.   *60*

1805   1807

36 **distress** the death of Wordsworth's brother John in 1805. 54 **the Kind** mankind. Cf. the poet's earliest criticism of the recluse or solitary in "Lines Left upon a Seat in a Yew-Tree."

LAODAMIA°

"With sacrifice before the rising morn
Vows have I made by fruitless hope inspired;
And from the infernal Gods, 'mid shades forlorn
Of night, my slaughtered Lord° have I required:
5 Celestial pity I again implore;—
Restore him to my sight—great Jove, restore!"

So speaking, and by fervent love endowed
With faith, the Suppliant heavenward lifts her hands;
While, like the sun emerging from a cloud,
10 Her countenance brightens—and her eye expands;
Her bosom heaves and spreads, her stature grows;
And she expects the issue in repose.

O terror! what hath she perceived?—O joy!
What doth she look on?—whom doth she behold?
15 Her Hero slain upon the beach of Troy?
His vital presence? his corporeal mould?
It is—if sense deceive her not—'tis He!
And a God leads him, wingèd Mercury!

Mild Hermes spake—and touched her with his wand
That calms all fear; "Such grace hath crowned thy
20   prayer,
Laodamía! that at Jove's command
Thy Husband walks the paths of upper air:
He comes to tarry with thee three hours' space;
Accept the gift, behold him face to face!"

25 Forth sprang the impassioned Queen her Lord to clasp;
Again that consummation she essayed;
But unsubstantial Form eludes her grasp
As often as that eager grasp was made.
The Phantom parts—but parts to re-unite,
30 And re-assume his place before her sight.

0 **Laodamia** In the *Aeneid* (VI. 440–49) Virgil puts Laodamia
among the lovers met by Aeneas in Hades. 4 **slaughtered Lord**
Protesilaus (see lines 31 ff.). The cause of his death is explained
in lines 43 ff.

"Protesiláus, lo! thy guide is gone!
Confirm, I pray, the vision with thy voice:
This is our palace,—yonder is thy throne;
Speak, and the floor thou tread'st on will rejoice.
Not to appal me have the gods bestowed 　　35
This precious boon; and blest a sad abode."

"Great Jove, Laodamía! doth not leave
His gifts imperfect:—Spectre though I be,
I am not sent to scare thee or deceive;
But in reward of thy fidelity. 　　40
And something also did my worth obtain;
For fearless virtue bringeth boundles_ gain.

"Thou knowest, the Delphic oracle foretold
That the first Greek who touched the Trojan strand
Should die; but me the threat could not withhold: 　　45
A generous cause a victim did demand;
And forth I leapt upon the sandy plain;
A self-devoted° chief—by Hector slain."

"Supreme of Heroes—bravest, noblest, best!
Thy matchless courage I bewail no more, 　　50
Which then, when tens of thousands were deprest
By doubt, propelled thee to the fatal shore;
Thou found'st—and I forgive thee—here thou art—
A nobler counsellor than my poor heart.

"But thou, though capable of sternest deed, 　　55
Wert kind as resolute, and good as brave;
And he, whose power restores thee, hath decreed
Thou should'st elude the malice of the grave:
Redundant° are thy locks, thy lips as fair
As when their breath enriched Thessalian air. 　　60

"No Spectre greets me,—no vain Shadow this;
Come, blooming Hero, place thee by my side!
Give, on this well-known couch, one nuptial kiss
To me, this day, a second time thy bride!"
Jove frowned in heaven: the conscious Parcae° threw 　　65
Upon those roseate lips a Stygian hue.

48 **self-devoted** self-sacrificed.　　59 **redundant** flowing.　　**65 conscious
Parcae** all-knowing goddesses of fate.

"This visage tells that my doom is past:
Nor should the change be mourned, even if the joys
Of sense were able to return as fast
70 And surely as they vanish. Earth destroys
Those raptures duly—Erebus disdains:
Calm pleasures there abide—majestic pains.

"Be taught, O faithful Consort, to control
Rebellious passion: for the Gods approve
75 The depth, and not the tumult, of the soul;
A fervent, not ungovernable, love.
Thy transports moderate; and meekly mourn
When I depart, for brief is my sojourn—"

"Ah, wherefore?—Did not Hercules by force
80 Wrest from the guardian Monster of the tomb
Alcestis, a reanimated corse°,
Given back to dwell on earth in vernal bloom?
Medea's spells dispersed the weight of years,
And Æson stood a youth 'mid youthful peers.

85 "The Gods to us are merciful—and they
Yet further may relent: for mightier far
Than strength of nerve and sinew, or the sway
Of magic potent over sun and star,
Is love, though oft to agony distrest,
90 And though his favourite seat be feeble woman's breast.

"But if thou goest, I follow—" "Peace!" he said,—
She looked upon him and was calmed and cheered;
The ghastly colour from his lips had fled;
In his deportment, shape, and mien, appeared
95 Elysian beauty, melancholy grace,
Brought from a pensive though a happy place.

He spake of love, such love as Spirits feel
In words whose course is equable and pure;
No fears to beat away—no strife to heal—
100 The past unsighed for, and the future sure;
Spake of heroic arts in graver mood
Revived, with finer harmony pursued;

81 **corse** corpse.

Of all that is most beauteous—imaged there
In happier beauty; more pellucid streams,
An ampler ether, a diviner air,   *105*
And fields invested with purpureal gleams;
Climes which the sun, who sheds the brightest day
Earth knows, is all unworthy to survey.

Yet there the Soul shall enter which hath earned
That privilege by virtue.—"Ill," said he,   *110*
"The end of man's existence I discerned,
Who from ignoble games and revelry
Could draw, when we had parted, vain delight,
While tears were thy best pastime, day and night;

"And while my youthful peers before my eyes   *115*
(Each hero following his peculiar bent)
Prepared themselves for glorious enterprise
By martial sports,—or, seated in the tent,
Chieftains and kings in council were detained;
What time the fleet at Aulis lay enchained.   *120*

"The wished-for wind was given:—I then revolved
The oracle, upon the silent sea;
And, if no worthier led the way, resolved
That, of a thousand vessels, mine should be
The foremost prow in pressing to the strand,—   *125*
Mine the first blood that tinged the Trojan sand.

"Yet bitter, oft-times bitter, was the pang
When of thy loss I thought, belovèd Wife!
On thee too fondly did my memory hang,
And on the joys we shared in mortal life,—   *130*
The paths which we had trod—these fountains, flowers;
My new-planned cities, and unfinished towers.

"But should suspense permit the Foe to cry,
'Behold they tremble!—haughty their array,
Yet of their number no one dares to die?'   *135*
In soul I swept the indignity away:
Old frailties then recurred:—but lofty thought,
In act embodied, my deliverance wrought.

"And Thou, though strong in love, art all too weak
140 In reason, in self-government too slow;
I counsel thee by fortitude to seek
Our blest re-union in the shades below.
The invisible world with thee hath sympathised;
Be thy affections raised and solemnised.

145 "Learn, by a mortal yearning, to ascend—
Seeking a higher object. Love was given,
Encouraged, sanctioned, chiefly for that end;
For this the passion to excess was driven—
That self might be annulled: her bondage prove
150 The fetters of a dream, opposed to love."—

Aloud she shrieked! for Hermes reappears!
Round the dear Shade she would have clung—'tis vain;
The hours are past—too brief had they been years;
And him no mortal effort can detain:
155 Swift, toward the realms that know not earthly day,
He through the portal takes his silent way,
And on the palace-floor a lifeless corse She lay.

Thus, all in vain exhorted and reproved,
She perished; and, as for a wilful crime,
160 By the just Gods whom no weak pity moved,
Was doomed to wear out her appointed time,
Apart from happy Ghosts, that gather flowers
Of blissful quiet 'mid unfading bowers.

—Yet tears to human suffering are due;
165 And mortal hopes defeated and o'erthrown
Are mourned by man, and not by man alone,
As fondly he believes.—Upon the side
Of Hellespont (such faith was entertained)
A knot of spiry trees for ages grew
170 From out the tomb of him for whom she died;
And ever, when such stature they had gained
That Ilium's walls were subject to their view,
The trees' tall summits withered at the sight;
A constant interchange of growth and blight!

POLITICAL SONNETS°

1801

I grieved for Buonaparté, with a vain
And an unthinking grief! The tenderest mood
Of that Man's mind—what can it be? what food
Fed his first hopes? what knowledge could *he* gain?
'Tis not in battles that from youth we train   *5*
The Governor who must be wise and good,
And temper with the sternness of the brain
Thoughts motherly, and meek as womanhood.
Wisdom doth live with children round her knees:
Books, leisure, perfect freedom, and the talk   *10*
Man holds with week-day man in the hourly walk
Of the mind's business: these are the degrees
By which true Sway doth mount; this is the stalk
True Power doth grow on; and her rights are these.

1802   1807

On the Extinction of the Venetian Republic°

Once did She hold the gorgeous east in fee;
And was the safeguard of the west: the worth
Of Venice did not fall below her birth,
Venice, the eldest Child of Liberty.
She was a maiden City, bright and free;   *5*
No guile seduced, no force could violate;
And, when she took unto herself a Mate,
She must espouse the everlasting Sea.°

0 **Political Sonnets** Wordsworth devoted a great deal of his time,
after 1800, to political poetry. Influenced by Milton, he used the
sonnet form in a consciously prophetic yet deeply journalistic way
to record his reactions to the Napoleonic wars. While rallying patri-
otic feeling, he also summoned the nation to self-criticism. The
poems reprinted here are from a group entitled "Sonnets Dedicated
to Liberty" in *Poems in Two Volumes* (1807).

0 **On the . . . Republic** Napoleon so decreed in 1797.   **7–8 And . . .
Sea** In a yearly rite the Doge "wedded" Venice to the Adriatic.

And what if she had seen those glories fade,
10   Those titles vanish, and that strength decay;
Yet shall some tribute of regret be paid
When her long life hath reached its final day:
Men are we, and must grieve when even the Shade
Of that which once was great, is passed away.

1802   1807

To Toussaint L'Ouverture°

Toussaint, the most unhappy man of men!
Whether the whistling Rustic tend his plough
Within thy hearing, or thy head be now
Pillowed in some deep dungeon's earless den;—
5   O miserable Chieftain! where and when
Wilt thou find patience? Yet die not; do thou
Wear rather in thy bonds a cheerful brow:
Though fallen thyself, never to rise again,
Live, and take comfort. Thou hast left behind
10   Powers that will work for thee; air, earth, and skies;
There's not a breathing of the common wind
That will forget thee; thou hast great allies;
Thy friends are exultations, agonies,
And love, and man's unconquerable mind.

1802   1807

September 1st, 1802°

We had a fellow-Passenger who came
From Calais with us, gaudy in array,
A Negro Woman like a Lady gay,

0 **To Toussaint L'Ouverture** addresses a former slave who led a
Negro rebellion against the reinstitution of slavery by the French
in Haiti. He was imprisoned in France and died there.
0 **September 1st, 1802** "Among the capricious acts of tyranny that
disgraced those times, was the chasing of all Negroes from France
by decree of the government. . . ." (Introductory Note). Words-
worth's "Calais" sonnets were a result of his journey to France
during the Peace of Amiens. I give the earliest published version.

Yet silent as a woman fearing blame;
Dejected, meek, yea pitiably tame,   5
She sate, from notice turning not away,
But on our proffer'd kindness still did lay
A weight of languid speech, or at the same
Was silent, motionless in eyes and face.
She was a Negro Woman driv'n from France,   10
Rejected, like all others of that race,
Not one of whom may now find footing there;
This the poor Out-cast did to us declare,
Nor murmur'd at the unfeeling Ordinance.

1802   1807

September, 1802. Near Dover

Inland, within a hollow vale, I stood;
And saw, while sea was calm and air was clear,
The coast of France—the coast of France how near!
Drawn almost into frightful neighbourhood.
I shrunk; for verily the barrier flood   5
Was like a lake, or river bright and fair,
A span of waters; yet what power is there!
What mightiness for evil and for good!
Even so doth God protect us if we be
Virtuous and wise. Winds blow, and waters roll,   10
Strength to the brave, and Power, and Deity;
Yet in themselves are nothing! One decree
Spake laws to *them,* and said that by the soul
Only, the Nations shall be great and free.

1802   1807

London, 1802

Milton! thou shouldst be living at this hour:
England hath need of thee: she is a fen
Of stagnant waters: altar, sword, and pen,
Fireside, the heroic wealth of hall and bower,
Have forfeited their ancient English dower   5
Of inward happiness. We are selfish men;

Oh! raise us up, return to us again;
And give us manners, virtue, freedom, power.
Thy soul was like a Star, and dwelt apart;
10 Thou hadst a voice whose sound was like the sea:
Pure as the naked heavens, majestic, free,
So didst thou travel on life's common way,
In cheerful godliness; and yet thy heart
The lowliest duties on herself did lay.

1802   1807

It Is Not To Be Thought of That the Flood

It is not to be thought of that the Flood
Of British freedom, which, to the open sea
Of the world's praise, from dark antiquity
Hath flowed, "with pomp of waters, unwithstood,"°
5 Roused though it be full often to a mood
Which spurns the check of salutary bands,
That this most famous Stream in bogs and sands
Should perish; and to evil and to good
Be lost for ever. In our halls is hung
10 Armoury of the invincible Knights of old:
We must be free or die, who speak the tongue
That Shakespeare spake; the faith and morals hold
Which Milton held.—In every thing we are sprung
Of Earth's first blood, have titles manifold.

1802–1803   1807

Thought of a Briton on the Subjugation of Switzerland°

Two Voices are there; one is of the sea,
One of the mountains;° each a mighty Voice:
In both from age to age thou didst rejoice,
They were thy chosen music, Liberty!

4 "with . . . unwithstood" from Samuel Daniel's *Civil Wars* II.7 (1609).

0 Switzerland Invaded by Napoleon in 1798 and subjugated in 1802.
1–2 sea . . . mountains Britain and Switzerland respectively.

There came a Tyrant, and with holy glee   5
Thou fought'st against him; but hast vainly striven:
Thou from thy Alpine holds at length art driven,
Where not a torrent murmurs heard by thee.
Of one deep bliss thine ear hath been bereft:
Then cleave, O cleave to that which still is left;   10
For, high-souled Maid, what sorrow would it be
That Mountain floods should thunder as before,
And Ocean bellow from his rocky shore,
And neither awful Voice be heard by thee!

1806–1807   1807

Written in London, September, 1802

O Friend! I know not which way I must look
For comfort, being, as I am, opprest,
To think that now our life is only drest
For show; mean handy-work of craftsman, cook,
Or groom!—We must run glittering like a brook   5
In the open sunshine, or we are unblest:
The wealthiest man among us is the best:
No grandeur now in nature or in book
Delights us. Rapine, avarice, expense,
This is idolatry; and these we adore: 10
Plain living and high thinking are no more:
The homely beauty of the good old cause
Is gone; our peace, our fearful innocence,
And pure religion breathing household laws.

1802   1807

England! The Time Is Come

England! the time is come when thou should'st wean
Thy heart from its emasculating food;
The truth should now be better understood;
Old things have been unsettled; we have seen
Fair seed-time, better harvest might have been   5
But for thy trespasses; and, at this day,
If for Greece, Egypt, India, Africa,
Aught good were destined, thou wouldst step between.

England! all nations in this charge° agree:
10   But worse, more ignorant in love and hate,
Far—far more abject, is thine Enemy:°
Therefore the wise pray for thee, though the freight
Of thy offences be a heavy weight:
Oh grief that Earth's best hopes rest all with Thee!

1803 (?)   1807

November, 1806

Another year!—another deadly blow!
Another mighty Empire° overthrown!
And We are left, or shall be left, alone;
The last that dare to struggle with the Foe.
5   'Tis well! from this day forward we shall know
That in ourselves our safety must be sought;
That by our own right hands it must be wrought;
That we must stand unpropped, or be laid low.
O dastard whom such foretaste doth not cheer!
10   We shall exult, if they who rule the land
Be men who hold its many blessings dear,
Wise, upright, valiant; not a servile band,
Who are to judge of danger which they fear,
And honour which they do not understand.

1806   1807

Lines

*Composed at Grasmere, during a walk one Evening,
after a stormy day, the Author having just read in a
Newspaper that the dissolution of Mr. Fox° was hourly
expected.*

Loud is the Vale! the Voice is up
With which she speaks when storms are gone,
A mighty Unison of streams!
Of all her Voices, One!

9 **this charge** set forth in the octave.   11 **Enemy** France.
2 **Empire** Prussia, in the battle of Jena, October 14, 1806.
0 **Mr. Fox** Charles James Fox, the great English statesman, died on
September 13, 1806. Wordsworth respected his policies concerning
France and the abolition of the slave trade.

Loud is the Vale;—this inland Depth 5
In peace is roaring like the Sea;
Yon Star upon the mountain-top
Is listening quietly.

Sad was I, ev'n to pain depressed,
Importunate and heavy load! 10
The Comforter hath found me here,
Upon this lonely road;

And many thousands now are sad,
Wait the fulfillment of their fear;
For He must die who is their Stay, 15
Their Glory disappear.

A Power is passing from the earth
To breathless Nature's dark abyss;
But when the Mighty pass away
What is it more than this, 20

That Man, who is from God sent forth,
Doth yet again to God return?—
Such ebb and flow must ever be,
Then wherefore should we mourn?

1806   1807

THE PRELUDE°
or
Growth of a Poet's Mind

An Autobiographical Poem

Book First

Introduction—Childhood and School-time

O there is blessing in this gentle breeze,
A visitant that while it fans my cheek

0 **The Prelude** Wordsworth considered this "Poem on his own life"
as an appendix to *The Recluse,* his unrealized "song of philosophic
Truth." The poem was kept in manuscript, undergoing numerous
changes between 1805 and its publication in 1850 by the poet's wife,
who first titled it *The Prelude.* The authorized version of 1850, here
reprinted, is sometimes less candid than the 1805 *Prelude,* but does
not differ substantially from it, and is usually more concise.

Doth seem half-conscious of the joy it brings
From the green fields, and from yon azure sky.
5 Whate'er its mission, the soft breeze can come
To none more grateful than to me; escaped
From the vast city, where I long had pined
A discontented sojourner: now free,
Free as a bird to settle where I will.
10 What dwelling shall receive me? in what vale
Shall be my harbour? underneath what grove
Shall I take up my home? and what clear stream
Shall with its murmur lull me into rest?
The earth is all before me.° With a heart
15 Joyous, nor scared at its own liberty,
I look about; and should the chosen guide
Be nothing better than a wandering cloud,
I cannot miss my way. I breathe again!
Trances of thought and mountings of the mind
20 Come fast upon me: it is shaken off,
That burthen of my own unnatural self,
The heavy weight of many a weary day
Not mine, and such as were not made for me.
Long months of peace (if such bold word accord
25 With any promises of human life),
Long months of ease and undisturbed delight
Are mine in prospect; whither shall I turn,
By road or pathway, or through trackless field,
Up hill or down, or shall some floating thing
30 Upon the river point me out my course?

Dear Liberty! Yet what would it avail
But for a gift° that consecrates the joy?
For I, methought, while the sweet breath of heaven
Was blowing on my body, felt within
35 A correspondent breeze, that gently moved
With quickening virtue,° but is now become
A tempest, a redundant energy,

---

14 **The earth . . . me.** See *Paradise Lost* XII. 646.   32 **gift** poetic
inspiration. Lines 33–38 describe how inspiration (the answering
or "correspondent" breeze born when Nature gently in-spires or
breathes upon him) grows to storm-wind intensity.   36 **quickening
virtue** revitalizing force.

Vexing its own creation. Thanks to both,
And their congenial powers, that, while they join
In breaking up a long-continued frost,   *40*
Bring with them vernal promises, the hope
Of active days urged on by flying hours,—
Days of sweet leisure, taxed with patient thought
Abstruse, nor wanting punctual service high,
Matins and vespers of harmonious verse!   *45*

  Thus far, O Friend!° did I, not used to make
A present joy the matter of a song,°
Pour forth that day° my soul in measured strains
That would not be forgotten, and are here
Recorded: to the open fields I told   *50*
A prophecy: poetic numbers came
Spontaneously to clothe in priestly robe
A renovated spirit singled out,
Such hope was mine, for holy services.
My own voice cheered me, and far more, the mind's   *55*
Internal echo of the imperfect sound;
To both I listened, drawing from them both
A cheerful confidence in things to come.

  Content and not unwilling now to give
A respite to this passion, I paced on   *60*
With brisk and eager steps; and came, at length,
To a green shady place, where down I sate
Beneath a tree, slackening my thoughts by choice,
And settling into gentler happiness.
'Twas autumn, and a clear and placid day,   *65*
With warmth, as much as needed, from a sun
Two hours declined towards the west; a day
With silver clouds, and sunshine on the grass,
And in the sheltered and the sheltering grove
A perfect stillness. Many were the thoughts   *70*
Encouraged and dismissed, till choice was made
Of a known Vale, whither my feet should turn,

46 **Friend** Coleridge, to whom *The Prelude* is addressed.   46–47
not used . . . song that is, inspired by present joy as opposed to
"emotion recollected in tranquillity."   48 **that day** in 1795 or per-
haps 1797 when Wordsworth first dreamed of settling in Grasmere.

Nor rest till they had reached the very door
Of the one cottage which methought I saw.
75 No picture of mere memory ever looked
So fair; and while upon the fancied scene
I gazed with growing love, a higher power°
Than Fancy gave assurance of some work
Of glory° there forthwith to be begun,
80 Perhaps too there performed. Thus long I mused,
Nor e'er lost sight of what I mused upon,
Save when, amid the stately grove of oaks,
Now here, now there, an acorn, from its cup
Dislodged, through sere leaves rustled, or at once
85 To the bare earth dropped with a startling sound.
From that soft couch I rose not, till the sun
Had almost touched the horizon; casting then
A backward glance upon the curling cloud
Of city smoke, by distance ruralised;
90 Keen as a Truant or a Fugitive,
But as a Pilgrim resolute, I took,
Even with the chance equipment of that hour,
The road that pointed toward the chosen Vale.
It was a splendid evening, and my soul
95 Once more made trial of her strength, nor lacked
Æolian° visitations; but the harp
Was soon defrauded, and the banded host
Of harmony dispersed in straggling sounds,
And lastly utter silence! "Be it so;
100 Why think of any thing but present good?"
So, like a home-found labourer I pursued
My way beneath the mellowing sun, that shed
Mild influence; nor left in me one wish
Again to bend the Sabbath of that time
105 To a servile yoke. What need of many words?
A pleasant loitering journey, through three days
Continued, brought me to my hermitage.
I spare to tell of what ensued, the life
In common things—the endless store of things,

77 **higher power** imagination. 78–79 **work of glory** his poem, *The Recluse,* to which this is the "prelude." 96 **Aeolian** from Aeolus, Greek god of winds. "Harp" introduces the image of the wind-harp, symbol for the poetic mind which is as musically responsive to Nature as the harp is to winds.

Rare, or at least so seeming, every day   *110*
Found all about me in one neighbourhood—
The self-congratulation, and, from morn
To night, unbroken cheerfulness serene.
But speedily an earnest longing rose
To brace myself to some determined aim,   *115*
Reading or thinking; either to lay up
New stores, or rescue from decay the old
By timely interference: and therewith
Came hopes still higher, that with outward life
I might endue some airy phantasies   *120*
That had been floating loose about for years,
And to such beings temperately deal forth
The many feelings that oppressed my heart.
That hope hath been discouraged; welcome light
Dawns from the east, but dawns to disappear   *125*
And mock me with a sky that ripens not
Into a steady morning: if my mind,
Remembering the bold promise of the past,
Would gladly grapple with some noble theme,
Vain is her wish; where'er she turns she finds   *130*
Impediments from day to day renewed.

  And now it would content me to yield up
Those lofty hopes awhile, for present gifts
Of humbler industry. But, oh, dear Friend!
The Poet, gentle creature as he is,   *135*
Hath, like the Lover, his unruly times;
His fits when he is neither sick nor well,
Though no distress be near him but his own
Unmanageable thoughts: his mind, best pleased
While she as duteous as the mother dove   *140*
Sits brooding, lives not always to that end,
But like the innocent bird, hath goadings on
That drive her as in trouble through the groves;
With me is now such passion, to be blamed
No otherwise than as it lasts too long.   *145*

  When, as becomes a man who would prepare
For such an arduous work, I through myself
Make rigorous inquisition, the report

Is often cheering; for I neither seem
150 To lack that first great gift, the vital soul,
Nor general Truths, which are themselves a sort
Of Elements and Agents, Under-powers,
Subordinate helpers of the living mind:
Nor am I naked of external things,
155 Forms, images, nor numerous other aids
Of less regard, though won perhaps with toil
And needful to build up a Poet's praise.
Time, place, and manners do I seek, and these
Are found in plenteous store, but nowhere such
160 As may be singled out with steady choice;
No little band of yet remembered names
Whom I, in perfect confidence, might hope
To summon back from lonesome banishment,
And make them dwellers in the hearts of men
165 Now living, or to live in future years.
Sometimes the ambitious Power of choice, mistaking
Proud spring-tide swellings for a regular sea,
Will settle on some British theme, some old
Romantic tale by Milton left unsung;
170 More often turning to some gentle place
Within the groves of Chivalry, I pipe
To shepherd swains, or seated harp in hand,
Amid reposing knights by a river side
Or fountain, listen to the grave reports
175 Of dire enchantments faced and overcome
By the strong mind, and tales of warlike feats,
Where spear encountered spear, and sword with sword
Fought, as if conscious of the blazonry
That the shield bore, so glorious was the strife;
180 Whence inspiration for a song that winds
Through ever-changing scenes of votive quest
Wrongs to redress, harmonious tribute paid
To patient courage and unblemished truth,
To firm devotion, zeal unquenchable,
185 And Christian meekness hallowing faithful loves.
Sometimes, more sternly moved,° I would relate

186 **more sternly moved** From Romance Wordsworth turns to history and heroes (Mithridates, etc.) associated with national liberation movements.

How vanquished Mithridates northward passed,
And, hidden in the cloud of years, became
Odin, the Father of a race by whom
Perished the Roman Empire: how the friends   *190*
And followers of Sertorius, out of Spain
Flying, found shelter in the Fortunate Isles,
And left their usages, their arts and laws,
To disappear by a slow gradual death,
To dwindle and to perish one by one,   *195*
Starved in those narrow bounds: but not the soul
Of Liberty, which fifteen hundred years
Survived, and, when the European came
With skill and power that might not be withstood,
Did, like a pestilence, maintain its hold   *200*
And wasted down by glorious death that race
Of natural heroes: or I would record
How, in tyrannic times, some high-souled man,
Unnamed among the chronicles of kings,
Suffered in silence for Truth's sake: or tell,   *205*
How that one Frenchman, through continued force
Of meditation on the inhuman deeds
Of those who conquered first the Indian Isles,
Went single in his ministry across
The Ocean; not to comfort the oppressed,   *210*
But, like a thirsty wind, to roam about
Withering the Oppressor: how Gustavus sought
Help at his need in Dalecarlia's mines;
How Wallace fought for Scotland; left the name
Of Wallace to be found, like a wild flower,   *215*
All over his dear Country; left the deeds
Of Wallace, like a family of Ghosts,
To people the steep rocks and river banks,
Her natural sanctuaries, with a local soul
Of independence and stern liberty.   *220*
Sometimes it suits me better to invent
A tale from my own heart, more near akin
To my own passions and habitual thoughts;
Some variegated story, in the main
Lofty, but the unsubstantial structure melts   *225*
Before the very sun that brightens it,
Mist into air dissolving! Then a wish,

My best and favourite aspiration, mounts
With yearning toward some philosophic song
230 Of Truth that cherishes our daily life;
With meditations passionate from deep
Recesses in man's heart, immortal verse
Thoughtfully fitted to the Orphean lyre;
But from this awful burthen I full soon
235 Take refuge and beguile myself with trust
That mellower years will bring a riper mind
And clearer insight. Thus my days are past
In contradiction; with no skill to part
Vague longing, haply bred by want of power,
240 From paramount impulse not to be withstood,
A timorous capacity from prudence,
From circumspection, infinite delay.
Humility and modest awe themselves
Betray me, serving often for a cloak
245 To a more subtle selfishness; that now
Locks every function up in blank reserve,
Now dupes me, trusting to an anxious eye
That with intrusive restlessness beats off
Simplicity and self-presented truth.
250 Ah! better far than this, to stray about
Voluptuously through fields and rural walks,
And ask no record of the hours, resigned
To vacant musing, unreproved neglect
Of all things, and deliberate holiday.
255 Far better never to have heard the name
Of zeal and just ambition, than to live
Baffled and plagued by a mind that every hour
Turns recreant to her task; takes heart again,
Then feels immediately some hollow thought
260 Hang like an interdict upon her hopes.
This is my lot; for either still I find
Some imperfection in the chosen theme,
Or see of absolute accomplishment
Much wanting, so much wanting, in myself,
265 That I recoil and droop, and seek repose
In listlessness from vain perplexity,
Unprofitably travelling toward the grave,

Like a false steward° who hath much received
And renders nothing back.
                        Was it for this
That one, the fairest of all rivers, loved   270
To blend his murmurs with my nurse's song,
And, from his alder shades and rocky falls,
And from his fords and shallows, sent a voice
That flowed along my dreams? For this, didst thou,
O Derwent! winding among grassy holms   275
Where I was looking on, a babe in arms,
Make ceaseless music that composed my thoughts
To more than infant softness, giving me
Amid the fretful dwellings of mankind
A foretaste, a dim earnest, of the calm   280
That Nature breathes among the hills and groves.

    When he had left the mountains and received
On his smooth breast the shadow of those towers°
That yet survive, a shattered monument
Of feudal sway, the bright blue river passed   285
Along the margin of our terrace walk;
A tempting playmate whom we dearly loved.
Oh, many a time have I, a five years' child,
In a small mill-race severed from his stream,
Made one long bathing of a summer's day;   290
Basked in the sun, and plunged and basked again
Alternate, all a summer's day, or scoured
The sandy fields, leaping through flowery groves
Of yellow ragwort; or, when rock and hill,
The woods, and distant Skiddaw's lofty height,   295
Were bronzed with deepest radiance, stood alone
Beneath the sky, as if I had been born
On Indian plains, and from my mother's hut
Had run abroad in wantonness, to sport
A naked savage, in the thunder shower.   300

    Fair seed-time had my soul, and I grew up
Fostered alike by beauty and by fear:
Much favoured in my birth-place, and no less

268 **false steward** See Luke 16.   283 **towers** of the castle at Cocker-
mouth, Wordsworth's birthplace.

In that beloved Vale° to which erelong
305 We were transplanted—there were we let loose
For sports of wider range. Ere I had told
Ten birth-days, when among the mountain slopes
Frost, and the breath of frosty wind had snapped
The last autumnal crocus, 'twas my joy
310 With store of springes o'er my shoulder hung
To range the open heights where woodcocks run
Along the smooth green turf. Through half the night,
Scudding away from snare to snare, I plied
That anxious visitation;—moon and stars
315 Were shining o'er my head. I was alone,
And seemed to be a trouble to the peace
That dwelt among them. Sometimes it befel
In these night wanderings, that a strong desire
O'erpowered my better reason, and the bird
320 Which was the captive of another's toil
Became my prey; and when the deed was done
I heard among the solitary hills
Low breathings coming after me, and sounds
Of undistinguishable motion, steps
325 Almost as silent as the turf they trod.

Nor less when spring had warmed the cultured Vale,
Moved we as plunderers where the mother-bird
Had in high places built her lodge; though mean
Our object and inglorious, yet the end
330 Was not ignoble. Oh! when I have hung
Above the raven's nest, by knots of grass
And half-inch fissures in the slippery rock
But ill sustained, and almost (so it seemed)
Suspended by the blast that blew amain,
335 Shouldering the naked crag, oh, at that time
While on the perilous ridge I hung alone,
With what strange utterance did the loud dry wind
Blow through my ear! the sky seemed not a sky
Of earth—and with what motion moved the clouds!

340 Dust as we are, the immortal spirit grows
Like harmony in music; there is a dark

304 **Vale** Esthwaite valley.

Inscrutable workmanship that reconciles
Discordant elements, makes them cling together
In one society. How strange that all
The terrors, pains, and early miseries,   345
Regrets, vexations, lassitudes interfused
Within my mind, should e'er have borne a part,
And that a needful part, in making up
The calm existence that is mine when I
Am worthy of myself! Praise to the end!   350
Thanks to the means which Nature deigned to employ;
Whether her fearless visitings, or those
That came with soft alarm, like hurtless light
Opening the peaceful clouds; or she may use
Severer interventions, ministry   355
More palpable, as best might suit her aim.

    One summer evening (led by her) I found
A little boat tied to a willow tree
Within a rocky cove, its usual home.
Straight I unloosed her chain, and stepping in   360
Pushed from the shore. It was an act of stealth
And troubled pleasure, nor without the voice
Of mountain-echoes did my boat move on;
Leaving behind her still, on either side,
Small circles glittering idly in the moon,   365
Until they melted all into one track
Of sparkling light. But now, like one who rows,
Proud of his skill, to reach a chosen point
With an unswerving line, I fixed my view
Upon the summit of a craggy ridge,   370
The horizon's utmost boundary; far above
Was nothing but the stars and the grey sky.
She was an elfin pinnace; lustily
I dipped my oars into the silent lake,
And, as I rose upon the stroke, my boat   375
Went heaving through the water like a swan;
When, from behind that craggy steep till then
The horizon's bound, a huge peak, black and huge,
As if with voluntary power instinct
Upreared its head. I struck and struck again,   380
And growing still in stature the grim shape

Towered up between me and the stars, and still,
For so it seemed, with purpose of its own
And measured motion like a living thing,
385 Strode after me. With trembling oars I turned,
And through the silent water stole my way
Back to the covert of the willow tree;
There in her mooring-place I left my bark,—
And through the meadows homeward went, in grave
390 And serious mood; but after I had seen
That spectacle, for many days, my brain
Worked with a dim and undetermined sense
Of unknown modes of being; o'er my thoughts
There hung a darkness, call it solitude
395 Or blank desertion. No familiar shapes
Remained, no pleasant images of trees,
Of sea or sky, no colours of green fields;
But huge and mighty forms, that do not live
Like living men, moved slowly through the mind
400 By day, and were a trouble to my dreams.

Wisdom and Spirit of the universe!
Thou Soul that art the eternity of thought
That givest to forms and images a breath
And everlasting motion, not in vain
405 By day or star-light thus from my first dawn
Of childhood didst thou intertwine for me
The passions that build up our human soul;
Not with the mean and vulgar works of man,
But with high objects, with enduring things—
410 With life and nature, purifying thus
The elements of feeling and of thought,
And sanctifying, by such discipline,
Both pain and fear, until we recognise
A grandeur in the beatings of the heart.
415 Nor was this fellowship vouchsafed to me
With stinted kindness. In November days,
When vapours rolling down the valley made
A lonely scene more lonesome, among woods,
At noon and 'mid the calm of summer nights,
420 When, by the margin of the trembling lake,

Beneath the gloomy hills homeward I went
In solitude, such intercourse was mine;
Mine was it in the fields both day and night,
And by the waters, all the summer long.

　　And in the frosty season, when the sun　　425
Was set, and visible for many a mile
The cottage windows blazed through twilight gloom,
I heeded not their summons: happy time
It was indeed for all of us—for me
It was a time of rapture! Clear and loud　　430
The village clock tolled six,—I wheeled about,
Proud and exulting like an untired horse
That cares not for his home. All shod with steel,
We hissed along the polished ice in games
Confederate, imitative of the chase　　435
And woodland pleasures,—the resounding horn,
The pack loud chiming, and the hunted hare.
So through the darkness and the cold we flew,
And not a voice was idle; with the din
Smitten, the precipices rang aloud;　　440
The leafless trees and every icy crag
Tinkled like iron; while far distant hills
Into the tumult sent an alien sound
Of melancholy not unnoticed, while the stars
Eastward were sparkling clear, and in the west　　445
The orange sky of evening died away.
Not seldom from the uproar I retired
Into a silent bay, or sportively
Glanced sideway, leaving the tumultuous throng,
To cut across the reflex of a star　　450
That fled, and, flying still before me, gleamed
Upon the glassy plain; and oftentimes,
When we had given our bodies to the wind,
And all the shadowy banks on either side
Came sweeping through the darknesss, spinning
　　　still　　455
The rapid line of motion, then at once
Have I, reclining back upon my heels,
Stopped short; yet still the solitary cliffs

Wheeled by me—even as if the earth had rolled
460 With visible motion her diurnal round!
Behind me did they stretch in solemn train,
Feebler and feebler, and I stood and watched
Till all was tranquil as a dreamless sleep.

Ye Presences of Nature in the sky
465 And on the earth! Ye Visions of the hills!
And Souls of lonely places! can I think
A vulgar hope was yours when ye employed
Such ministry, when ye through many a year
Haunting me thus among my boyish sports,
470 On caves and trees, upon the woods and hills,
Impressed upon all forms the characters
Of danger or desire; and thus did make
The surface of the universal earth
With triumph and delight, with hope and fear,
Work like a sea?
475   Not uselessly employed,
Might I pursue this theme through every change
Of exercise and play, to which the year
Did summon us in his delightful round.

We were a noisy crew; the sun in heaven
480 Beheld not vales more beautiful than ours;
Nor saw a band in happiness and joy
Richer, or worthier of the ground they trod.
I could record with no reluctant voice
The woods of autumn, and their hazel bowers
485 With milk-white clusters hung; the rod and line,
True symbol of hope's foolishness, whose strong
And unreproved enchantment led us on
By rocks and pools shut out from every star,
All the green summer, to forlorn cascades
490 Among the windings hid of mountain brooks.
—Unfading recollections! at this hour
The heart is almost mine with which I felt,
From some hill-top on sunny afternoons,
The paper kite high among fleecy clouds
495 Pull at her rein like an impetuous courser;

Or, from the meadows sent on gusty days,
Beheld her breast the wind, then suddenly
Dashed headlong, and rejected by the storm.

Ye lowly cottages wherein we dwelt,
A ministration of your own was yours;   *500*
Can I forget you, being as you were
So beautiful among the pleasant fields
In which ye stood? or can I here forget
The plain and seemly countenance with which
Ye dealt out your plain comforts? Yet had ye   *505*
Delights and exultations of your own.
Eager and never weary we pursued
Our home-amusements by the warm peat-fire
At evening, when with pencil, and smooth slate
In square divisions parcelled out and all   *510*
With crosses and with cyphers scribbled o'er,
We schemed and puzzled, head opposed to head
In strife too humble to be named in verse:
Or round the naked table, snow-white deal,
Cherry or maple, sate in close array,   *515*
And to the combat, Loo or Whist, led on
A thick-ribbed army; not, as in the world,
Neglected and ungratefully thrown by
Even for the very service they had wrought,
But husbanded through many a long campaign.   *520*
Uncouth assemblage was it, where no few
Had changed their functions; some, plebeian cards
Which Fate, beyond the promise of their birth
Had dignified, and called to represent
The persons of departed potentates.   *525*
Oh, with what echoes on the board they fell!
Ironic diamonds,—clubs, hearts, diamonds, spades,
A congregation piteously akin!
Cheap matter offered they to boyish wit,
Those sooty knaves, precipitated down   *530*
With scoffs and taunts, like Vulcan out of heaven:
The paramount ace, a moon in her eclipse,
Queens gleaming through their splendour's last decay,
And monarchs surly at the wrongs sustained
By royal visages. Meanwhile abroad   *535*

Incessant rain was falling, or the frost
Raged bitterly, with keen and silent tooth;
And, interrupting oft that eager game,
From under Esthwaite's splitting fields of ice
540 The pent-up air, struggling to free itself,
Gave out to meadow grounds and hills a loud
Protracted yelling, like the noise of wolves
Howling in troops along the Bothnic Main.

    Nor, sedulous as I have been to trace
545 How Nature by extrinsic passion° first
Peopled the mind with forms sublime or fair,
And made me love them, may I here omit
How other pleasures have been mine, and joys
Of subtler origin; how I have felt,
550 Not seldom even in that tempestuous time,
Those hallowed and pure motions of the sense
Which seem, in their simplicity, to own
An intellectual charm; that calm delight
Which, if I err not, surely must belong
555 To those first-born affinities that fit
Our new existence to existing things,
And, in our dawn of being, constitute
The bond of union between life and joy.

    Yes, I remember when the changeful earth,
560 And twice five summers on my mind had stamped
The faces of the moving year, even then
I held unconscious intercourse with beauty
Old as creation, drinking in a pure
Organic pleasure from the silver wreaths
565 Of curling mist, or from the level plain
Of waters coloured by impending clouds.

    The sands of Westmoreland, the creeks and bays
Of Cumbria's rocky limits, they can tell
How, when the Sea threw off his evening shade,
570 And to the shepherd's hut on distant hill
Sent welcome notice of the rising moon,

545 **extrinsic passion** feeling that did not seem to have Nature as its
end.

How I have stood, to fancies such as these
A stranger, linking with the spectacle
No conscious memory of a kindred sight,
And bringing with me no peculiar sense   575
Of quietness or peace; yet have I stood,
Even while mine eye hath moved o'er many a league
Of shining water, gathering as it seemed,
Through every hair-breadth in that field of light
New pleasure like a bee among the flowers.   580

    Thus oft amid those fits of vulgar° joy
Which, through all seasons, on a child's pursuits
Are prompt attendants, 'mid that giddy bliss
Which, like a tempest, works along the blood
And is forgotten; even then I felt   585
Gleams like the flashing of a shield;—the earth
And common face of Nature spake to me
Rememberable things; sometimes, 'tis true,
By chance collisions and quaint accidents
(Like those ill-sorted unions, work supposed   590
Of evil-minded fairies), yet not vain
Nor profitless, if haply they impressed
Collateral objects° and appearances,
Albeit lifeless then, and doomed to sleep
Until maturer seasons called them forth   595
To impregnate and to elevate the mind.
—And if the vulgar joy by its own weight
Wearied itself out of the memory,
The scenes which were a witness of that joy
Remained in their substantial lineaments   600
Depicted on the brain, and to the eye
Were visible, a daily sight; and thus
By the impressive discipline of fear,
By pleasure and repeated happiness,
So frequently repeated, and by force   605
Of obscure feelings representative
Of things forgotten, these same scenes so bright,
So beautiful, so majestic in themselves,

---

581 **vulgar** ordinary.   593 **Collateral objects** not in the direct field
of vision or significance.

Though yet the day was distant, did become
610 Habitually dear, and all their forms
And changeful colours by invisible links
Were fastened to the affections.
                                    I began
My story early—not misled, I trust,
By an infirmity of love for days
615 Disowned by memory—fancying flowers where none
Not even the sweetest do or can survive
For him at least whose dawning day they cheered.
Nor will it seem to thee, O Friend! so prompt
In sympathy, that I have lengthened out
620 With fond and feeble tongue a tedious tale.
Meanwhile, my hope has been, that I might fetch
Invigorating thoughts from former years;
Might fix the wavering balance of my mind,
And haply meet reproaches too, whose power
625 May spur me on, in manhood now mature,
To honourable toil. Yet should these hopes
Prove vain and thus should neither I be taught
To understand myself, nor thou to know
With better knowledge how the heart was framed
630 Of him thou lovest; need I dread from thee
Harsh judgments, if the song be loth to quit
Those recollected hours that have the charm
Of visionary things, those lovely forms
And sweet sensations that throw back our life,
635 And almost make remotest infancy
A visible scene, on which the sun is shining?

One end at least hath been attained; my mind
Hath been revived, and if this genial mood
Desert me not, forthwith shall be brought down
640 Through later years the story of my life.
The road lies plain before me;—'tis a theme
Single and of determined bounds; and hence
I choose it rather at this time, than work
Of ampler or more varied argument,
645 Where I might be discomfited and lost:
And certain hopes are with me, that to thee
This labour will be welcome, honoured Friend!

Book Second

School-Time (*continued*)

Thus far, O Friend! have we, though leaving much
Unvisited, endeavoured to retrace
The simple ways in which my childhood walked;
Those chiefly that first led me to the love
Of rivers, woods, and fields. The passion yet   5
Was in its birth, sustained as might befal
By nourishment that came unsought; for still
From week to week, from month to month, we lived
A round of tumult. Duly were our games
Prolonged in summer till the daylight failed;   10
No chair remained before the doors; the bench
And threshold steps were empty; fast asleep
The labourer, and the old man who had sate
A later lingerer; yet the revelry
Continued and the loud uproar: at last,   15
When all the ground was dark, and twinkling stars
Edged the black clouds, home and to bed we went,
Feverish with weary joints and beating minds.
Ah! is there one who ever has been young,
Nor needs a warning voice to tame the pride   20
Of intellect and virtue's self-esteem?
One is there, though the wisest and the best
Of all mankind, who covets not at times
Union that cannot be;—who would not give,
If so he might, to duty and to truth   25
The eagerness of infantine desire?°
A tranquillising spirit presses now
On my corporeal frame, so wide appears
The vacancy between me and those days
Which yet have such self-presence in my mind,   30
That, musing on them, often do I seem
Two consciousnesses, conscious of myself
And of some other Being. A rude mass
Of native rock, left midway in the square
Of our small market village, was the goal   35
Or centre of these sports; and when, returned

24–26 **Union . . . desire** Cf. "Ode to Duty," second stanza.

After long absence, thither I repaired,
Gone was the old grey stone, and in its place
A smart Assembly-room usurped the ground
40 That had been ours. There let the fiddle scream,
And be ye happy! Yet, my Friends! I know
That more than one of you will think with me
Of those soft starry nights, and that old Dame
From whom the stone was named, who there had sate,
45 And watched her table with its huckster's wares
Assiduous, through the length of sixty years.

We ran a boisterous course; the year span round
With giddy motion. But the time approached
That brought with it a regular desire
50 For calmer pleasures, when the winning forms
Of Nature were collaterally attached
To every scheme of holiday delight
And every boyish sport, less grateful else
And languidly pursued.
                                When summer came,
55 Our pastime was, on bright half-holidays,
To sweep along the plain of Windermere
With rival oars; and the selected bourne
Was now an Island musical with birds
That sang and ceased not; now a Sister Isle
60 Beneath the oaks' umbrageous covert, sown
With lilies of the valley like a field;
And now a third small Island, where survived
In solitude the ruins of a shrine
Once to Our Lady dedicate, and served
65 Daily with chaunted rites. In such a race
So ended, disappointment could be none,
Uneasiness, or pain, or jealousy:
We rested in the shade, all pleased alike,
Conquered and conqueror. Thus the pride of strength,
70 And the vain-glory of superior skill,
Were tempered; thus was gradually produced
A quiet independence of the heart;
And to my Friend who knows me I may add,
Fearless of blame, that hence for future days
75 Ensued a diffidence and modesty,

And I was taught to feel, perhaps too much,
The self-sufficing power of Solitude.

    Our daily meals were frugal, Sabine fare!
More than we wished we knew the blessing then
Of vigorous hunger—hence corporeal strength   *80*
Unsapped by delicate viands; for, exclude
A little weekly stipend, and we lived
Through three divisions of the quartered year
In penniless poverty. But now to school
From the half-yearly holidays returned,   *85*
We came with weightier purses, that sufficed
To furnish treats more costly than the Dame
Of the old grey stone, from her scant board, supplied.
Hence rustic dinners on the cool green ground,
Or in the woods, or by a river side   *90*
Or shady fountains, while among the leaves
Soft airs were stirring, and the mid-day sun
Unfelt shone brightly round us in our joy.
Nor is my aim neglected if I tell
How sometimes, in the length of those half-years,   *95*
We from our funds drew largely;—proud to curb,
And eager to spur on, the galloping steed;
And with the cautious inn-keeper, whose stud
Supplied our want, we haply might employ
Sly subterfuge, if the adventure's bound   *100*
Were distant: some famed temple where of yore
The Druids worshipped, or the antique walls
Of that large abbey, where within the Vale
Of Nightshade, to St. Mary's honour built,
Stands yet a mouldering pile with fractured arch,   *105*
Belfry, and images, and living trees,
A holy scene! Along the smooth green turf
Our horses grazed. To more than inland peace,
Left by the west wind sweeping overhead
From a tumultuous ocean, trees and towers   *110*
In that sequestered valley may be seen,
Both silent and both motionless alike;
Such the deep shelter that is there, and such
The safeguard for repose and quietness.

115   Our steeds remounted and the summons given,
With whip and spur we through the chauntry° flew
In uncouth race, and left the cross-legged knight,
And the stone-abbot, and that single wren
Which one day sang so sweetly in the nave
120 Of the old church, that—though from recent showers
The earth was comfortless, and touched by faint
Internal breezes, sobbings of the place
And respirations, from the roofless walls
The shuddering ivy dripped large drops—yet still
125 So sweetly 'mid the gloom the invisible bird
Sang to herself, that there I could have made
My dwelling-place, and lived for ever there
To hear such music. Through the walls we flew
And down the valley, and, a circuit made
130 In wantonness of heart, through rough and smooth
We scampered homewards. Oh, ye rocks and streams,
And that still spirit shed from evening air!
Even in this joyous time I sometimes felt
Your presence, when with slackened step we breathed
135 Along the sides of the steep hills, or when
Lighted by gleams of moonlight from the sea
We beat with thundering hoofs the level sand.

     Midway on long Winander's eastern shore,
Within the crescent of a pleasant bay,
140 A tavern stood; no homely-featured house,
Primeval like its neighbouring cottages,
But 'twas a splendid place, the door beset
With chaises, grooms, and liveries, and within
Decanters, glasses, and blood-red wine.
145 In ancient times, or ere the Hall was built
On the large island, had this dwelling been
More worthy of a poet's love, a hut,
Proud of its one bright fire and sycamore shade.
But—though the rhymes were gone that once inscribed
150 The threshold, and large golden characters,
Spread o'er the spangled sign-board, had dislodged
The old Lion and usurped his place, in slight

116 **chauntry** chantry; chapel.

And mockery of the rustic painter's hand—
Yet, to this hour, the spot to me is dear
With all its foolish pomp. The garden lay   *155*
Upon a slope surmounted by a plain
Of a small bowling-green; beneath us stood
A grove, with gleams of water through the trees
And over the tree-tops; nor did we want
Refreshment, strawberries and mellow cream.   *160*
There, while through half an afternoon we played
On the smooth platform, whether skill prevailed
Or happy blunder triumphed, bursts of glee
Made all the mountains ring. But, ere night-fall,
When in our pinnace we returned at leisure   *165*
Over the shadowy lake, and to the beach
Of some small island steered our course with one,
The Minstrel of the Troop, and left him there,
And rowed off gently, while he blew his flute
Alone upon the rock—oh, then, the calm   *170*
And dead still water lay upon my mind
Even with a weight of pleasure, and the sky,
Never before so beautiful, sank down
Into my heart, and held me like a dream!
Thus were my sympathies enlarged, and thus   *175*
Daily the common range of visible things
Grew dear to me: already I began
To love the sun; a boy I loved the sun,
Not as I since have loved him, as a pledge
And surety of our earthly life, a light   *180*
Which we behold and feel we are alive;
Nor for his bounty to so many worlds—
But for this cause, that I had seen him lay
His beauty on the morning hills, had seen
The western mountain touch his setting orb,   *185*
In many a thoughtless hour, when, from excess
Of happiness, my blood appeared to flow
For its own pleasure, and I breathed with joy.
And, from like feelings, humble though intense,
To patriotic and domestic love   *190*
Analogous, the moon to me was dear;
For I could dream away my purposes,

Standing to gaze upon her while she hung
Midway between the hills, as if she knew
195 No other region, but belonged to thee,
Yea, appertained by a peculiar right
To thee and thy grey huts, thou one dear Vale!

Those incidental charms which first attached
My heart to rural objects, day by day
200 Grew weaker, and I hasten on to tell
How Nature, intervenient till this time
And secondary, now at length was sought
For her own sake. But who shall parcel out
His intellect by geometric rules,
205 Split like a province into round and square?
Who knows the individual hour in which
His habits were first sown, even as a seed?
Who that shall point as with a wand and say
"This portion of the river of my mind
210 Came from yon fountain?" Thou, my Friend! art one
More deeply read in thy own thoughts; to thee
Science appears but what in truth she is,
Not as our glory and our absolute boast,
But as a succedaneum,° and a prop
215 To our infirmity. No officious slave
Art thou of that false secondary power°
By which we multiply distinctions, then
Deem that our puny boundaries are things
That we perceive, and not that we have made.
220 To thee, unblinded by these formal arts,
The unity of all hath been revealed,
And thou wilt doubt with me, less aptly skilled
Than many are to range the faculties
In scale and order, class the cabinet
225 Of their sensations, and in voluble phrase
Run through the history and birth of each
As of a single independent thing.
Hard task, vain hope, to analyse the mind,
If each most obvious and particular thought,

214 **succedaneum** substitute.   216 **false secondary power** of the intellect that asserts the reality of its purely analytic distinctions and so usurps the primary, unifying power of imagination.

Not in a mystical and idle sense,   230
But in the words of Reason deeply weighed,
Hath no beginning.
            Blest the infant Babe,
(For with my best conjecture I would trace
Our Being's earthly progress,) blest the Babe,
Nursed in his Mother's arms, who sinks to sleep   235
Rocked on his Mother's breast; who with his soul
Drinks in the feelings of his Mother's eye!
For him, in one dear Presence, there exists
A virtue which irradiates and exalts
Objects through widest intercourse of sense.   240
No outcast he, bewildered and depressed:
Along his infant veins are interfused
The gravitation and the filial bond
Of nature that connect him with the world.
Is there a flower, to which he points with hand   245
Too weak to gather it, already love
Drawn from love's purest earthly fount for him
Hath beautified that flower; already shades
Of pity cast from inward tenderness
Do fall around him upon aught that bears   250
Unsightly marks of violence or harm.
Emphatically such a Being lives,
Frail creature as he is, helpless as frail,
An inmate of this active universe.
For feeling has to him imparted power   255
That through the growing faculties of sense
Doth like an agent of the one great Mind
Create, creator and receiver both,
Working but in alliance with the works
Which it beholds.—Such, verily, is the first   260
Poetic spirit of our human life,
By uniform control of after years,
In most, abated or suppressed; in some,
Through every change of growth and of decay,
Pre-eminent till death.
            From early days,   265
Beginning not long after that first time
In which, a Babe, by intercourse of touch
I held mute dialogues with my Mother's heart,

I have endeavoured to display the means
270 Whereby this infant sensibility,
Great birthright of our being, was in me
Augmented and sustained. Yet is a path
More difficult before me; and I fear
That in its broken windings we shall need
275 The chamois' sinews, and the eagle's wing:
For now a trouble came into my mind
From unknown causes.° I was left alone
Seeking the visible world, nor knowing why.
The props of my affections were removed,
280 And yet the building stood, as if sustained
By its own spirit! All that I beheld
Was dear, and hence to finer influxes
The mind lay open, to a more exact
And close communion. Many are our joys
285 In youth, but oh! what happiness to live
When every hour brings palpable access
Of knowledge, when all knowledge is delight,
And sorrow is not there! The seasons came,
And every season wheresoe'er I moved
290 Unfolded transitory qualities,
Which, but for this most watchful power of love,
Had been neglected; left a register
Of permanent relations, else unknown.
Hence life, and change, and beauty, solitude
295 More active ever than "best society"°—
Society made sweet as solitude
By inward concords, silent, inobtrusive,
And gentle agitations of the mind
From manifold distinctions, difference
300 Perceived in things, where, to the unwatchful eye,
No difference is, and hence, from the same source,
Sublimer joy; for I would walk alone,
Under the quiet stars, and at that time
Have felt whate'er there is of power in sound
305 To breathe an elevated mood, by form

277 **unknown causes** The known cause was his mother's death when he was eight. Less easily understood was why her death did not weaken his relationship to the external world.   295 **"best society"** *Paradise Lost* IX. 249.

Or image unprofaned; and I would stand,
If the night blackened with a coming storm,
Beneath some rock, listening to notes that are
The ghostly language of the ancient earth,
Or make their dim abode in distant winds.   *310*
Thence did I drink the visionary power;
And deem not profitless those fleeting moods
Of shadowy exultation: not for this,
That they are kindred to our purer mind
And intellectual life; but that the soul,   *315*
Remembering how she felt, but what she felt
Remembering not, retains an obscure sense
Of possible sublimity, whereto
With growing faculties she doth aspire,
With faculties still growing, feeling still   *320*
That whatsoever point they gain, they yet
Have something to pursue.
                    And not alone,
'Mid gloom and tumult, but no less 'mid fair
And tranquil scenes, that universal power
And fitness in the latent qualities   *325*
And essences of things, by which the mind
Is moved with feelings of delight, to me
Came, strengthened with a superadded soul,
A virtue not its own. My morning walks
Were early;—oft before the hours of school   *330*
I travelled round our little lake, five miles
Of pleasant wandering. Happy time! more dear
For this, that one was by my side, a Friend,
Then passionately loved; with heart how full
Would he peruse these lines! For many years   *335*
Have since flowed in between us, and, our minds
Both silent to each other, at this time
We live as if those hours had never been.
Nor seldom did I lift our cottage latch
Far earlier, ere one smoke-wreath had risen   *340*
From human dwelling, or the thrush, high-perched,
Piped to the woods his shrill reveillé, sate
Alone upon some jutting eminence,
At the first gleam of dawn-light, when the Vale,
Yet slumbering, lay in utter solitude.   *345*

How shall I seek the origin? where find
Faith in the marvellous things which then I felt?
Oft in these moments such a holy calm
Would overspread my soul, that bodily eyes
350 Were utterly forgotten, and what I saw
Appeared like something in myself, a dream,
A prospect in the mind.
     'Twere long to tell
What spring and autumn, what the winter snows,
And what the summer shade, what day and night,
355 Evening and morning, sleep and waking, thought
From sources inexhaustible, poured forth
To feed the spirit of religious love
In which I walked with Nature. But let this
Be not forgotten, that I still retained
360 My first creative sensibility;
That by the regular action of the world
My soul was unsubdued. A plastic power
Abode with me; a forming hand, at times
Rebellious, acting in a devious mood;
365 A local spirit of his own, at war
With general tendency, but, for the most,
Subservient strictly to external things
With which it communed. An auxiliar light
Came from my mind, which on the setting sun
370 Bestowed new splendour; the melodious birds,
The fluttering breezes, fountains that run on
Murmuring so sweetly in themselves, obeyed
A like dominion, and the midnight storm
Grew darker in the presence of my eye:
375 Hence my obeisance, my devotion hence,
And hence my transport.
     Nor should this, perchance,
Pass unrecorded, that I still had loved
The exercise and produce of a toil,
Than analytic industry to me
380 More pleasing, and whose character I deem
Is more poetic as resembling more
Creative agency. The song would speak
Of that interminable building reared
By observation of affinities

In objects where no brotherhood exists   *385*
To passive minds. My seventeenth year was come;
And, whether from this habit rooted now
So deeply in my mind, or from excess
In the great social principle of life
Coercing all things into sympathy,   *390*
To unorganic natures were transferred
My own enjoyments; or the power of truth
Coming in revelation, did converse
With things that really are; I, at this time,
Saw blessings spread around me like a sea.   *395*
Thus while the days flew by, and years passed on,
From Nature and her overflowing soul,
I had received so much, that all my thoughts
Were steeped in feeling; I was only then
Contented, when with bliss ineffable   *400*
I felt the sentiment of Being spread
O'er all that moves and all that seemeth still;
O'er all that, lost beyond the reach of thought
And human knowledge, to the human eye
Invisible, yet liveth to the heart;   *405*
O'er all that leaps and runs, and shouts and sings,
Or beats the gladsome air; o'er all that glides
Beneath the wave, yea, in the wave itself,
And mighty depth of waters. Wonder not
If high the transport, great the joy I felt,   *410*
Communing in this sort through earth and heaven
With every form of creature, as it looked
Towards the Uncreated with a countenance
Of adoration, with an eye of love.°
One song they sang, and it was audible,   *415*
Most audible, then, when the fleshly ear,
O'ercome by humblest prelude of that strain,
Forgot her functions, and slept undisturbed.

    If this be error, and another faith
Find easier access to the pious mind,   *420*

410–14 **great the joy . . . eye of love** One of Wordsworth's most
sanctimonious interpolations. The 1805 *Prelude* reads simply "in all
things now / I saw one life, and felt that it was joy."

Yet were I grossly destitute of all
Those human sentiments that make this earth
So dear, if I should fail with grateful voice
To speak of you, ye mountains, and ye lakes
425 And sounding cataracts, ye mists and winds
That dwell among the hills where I was born.
If in my youth I have been pure in heart,
If, mingling with the world, I am content
With my own modest pleasures, and have lived
430 With God and Nature communing, removed
From little enmities and low desires,
The gift is yours; if in these times of fear,
This melancholy waste of hopes o'erthrown,
If, 'mid indifference and apathy,
435 And wicked exultation when good men
On every side fall off, we know not how,
To selfishness, disguised in gentle names
Of peace and quiet and domestic love,
Yet mingled not unwillingly with sneers
440 On visionary minds; if, in this time
Of dereliction and dismay, I yet
Despair not of our nature, but retain
A more than Roman confidence, a faith
That fails not, in all sorrow my support,
445 The blessing of my life; the gift is yours,
Ye winds and sounding cataracts! 'tis yours,
Ye mountains! thine, O Nature! Thou hast fed
My lofty speculations; and in thee,
For this uneasy heart of ours, I find
450 A never-failing principle of joy
And purest passion.
                    Thou, my Friend! wert reared
In the great city, 'mid far other scenes;
But we, by different roads, at length have gained
The selfsame bourne. And for this cause to thee
455 I speak, unapprehensive of contempt,
The insinuated scoff of coward tongues,
And all that silent language which so oft
In conversation between man and man
Blots from the human countenance all trace
460 Of beauty and of love. For thou hast sought

The truth in solitude, and, since the days
That gave thee liberty, full long desired,
To serve in Nature's temple, thou hast been
The most assiduous of her ministers;
In many things my brother, chiefly here   *465*
In this our deep devotion.
                Fare thee well!°
Health and the quiet of a healthful mind
Attend thee! seeking oft the haunts of men,
And yet more often living with thyself,
And for thyself, so haply shall thy days   *470*
Be many, and a blessing to mankind.

Book Third

Residence at Cambridge

It was a dreary morning when the wheels
Rolled over a wide plain o'erhung with clouds,
And nothing cheered our way till first we saw
The long-roofed chapel of King's College lift
Turrets and pinnacles in answering files,   *5*
Extended high above a dusky grove.

Advancing, we espied upon the road
A student clothed in gown and tasselled cap,
Striding along as if o'ertasked by Time,
Or covetous of exercise and air;   *10*
He passed—nor was I master of my eyes
Till he was left an arrow's flight behind.
As near and nearer to the spot we drew,
It seemed to suck us in with an eddy's force.
Onward we drove beneath the Castle; caught,   *15*
While crossing Magdalene Bridge, a glimpse of Cam;°
And at the *Hoop* alighted, famous Inn.

My spirit was up, my thoughts were full of hope;
Some friends I had, acquaintances who there

---

466 **Fare thee well** Coleridge left England for Malta in 1804 to seek
"Health and . . . a healthful mind."

16 **Cam** river flowing through Cambridge.

Seemed friends, poor simple school-boys, now hung
20   round
With honour and importance: in a world
Of welcome faces up and down I roved;
Questions, directions, warnings and advice,
Flowed in upon me, from all sides; fresh day
25 Of pride and pleasure! to myself I seemed
A man of business and expense, and went
From shop to shop about my own affairs,
To Tutor or to Tailor, as befel,
From street to street with loose and careless mind.

30   I was the Dreamer, they the Dream; I roamed
Delighted through the motley spectacle;
Gowns grave, or gaudy, doctors, students, streets,
Courts, cloisters, flocks of churches, gateways, towers:
Migration strange for a stripling of the hills,
A northern villager.
35   As if the change
Had waited on some Fairy's wand, at once
Behold me rich in monies, and attired
In splendid garb, with hose of silk, and hair
Powdered like rimy trees, when frost is keen.
40 My lordly dressing-gown, I pass it by,
With other signs of manhood that supplied
The lack of beard.—The weeks went roundly on,
With invitations, suppers, wine and fruit,
Smooth housekeeping within, and all without
45 Liberal, and suiting gentleman's array.

The Evangelist St. John my patron was:°
Three Gothic courts are his, and in the first
Was my abiding-place, a nook obscure;
Right underneath, the College kitchens made
50 A humming sound, less tuneable than bees,
But hardly less industrious; with shrill notes
Of sharp command and scolding intermixed.
Near me hung Trinity's loquacious clock,
Who never let the quarters, night or day,

46 **The Evangelist . . . was** Wordsworth entered St. John's College
in October, 1787.

Slip by him unproclaimed, and told the hours   55
Twice over with a male and female voice.
Her pealing organ was my neighbour too;
And from my pillow, looking forth by light
Of moon or favouring stars, I could behold
The antechapel where the statue stood   60
Of Newton with his prism and silent face,
The marble index of a mind for ever
Voyaging through strange seas of Thought, alone.

*   *   *   *

Oft when the dazzling show no longer new   90
Had ceased to dazzle, ofttimes did I quit
My comrades, leave the crowd, buildings and groves,
And as I paced alone the level fields
Far from those lovely sights and sounds sublime
With which I had been conversant, the mind   95
Drooped not; but there into herself returning,
With prompt rebound seemed fresh as heretofore.
At least I more distinctly recognised
Her native instincts: let me dare to speak
A higher language, say that now I felt   100
What independent solaces were mine,
To mitigate the injurious sway of place
Or circumstance, how far soever changed
In youth, or *to* be changed in manhood's prime;
Or for the few who shall be called to look   105
On the long shadows in our evening years,
Ordained precursors to the night of death.
As if awakened, summoned, roused, constrained,
I looked for universal things; perused
The common countenance of earth and sky: 110
Earth, nowhere unembellished by some trace
Of that first Paradise whence man was driven;
And sky, whose beauty and bounty are expressed
By the proud name she bears—the name of Heaven.
I called on both to teach me what they might;   115
Or turning the mind in upon herself
Pored, watched, expected, listened, spread my thoughts
And spread them with a wider creeping; felt
Incumbencies more awful, visitings

120 Of the Upholder of the tranquil soul,
That tolerates the indignities of Time,
And, from the centre of Eternity
All finite motions overruling, lives
In glory immutable. But peace! enough
125 Here to record I had ascended now
To such community with highest truth—
A track pursuing, not untrod before,
From strict analogies by thought supplied
Or consciousnesses not to be subdued.
130 To every natural form, rock, fruit or flower,
Even the loose stones that cover the high-way,
I gave a moral life: I saw them feel,
Or linked them to some feeling: the great mass
Lay bedded in a quickening soul, and all
135 That I beheld respired with inward meaning.
Add that whate'er of Terror or of Love
Or Beauty, Nature's daily face put on
From transitory passion, unto this
I was as sensitive as waters are
140 To the sky's influence, in a kindred mood
Of passion; was obedient as a lute
That waits upon the touches of the wind.
Unknown, unthought of, yet I was most rich—
I had a world about me—'twas my own;
145 I made it, for it only lived to me,
And to the God who sees into the heart.
Such sympathies, though rarely, were betrayed
By outward gestures and by visible looks:
Some called it madness—so indeed it was,
150 If child-like fruitfulness in passing joy,
If steady moods of thoughtfulness matured
To inspiration, sort with such a name;
If prophecy be madness; if things viewed
By poets in old time, and higher up
155 By the first men, earth's first inhabitants,
May in these tutored days no more be seen
With undisordered sight. But leaving this,
It was no madness, for the bodily eye
Amid my strongest workings evermore

Was searching out the lines of difference 160
As they lie hid in all external forms,
Near or remote, minute or vast, an eye
Which from a tree, a stone, a withered leaf,
To the broad ocean and the azure heavens
Spangled with kindred multitudes of stars, 165
Could find no surface where its power might sleep;
Which spake perpetual logic to my soul,
And by an unrelenting agency
Did bind my feelings even as in a chain.

And here, O Friend! have I retraced my life 170
Up to an eminence, and told a tale
Of matters which not falsely may be called
The glory of my youth. Of genius, power,
Creation and divinity itself
I have been speaking, for my theme has been 175
What passed within me. Not of outward things
Done visibly for other minds, words, signs,
Symbols or actions, but of my own heart
Have I been speaking, and my youthful mind.
O Heavens! how awful is the might of souls, 180
And what they do within themselves while yet
The yoke of earth is new to them, the world
Nothing but a wild field where they were sown.
This is, in truth, heroic argument,°
This genuine prowess, which I wished to touch 185
With hand however weak, but in the main
It lies far hidden from the reach of words.
Points have we all of us within our souls
Where all stand single; this I feel, and make
Breathings for incommunicable powers; 190
But is not each a memory to himself?
And, therefore, now that we must quit this theme,
I am not heartless, for there's not a man
That lives who hath not known his god-like hours,
And feels not what an empire we inherit 195
As natural beings in the strength of Nature.

184 **heroic argument** Cf. *Paradise Lost* IX. 13–14, 28–29.

No more: for now into a populous plain
We must descend. A Traveller I am,
Whose tale is only of himself; even so,
200 So be it, if the pure of heart be prompt
To follow, and if thou, my honoured Friend!
Who in these thoughts art ever at my side,
Support, as heretofore, my fainting steps.

It hath been told, that when the first delight
205 That flashed upon me from this novel show
Had failed, the mind returned into herself;
Yet true it is, that I had made a change
In climate, and my nature's outward coat
Changed also slowly and insensibly.
210 Full oft the quiet and exalted thoughts
Of loneliness gave way to empty noise
And superficial pastimes; now and then
Forced labour, and more frequently forced hopes;
And, worst of all, a treasonable growth
215 Of indecisive judgments, that impaired
And shook the mind's simplicity.—And yet
This was a gladsome time. Could I behold—
Who, less insensible than sodden clay
In a sea-river's bed at ebb of tide,
220 Could have beheld,—with undelighted heart,
So many happy youths, so wide and fair
A congregation in its budding-time
Of health, and hope, and beauty, all at once
So many divers samples from the growth
225 Of life's sweet season—could have seen unmoved
That miscellaneous garland of wild flowers
Decking the matron temples of a place
So famous through the world? To me, at least,
It was a goodly prospect: for, in sooth,
230 Though I had learnt betimes to stand unpropped,
And independent musings pleased me so
That spells seemed on me when I was alone,
Yet could I only cleave to solitude
In lonely places; if a throng was near
235 That way I leaned by nature; for my heart
Was social, and loved idleness and joy.

Not seeking those who might participate
My deeper pleasures (nay, I had not once,
Though not unused to mutter lonesome songs,
Even with myself divided such delight,   240
Or looked that way for aught that might be clothed
In human language), easily I passed
From the remembrances of better things,
And slipped into the ordinary works
Of careless youth, unburthened, unalarmed.   245
Caverns there were within my mind which sun
Could never penetrate, yet did there not
Want store of leafy *arbours* where the light
Might enter in at will. Companionships,
Friendships, acquaintances, were welcome all.   250
We sauntered, played, or rioted; we talked
Unprofitable talk at morning hours;
Drifted about along the streets and walks,
Read lazily in trivial books, went forth
To gallop through the country in blind zeal   255
Of senseless horsemanship, or on the breast
Of Cam sailed boisterously, and let the stars
Come forth, perhaps without one quiet thought.

Such was the tenor of the second act
In this new life. Imagination slept,   260
And yet not utterly. I could not print
Ground where the grass had yielded to the steps
Of generations of illustrious men,
Unmoved. I could not always lightly pass
Through the same gateways, sleep where they had slept, 265
Wake where they waked, range that inclosure old,
That garden of great intellects, undisturbed.
Place also by the side of this dark sense
Of nobler feeling, that those spiritual men,
Even the great Newton's own ethereal self,   270
Seemed humbled in these precincts, thence to be
The more endeared. Their several memories here
(Even like their persons in their portraits clothed
With the accustomed garb of daily life)
Put on a lowly and a touching grace   275

Of more distinct humanity, that left
All genuine admiration unimpaired.

Beside the pleasant Mill of Trompington°
I laughed with Chaucer, in the hawthorn shade
280 Heard him, while birds were warbling, tell his tales
Of amorous passion. And that gentle Bard,
Chosen by the Muses for their Page of State—
Sweet Spenser, moving through his clouded heaven
With the moon's beauty and the moon's soft pace,
285 I called him Brother, Englishman, and Friend!
Yea, our blind Poet, who, in his later day,
Stood almost single; uttering odious truth—
Darkness before, and danger's voice behind,
Soul awful—if the earth has ever lodged
290 An awful soul—I seemed to see him here
Familiarly, and in his scholar's dress
Bounding before me, yet a stripling youth—
A boy, no better, with his rosy cheeks
Angelical, keen eye, courageous look,
295 And conscious step of purity and pride.
Among the band of my compeers was one
Whom chance had stationed in the very room
Honoured by Milton's name. O temperate Bard!
Be it confest that, for the first time, seated
300 Within thy innocent lodge and oratory,
One of a festive circle, I poured out
Libations, to thy memory drank, till pride
And gratitude grew dizzy in a brain
Never excited by the fumes of wine
305 Before that hour, or since. Then, forth I ran
From the assembly; through a length of streets,
Ran, ostrich-like, to reach our chapel door
In not a desperate or opprobrious time,
Albeit long after the importunate bell
310 Had stopped, with wearisome Cassandra voice
No longer haunting the dark winter night.
Call back, O Friend! a moment to thy mind
The place itself and fashion of the rites.

278 **Trompington** scene of the Reeve's tale in Chaucer's *Canterbury Tales.*

With careless ostentation shouldering up
My surplice, through the inferior throng I clove   *315*
Of the plain Burghers, who in audience stood
On the last skirts of their permitted ground,
Under the pealing organ. Empty thoughts!
I am ashamed of them: and that great Bard,
And thou, O Friend! who in thy ample mind   *320*
Hast placed me high above my best deserts,
Ye will forgive the weakness of that hour,
In some of its unworthy vanities,
Brother to many more.
                              In this mixed sort
The months passed on, remissly, not given up   *325*
To wilful alienation from the right,
Or walks of open scandal, but in vague
And loose indifference, easy likings, aims
Of a low pitch—duty and zeal dismissed,
Yet Nature, or a happy course of things   *330*
Not doing in their stead the needful work.
The memory languidly revolved, the heart
Reposed in noontide rest, the inner pulse
Of contemplation almost failed to beat.

                 *   *   *   *

     Yet was this deep vacation° not given up
To utter waste. Hitherto I had stood
In my own mind remote from social life,
(At least from what we commonly so name,)   *515*
Like a lone shepherd on a promontory
Who lacking occupation looks far forth
Into the boundless sea, and rather makes
Than finds what he beholds. And sure it is,
That this first transit from the smooth delights   *520*
And wild outlandish walks of simple youth
To something that resembles an approach
Towards human business, to a privileged world
Within a world, a midway residence
With all its intervenient imagery,   *525*
Did better suit my visionary mind,
Far better, than to have been bolted forth,

512 **vacation** retains the root meaning "vacancy."

Thrust out abruptly into Fortune's way
Among the conflicts of substantial life;
530 By a more just gradation did lead on
To higher things; more naturally matured,
For permanent possession, better fruits,
Whether of truth or virtue, to ensue.
In serious mood, but oftener, I confess,
535 With playful zest of fancy did we note
(How could we less?) the manners and the ways
Of those who lived distinguished by the badge
Of good or ill report; or those with whom
By frame of Academic discipline
540 We were perforce connected, men whose sway
And known authority of office served
To set our minds on edge, and did no more.
Nor wanted we rich pastime of this kind,
Found everywhere, but chiefly in the ring
545 Of the grave Elders, men unscoured, grotesque
In character, tricked out like aged trees
Which through the lapse of their infirmity
Give ready place to any random seed
That chooses to be reared upon their trunks.

550   Here on my view, confronting vividly
Those shepherd swains whom I had lately left,
Appeared a different aspect of old age;
How different! yet both distinctly marked,
Objects embossed to catch the general eye,
555 Or portraitures for special use designed,
As some might seem, so aptly do they serve
To illustrate Nature's book of rudiments—
That book upheld as with maternal care
When she would enter on her tender scheme
560 Of teaching comprehension with delight,
And mingling playful with pathetic thoughts.

The surfaces of artificial life
And manners finely wrought, the delicate race
Of colours, lurking, gleaming up and down
565 Through that state arras woven with silk and gold;
This wily interchange of snaky hues,

Willingly or unwillingly revealed,
I neither knew nor cared for; and as such
Were wanting here, I took what might be found
Of less elaborate fabric. At this day   570
I smile, in many a mountain solitude
Conjuring up scenes as obsolete in freaks
Of character, in points of wit as broad,
As aught by wooden images performed
For entertainment of the gaping crowd   575
At wake or fair. And oftentimes do flit
Remembrances before me of old men—
Old humourists, who have been long in their graves,
And having almost in my mind put off
Their human names, have into phantoms passed   580
Of texture midway between life and books.

            *   *   *   *

   Thus in submissive idleness, my Friend!
The labouring time of autumn, winter, spring,
Eight months! rolled pleasingly away; the ninth
Came and returned me to my native hills.   635

Book Fourth

Summer Vacation

Bright was the summer's noon when quickening steps
Followed each other till a dreary moor
Was crossed, a bare ridge clomb, upon whose top
Standing alone, as from a rampart's edge,
I overlooked the bed of Windermere,   5
Like a vast river, stretching in the sun.
With exultation, at my feet I saw
Lake, islands, promontories, gleaming bays,
A universe of Nature's fairest forms
Proudly revealed with instantaneous burst,   10
Magnificent, and beautiful, and gay.

            *   *   *   *

                 When first I made
Once more the circuit of our little lake,
If ever happiness hath lodged with man,

140 That day consummate happiness was mine,
Wide-spreading, steady, calm, contemplative.
The sun was set, or setting, when I left
Our cottage door, and evening soon brought on
A sober hour, not winning or serene,
145 For cold and raw the air was, and untuned:
But as a face we love is sweetest then
When sorrow damps it, or, whatever look
It chance to wear, is sweetest if the heart
Have fulness in herself; even so with me
150 It fared that evening. Gently did my soul
Put off her veil, and, self-transmuted, stood
Naked, as in the presence of her God.
While on I walked, a comfort seemed to touch
A heart that had not been disconsolate:
155 Strength came where weakness was not known to be,
At least not felt; and restoration came
Like an intruder knocking at the door
Of unacknowledged weariness. I took
The balance, and with firm hand weighed myself.
160 —Of that external scene which round me lay,
Little, in this abstraction,° did I see;
Remembered less; but I had inward hopes
And swellings of the spirit, was rapt and soothed,
Conversed with promises, had glimmering views
165 How life pervades the undecaying mind;
How the immortal soul with God-like power
Informs, creates, and thaws the deepest sleep
That time can lay upon her; how on earth,
Man, if he do but live within the light
170 Of high endeavours, daily spreads abroad
His being armed with strength that cannot fail.

*   *   *   *

Nor less do I remember to have felt,
Distinctly manifested at this time,
A human-heartedness about my love
For objects hitherto the absolute wealth
235 Of my own private being and no more:
Which I had loved, even as a blessed spirit

161 **abstraction** abstracted state of mind.

Or Angel, if he were to dwell on earth,
Might love in individual happiness.
But now there opened on me other thoughts,
Of change, congratulation or regret,   *240*
A pensive feeling! It spread far and wide;
The trees, the mountains shared it, and the brooks,
The stars of Heaven, now seen in their old haunts—
White Sirius glittering o'er the southern crags,
Orion with his belt, and those fair Seven,°   *245*
Acquaintances of every little child,
And Jupiter, my own belovèd star!
Whatever shadings of mortality,
Whatever imports from the world of death
Had come among these objects heretofore,   *250*
Were, in the main, of mood less tender: strong,
Deep, gloomy were they, and severe; the scatterings
Of awe or tremulous dread, that had given way
In later youth to yearnings of a love
Enthusiastic, to delight and hope.   *255*

    As one who hangs down-bending from the side
Of a slow-moving boat, upon the breast
Of a still water, solacing himself
With such discoveries as his eye can make
Beneath him in the bottom of the deep,   *260*
Sees many beauteous sights—weeds, fishes, flowers,
Grots, pebbles, roots of trees, and fancies more,
Yet often is perplexed and cannot part
The shadow from the substance, rocks and sky,
Mountains and clouds, reflected in the depth   *265*
Of the clear flood, from things which there abide
In their true dwelling; now is crossed by gleam
Of his own image, by a sun-beam now,
And wavering motions sent he knows not whence,
Impediments that make his task more sweet;   *270*
Such pleasant office have we long pursued
Incumbent o'er the surface of past time
With like success, nor often have appeared
Shapes fairer or less doubtfully discerned
Than these to which the Tale, indulgent Friend!   *275*

245 Seven Big Dipper.

Would now direct thy notice. Yet in spite
Of pleasure won, and knowledge not withheld,
There was an inner falling off—I loved,
Loved deeply all that had been loved before,
280 More deeply even than ever: but a swarm
Of heady schemes jostling each other, gawds,
And feast and dance, and public revelry,
And sports and games (too grateful° in themselves,
Yet in themselves less grateful, I believe,
285 Than as they were a badge glossy and fresh
Of manliness and freedom) all conspired
To lure my mind from firm habitual quest
Of feeding pleasures, to depress the zeal
And damp those daily yearnings which had once been
mine—
290 A wild, unworldly-minded youth, given up
To his own eager thoughts. It would demand
Some skill, and longer time than may be spared,
To paint these vanities, and how they wrought
In haunts where they, till now, had been unknown.
295 It seemed the very garments that I wore
Preyed on my strength, and stopped the quiet stream
Of self-forgetfulness.
                          Yes, that heartless chase
Of trivial pleasures was a poor exchange
For books and nature at that early age.
300 'Tis true, some casual knowledge might be gained
Of character or life; but at that time,
Of manners put to school I took small note,
And all my deeper passions lay elsewhere.
Far better had it been to exalt the mind
305 By solitary study, to uphold
Intense desire through meditative peace;
And yet, for chastisement of these regrets,
The memory of one particular hour
Doth here rise up against me. 'Mid a throng
310 Of maids and youths, old men, and matrons staid,
A medley of all tempers, I had passed
The night in dancing, gaiety, and mirth,

283 grateful satisfying.

With din of instruments and shuffling feet,
And glancing forms, and tapers glittering,
And unaimed prattle flying up and down; 315
Spirits upon the stretch, and here and there
Slight shocks of young love-liking interspersed,
Whose transient pleasure mounted to the head,
And tingled through the veins. Ere we retired,
The cock had crowed, and now the eastern sky 320
Was kindling, not unseen, from humble copse
And open field, through which the pathway wound,
And homeward led my steps. Magnificent
The morning rose, in memorable pomp,
Glorious as e'er I had beheld—in front, 325
The sea lay laughing at a distance; near,
The solid mountains shone, bright as the clouds,
Grain-tinctured,° drenched in empyrean light;
And in the meadows and the lower grounds
Was all the sweetness of a common dawn— 330
Dews, vapours, and the melody of birds,
And labourers going forth to till the fields.

Ah! need I say, dear Friend! that to the brim
My heart was full; I made no vows, but vows
Were then made for me; bond unknown to me 335
Was given, that I should be, else sinning greatly,
A dedicated Spirit. On I walked
In thankful blessedness, which yet survives.

     *   *   *   *

When from our better selves we have too long
Been parted by the hurrying world, and droop, 355
Sick of its business, of its pleasures tired,
How gracious, how benign, is Solitude;
How potent a mere image of her sway;
Most potent when impressed upon the mind
With an appropriate human centre—hermit, 360
Deep in the bosom of the wilderness;
Votary (in vast cathedral, where no foot
Is treading, where no other face is seen)
Kneeling at prayers; or watchman on the top

328 **Grain-tinctured** crimson.

365 Of lighthouse, beaten by Atlantic waves;
Or as the soul of that great Power is met
Sometimes embodied on a public road,
When, for the night deserted, it assumes
A character of quiet more profound
Than pathless wastes.

370   Once, when those summer months
Were flown, and autumn brought its annual show
Of oars with oars contending, sails with sails,
Upon Winander's spacious breast, it chanced
That—after I had left a flower-decked room

375 (Whose in-door pastime, lighted up, survived
To a late hour), and spirits overwrought
Were making night do penance for a day
Spent in a round of strenuous idleness—
My homeward course led up a long ascent,

380 Where the road's watery surface, to the top
Of that sharp rising, glittered to the moon
And bore the semblance of another stream
Stealing with silent lapse to join the brook
That murmured in the vale. All else was still;

385 No living thing appeared in earth or air,
And, save the flowing water's peaceful voice,
Sound there was none—but, lo! an uncouth shape,
Shown by a sudden turning of the road,
So near that, slipping back into the shade

390 Of a thick hawthorn, I could mark him well,
Myself unseen. He was of stature tall,
A span above man's common measure, tall,
Stiff, lank, and upright; a more meagre man
Was never seen before by night or day.

395 Long were his arms, pallid his hands; his mouth
Looked ghastly in the moonlight: from behind,
A mile-stone propped him; I could also ken
That he was clothed in military garb,
Though faded, yet entire. Companionless,

400 No dog attending, by no staff sustained,
He stood, and in his very dress appeared
A desolation, a simplicity,
To which the trappings of a gaudy world
Make a strange back-ground. From his lips, ere long,

Issued low muttered sounds, as if of pain   *405*
Or some uneasy thought; yet still his form
Kept the same awful steadiness—at his feet
His shadow lay, and moved not. From self-blame
Not wholly free, I watched him thus; at length
Subduing my heart's specious cowardice,   *410*
I left the shady nook where I had stood
And hailed him. Slowly from his resting-place
He rose, and with a lean and wasted arm
In measured gesture lifted to his head
Returned my salutation; then resumed   *415*
His station as before; and when I asked
His history, the veteran, in reply,
Was neither slow nor eager; but, unmoved,
And with a quiet uncomplaining voice,
A stately air of mild indifference,   *420*
He told in few plain words a soldier's tale—
That in the Tropic Islands he had served,
Whence he had landed scarcely three weeks past;
That on his landing he had been dismissed,
And now was travelling towards his native home.   *425*
This heard, I said, in pity, "Come with me."
He stooped, and straightway from the ground took up
An oaken staff by me yet unobserved—
A staff which must have dropped from his slack hand
And lay till now neglected in the grass.   *430*
Though weak his step and cautious, he appeared
To travel without pain, and I beheld,
With an astonishment but ill suppressed,
His ghastly figure moving at my side;
Nor could I, while we journeyed thus, forbear   *435*
To turn from present hardships to the past,
And speak of war, battle, and pestilence,
Sprinkling this talk with questions, better spared,
On what he might himself have seen or felt.
He all the while was in demeanour calm,   *440*
Concise in answer; solemn and sublime
He might have seemed, but that in all he said
There was a strange half-absence, as of one
Knowing too well the importance of his theme,
But feeling it no longer. Our discourse   *445*

Soon ended, and together on we passed
In silence through a wood gloomy and still.
Up-turning, then, along an open field,
We reached a cottage. At the door I knocked,
450 And earnestly to charitable care
Commended him as a poor friendless man,
Belated and by sickness overcome.
Assured that now the traveller would repose
In comfort, I entreated that henceforth
455 He would not linger in the public ways,
But ask for timely furtherance and help
Such as his state required. At this reproof,
With the same ghastly mildness in his look,
He said, "My trust is in the God of Heaven,
460 And in the eye of him who passes me!"

*   *   *   *

Book Fifth

Books

*   *   *   *

Hitherto,
In progress through this Verse, my mind hath looked
Upon the speaking face of earth and heaven
As her prime teacher, intercourse with man
15 Established by the sovereign Intellect,
Who through that bodily image hath diffused,
As might appear to the eye of fleeting time,
A deathless spirit. Thou also, man! hast wrought,
For commerce of thy nature with herself,
20 Things that aspire to unconquerable life;°
And yet we feel—we cannot choose but feel—
That they must perish. Tremblings of the heart
It gives, to think that our immortal being
No more shall need such garments; and yet man,
25 As long as he shall be the child of earth,
Might almost "weep to have"° what he may lose,
Nor be himself extinguished, but survive,

20 **Things . . . life** that is, books. 26 **"weep to have"** Shakespeare,
Sonnet 64.

Abject, depressed, forlorn, disconsolate.
A thought is with me sometimes, and I say,—
Should the whole frame of earth by inward throes   *30*
Be wrenched, or fire come down from far to scorch
Her pleasant habitations, and dry up
Old Ocean, in his bed left singed and bare,
Yet would the living Presence still subsist
Victorious, and composure would ensue,   *35*
And kindlings like the morning—presage sure
Of day returning and of life revived.
But all the meditations of mankind,
Yea, all the adamantine holds of truth
By reason built, or passion, which itself   *40*
Is highest reason in a soul sublime;
The consecrated works of Bard and Sage,
Sensuous or intellectual, wrought by men,
Twin labourers and heirs of the same hopes;
Where would they be? Oh! why hath not the Mind   *45*
Some element to stamp her image on
In nature somewhat nearer to her own?
Why, gifted with such powers to send abroad
Her spirit, must it lodge in shrines so frail?

    One day, when from my lips a like complaint   *50*
Had fallen in presence of a studious friend,
He with a smile made answer, that in truth
'Twas going far to seek disquietude;
But on the front of his reproof confessed
That he himself had oftentimes given way   *55*
To kindred hauntings. Whereupon I told,
That once in the stillness of a summer's noon,
While I was seated in a rocky cave
By the sea-side, perusing, so it chanced,
The famous history of the errant knight°   *60*
Recorded by Cervantes, these same thoughts
Beset me, and to height unusual rose,
While listlessly I sate, and, having closed
The book, had turned my eyes toward the wide sea.
On poetry and geometric truth,   *65*

60 **knight** Don Quixote.

And their high privilege of lasting life,
From all internal injury exempt,
I mused, upon these chiefly: and at length,
My senses yielding to the sultry air,
70   Sleep seized me, and I passed into a dream.
I saw before me stretched a boundless plain
Of sandy wilderness, all black and void,
And as I looked around, distress and fear
Came creeping over me, when at my side,
75   Close at my side, an uncouth shape appeared
Upon a dromedary, mounted high.
He seemed an Arab of the Bedouin tribes:
A lance he bore, and underneath one arm
A stone, and in the opposite hand a shell
80   Of a surpassing brightness. At the sight
Much I rejoiced, not doubting but a guide
Was present, one who with unerring skill
Would through the desert lead me; and while yet
I looked and looked, self-questioned what this freight
85   Which the new-comer carried through the waste
Could mean, the Arab told me that the stone
(To give it in the language of the dream)
Was "Euclid's Elements;" and "This," said he,
"Is something of more worth;" and at the word
90   Stretched forth the shell, so beautiful in shape,
In colour so resplendent, with command
That I should hold it to my ear. I did so,
And heard that instant in an unknown tongue,
Which yet I understood, articulate sounds,
95   A loud prophetic blast of harmony;
An Ode, in passion uttered, which foretold
Destruction to the children of the earth
By deluge, now at hand. No sooner ceased
The song, than the Arab with calm look declared
100   That all would come to pass of which the voice
Had given forewarning, and that he himself
Was going then to bury those two books:
The one that held acquaintance with the stars,
And wedded soul to soul in purest bond
105   Of reason, undisturbed by space or time;
The other that was a god, yea many gods,

Had voices more than all the winds, with power
To exhilarate the spirit, and to soothe,
Through every clime, the heart of human kind.
While this was uttering, strange as it may seem,   *110*
I wondered not, although I plainly saw
The one to be a stone, the other a shell;
Nor doubted once but that they both were books,
Having a perfect faith in all that passed.
Far stronger, now, grew the desire I felt   *115*
To cleave unto this man; but when I prayed
To share his enterprise, he hurried on
Reckless° of me: I followed, not unseen,
For oftentimes he cast a backward look,
Grasping his twofold treasure.—Lance in rest,   *120*
He rode, I keeping pace with him; and now
He, to my fancy, had become the knight
Whose tale Cervantes tells; yet not the knight,
But was an Arab of the desert too;
Of these was neither, and was both at once.   *125*
His countenance, meanwhile, grew more disturbed;
And, looking backwards when he looked, mine eyes
Saw, over half the wilderness diffused,
A bed of glittering light: I asked the cause:
"It is," said he, "the waters of the deep   *130*
Gathering upon us;" quickening then the pace
Of the unwieldly creature he bestrode,
He left me: I called after him aloud;
He heeded not; but, with his twofold charge
Still in his grasp, before me, full in view,   *135*
Went hurrying o'er the illimitable waste,
With the fleet waters of a drowning world
In chase of him; whereat I waked in terror,
And saw the sea before me, and the book,
In which I had been reading, at my side.   *140*

   Full often, taking from the world of sleep
This Arab phantom, which I thus beheld,
This semi-Quixote, I to him have given
A substance, fancied him a living man,

118 **Reckless** heedless.

145 A gentle dweller in the desert, crazed
By love and feeling, and internal thought
Protracted among endless solitudes;
Have shaped him wandering upon this quest!
Nor have I pitied him; but rather felt
150 Reverence was due to a being thus employed;
And thought that, in the blind and awful lair
Of such a madness, reason did lie couched.
Enow there are on earth to take in charge
Their wives, their children, and their virgin loves,
155 Or whatsoever else the heart holds dear;
Enow to stir for these; yea, will I say,
Contemplating in soberness the approach
Of an event so dire, by signs in earth
Or heaven made manifest, that I could share
160 That maniac's fond anxiety, and go
Upon like errand. Oftentimes at least
Me hath such strong entrancement overcome,
When I have held a volume in my hand,
Poor earthly casket of immortal verse,
165 Shakespeare, or Milton, labourers divine!

*   *   *   *

I rejoice,
225 And, by these thoughts admonished, will pour out
Thanks with uplifted heart, that I was reared
Safe from an evil which these days have laid
Upon the children of the land, a pest
That might have dried me up, body and soul.
230 This verse is dedicate to Nature's self,
And things that teach as Nature teaches: then,
Oh! where had been the Man, the Poet where,
Where had we been, we two, belovèd Friend!
If in the season of unperilous choice,
235 In lieu of wandering, as we did, through vales
Rich with indigenous produce, open ground
Of Fancy, happy pastures ranged at will,
We had been followed, hourly watched, and noosed,
Each in his several melancholy walk
240 Stringed like a poor man's heifer at its feed,
Led through the lanes in forlorn servitude;

Or rather like a stallèd ox debarred
From touch of growing grass, that may not taste
A flower till it have yielded up its sweets
A prelibation to the mower's scythe.   *245*

* * * *

        ... that common sense
May try this modern system by its fruits,   *295*
Leave let me take to place before her sight
A specimen pourtrayed with faithful hand.
Full early trained to worship seemliness,
This model of a child is never known
To mix in quarrels; that were far beneath   *800*
Its dignity; with gifts he bubbles o'er
As generous as a fountain; selfishness
May not come near him, nor the little throng
Of flitting pleasures tempt him from his path;
The wandering beggars propagate his name,   *805*
Dumb creatures find him tender as a nun,
And natural or supernatural fear,
Unless it leap upon him in a dream,
Touches him not.

* * * *

... ever as a thought of purer birth
Rises to lead him toward a better clime,
Some intermeddler still is on the watch
To drive him back, and pound him, like a stray,   *835*
Within the pinfold of his own conceit.
Meanwhile old grandame earth is grieved to find
The playthings, which her love designed for him,
Unthought of: in their woodland beds the flowers
Weep, and the river sides are all forlorn.   *840*
Oh! give us once again the wishing cap
Of Fortunatus, and the invisible coat
Of Jack the Giant-killer, Robin Hood,
And Sabra in the forest with St. George!
The child, whose love is here, at least, doth reap   *845*
One precious gain, that he forgets himself.

    These mighty workmen of our later age,
Who, with a broad highway, have overbridged

The froward chaos of futurity,
350 Tamed to their bidding; they who have the skill
To manage books, and things, and make them act
On infant minds as surely as the sun
Deals with a flower; the keepers of our time,
The guides and wardens of our faculties,
355 Sages who in their prescience would control
All accidents, and to the very road
Which they have fashioned would confine us down,
Like engines; when will their presumption learn,
That in the unreasoning progress of the world
360 A wiser spirit is at work for us,
A better eye than theirs, most prodigal
Of blessings, and most studious of our good,
Even in what seem our most unfruitful hours?

There was a Boy: ye knew him well, ye cliffs
365 And islands of Winander!——many a time
At evening, when the earliest stars began
To move along the edges of the hills,
Rising or setting, would he stand alone
Beneath the trees or by the glimmering lake,
370 And there, with fingers interwoven, both hands
Pressed closely palm to palm, and to his mouth
Uplifted, he, as through an instrument,
Blew mimic hootings to the silent owls,
That they might answer him; and they would shout
375 Across the watery vale, and shout again,
Responsive to his call, with quivering peals,
And long halloos and screams, and echoes loud,
Redoubled and redoubled, concourse wild
Of jocund din; and, when a lengthened pause
380 Of silence came and baffled his best skill,
Then sometimes, in that silence while he hung
Listening, a gentle shock of mild surprise
Has carried far into his heart the voice
Of mountain torrents; or the visible scene
385 Would enter unawares into his mind,
With all its solemn imagery, its rocks,
Its woods, and that uncertain heaven, received
Into the bosom of the steady lake.

    This Boy was taken from his mates, and died
In childhood, ere he was full twelve years old.   *890*
Fair is the spot, most beautiful the vale
Where he was born; the grassy churchyard hangs
Upon a slope above the village school,
And through that churchyard when my way has led
On summer evenings, I believe that there   *895*
A long half hour together I have stood
Mute, looking at the grave in which he lies!
Even now appears before the mind's clear eye
That self-same village church; I see her sit
(The thronèd Lady° whom erewhile we hailed)   *400*
On her green hill, forgetful of this Boy
Who slumbers at her feet,—forgetful, too,
Of all her silent neighbourhood of graves,
And listening only to the gladsome sounds
That, from the rural school ascending, play   *405*
Beneath her and about her. May she long
Behold a race of young ones like to those
With whom I herded!—(easily, indeed,
We might have fed upon a fatter soil
Of arts and letters—but be that forgiven)—   *410*
A race of real children; not too wise,
Too learned, or too good; but wanton, fresh,
And bandied up and down by love and hate;
Not unresentful where self-justified;
Fierce, moody, patient, venturous, modest, shy;   *415*
Mad at their sports like withered leaves in winds;
Though doing wrong and suffering, and full oft
Bending beneath our life's mysterious weight
Of pain, and doubt, and fear, yet yielding not
In happiness to the happiest upon earth.   *420*
Simplicity in habit, truth in speech,
Be these the daily strengtheners of their minds;
May books and Nature be their early joy!
And knowledge, rightly honoured with that name—
Knowledge not purchased by the loss of power!   *425*

   Well do I call to mind the very week

400 **Lady** the church overlooking Hawkshead village, where Words-
worth had attended school.

When I was first intrusted to the care
Of that sweet Valley; when its paths, its shores,
And brooks were like a dream of novelty
430 To my half-infant thoughts; that very week,
While I was roving up and down alone,
Seeking I knew not what, I chanced to cross
One of those open fields, which, shaped like ears,
Make green peninsulas on Esthwaite's Lake:
435 Twilight was coming on, yet through the gloom
Appeared distinctly on the opposite shore
A heap of garments, as if left by one
Who might have there been bathing. Long I watched,
But no one owned them; meanwhile the calm lake
440 Grew dark with all the shadows on its breast,
And, now and then, a fish up-leaping snapped
The breathless stillness. The succeeding day,
Those unclaimed garments telling a plain tale
Drew to the spot an anxious crowd; some looked
445 In passive expectation from the shore,
While from a boat others hung o'er the deep,
Sounding with grappling irons and long poles.
At last, the dead man, 'mid that beauteous scene
Of trees and hills and water, bolt upright
450 Rose, with his ghastly face, a spectre shape
Of terror; yet no soul-debasing fear,
Young as I was, a child not nine years old,
Possessed me, for my inner eye had seen
Such sights before, among the shining streams
455 Of faëry land, the forest of romance.
Their spirit hallowed the sad spectacle
With decoration of ideal grace;
A dignity, a smoothness, like the works
Of Grecian art, and purest poesy.

*   *   *   *

A gracious spirit o'er this earth presides,
And o'er the heart of man: invisibly
It comes, to works of unreproved delight,
And tendency benign, directing those
495 Who care not, know not, think not what they do.
The tales that charm away the wakeful night

In Araby; romances; legends penned
For solace by dim light of monkish lamps;
Fictions, for ladies of their love, devised
By youthful squires; adventures endless, spun   500
By the dismantled warrior in old age,
Out of the bowels of those very schemes
In which his youth did first extravagate;
These spread like day, and something in the shape
Of these will live till man shall be no more.   505
Dumb yearnings, hidden appetites, are ours,
And *they must* have their food. Our childhood sits,
Our simple childhood, sits upon a throne
That hath more power than all the elements.
I guess not what this tells of Being past,   510
Nor what it augurs of the life to come;
But so it is; and, in that dubious hour,
That twilight when we first begin to see
This dawning earth, to recognise, expect,
And in the long probation that ensues,   515
The time of trial, ere we learn to live
In reconcilement with our stinted powers;
To endure this state of meagre vassalage,
Unwilling to forego, confess, submit,
Uneasy and unsettled, yoke-fellows   520
To custom, mettlesome, and not yet tamed
And humbled down; oh! then we feel, we feel,
We know where we have friends.

*   *   *   *

. . . he, who in his youth
A daily wanderer among woods and fields
With living Nature hath been intimate,
Not only in that raw unpractised time
Is stirred to exstasy, as others are,   590
By glittering verse; but further, doth receive,
In measure only dealt out to himself,
Knowledge and increase of enduring joy
From the great Nature that exists in works
Of mighty Poets. Visionary power   595
Attends the motions of the viewless winds,
Embodied in the mystery of words:

There, darkness makes abode, and all the host
Of shadowy things work endless changes,—there,
600 As in a mansion like their proper home,
Even forms and substances are circumfused
By that transparent veil with light divine,
And, through the turnings intricate of verse,
Present themselves as objects recognised,
605 In flashes, and with glory not their own.

*   *   *   *

Book Sixth

Cambridge and the Alps

                              ... Of rivers, fields,
265 And groves I speak to thee, my Friend!° to thee,
Who, yet a liveried schoolboy, in the depths
Of the huge city, on the leaded roof
Of that wide edifice, thy school and home,
Wert used to lie and gaze upon the clouds
270 Moving in heaven; or, of that pleasure tired,
To shut thine eyes, and by internal light
See trees, and meadows, and thy native stream,
Far distant, thus beheld from year to year
Of a long exile. Nor could I forget,
275 In this late portion of my argument,
That scarcely, as my term of pupilage
Ceased, had I left those academic bowers
When thou wert thither guided. From the heart
Of London, and from cloisters there, thou camest,
280 And didst sit down in temperance and peace,
A rigorous student. What a stormy course
Then followed. Oh! it is a pang that calls
For utterance, to think what easy change
Of circumstances might to thee have spared
285 A world of pain, ripened a thousand hopes,
For ever withered. Through this retrospect
Of my collegiate life I still have had
Thy after-sojourn in the self-same place
Present before my eyes, have played with times

265 **my Friend** Coleridge.

And accidents as children do with cards,   290
Or as a man, who, when his house is built,
A frame locked up in wood and stone, doth still,
As impotent fancy prompts, by his fireside,
Rebuild it to his liking. I have thought
Of thee, thy learning, gorgeous eloquence,   295
And all the strength and plumage of thy youth,
Thy subtle speculations, toils abstruse
Among the schoolmen, and Platonic forms
Of wild ideal pageantry, shaped out
From things well-matched or ill, and words for things,   300
The self-created sustenance of a mind
Debarred from Nature's living images,
Compelled to be a life unto herself,
And unrelentingly possessed by thirst
Of greatness, love, and beauty. Not alone,   305
Ah! surely not in singleness of heart
Should I have seen the light of evening fade
From smooth Cam's silent waters: had we met,
Even at that early time, needs must I trust
In the belief, that my maturer age,   310
My calmer habits, and more steady voice,
Would with an influence benign have soothed,
Or chased away, the airy wretchedness
That battened on thy youth. But thou hast trod
A march of glory, which doth put to shame   315
These vain regrets; health suffers in thee, else
Such grief for thee would be the weakest thought
That ever harboured in the breast of man.

                    *   *   *   *

When the third summer° freed us from restraint,
A youthful friend, he too a mountaineer,
Not slow to share my wishes, took his staff,
And sallying forth, we journeyed side by side,   325
Bound to the distant Alps. A hardy slight
Did this unprecedented course imply
Of college studies and their set rewards;
Nor had, in truth, the scheme been formed by me
Without uneasy forethought of the pain,   330

322 **third summer** 1790.

The censures, and ill-omening of those
To whom my worldly interests were dear.
But Nature then was sovereign in my mind,
And mighty forms, seizing a youthful fancy,
835 Had given a charter to irregular hopes.
In any age of uneventful calm
Among the nations, surely would my heart
Have been possessed by similar desire;
But Europe at that time was thrilled with joy,
840 France standing on the top of golden hours,
And human nature seeming born again.

Lightly equipped, and but a few brief looks
Cast on the white cliffs of our native shore
From the receding vessel's deck, we chanced
845 To land at Calais on the very eve
Of that great federal day;° and there we saw,
In a mean city, and among a few,
How bright a face is worn when joy of one
Is joy for tens of millions. Southward thence
850 We held our way, direct through hamlets, towns,
Gaudy with reliques of that festival,
Flowers left to wither on triumphal arcs,
And window-garlands. On the public roads,
And, once, three days successively, through paths
855 By which our toilsome journey was abridged,
Among sequestered villages we walked
And found benevolence and blessedness
Spread like a fragrance everywhere, when spring
Hath left no corner of the land untouched:
860 Where elms for many and many a league in files
With their thin umbrage, on the stately roads
Of that great kingdom, rustled o'er our heads,
For ever near us as we paced along:
How sweet at such a time, with such delight
865 On every side, in prime of youthful strength,
To feed a Poet's tender melancholy
And fond conceit of sadness, with the sound
Of undulations varying as might please
The wind that swayed them; once, and more than once,

346 **federal day** July 14, 1790, first anniversary of Bastille Day.

Unhoused beneath the evening star we saw   870
Dances of liberty, and, in late hours
Of darkness, dances in the open air
Deftly prolonged, though grey-haired lookers on
Might waste their breath in chiding.
                                    Under hills—
The vine-clad hills and slopes of Burgundy,   875
Upon the bosom of the gentle Saone
We glided forward with the flowing stream.
Swift Rhone! thou wert the *wings* on which we cut
A winding passage with majestic ease
Between thy lofty rocks. Enchanting show   880
Those woods and farms and orchards did present,
And single cottages and lurking towns,
Reach after reach, succession without end
Of deep and stately vales! A lonely pair
Of strangers, till day closed, we sailed along   885
Clustered together with a merry crowd
Of those emancipated, a blithe host
Of travellers, chiefly delegates returning
From the great spousals° newly solemnised
At their chief city, in the sight of Heaven.   890
Like bees they swarmed, gaudy and gay as bees;
Some vapoured in the unruliness of joy,
And with their swords flourished as if to fight
The saucy air. In this proud company
We landed—took with them our evening meal,   895
Guests welcome almost as the angels were
To Abraham of old.° The supper done,
With flowing cups elate and happy thoughts
We rose at signal given, and formed a ring
And, hand in hand, danced round and round the board; 400
All hearts were open, every tongue was loud
With amity and glee; we bore a name
Honoured in France, the name of Englishmen,
And hospitably did they give us hail,
As their forerunners in a glorious course;   405
And round and round the board we danced again.

389 **spousals** ceremonies in which the delegates swore allegiance to
the new Assembly.   396–97 **Guests . . . old** Genesis 18.

With these blithe friends our voyage we renewed
At early dawn. The monastery bells
Made a sweet jingling in our youthful ears;
410 The rapid river flowing without noise,
And each uprising or receding spire
Spake with a sense of peace, at intervals
Touching the heart amid the boisterous crew
By whom we were encompassed. Taking leave
415 Of this glad throng, foot-travellers side by side,
Measuring our steps in quiet, we pursued
Our journey, and ere twice the sun had set
Beheld the Convent of Chartreuse, and there
Rested within an awful *solitude*:
420 Yes, for even then no other than a place
Of soul-affecting *solitude* appeared
That far-famed region, though our eyes had seen,
As toward the sacred mansion we advanced,
Arms flashing, and a military glare
425 Of riotous men commissioned to expel
The blameless inmates, and belike subvert
That frame of social being, which so long
Had bodied forth the ghostliness of things
In silence visible and perpetual calm.
430 —"Stay, stay your sacrilegious hands!"—The voice
Was Nature's, uttered from her Alpine throne;
I heard it then and seem to hear it now—
"Your impious work forbear, perish what may,
Let this one temple last, be this one spot
435 Of earth devoted to eternity."
She ceased to speak, but while St. Bruno's pines
Waved their dark tops, not silent as they waved,
And while below, along their several beds,
Murmured the sister streams of Life and Death,°
440 Thus by conflicting passions pressed, my heart
Responded; "Honour to the patriot's zeal!
Glory and hope to new-born Liberty!
Hail to the mighty projects of the time!
Discerning sword that Justice wields, do thou

439 **Life and Death** translates *Guiers vif* and *Guiers mort*, streams
in the valley of the Grande Chartreuse.

Go forth and prosper; and, ye purging fires,   445
Up to the loftiest towers of Pride ascend,
Fanned by the breath of angry Providence.
But oh! if Past and Future be the wings
On whose support harmoniously conjoined
Moves the great spirit of human knowledge, spare   450
These courts of mystery, where a step advanced
Between the portals of the shadowy rocks
Leaves far behind life's treacherous vanities,
For penitential tears and trembling hopes
Exchanged—to equalise in God's pure sight   455
Monarch and peasant: be the house redeemed
With its unworldly votaries, for the sake
Of conquest over sense, hourly achieved
Through faith and meditative reason, resting
Upon the word of heaven-imparted truth,   460
Calmly triumphant; and for humbler claim
Of that imaginative impulse sent
From these majestic floods, yon shining cliffs,
The untransmuted shapes of many worlds,
Cerulean ether's pure inhabitants,   465
These forests unapproachable by death,
That shall endure as long as man endures,
To think, to hope, to worship, and to feel,
To struggle, to be lost within himself
In trepidation, from the blank abyss   470
To look with bodily eyes, and be consoled."
Not seldom since that moment have I wished
That thou, O Friend! the trouble or the calm
Hadst shared, when, from profane regards apart,
In sympathetic reverence we trod   475
The floors of those dim cloisters, till that hour,
From their foundation, strangers to the presence
Of unrestricted and unthinking man.
Abroad, how cheeringly the sunshine lay
Upon the open lawns! Vallombre's groves   480
Entering, we fed the soul with darkness; thence
Issued, and with uplifted eyes beheld,
In different quarters of the bending sky,
The cross of Jesus stand erect, as if
Hands of angelic powers had fixed it there,   485

Memorial reverenced by a thousand storms;
Yet then, from the undiscriminating sweep
And rage of one State-whirlwind, insecure.

'Tis not my present purpose to retrace
490 That variegated journey step by step.
A march it was of military speed,
And Earth did change her images and forms
Before us, fast as clouds are changed in heaven.
Day after day, up early and down late,
495 From hill to vale we dropped, from vale to hill
Mounted—from province on to province swept,
Keen hunters in a chase of fourteen weeks,
Eager as birds of prey, or as a ship
Upon the stretch, when winds are blowing fair:
500 Sweet coverts did we cross of pastoral life,
Enticing valleys, greeted them and left
Too soon, while yet the very flash and gleam
Of salutation were not passed away.
Oh! sorrow for the youth who could have seen
505 Unchastened, unsubdued, unawed, unraised
To patriarchal dignity of mind,
And pure simplicity of wish and will,
Those sanctified abodes of peaceful man,
Pleased (though to hardship born, and compassed round
510 With danger, varying as the seasons change),
Pleased with his daily task, or, if not pleased,
Contented, from the moment that the dawn
(Ah! surely not without attendant gleams
Of soul-illumination) calls him forth
515 To industry, by glistenings flung on rocks,
Whose evening shadows lead him to repose.

Well might a stranger look with bounding heart
Down on a green recess, the first I saw
Of those deep haunts, an aboriginal vale,
520 Quiet and lorded over and possessed
By naked huts, wood-built, and sown like tents
Or Indian cabins over the fresh lawns
And by the river side.

That very day,
From a bare ridge we also first beheld
Unveiled the summit of Mont Blanc, and grieved   *525*
To have a soulless image on the eye
That had usurped upon a living thought°
That never more could be. The wondrous Vale
Of Chamouny stretched far below, and soon
With its dumb cataracts and streams of ice,   *530*
A motionless array of mighty waves,
Five rivers broad and vast, made rich amends,
And reconciled us to realities;
There small birds warble from the leafy trees,
The eagle soars high in the element,   *535*
There doth the reaper bind the yellow sheaf,
The maiden spread the haycock in the sun,
While Winter like a well-tamed lion walks,
Descending from the mountain to make sport
Among the cottages by beds of flowers.   *540*

Whate'er in this wide circuit we beheld,
Or heard, was fitted to our unripe state
Of intellect and heart. With such a book
Before our eyes, we could not choose but read
Lessons of genuine brotherhood, the plain   *545*
And universal reason of mankind,
The truths of young and old. Nor, side by side
Pacing, two social pilgrims, or alone
Each with his humour, could we fail to abound
In dreams and fictions, pensively composed: *550*
Dejection taken up for pleasure's sake,
And gilded sympathies, the willow wreath,
And sober posies of funereal flowers,
Gathered among those solitudes sublime
From formal gardens of the lady Sorrow,   *555*
Did sweeten many a meditative hour.

Yet still in me with those soft luxuries
Mixed something of stern mood, an under-thirst

526–27 **soulless . . . thought** The expectation was greater than the
reality. Cf. the disappointment (and compensation) in lines 560–640.

Of vigour seldom utterly allayed.
560 And from that source how different a sadness
Would issue, let one incident make known.
When from the Vallais we had turned, and clomb
Along the Simplon's steep and rugged road,°
Following a band of muleteers, we reached
565 A halting-place, where all together took
Their noon-tide meal. Hastily rose our guide,
Leaving us at the board; awhile we lingered,
Then paced the beaten downward way that led
Right to a rough stream's edge, and there broke off;
570 The only track now visible was one
That from the torrent's further brink held forth
Conspicuous invitation to ascend
A lofty mountain. After brief delay
Crossing the unbridged stream, that road we took,
575 And clomb with eagerness, till anxious fears
Intruded, for we failed to overtake
Our comrades gone before. By fortunate chance,
While every moment added doubt to doubt,
A peasant met us, from whose mouth we learned
580 That to the spot which had perplexed us first
We must descend, and there should find the road,
Which in the stony channel of the stream
Lay a few steps, and then along its banks;
And, that our future course, all plain to sight,
585 Was downwards, with the current of that stream.
Loth to believe what we so grieved to hear,
For still we had hopes that pointed to the clouds,
We questioned him again, and yet again;
But every word that from the peasant's lips
590 Came in reply, translated by our feelings,
Ended in this,—*that we had crossed the Alps.*

Imagination—here° the Power so called
Through sad incompetence of human speech,
That awful Power rose from the mind's abyss

563 **Simplon's . . . road** over the Alps.   592 **Imagination—here** This
apostrophe (lines 592–616) is an inspired afterthought on the ex-
perience and interrupts the straight line of the narrative (line 617
connects with 591). "Here" refers to the poet in the act of composi-
tion or reflection fourteen years after the event.

Like an unfathered vapour that enwraps,   595
At once, some lonely traveller. I was lost;
Halted without an effort to break through;
But to my conscious soul I now can say—
"I recognise thy glory:" in such strength
Of usurpation, when the light of sense   600
Goes out, but with a flash that has revealed
The invisible world, doth greatness make abode,
There harbours; whether we be young or old,
Our destiny, our being's heart and home,
Is with infinitude, and only there;   605
With hope it is, hope that can never die,
Effort, and expectation, and desire,
And something evermore about to be.
Under such banners militant, the soul
Seeks for no trophies, struggles for no spoils   610
That may attest her prowess, blest in thoughts
That are their own perfection and reward,
Strong in herself and in beatitude
That hides her, like the mighty flood of Nile
Poured from his fount of Abyssinian clouds   615
To fertilise the whole Egyptian plain.

   The melancholy slackening that ensued
Upon those tidings by the peasant given
Was soon dislodged. Downwards we hurried fast,
And, with the half-shaped road which we had missed,   620
Entered a narrow chasm. The brook and road
Were fellow-travellers in this gloomy strait,
And with them did we journey several hours
At a slow pace. The immeasurable height
Of woods decaying, never to be decayed,   625
The stationary blasts of waterfalls,
And in the narrow rent at every turn
Winds thwarting winds, bewildered and forlorn,
The torrents shooting from the clear blue sky,
The rocks that muttered close upon our ears,   630
Black drizzling crags that spake by the way-side
As if a voice were in them, the sick sight
And giddy prospect of the raving stream,
The unfettered clouds and region of the Heavens,

635 Tumult and peace, the darkness and the light—
Were all like workings of one mind, the features
Of the same face, blossoms upon one tree;
Characters of the great Apocalypse,
The types and symbols of Eternity,
640 Of first, and last, and midst, and without end.

That night our lodging was a house that stood
Alone within the valley, at a point
Where, tumbling from aloft, a torrent swelled
The rapid stream whose margin we had trod;
645 A dreary mansion, large beyond all need,
With high and spacious rooms, deafened and stunned
By noise of waters, making innocent sleep
Lie melancholy among weary bones.

Uprisen betimes, our journey we renewed,
650 Led by the stream, ere noon-day magnified
Into a lordly river, broad and deep,
Dimpling along in silent majesty,
With mountains for its neighbours, and in view
Of distant mountains and their snowy tops,
655 And thus proceeding to Locarno's Lake,
Fit resting-place for such a visitant.
Locarno! spreading out in width like Heaven,
How dost thou cleave to the poetic heart,
Back in the sunshine of the memory;
660 And Como! thou, a treasure whom the earth
Keeps to herself, confined as in a depth
Of Abyssinian privacy. I spake°
Of thee, thy chestnut woods, and garden plots
Of Indian corn tended by dark-eyed maids;
665 Thy lofty steeps, and pathways roofed with vines,
Winding from house to house, from town to town,
Sole link that binds them to each other; walks,
League after league, and cloistral avenues,
Where silence dwells if music be not there:
670 While yet a youth undisciplined in verse,
Through fond ambition of that hour I strove
To chant your praise; nor can approach you now

662 **I spake** in *Descriptive Sketches* (1793), lines 77–140.

Ungreeted by a more melodious Song,
Where tones of Nature smoothed by learnèd Art
May flow in lasting current. Like a breeze   675
Or sunbeam over your domain I passed
In motion without pause; but ye have left
Your beauty with me, a serene accord
Of forms and colours, passive, yet endowed
In their submissiveness with power as sweet   680
And gracious, almost, might I dare to say,
As virtue is, or goodness; sweet as love,
Or the remembrance of a generous deed,
Or mildest visitations of pure thought,
When God, the giver of all joy, is thanked   685
Religiously, in silent blessedness;
Sweet as this last herself, for such it is.

    With those delightful pathways we advanced,
For two days' space in presence of the Lake,
That, stretching far among the Alps, assumed   690
A character more stern. The second night,
From sleep awakened, and misled by sound
Of the church clock telling the hours with strokes
Whose import then we had not learned, we rose
By moonlight, doubting not that day was nigh,   695
And that meanwhile, by no uncertain path,
Along the winding margin of the lake,
Led, as before, we should behold the scene
Hushed in profound repose. We left the town
Of Gravedona with this hope; but soon   700
Were lost, bewildered among woods immense,
And on a rock sate down, to wait for day.
An open place it was, and overlooked,
From high, the sullen water far beneath,
On which a dull red image of the moon   705
Lay bedded, changing oftentimes its form
Like an uneasy snake. From hour to hour
We sate and sate, wondering, as if the night
Had been ensnared by witchcraft. On the rock
At last we stretched our weary limbs for sleep,   710
But *could not* sleep, tormented by the stings
Of insects, which, with noise like that of noon,

Filled all the woods; the cry of unknown birds;
The mountains more by blackness visible
715 And their own size, than any outward light;
The breathless wilderness of clouds; the clock
That told, with unintelligible voice,
The widely parted hours; the noise of streams,
And sometimes rustling motions nigh at hand,
720 That did not leave us free from personal fear;
And, lastly, the withdrawing moon, that set
Before us, while she still was high in heaven;—
These were our food; and such a summer's night
Followed that pair of golden days that shed
725 On Como's Lake, and all that round it lay,
Their fairest, softest, happiest influence.

* * * *

Let this alone
Be mentioned as a parting word, that not
In hollow exultation, dealing out
Hyperboles of praise comparative;
735 Not rich one moment to be poor for ever;
Not prostrate, overborne, as if the mind
Herself were nothing, a mere pensioner
On outward forms—did we in presence stand
Of that magnificent region. On the front
740 Of this whole Song is written that my heart
Must, in such Temple, needs have offered up
A different worship. Finally, whate'er
I saw, or heard, or felt, was but a stream
That flowed into a kindred stream; a gale,
745 Confederate with the current of the soul,
To speed my voyage; every sound or sight,
In its degree of power, administered
To grandeur or to tenderness,—to the one
Directly, but to tender thoughts by means
750 Less often instantaneous in effect;
Led me to these by paths that, in the main,
Were more circuitous, but not less sure
Duly to reach the point marked out by Heaven.

Oh, most belovèd Friend! a glorious time,
755 A happy time that was; triumphant looks

Were then the common language of all eyes;
As if awaked from sleep, the Nations hailed
Their great expectancy: the fife of war
Was then a spirit-stirring sound indeed,
A blackbird's whistle in a budding grove.   *760*
We left the Swiss exulting in the fate
Of their near neighbours; and, when shortening fast
Our pilgrimage, nor distant far from home,
We crossed the Brabant armies on the fret
For battle in the cause of Liberty.°   *765*
A stripling, scarcely of the household then
Of social life, I looked upon these things
As from a distance; heard, and saw, and felt,
Was touched, but with no intimate concern;
I seemed to move along them, as a bird   *770*
Moves through the air, or as a fish pursues
Its sport, or feeds in its proper element;
I wanted not that joy, I did not need
Such help; the ever-living universe,
Turn where I might, was opening out its glories,   *775*
And the independent spirit of pure youth
Called forth, at every season, new delights,
Spread round my steps like sunshine o'er green fields.

Book Seventh

Residence in London

Six changeful years have vanished since I first
Poured out (saluted by that quickening breeze
Which met me issuing from the City's walls)
A glad preamble° to this Verse: I sang
Aloud, with fervour irresistible   *5*
Of short-lived transport, like a torrent bursting,
From a black thunder-cloud, down Scafell's side
To rush and disappear. But soon broke forth
(So willed the Muse) a less impetuous stream,

764–65 **Brabant . . . Liberty** The Belgians are ready to defend themselves against the Austrians.

4 **glad preamble** See Book I. 1–45.

10   That flowed awhile with unabating strength,
Then stopped for years; not audible again
Before last primrose-time. Belovèd Friend!
The assurance which then cheered some heavy thoughts
On thy departure to a foreign land
15   Has failed; too slowly moves the promised work.
Through the whole summer have I been at rest,
Partly from voluntary holiday,
And part through outward hindrance. But I heard,
After the hour of sunset yester-even,
20   Sitting within doors between light and dark,
A choir of redbreasts gathered somewhere near
My threshold,—minstrels from the distant woods
Sent in on Winter's service, to announce,
With preparation artful and benign,
25   That the rough lord had left the surly North
On his accustomed journey. The delight,
Due to this timely notice, unawares
Smote me, and, listening, I in whispers said,
"Ye heartsome Choristers, ye and I will be
30   Associates, and, unscared by blustering winds,
Will chant together." Thereafter, as the shades
Of twilight deepened, going forth, I spied
A glow-worm underneath a dusky plume
Or canopy of yet unwithered fern,
35   Clear-shining, like a hermit's taper seen
Through a thick forest. Silence touched me here
No less than sound had done before; the child
Of Summer, lingering, shining, by herself,
The voiceless worm on the unfrequented hills,
40   Seemed sent on the same errand with the choir
Of Winter that had warbled at my door,
And the whole year breathed tenderness and love.

    The last night's genial feeling overflowed
Upon this morning, and my favourite grove,
45   Tossing in sunshine its dark boughs aloft,
As if to make the strong wind visible,
Wakes in me agitations like its own,
A spirit friendly to the Poet's task,
Which we will now resume with lively hope,

Nor checked by aught of tamer argument   50
That lies before us, needful to be told.

   Returned from that excursion, soon I bade
Farewell for ever to the sheltered seats
Of gownèd students, quitted hall and bower,
And every comfort of that privileged ground,   55
Well pleased to pitch a vagrant tent among
The unfenced regions of society.

   Yet, undetermined to what course of life
I should adhere, and seeming to possess
A little space of intermediate time   60
At full command, to London first I turned,
In no disturbance of excessive hope,
By personal ambition unenslaved,
Frugal as there was need, and, though self-willed,
From dangerous passions free. Three years had flown 65
Since I had felt in heart and soul the shock
Of the huge town's first presence, and had paced
Her endless streets, a transient visitant:
Now, fixed amid that concourse of mankind
Where Pleasure whirls about incessantly,   70
And life and labour seem but one, I filled
An idler's place; an idler well content
To have a house (what matter for a home?)
That owned him; living cheerfully abroad
With unchecked fancy ever on the stir,   75
And all my young affections out of doors.

    *   *   *   *

   Rise up, thou monstrous ant-hill on the plain
Of a too busy world! Before me flow,   150
Thou endless stream of men and moving things!
Thy every-day appearance, as it strikes—
With wonder heightened, or sublimed by awe—
On strangers, of all ages; the quick dance
Of colours, lights, and forms; the deafening din;   155
The comers and the goers face to face,
Face after face; the string of dazzling wares,
Shop after shop, with symbols, blazoned names,

And all the tradesman's honours overhead:
160 Here, fronts of houses, like a title-page,
    With letters huge inscribed from top to toe;
    Stationed above the door, like guardian saints,
    There, allegoric shapes, female or male,
    Or physiognomies of real men,
165 Land-warriors, kings, or admirals of the sea,
    Boyle,° Shakespeare, Newton, or the attractive° head
    Of some quack-doctor, famous in his day.

    Meanwhile the roar continues, till at length,
    Escaped as from an enemy, we turn
170 Abruptly into some sequestered nook,
    Still as a sheltered place when winds blow loud!
    At leisure, thence, through tracts of thin resort,
    And sights and sounds that come at intervals,
    We take our way. A raree-show is here,
175 With children gathered round; another street
    Presents a company of dancing dogs,
    Or dromedary, with an antic pair
    Of monkeys on his back; a minstrel band
    Of Savoyards; or, single and alone,
180 An English ballad-singer. Private courts,
    Gloomy as coffins, and unsightly lanes
    Thrilled by some female vendor's scream, belike
    The very shrillest of all London cries,
    May then entangle our impatient steps;
185 Conducted through those labyrinths, unawares,
    To privileged regions and inviolate,
    Where from their airy lodges studious lawyers
    Look out on waters, walks, and gardens green.

        *   *   *   *

    Four rapid years had scarcely then been told
    Since, travelling southward from our pastoral hills,
    I heard, and for the first time in my life,
885 The voice of woman utter blasphemy—
    Saw woman as she is, to open shame
    Abandoned, and the pride of public vice;
    I shuddered, for a barrier seemed at once

166 **Boyle** Robert Boyle (1627–91), English chemist.   166 **attractive** attracting.

Thrown in, that from humanity divorced
Humanity, splitting the race of man   *890*
In twain, yet leaving the same outward form.
Distress of mind ensued upon the sight,
And ardent meditation. Later years
Brought to such spectacle a milder sadness,
Feelings of pure commiseration, grief   *895*
For the individual and the overthrow
Of her soul's beauty; farther I was then
But seldom led, or wished to go; in truth
The sorrow of the passion stopped me there.

* * * *

The matter that detains us now may seem,
To many, neither dignified enough
Nor arduous, yet will not be scorned by them,   *460*
Who, looking inward, have observed the ties
That bind the perishable hours of life
Each to the other, and the curious props
By which the world of memory and thought
Exists and is sustained. More lofty themes,   *465*
Such as at least do wear a prouder face,
Solicit our regard; but when I think
Of these, I feel the imaginative power
Languish within me; even then it slept,
When, pressed by tragic sufferings, the heart   *470*
Was more than full; amid my sobs and tears
It slept, even in the pregnant season of youth.
For though I was most passionately moved
And yielded to all changes of the scene
With an obsequious promptness, yet the storm   *475*
Passed not beyond the suburbs of the mind;
Save when realities of act and mien,
The incarnation of the spirits that move
In harmony amid the Poet's world,
Rose to ideal grandeur, or, called forth   *480*
By power of contrast, made me recognise,
As at a glance, the things which I had shaped,
And yet not shaped, had seen and scarcely seen,
When, having closed the mighty Shakspeare's page,
I mused, and thought, and felt, in solitude.   *485*

*   *   *   *

As the black storm upon the mountain top
620 Sets off the sunbeam in the valley, so
That huge fermenting mass of human-kind
Serves as a solemn back-ground, or relief,
To single forms and objects, whence they draw,
For feeling and contemplative regard,
625 More than inherent liveliness and power.
How oft, amid those overflowing streets,
Have I gone forward with the crowd, and said
Unto myself, "The face of every one
That passes by me is a mystery!"
630 Thus have I looked, nor ceased to look, oppressed
By thoughts of what and whither, when and how,
Until the shapes before my eyes became
A second-sight procession, such as glides
Over still mountains, or appears in dreams;
635 And once, far-travelled in such mood, beyond
The reach of common indication, lost
Amid the moving pageant, I was smitten
Abruptly, with the view (a sight not rare)
Of a blind Beggar, who, with upright face,
640 Stood, propped against a wall, upon his chest
Wearing a written paper, to explain
His story, whence he came, and who he was.
Caught by the spectacle my mind turned round
As with the might of waters; an apt type
645 This label seemed of the utmost we can know,
Both of ourselves and of the universe;
And, on the shape of that unmoving man,
His steadfast face and sightless eyes, I gazed,
As if admonished from another world.

650   Though reared upon the base of outward things,
Structures like these the excited spirit mainly
Builds for herself; scenes different there are,
Full-formed, that take, with small internal help,
Possession of the faculties,—the peace
655 That comes with night; the deep solemnity
Of nature's intermediate hours of rest,

When the great tide of human life stands still;
The business of the day to come, unborn,
Of that gone by, locked up, as in the grave;
The blended calmness of the heavens and earth,   660
Moonlight and stars, and empty streets, and sounds
Unfrequent as in deserts; at late hours
Of winter evenings, when unwholesome rains
Are falling hard, with people yet astir,
The feeble salutation from the voice   665
Of some unhappy woman, now and then
Heard as we pass, when no one looks about,
Nothing is listened to. But these,° I fear,
Are falsely catalogued; things that are, are not,
As the mind answers to them, or the heart   670
Is prompt, or slow, to feel. What say you, then,
To times, when half the city shall break out
Full of one passion, vengeance, rage, or fear?
To executions, to a street on fire,
Mobs, riots, or rejoicings? From these sights   675
Take one,—that ancient festival, the Fair,
Holden where martyrs suffered in past time,
And named of St. Bartholomew; there, see
A work completed to our hands, that lays,
If any spectacle on earth can do,   680
The whole creative powers of man asleep!—
For once, the Muse's help will we implore,
And she shall lodge us, wafted on her wings,
Above the press and danger of the crowd,
Upon some showman's platform. What a shock   685
For eyes and ears! what anarchy and din,
Barbarian and infernal,—a phantasma,
Monstrous in colour, motion, shape, sight, sound!
Below, the open space, through every nook
Of the wide area, twinkles, is alive   690
With heads; the midway region, and above,
Is thronged with staring pictures and huge scrolls,
Dumb proclamations of the Prodigies;
With chattering monkeys dangling from their poles,

668 these the "scenes" (line 652). Wordsworth suggests that there
is a life in things independent of our subjective responses.

695 And children whirling in their roundabouts;
     With those that stretch the neck and strain the eyes,
     And crack the voice in rivalship, the crowd
     Inviting; with buffoons against buffoons
     Grimacing, writhing, screaming,—him who grinds
700 The hurdy-gurdy, at the fiddle weaves,
     Rattles the salt-box, thumps the kettle-drum,
     And him who at the trumpet puffs his cheeks,
     The silver-collared Negro with his timbrel,
     Equestrians, tumblers, women, girls, and boys,
705 Blue-breeched, pink-vested, with high-towering plumes.
     All moveables of wonder, from all parts,
     Are here—Albinos, painted Indians, Dwarfs,
     The Horse of knowledge, and the learned Pig,
     The Stone-eater, the man that swallows fire,
710 Giants, Ventriloquists, the Invisible Girl,
     The Bust that speaks and moves its goggling eyes,
     The Wax-work, Clock-work, all the marvellous craft
     Of modern Merlins, Wild Beasts, Puppet-shows,
     All out-o'-the-way, far-fetched, perverted things,
715 All freaks of nature, all Promethean thoughts
     Of man, his dullness, madness, and their feats
     All jumbled up together, to compose
     A Parliament of Monsters. Tents and Booths
     Meanwhile, as if the whole were one vast mill,
720 Are vomiting, receiving on all sides,
     Men, Women, three-years' Children, Babes in arms.

      Oh, blank confusion! true epitome
     Of what the mighty City is herself,
     To thousands upon thousands of her sons,
725 Living amid the same perpetual whirl
     Of trivial objects, melted and reduced
     To one identity, by differences
     That have no law, no meaning, and no end—
     Oppression, under which even highest minds
730 Must labour, whence the strongest are not free.
     But though the picture weary out the eye,
     By nature an unmanageable sight,
     It is not wholly so to him who looks
     In steadiness, who hath among least things

An under-sense of greatest; sees the parts 735
As parts, but with a feeling of the whole.

*   *   *   *

Book Eighth

Retrospect—Love of Nature Leading to Love of Man

*   *   *   *

With deep devotion, Nature, did I feel, 70
In that enormous City's turbulent world
Of men and things, what benefit I owed
To thee, and those domains of rural peace,
Where to the sense of beauty first my heart
Was opened; tract more exquisitely fair 75
Than that famed paradise of ten thousand trees,
Or Gehol's matchless gardens, for delight
Of the Tartarian dynasty composed
(Beyond that mighty wall, not fabulous,
China's stupendous mound) by patient toil 80
Of myriads and boon nature's lavish help;
There, in a clime from widest empire chosen,
Fulfilling (could enchantment have done more?)
A sumptuous dream of flowery lawns, with domes
Of pleasure sprinkled over, shady dells 85
For eastern monasteries, sunny mounts
With temples crested, bridges, gondolas,
Rocks, dens, and groves of foliage taught to melt
Into each other their obsequious hues,
Vanished and vanishing in subtle chase, 90
Too fine to be pursued; or standing forth
In no discordant opposition, strong
And gorgeous as the colours side by side
Bedded among rich plumes of tropic birds;
And mountains over all, embracing all; 95
And all the landscape, endlessly enriched
With waters running, falling, or asleep.

But lovelier far than this, the paradise
Where I was reared; in Nature's primitive gifts

100 Favoured no less, and more to every sense
    Delicious, seeing that the sun and sky,
    The elements, and seasons as they change,
    Do find a worthy fellow-labourer there—
    Man free, man working for himself, with choice
105 Of time, and place, and object; by his wants,
    His comforts, native occupations, cares,
    Cheerfully led to individual ends
    Or social, and still followed by a train
    Unwooed, unthought-of even—simplicity,
110 And beauty, and inevitable grace.

    Yea, when a glimpse of those imperial bowers
    Would to a child be transport over-great,
    When but a half-hour's roam through such a place
    Would leave behind a dance of images,
115 That shall break in upon his sleep for weeks;
    Even then the common haunts of the green earth,
    And ordinary interests of man,
    Which they embosom, all without regard
    As both may seem, are fastening on the heart
120 Insensibly, each with the other's help.
    For me, when my affections first were led
    From kindred, friends, and playmates, to partake
    Love for the human creature's absolute self,
    That noticeable kindliness of heart
125 Sprang out of fountains, there abounding most
    Where sovereign Nature dictated the tasks
    And occupations which her beauty adorned,
    And Shepherds were the men that pleased me first. . . .

    *   *   *   *

    When up the lonely brooks on rainy days
    Angling I went, or trod the trackless hills
    By mists bewildered, suddenly mine eyes
265 Have glanced upon him distant a few steps,
    In size a giant, stalking through thick fog,
    His sheep like Greenland bears; or, as he stepped
    Beyond the boundary line of some hill-shadow,
    His form hath flashed upon me, glorified
270 By the deep radiance of the setting sun:

Or him have I descried in distant sky,
A solitary object and sublime,
Above all height! like an aerial cross
Stationed alone upon a spiry rock
Of the Chartreuse, for worship. Thus was man   275
Ennobled outwardly before my sight,
And thus my heart was early introduced
To an unconscious love and reverence
Of human nature; hence the human form
To me became an index of delight,   280
Of grace and honour, power and worthiness.
Meanwhile this creature—spiritual almost
As those of books, but more exalted far;
Far more of an imaginative form
Than the gay Corin of the groves, who lives   285
For his own fancies, or to dance by the hour,
In coronal, with Phyllis° in the midst—
Was, for the purposes of kind, a man
With the most common; husband, father; learned,
Could teach, admonish; suffered with the rest   290
From vice and folly, wretchedness and fear;
Of this I little saw, cared less for it,
But something must have felt.
                    Call ye these appearances—
Which I beheld of shepherds in my youth,
This sanctity of Nature given to man—   295
A shadow, a delusion, ye who pore
On the dead letter, miss the spirit of things;
Whose truth is not a motion or a shape
Instinct with vital functions, but a block
Or waxen image which yourselves have made,   800
And ye adore! But blessed be the God
Of Nature and of Man that this was so;
That men before my inexperienced eyes
Did first present themselves thus purified,
Removed, and to a distance that was fit: 805
And so we all of us in some degree
Are led to knowledge, whencesoever led,

285–87 **Corin . . . Phyllis** figures from bookish pastoral poetry.

And howsoever; were it otherwise,
And we found evil fast as we find good
810 In our first years, or think that it is found,
How could the innocent heart bear up and live!
But doubly fortunate my lot; not here
Alone, that something of a better life
Perhaps was round me than it is the privilege
815 Of most to move in, but that first I looked
At Man through objects that were great or fair;
First communed with him by their help. And thus
Was founded a sure safeguard and defence
Against the weight of meanness, selfish cares,
820 Coarse manners, vulgar passions, that beat in
On all sides from the ordinary world
In which we traffic. Starting from this point
I had my face turned toward the truth, began
With an advantage furnished by that kind
825 Of prepossession, without which the soul
Receives no knowledge that can bring forth good,
No genuine insight ever comes to her.
From the restraint of over-watchful eyes
Preserved, I moved about, year after year,
830 Happy, and now most thankful that my walk
Was guarded from too early intercourse
With the deformities of crowded life,
And those ensuing laughters and contempts,
Self-pleasing, which, if we would wish to think
835 With a due reverence on earth's rightful lord,
Here placed to be the inheritor of heaven,
Will not permit us; but pursue the mind,
That to devotion willingly would rise,
Into the temple and the temple's heart.

840   Yet deem not, Friend! that human kind with me
Thus early took a place pre-eminent;
Nature herself was, at this unripe time,
But secondary to my own pursuits
And animal activities, and all
845 Their trivial pleasures; and when these had drooped
And gradually expired, and Nature, prized
For her own sake, became my joy, even then—

And upwards through late youth, until not less
Than two-and-twenty summers had been told—
Was Man in my affections and regards   *850*
Subordinate to her, her visible forms
And viewless agencies: a passion, she,
A rapture often, and immediate love
Ever at hand; he, only a delight
Occasional, an accidental grace,   *855*
His hour being not yet come. . . .

*   *   *   *

But when that first poetic faculty   *865*
Of plain Imagination and severe,
No longer a mute influence of the soul,
Ventured, at some rash Muse's earnest call,
To try her strength among harmonious words;
And to book-notions and the rules of art   *870*
Did knowingly conform itself; there came
Among the simple shapes of human life
A wilfulness of fancy and conceit;
And Nature and her objects beautified
These fictions, as in some sort, in their turn,   *875*
They burnished her. From touch of this new power
Nothing was safe: the elder-tree that grew
Beside the well-known charnel-house had then
A dismal look: the yew-tree had its ghost,
That took his station there for ornament: *880*
The dignities of plain occurrence then
Were tasteless, and truth's golden mean, a point
Where no sufficient pleasure could be found.
Then, if a widow, staggering with the blow
Of her distress, was known to have turned her steps   *885*
To the cold grave in which her husband slept,
One night, or haply more than one, through pain
Or half-insensate impotence of mind,
The fact was caught at greedily, and there
She must be visitant the whole year through,   *890*
Wetting the turf with never-ending tears.

Through quaint obliquities I might pursue
These cravings; when the fox-glove, one by one,

Upwards through every stage of the tall stem,
395 Had shed beside the public way its bells,
And stood of all dismantled, save the last
Left at the tapering ladder's top, that seemed
To bend as doth a slender blade of grass
Tipped with a rain-drop, Fancy loved to seat,
400 Beneath the plant despoiled, but crested still
With this last relic, soon itself to fall,
Some vagrant mother, whose arch little ones,
All unconcerned by her dejected plight,
Laughed as with rival eagerness their hands
405 Gathered the purple cups that round them lay,
Strewing the turf's green slope.
                                        A diamond light
(Whene'er the summer sun, declining, smote
A smooth rock wet with constant springs) was seen
Sparkling from out a copse-clad bank that rose
410 Fronting our cottage. Oft besides the hearth
Seated, with open door, often and long
Upon this restless lustre have I gazed,
That made my fancy restless as itself.
'Twas now for me a burnished silver shield
415 Suspended over a knight's tomb, who lay
Inglorious, buried in the dusky wood:
An entrance now into some magic cave
Or palace built by fairies of the rock;
Nor could I have been bribed to disenchant
420 The spectacle, by visiting the spot.
Thus wilful Fancy, in no hurtful mood,
Engrafted far-fetched shapes on feeling bred
By pure Imagination:° busy Power
She was, and with her ready pupil turned
425 Instinctively to human passions, then
Least understood. Yet, 'mid the fervent swarm
Of these vagaries, with an eye so rich
As mine was through the bounty of a grand
And lovely region, I had forms distinct
430 To steady me: each airy thought revolved

421–23 **Fancy . . . Imagination** The terms are variously used and
defined by Wordsworth. See, for example, "Fancy and Imagina-
tion," pp. 430 ff. below.

Round a substantial centre, which at once
Incited it to motion, and controlled.
I did not pine like one in cities bred,
As was thy melancholy lot, dear Friend!
Great Spirit as thou art, in endless dreams   *435*
Of sickliness, disjoining, joining, things
Without the light of knowledge. Where the harm,
If, when the woodman languished with disease
Induced by sleeping nightly on the ground
Within his sod-built cabin, Indian-wise,   *440*
I called the pangs of disappointed love,
And all the sad etcetera of the wrong,
To help him to his grave? Meanwhile the man,
If not already from the woods retired
To die at home, was haply, as I knew,   *445*
Withering by slow degrees, 'mid gentle airs,
Birds, running streams, and hills so beautiful
On golden evenings, while the charcoal pile
Breathed up its smoke, an image of his ghost
Or spirit that full soon must take her flight.   *450*

*   *   *   *

Grave Teacher, stern Preceptress! for at times   *530*
Thou canst put on an aspect most severe;
London, to thee I willingly return.
Erewhile my verse played idly with the flowers
Enwrought upon thy mantle; satisfied
With that amusement, and a simple look   *535*
Of child-like inquisition now and then
Cast upwards on thy countenance, to detect
Some inner meanings which might harbour there.
But how could I in mood so light indulge,
Keeping such fresh remembrance of the day,   *540*
When, having thridded° the long labyrinth
Of the suburban villages, I first
Entered thy vast dominion? On the roof
Of an itinerant vehicle I sate,
With vulgar men about me, trivial forms   *545*
Of houses, pavement, streets, of men and things,—
Mean shapes on every side: but, at the instant,

541 **thridded** threaded.

When to myself it fairly might be said,
The threshold now is overpast, (how strange
550 That aught external to the living mind
Should have such mighty sway! yet so it was),
A weight of ages did at once descend
Upon my heart; no thought embodied, no
Distinct remembrances, but weight and power,—
555 Power growing under weight: alas! I feel
That I am trifling: 'twas a moment's pause,—
All that took place within me came and went
As in a moment; yet with Time it dwells,
And grateful memory, as a thing divine.

*   *   *   *

. . . less
Than other intellects had mine been used
To lean upon extrinsic circumstance
625 Of record or tradition; but a sense
Of what in the Great City had been done
And suffered, and was doing, suffering, still,
Weighed with me, could support the test of thought;
And, in despite of all that had gone by,
630 Or was departing never to return,
There I conversed with majesty and power
Like independent natures. Hence the place
Was thronged with impregnations like the Wilds
In which my early feelings had been nursed—
635 Bare hills and valleys, full of caverns, rocks,
And audible seclusions, dashing lakes,
Echoes and waterfalls, and pointed crags
That into music touch the passing wind.
Here then my young imagination found
640 No uncongenial element; could here
Among new objects serve or give command,
Even as the heart's occasions might require,
To forward reason's else too scrupulous march.
The effect was, still more elevated views
645 Of human nature. Neither vice nor guilt,
Debasement undergone by body or mind,
Nor all the misery forced upon my sight,
Misery not lightly passed, but sometimes scanned

Most feelingly, could overthrow my trust
In what we *may* become; induce belief   650
That I was ignorant, had been falsely taught,
A solitary, who with vain conceits
Had been inspired, and walked about in dreams.
From those sad scenes when meditation turned,
Lo! every thing that was indeed divine   655
Retained its purity inviolate,
Nay brighter shone, by this portentous gloom
Set off; such opposition as aroused
The mind of Adam, yet in Paradise
Though fallen from bliss, when in the East he saw   660
Darkness ere day's mid course, and morning light
More orient in the western cloud, that drew
O'er the blue firmament a radiant white,
Descending slow with something heavenly fraught.°

*   *   *   *

   Thus from a very early age, O Friend!
My thoughts by slow gradations had been drawn
To human-kind, and to the good and ill
Of human life: Nature had led me on;
And oft amid the "busy hum"° I seemed   680
To travel independent of her help,
As if I had forgotten her; but no,
The world of human-kind outweighed not hers
In my habitual thoughts; the scale of love,
Though filling daily, still was light, compared   685
With that in which *her* mighty objects lay.

Book Ninth

Residence in France

Even as a river,—partly (it might seem)
Yielding to old remembrances, and swayed
In part by fear to shape a way direct,
That would engulph him soon in the ravenous sea—

660–64 **East . . . fraught.** Cf. *Paradise Lost* XI. 204 ff.   680 **"busy
hum"** Milton, "L'Allegro," line 118.

5   Turns, and will measure back his course, far back,
Seeking the very regions which he crossed
In his first outset; so have we, my Friend!
Turned and returned with intricate delay.
Or as a traveller, who has gained the brow
10   Of some aerial Down, while there he halts
For breathing-time, is tempted to review
The region left behind him; and, if aught
Deserving notice have escaped regard,
Or been regarded with too careless eye,
15   Strives, from that height, with one and yet one more
Last look, to make the best amends he may:
So have we lingered. Now we start afresh
With courage, and new hope risen on our toil.
Fair greetings to this shapeless eagerness,
20   Whene'er it comes! needful in work so long,
Thrice needful to the argument which now
Awaits us! Oh, how much unlike the past!

Free as a colt at pasture on the hill,
I ranged at large, through London's wide domain,
25   Month after month. Obscurely did I live,
Not seeking frequent intercourse with men,
By literature, or elegance, or rank,
Distinguished. Scarcely was a year thus spent
Ere I forsook the crowded solitude,
30   With less regret for its luxurious pomp,
And all the nicely-guarded shows of art,
Than for the humble book-stalls in the streets,
Exposed to eye and hand where'er I turned.

France lured me forth; the realm that I had crossed
35   So lately, journeying toward the snow-clad Alps.
But now, relinquishing the scrip° and staff,
And all enjoyment which the summer sun
Sheds round the steps of those who meet the day
With motion constant as his own, I went
40   Prepared to sojourn in a pleasant town,
Washed by the current of the stately Loire.

36 scrip knapsack.

Through Paris lay my readiest course, and there
Sojourning a few days, I visited,
In haste, each spot of old or recent fame,
The latter chiefly; from the field of Mars   45
Down to the suburbs of St. Antony,
And from Mont Martyr southward to the Dome
Of Geneviève. In both her clamorous Halls,
The National Synod and the Jacobins,
I saw the Revolutionary Power   50
Toss like a ship at anchor, rocked by storms;
The Arcades I traversed, in the Palace huge
Of Orleans; coasted round and round the line
Of Tavern, Brothel, Gaming-house, and Shop,
Great rendezvous of worst and best, the walk   55
Of all who had a purpose, or had not;
I stared and listened, with a stranger's ears,
To Hawkers and Haranguers, hubbub wild!
And hissing Factionists with ardent eyes,
In knots, or pairs, or single. Not a look   60
Hope takes, or Doubt or Fear is forced to wear,
But seemed there present; and I scanned them all,
Watched every gesture uncontrollable,
Of anger, and vexation, and despite,
All side by side, and struggling face to face,   65
With gaiety and dissolute idleness.

Where silent zephyrs sported with the dust
Of the Bastille, I sate in the open sun,
And from the rubbish gathered up a stone,
And pocketed the relic, in the guise   70
Of an enthusiast; yet, in honest truth,
I looked for something that I could not find,
Affecting more emotion than I felt;
For 'tis most certain, that these various sights,
However potent their first shock, with me   75
Appeared to recompense the traveller's pains
Less than the painted Magdalene of Le Brun,°
A beauty exquisitely wrought, with hair
Dishevelled, gleaming eyes, and rueful cheek
Pale and bedropped with everflowing tears.   80

77 **Le Brun** Charles Le Brun (1619–90).

But hence to my more permanent abode
I hasten; there, by novelties in speech,
Domestic manners, customs, gestures, looks,
And all the attire of ordinary life,
85 Attention was engrossed; and, thus amused,
I stood, 'mid those concussions, unconcerned,
Tranquil almost, and careless as a flower
Glassed in a green-house, or a parlour shrub
That spreads its leaves in unmolested peace,
90 While every bush and tree, the country through,
Is shaking to the roots: indifference this
Which may seem strange: but I was unprepared
With needful knowledge, had abruptly passed
Into a theatre, whose stage was filled
95 And busy with an action far advanced.

*   *   *   *

125   A band of military Officers,
Then stationed in the city, were the chief
Of my associates: some of these wore swords
That had been seasoned in the wars, and all
Were men well-born; the chivalry of France.
130 In age and temper differing, they had yet
One spirit ruling in each heart; alike
(Save only one, hereafter to be named)
Were bent upon undoing what was done:
This was their rest and only hope; therewith
135 No fear had they of bad becoming worse,
For worst to them was come; nor would have stirred,
Or deemed it worth a moment's thought to stir,
In any thing, save only as the act
Looked thitherward. One, reckoning by years,
140 Was in the prime of manhood, and erewhile
He had sate lord in many tender hearts;
Though heedless of such honours now, and changed:
His temper was quite mastered by the times,
And they had blighted him, had eat away
145 The beauty of his person, doing wrong
Alike to body and to mind: his port,
Which once had been erect and open, now
Was stooping and contracted, and a face,

Endowed by Nature with her fairest gifts
Of symmetry and light and bloom, expressed,   *150*
As much as any that was ever seen,
A ravage out of season, made by thoughts
Unhealthy and vexatious. With the hour,
That from the press of Paris duly brought
Its freight of public news, the fever came,   *155*
A punctual visitant, to shake this man,
Disarmed his voice and fanned his yellow cheek
Into a thousand colours; while he read,
Or mused, his sword was haunted by his touch
Continually, like an uneasy place   *160*
In his own body. 'Twas in truth an hour
Of universal ferment; mildest men
Were agitated; and commotions, strife
Of passion and opinion, filled the walls
Of peaceful houses with unquiet sounds.   *165*
The soil of common life was, at that time,
Too hot to tread upon. Oft said I then,
And not then only, "What a mockery this
Of history, the past and that to come!
Now do I feel how all men are deceived,   *170*
Reading of nations and their works, in faith,
Faith given to vanity and emptiness;
Oh! laughter for the page that would reflect
To future times the face of what now is!"
The land all swarmed with passion, like a plain   *175*
Devoured by locusts,—Carra, Gorsas,°—add
A hundred other names, forgotten now,
Nor to be heard of more; yet, they were powers,
Like earthquakes, shocks repeated day by day,
And felt through every nook of town and field.   *180*

* * * *

... born in a poor district, and which yet   *215*
Retaineth more of ancient homeliness,
Than any other nook of English ground,
It was my fortune scarcely to have seen,
Through the whole tenor of my school-day time,
The face of one, who, whether boy or man,   *220*

176 **Carra, Gorsas** Girondist sympathizers executed in October, 1793.

Was vested with attention or respect
Through claims of wealth or blood; nor was it least
Of many benefits, in later years
Derived from academic institutes
225 And rules, that they held something up to view
Of a Republic, where all stood thus far
Upon equal ground; that we were brothers all
In honour, as in one community,
Scholars and gentlemen; where, furthermore,
230 Distinction lay open to all that came,
And wealth and titles were in less esteem
Than talents, worth, and prosperous industry.
Add unto this, subservience from the first
To presences of God's mysterious power
235 Made manifest in Nature's sovereignty,
And fellowship with venerable books,
To sanction the proud workings of the soul,
And mountain liberty. It could not be
But that one tutored thus should look with awe
240 Upon the faculties of man, receive
Gladly the highest promises, and hail,
As best, the government of equal rights
And individual worth. And hence, O Friend!
If at the first great outbreak I rejoiced
245 Less than might well befit my youth, the cause
In part lay here, that unto me the events
Seemed nothing out of nature's certain course,
A gift that was come rather late than soon.

* * * *

Among that band of Officers was one,°
Already hinted at, of other mould—
290 A patriot, thence rejected by the rest,
And with an oriental loathing spurned,
As of a different caste. A meeker man
Than this lived never, nor a more benign,
Meek though enthusiastic. Injuries
295 Made *him* more gracious, and his nature then

---

288 **one** Michel Beaupuy (1755-96), an aristocrat and officer in
the regular army who nonetheless supported the new Republic. His
character and discourse profoundly affected Wordsworth's attitudes
toward the Revolution.

Did breathe its sweetness out most sensibly,
As aromatic flowers on Alpine turf,
When foot hath crushed them. He through the events
Of that great change wandered in perfect faith,
As through a book, an old romance, or tale   300
Of Fairy, or some dream of actions wrought
Behind the summer clouds. By birth he ranked
With the most noble, but unto the poor
Among mankind he was in service bound,
As by some tie invisible, oaths professed   305
To a religious order. Man he loved
As man; and, to the mean and the obscure,
And all the homely in their homely works,
Transferred a courtesy which had no air
Of condescension; but did rather seem   310
A passion and a gallantry, like that
Which he, a soldier, in his idler day
Had paid to woman: somewhat vain he was,
Or seemed so, yet it was not vanity,
But fondness, and a kind of radiant joy   315
Diffused around him, while he was intent
On works of love or freedom, or revolved
Complacently° the progress of a cause,
Whereof he was a part: yet this was meek
And placid, and took nothing from the man   320
That was delightful. Oft in solitude
With him did I discourse about the end
Of civil government, and its wisest forms;
Of ancient loyalty, and chartered rights,
Custom and habit, novelty and change;   325
Of self-respect, and virtue in the few
For patrimonial honour set apart,
And ignorance in the labouring multitude.
For he, to all intolerance indisposed,
Balanced these contemplations in his mind;   330
And I, who at that time was scarcely dipped
Into the turmoil, bore a sounder judgment
Than later days allowed; carried about me,
With less alloy to its integrity,
The experience of past ages, as, through help   335

317–18 **revolved Complacently** thought confidently about.

Of books and common life, it makes sure way
To youthful minds, by objects over near
Not pressed upon, nor dazzled or misled
By struggling with the crowd for present ends.

*   *   *   *

Along that very Loire, with festal mirth
Resounding at all hours, and innocent yet
Of civil slaughter, was our frequent walk;
Or in wide forests of continuous shade,
435 Lofty and over-arched, with open space
Beneath the trees, clear footing many a mile—
A solemn region. Oft amid those haunts,
From earnest dialogues I slipped in thought,
And let remembrance steal to other times,
440 When, o'er those interwoven roots, moss-clad,
And smooth as marble or a waveless sea,
Some Hermit, from his cell forth-strayed, might pace
In sylvan meditation undisturbed;
As on the pavement of a Gothic church
445 Walks a lone Monk, when service hath expired,
In peace and silence. But if e'er was heard,—
Heard, though unseen,—a devious traveller,
Retiring or approaching from afar
With speed and echoes loud of trampling hoofs
450 From the hard floor reverberated, then
It was Angelica° thundering through the woods
Upon her palfrey, or that gentle maid
Erminia,° fugitive as fair as she.
Sometimes methought I saw a pair of knights
455 Joust underneath the trees, that as in storm
Rocked high above their heads; anon, the din
Of boisterous merriment, and music's roar,
In sudden proclamation, burst from haunt
Of Satyrs in some viewless glade, with dance
460 Rejoicing o'er a female in the midst,
A mortal beauty, their unhappy thrall.
The width of those huge forests, unto me
A novel scene, did often in this way

451 **Angelica** heroine of Ariosto's *Orlando Furioso*.   453 **Erminia**
heroine of Tasso's *Gerusalemme Liberata*.

Master my fancy while I wandered on
With that revered companion. And sometimes—   465
When to a convent in a meadow green,
By a brook-side, we came, a roofless pile,
And not by reverential touch of Time
Dismantled, but by violence abrupt—
In spite of those heart-bracing colloquies,   470
In spite of real fervour, and of that
Less genuine and wrought up within myself—
I could not but bewail a wrong so harsh,
And for the Matin-bell to sound no more
Grieved, and the twilight taper, and the cross   475
High on the topmost pinnacle, a sign
(How welcome to the weary traveller's eyes!)
Of hospitality and peaceful rest.
And when the partner of those varied walks
Pointed upon occasion to the site   480
Of Romorentin, home of ancient kings,
To the imperial edifice of Blois,
Or to that rural castle, name now slipped
From my remembrance, where a lady lodged,
By the first Francis wooed, and bound to him   485
In chains of mutual passion, from the tower,
As a tradition of the country tells,
Practised to commune with her royal knight
By cressets and love-beacons, intercourse
'Twixt her high-seated residence and his   490
Far off at Chambord on the plain beneath;
Even here, though less than with the peaceful house
Religious, 'mid those frequent monuments
Of Kings, their vices and their better deeds,
Imagination, potent to inflame   495
At times with virtuous wrath and noble scorn,
Did also often mitigate the force
Of civic prejudice, the bigotry,
So call it, of a youthful patriot's mind;
And on these spots with many gleams I looked   500
Of chivalrous delight. Yet not the less,
Hatred of absolute rule, where will of one
Is law for all, and of that barren pride
In them who, by immunities unjust,

505 Between the sovereign and the people stand,
His helper and not theirs, laid stronger hold
Daily upon me, mixed with pity too
And love; for where hope is, there love will be
For the abject multitude. And when we chanced
510 One day to meet a hunger-bitten girl,
Who crept along fitting her languid gait
Unto a heifer's motion, by a cord
Tied to her arm, and picking thus from the lane
Its sustenance, while the girl with pallid hands
515 Was busy knitting in a heartless mood
Of solitude, and at the sight my friend
In agitation said, " 'Tis against *that*
That we are fighting," I with him believed
That a benignant spirit was abroad
520 Which might not be withstood, that poverty
Abject as this would in a little time
Be found no more, that we should see the earth
Unthwarted in her wish to recompense
The meek, the lowly, patient child of toil,
525 All institutes for ever blotted out
That legalised exclusion, empty pomp
Abolished, sensual state and cruel power,
Whether by edict of the one or few;
And finally, as sum and crown of all,
530 Should see the people having a strong hand
In framing their own laws. . . .

* * * *

Book Tenth

Residence in France (Continued)

It was a beautiful and silent day
That overspread the countenance of earth,
Then fading with unusual quietness,—
A day as beautiful as e'er was given
5 To soothe regret, though deepening what it soothed,
When by the gliding Loire I paused, and cast
Upon his rich domains, vineyard and tilth,

Green meadow-ground, and many-coloured woods,
Again, and yet again, a farewell look;
Then from the quiet of that scene passed on,   10
Bound to the fierce Metropolis. From his throne
The King had fallen, and that invading host—
Presumptuous cloud, on whose black front was written
The tender mercies of the dismal wind
That bore it—on the plains of Liberty   15
Had burst innocuous. Say in bolder words,
They—who had come elate as eastern hunters
Banded beneath the Great Mogul,° when he
Erewhile went forth from Agra or Lahore,
Rajahs and Omrahs in his train, intent   20
To drive their prey enclosed within a ring
Wide as a province, but, the signal given,
Before the point of the life-threatening spear
Narrowing itself by moments—they, rash men,
Had seen the anticipated quarry turned   25
Into avengers, from whose wrath they fled
In terror. Disappointment and dismay
Remained for all whose fancies had run wild
With evil expectations; confidence
And perfect triumph for the better cause.   30

  The State, as if to stamp the final seal
On her security, and to the world
Show what she was, a high and fearless soul,
Exulting in defiance, or heart-stung
By sharp resentment, or belike to taunt   35
With spiteful gratitude the baffled League,°
That had stirred up her slackening faculties
To a new transition, when the King was crushed,
Spared not the empty throne, and in proud haste
Assumed the body and venerable name   40
Of a Republic. Lamentable crimes,
'Tis true, had gone before this hour, dire work
Of massacre, in which the senseless sword
Was prayed to as a judge; but these were past,
Earth free from them for ever, as was thought,—   45

18 **Great Mogul** Cf. *Paradise Lost* XI. 391.   36 **the baffled League**
Britain and her allies.

Ephemeral monsters, to be seen but once!
Things that could only show themselves and die.

Cheered with this hope, to Paris I returned,
And ranged, with ardour heretofore unfelt,
50　The spacious city, and in progress passed
The prison where the unhappy Monarch lay,
Associate with his children and his wife
In bondage; and the palace, lately stormed
With roar of cannon by a furious host.
55　I crossed the square (an empty area then!)
Of the Carrousel, where so late had lain
The dead, upon the dying heaped, and gazed
On this and other spots, as doth a man
Upon a volume whose contents he knows
60　Are memorable, but from him locked up,
Being written in a tongue he cannot read,
So that he questions the mute leaves with pain,
And half upbraids their silence. But that night
I felt most deeply in what world I was,
65　What ground I trod on, and what air I breathed.
High was my room and lonely, near the roof
Of a large mansion or hotel, a lodge
That would have pleased me in more quiet times;
Nor was it wholly without pleasure then
70　With unextinguished taper I kept watch,
Reading at intervals; the fear gone by
Pressed on me almost like a fear to come.
I thought of those September massacres,°
Divided from me by one little month,
75　Saw them and touched: the rest was conjured up
From tragic fictions or true history,
Remembrances and dim admonishments.
The horse is taught his manage, and no star
Of wildest course but treads back his own steps;
80　For the spent hurricane the air provides
As fierce a successor; the tide retreats
But to return out of its hiding-place

73 **September massacres** In early September, 1792, mobs of "patri-
ots" butchered more than a thousand prisoners and others suspected
of Royalist sympathies.

In the great deep; all things have second birth;
The earthquake is not satisfied at once;
And in this way I wrought upon myself,   85
Until I seemed to hear a voice that cried,
To the whole city, "Sleep no more."° The trance
Fled with the voice to which it had given birth;
But vainly comments of a calmer mind
Promised soft peace and sweet forgetfulness.   90
The place, all hushed and silent as it was,
Appeared unfit for the repose of night,
Defenceless as a wood where tigers roam.

With early morning towards the Palace-walk
Of Orleans eagerly I turned; as yet   95
The streets were still; not so those long Arcades;
There, 'mid a peal of ill-matched sounds and cries,
That greeted me on entering, I could hear
Shrill voices from the hawkers in the throng,
Bawling, "Denunciation of the Crimes   100
Of Maximilian Robespierre;" the hand,
Prompt as the voice, held forth a printed speech,
The same that had been recently pronounced,
When Robespierre, not ignorant for what mark
Some words of indirect reproof had been   105
Intended, rose in hardihood, and dared
The man who had an ill surmise of him
To bring his charge in openness; whereat,
When a dead pause ensued, and no one stirred,
In silence of all present, from his seat   110
Louvet walked single through the avenue,
And took his station in the Tribune, saying,
"I, Robespierre, accuse thee!" Well is known
The inglorious issue of that charge, and how
He, who had launched the startling thunderbolt,   115
The one bold man,° whose voice the attack had
          sounded,
Was left without a follower to discharge
His perilous duty, and retire lamenting
That Heaven's best aid is wasted upon men

87 **"Sleep no more"** *Macbeth*, **II. ii. 36.   116 the one bold man** Cf.
Paradise Lost V. 901–903.

Who to themselves are false.
120   But these are things
Of which I speak, only as they were storm
Or sunshine to my individual mind,
No further. Let me then relate that now—
In some sort seeing with my proper eyes
125 That Liberty, and Life, and Death would soon
To the remotest corners of the land
Lie in the arbitrement of those who ruled
The capital City; what was struggled for,
And by what combatants victory must be won;
130 The indecision on their part whose aim
Seemed best, and the straightforward path of those
Who in attack or in defence were strong
Through their impiety—my inmost soul
Was agitated; yea, I could almost
135 Have prayed that throughout earth upon all men,
By patient exercise of reason made
Worthy of liberty, all spirits filled
With zeal expanding in Truth's holy light,
The gift of tongues might fall, and power arrive
140 From the four quarters of the winds to do
For France, what without help she could not do,
A work of honour; think not that to this
I added, work of safety: from all doubt
Or trepidation for the end of things
145 Far was I, far as angels are from guilt.

     Yet did I grieve, nor only grieved, but thought
Of opposition and of remedies:
An insignificant stranger and obscure,
And one, moreover, little graced with power
150 Of eloquence even in my native speech,
And all unfit for tumult or intrigue,
Yet would I at this time with willing heart
Have undertaken for a cause so great
Service however dangerous. I revolved,
155 How much the destiny of Man had still
Hung upon single persons; that there was,
Transcendent to all local patrimony,
One nature, as there is one sun in heaven;

That objects, even as they are great, thereby
Do come within the reach of humblest eyes;   *160*
That man is only weak through his mistrust
And want of hope where evidence divine
Proclaims to him that hope should be most sure. . . .

*   *   *   *

         In this frame of mind,
Dragged by a chain of harsh necessity,°
So seemed it,—now I thankfully acknowledge,
Forced by the gracious providence of Heaven,—
To England I returned, else (though assured   *225*
That I both was and must be of small weight,
No better than a landsman on the deck
Of a ship struggling with a hideous storm)
Doubtless, I should have then made common cause
With some who perished; haply perished too,   *230*
A poor mistaken and bewildered offering,—
Should to the breast of Nature have gone back,
With all my resolutions, all my hopes,
A Poet only to myself, to men
Useless, and even, beloved Friend! a soul   *235*
To thee unknown!°
         Twice had the trees let fall
Their leaves, as often Winter had put on
His hoary crown, since I had seen the surge
Beat against Albion's shore, since ear of mine
Had caught the accents of my native speech   *240*
Upon our native country's sacred ground.
A patriot of the world, how could I glide
Into communion with her sylvan shades,
Erewhile my tuneful haunt? It pleased me more
To abide in the great City, where I found   *245*
The general air still busy with the stir
Of that first memorable onset made
By a strong levy of humanity
Upon the traffickers in Negro blood;°

222 **necessity** He had run out of money.   236 **unknown** Wordsworth
met Coleridge in 1795.   247–49 **first . . . blood** The House of Com-
mons, in April, 1792, passed a resolution to end the slave trade, but
the measure was delayed in the House of Lords.

250 Effort which, though defeated, had recalled
To notice old forgotten principles,
And through the nation spread a novel heat
Of virtuous feeling. For myself, I own
That this particular strife had wanted power
255 To rivet my affections; nor did now
Its unsuccessful issue much excite
My sorrow; for I brought with me the faith
That, if France prospered, good men would not long
Pay fruitless worship to humanity,
260 And this most rotten branch of human shame,
Object, so seemed it, of superfluous pains,
Would fall together with its parent tree.
What, then, were my emotions, when in arms
Britain put forth her free-born strength in league,
265 Oh, pity and shame! with those confederate Powers!°
Not in my single self alone I found,
But in the minds of all ingenuous youth,
Change and subversion from that hour. No shock
Given to my moral nature had I known
270 Down to that very moment; neither lapse
Nor turn of sentiment that might be named
A revolution, save at this one time;
All else was progress on the self-same path
On which, with a diversity of pace,
275 I had been travelling: this a stride at once
Into another region. As a light
And pliant harebell, swinging in the breeze
On some grey rock—its birth-place—so had I
Wantoned, fast rooted on the ancient tower
280 Of my belovèd country, wishing not
A happier fortune than to wither there:
Now was I from that pleasant station torn
And tossed about in whirlwind. I rejoiced,
Yea, afterwards—truth most painful to record!—
285 Exulted, in the triumph of my soul,
When Englishmen by thousands were o'erthrown,
Left without glory on the field, or driven,
Brave hearts! to shameful flight. It was a grief,—

263–65 **when . . . Powers** In February, 1793, Britain joined the other powers at war with France.

Grief call it not, 'twas anything but that,—
A conflict of sensations without name,   290
Of which *he* only, who may love the sight
Of a village steeple, as I do, can judge,
When, in the congregation bending all
To their great Father, prayers were offered up,
Or praises for our country's victories;   295
And, 'mid the simple worshippers, perchance
I only, like an uninvited guest
Whom no one owned, sate silent, shall I add,
Fed on the day of vengeance yet to come.

Oh! much have they to account for, who could tear,   300
By violence, at one decisive rent,
From the best youth in England their dear pride,
Their joy, in England; this, too, at a time
In which worst losses easily might wear
The best of names, when patriotic love   305
Did of itself in modesty give way,
Like the Precursor when the Deity
Is come Whose harbinger he was; a time
In which apostasy from ancient faith
Seemed but conversion to a higher creed;   310
Withal a season dangerous and wild,
A time when sage Experience would have snatched
Flowers out of any hedge-row to compose
A chaplet in contempt of his grey locks.

When the proud fleet° that bears the red-cross flag   315
In that unworthy service was prepared
To mingle, I beheld the vessels lie,
A brood of gallant creatures, on the deep;
I saw them in their rest, a sojourner
Through a whole month of calm and glassy days   320
In that delightful island° which protects
Their place of convocation—there I heard,
Each evening, pacing by the still sea-shore,
A monitory sound that never failed,—
The sunset cannon. While the orb went down   325

315 **fleet** of Britain.   321 **island** The Isle of Wight near Portsmouth
Harbor.

In the tranquillity of nature, came
That voice, ill requiem! seldom heard by me
Without a spirit overcast by dark
Imaginations, sense of woes to come,
330 Sorrow for human kind, and pain of heart.

In France, the men, who, for their desperate ends,
Had plucked up mercy by the roots, were glad
Of this new enemy. Tyrants, strong before
In wicked pleas, were strong as demons now;
335 And thus, on every side beset with foes,
The goaded land waxed mad; the crimes of few
Spread into madness of the many; blasts
From hell came sanctified like airs from heaven.
The sternness of the just, the faith of those
340 Who doubted not that Providence had times
Of vengeful retribution, theirs who throned
The human Understanding paramount
And made of that their God, the hopes of men
Who were content to barter short-lived pangs
345 For a paradise of ages, the blind rage
Of insolent tempers, the light vanity
Of intermeddlers, steady purposes
Of the suspicious, slips of the indiscreet,
And all the accidents of life were pressed
350 Into one service, busy with one work.
The Senate stood aghast, her prudence quenched,
Her wisdom stifled, and her justice scared,
Her frenzy only active to extol
Past outrages, and shape the way for new,
355 Which no one dared to oppose or mitigate.

Domestic carnage now filled the whole year
With feast-days; old men from the chimney-nook,
The maiden from the bosom of her love,
The mother from the cradle of her babe,
360 The warrior from the field—all perished, all—
Friends, enemies, of all parties, ages, ranks,
Head after head, and never heads enough
For those that bade them fall. They found their joy,
They made it proudly, eager as a child,

(If like desires of innocent little ones   365
May with such heinous appetites be compared),
Pleased in some open field to exercise
A toy that mimics with revolving wings
The motion of a wind-mill; though the air
Do of itself blow fresh, and make the vanes   370
Spin in his eyesight, *that* contents him not,
But with the plaything at arm's length, he sets
His front against the blast, and runs amain,
That it may whirl the faster.

                   Amid the depth
Of those enormities, even thinking minds   375
Forgot, at seasons, whence they had their being,
Forgot that such a sound was ever heard
As Liberty upon earth: yet all beneath
Her innocent authority was wrought,
Nor could have been, without her blessed name.   380
The illustrious wife of Roland, in the hour
Of her composure, felt that agony,
And gave it vent in her last words.° O Friend!
It was a lamentable time for man,
Whether a hope had e'er been his or not;   385
A woful time for them whose hopes survived
The shock; most woful for those few who still
Were flattered, and had trust in human kind:
They had the deepest feeling of the grief.
Meanwhile the Invaders fared as they deserved: 390
The Herculean Commonwealth had put forth her arms,
And throttled with an infant godhead's might
The snakes about her cradle; that was well,
And as it should be; yet no cure for them
Whose souls were sick with pain of what would be   395
Hereafter brought in charge against mankind.
Most melancholy at that time, O Friend!
Were my day-thoughts,—my nights were miserable;
Through months, through years, long after the last beat
Of those atrocities, the hour of sleep   400
To me came rarely charged with natural gifts,

381–83 **wife . . . words** Madame Roland, a Girondist, before being guillotined on November 8, 1793, cried "O Liberty, what crimes they commit in your name!"

Such ghastly visions had I of despair
And tyranny, and implements of death;
And innocent victims sinking under fear,
405 And momentary hope, and worn-out prayer,
Each in his separate cell, or penned in crowds
For sacrifice, and struggling with forced mirth
And levity in dungeons, where the dust
Was laid with tears. Then suddenly the scene
410 Changed, and the unbroken dream entangled me
In long orations, which I strove to plead
Before unjust tribunals,—with a voice
Labouring, a brain confounded, and a sense,
Death-like, of treacherous desertion, felt
415 In the last place of refuge—my own soul.

When I began in youth's delightful prime
To yield myself to Nature, when that strong
And holy passion overcame me first,
Nor day nor night, evening or morn, was free
420 From its oppression. But, O Power Supreme!
Without Whose call this world would cease to breathe,
Who from the fountain of Thy grace dost fill
The veins that branch through every frame of life,
Making man what he is, creature divine,
425 In single or in social eminence,
Above the rest raised infinite ascents
When reason that enables him to be
Is not sequestered—what a change is here!
How different ritual for this after-worship,
430 What countenance to promote this second love!
The first was service paid to things which lie
Guarded within the bosom of Thy will.
Therefore to serve was high beatitude;
Tumult was therefore gladness, and the fear
435 Ennobling, venerable; sleep secure,
And waking thoughts more rich than happiest dreams.

But as the ancient Prophets, borne aloft
In vision, yet constrained by natural laws
With them to take a troubled human heart,
440 Wanted not consolations, nor a creed

Of reconcilement, then when they denounced,
On towns and cities, wallowing in the abyss
Of their offences, punishment to come;
Or saw, like other men, with bodily eyes,
Before them, in some desolated place,   445
The wrath consummate and the threat fulfilled;
So, with devout humility be it said,
So did a portion of that spirit fall
On me uplifted from the vantage-ground
Of pity and sorrow to a state of being   450
That through the time's exceeding fierceness saw
Glimpses of retribution, terrible,
And in the order of sublime behests:
But, even if that were not, amid the awe
Of unintelligible chastisement,   455
Not only acquiescences of faith
Survived, but daring sympathies with power,
Motions not treacherous or profane, else why
Within the folds of no ungentle breast
Their dread vibration to this hour prolonged?   460
Wild blasts of music thus could find their way
Into the midst of turbulent events;
So that worst tempests might be listened to.

    *   *   *   *

  O Friend! few happier moments have been mine
Than that which told the downfall of this Tribe°
So dreaded, so abhorred. The day deserves
A separate record. Over the smooth sands
Of Leven's ample estuary lay   515
My journey,° and beneath a genial sun,
With distant prospect among gleams of sky
And clouds and intermingling mountain tops,
In one inseparable glory° clad,
Creatures of one ethereal substance met   520
In consistory, like a diadem
Or crown of burning seraphs as they sit

512 **Tribe** of Robespierre, who was guillotined on July 28, 1794.
514–16 **Over . . . journey** He was probably returning to visit a vil-
lage in Lancashire in the summer of 1794. 519 **glory** retains its
connotation of halo (cf. lines 521–22).

In the empyrean. Underneath that pomp
Celestial, lay unseen the pastoral vales
525 Among whose happy fields I had grown up
From childhood. On the fulgent spectacle,
That neither passed away nor changed, I gazed
Enrapt; but brightest things are wont to draw
Sad opposites out of the inner heart,
530 As even their pensive influence drew from mine.
How could it otherwise? for not in vain
That very morning had I turned aside
To seek the ground where, 'mid a throng of graves,
An honoured teacher° of my youth was laid,
535 And on the stone were graven by his desire
Lines from the churchyard elegy of Gray.
This faithful guide, speaking from his death-bed,
Added no farewell to his parting counsel,
But said to me, "My head will soon lie low;"
540 And when I saw the turf that covered him,
After the lapse of full eight years, those words,
With sound of voice and countenance of the Man,
Came back upon me, so that some few tears
Fell from me in my own despite. But now
545 I thought, still traversing that widespread plain,
With tender pleasure of the verses graven
Upon his tombstone, whispering to myself:
He loved the Poets, and, if now alive,
Would have loved me, as one not destitute
550 Of promise, nor belying the kind hope
That he had formed, when I, at his command,
Began to spin, with toil, my earliest songs.

As I advanced, all that I saw or felt
Was gentleness and peace. Upon a small
555 And rocky island near, a fragment stood,
(Itself like a sea rock) the low remains
(With shells encrusted, dark with briny weeds)
Of a dilapidated structure, once
A Romish chapel, where the vested priest
560 Said matins at the hour that suited those

534 teacher Rev. William Taylor (1754–86).

Who crossed the sands with ebb of morning tide.
Not far from that still ruin all the plain
Lay spotted with a variegated crowd
Of vehicles and travellers, horse and foot,
Wading beneath the conduct of their guide   565
In loose procession through the shallow stream
Of inland waters; the great sea meanwhile
Heaved at safe distance, far retired. I paused,
Longing for skill to paint a scene so bright
And cheerful, but the foremost of the band   570
As he approached, no salutation given
In the familiar language of the day,
Cried, "Robespierre is dead!"

*   *   *   *

Book Eleventh

France (concluded)

From that time forth, Authority in France
Put on a milder face; Terror had ceased,
Yet everything was wanting that might give
Courage to them who looked for good by light
Of rational Experience, for the shoots   5
And hopeful blossoms of a second spring:
Yet, in me, confidence was unimpaired;
The Senate's language, and the public acts
And measures of the Government, though both
Weak, and of heartless omen, had not power   10
To daunt me; in the People was my trust:
And, in the virtues, which mine eyes had seen.

*   *   *   *

This intuition led me to confound
One victory with another, higher far,—
Triumphs of unambitious peace at home,   20
And noiseless fortitude. Beholding still
Resistance strong as heretofore, I thought
That what was in degree the same was likewise
The same in quality,—that, as the worse
Of the two spirits then at strife remained   25
Untired, the better, surely, would preserve

The heart that first aroused him. Youth maintains,
In all conditions of society,
Communion more direct and intimate
30 With Nature,—hence, ofttimes, with reason too—
Than age or manhood, even. To Nature, then,
Power had reverted: habit, custom, law,
Had left an interregnum's open space
For *her* to move about in, uncontrolled.
35 Hence could I see how Babel-like their task,
Who, by the recent deluge stupified,
With their whole souls went culling from the day
Its petty promises, to build a tower
For their own safety; laughed with my compeers
40 At gravest heads, by enmity to France
Distempered, till they found, in every blast
Forced from the street-disturbing newsman's horn,
For her great cause record or prophecy,
Of utter ruin. How might we believe
45 That wisdom could, in any shape, come near
Men clinging to delusions so insane?
And thus, experience proving that no few
Of our opinions had been just, we took
Like credit to ourselves where less was due,
50 And thought that other notions were as sound,
Yea, could not but be right, because we saw
That foolish men opposed them.
                              To a strain
More animated I might here give way,
And tell, since juvenile errors are my theme,
55 What in those days, through Britain, was performed
To turn *all* judgments out of their right course;
But this is passion over-near ourselves,
Reality too close and too intense,
And intermixed with something, in my mind,
60 Of scorn and condemnation personal,
That would profane the sanctity of verse.
Our Shepherds, they say merely, at that time
Acted, or seemed at least to act, like men
Thirsting to make the guardian crook of law
65 A tool of murder; they who ruled the State—
Though with such awful proof before their eyes

That he, who would sow death, reaps death, or worse,
And can reap nothing better—child-like longed
To imitate, not wise enough to avoid;
Or left (by mere timidity betrayed)   70
The plain straight road, for one no better chosen
Than if their wish had been to undermine
Justice, and make an end of Liberty.

*   *   *   *

   O pleasant exercise of hope and joy!   105
For mighty were the auxiliars which then stood
Upon our side, we who were strong in love!
Bliss was it in that dawn to be alive,
But to be young was very Heaven! O times,
In which the meagre, stale, forbidding ways   110
Of custom, law, and statute, took at once
The attraction of a country in romance!
When Reason seemed the most to assert her rights
When most intent on making of herself
A prime enchantress—to assist the work,   115
Which then was going forward in her name!
Not favoured spots alone, but the whole Earth,
The beauty wore of promise—that which sets
(As at some moments might not be unfelt
Among the bowers of Paradise itself)   120
The budding rose above the rose full blown.

*   *   *   *

Not in Utopia,—subterranean fields,—   140
Or some secreted island, Heaven knows where!
But in the very world, which is the world
Of all of us,—the place where, in the end,
We find our happiness, or not at all!

   Why should I not confess that Earth was then   145
To me, what an inheritance, new-fallen,
Seems, when the first time visited, to one
Who thither comes to find in it his home?
He walks about and looks upon the spot
With cordial transport, moulds it and remoulds,   150
And is half-pleased with things that are amiss,
'Twill be such joy to see them disappear.

An active partisan, I thus convoked
From every object pleasant circumstance
155 To suit my ends; I moved among mankind
With genial feelings still predominant;
When erring, erring on the better part,
And in the kinder spirit; placable,
Indulgent, as not uninformed that men
160 See as they have been taught, and that Antiquity
Gives rights to error; and aware, no less
That throwing off oppression must be work
As well of License as of Liberty;
And above all—for this was more than all—
165 Not caring if the wind did now and then
Blow keen upon an eminence that gave
Prospect so large into futurity;
In brief, a child of Nature, as at first,
Diffusing only those affections wider
170 That from the cradle had grown up with me,
And losing, in no other way than light
Is lost in light, the weak in the more strong.

In the main outline, such it might be said
Was my condition, till with open war
175 Britain opposed the liberties of France.
This threw me first out of the pale of love;
Soured and corrupted, upwards to the source,
My sentiments; was not, as hitherto,
A swallowing up of lesser things in great,
180 But change of them into their contraries;
And thus a way was opened for mistakes
And false conclusions, in degree as gross,
In kind more dangerous. What had been a pride,
Was now a shame; my likings and my loves
185 Ran in new channels, leaving old ones dry;
And hence a blow that, in maturer age,
Would but have touched the judgment, struck more
     deep
Into sensations near the heart: meantime,
As from the first, wild theories were afloat,
190 To whose pretensions, sedulously urged,
I had but lent a careless ear, assured

That time was ready to set all things right,
And that the multitude, so long oppressed,
Would be oppressed no more.
                              But when events
Brought less encouragement, and unto these   *195*
The immediate proof of principles no more
Could be entrusted, while the events themselves,
Worn out in greatness, stripped of novelty,
Less occupied the mind, and sentiments
Could through my understanding's natural growth   *200*
No longer keep their ground, by faith maintained
Of inward consciousness, and hope that laid
Her hand upon her object—evidence
Safer, of universal application, such
As could not be impeached, was sought elsewhere.   *205*

But now, become oppressors° in their turn,
Frenchmen had changed a war of self-defence
For one of conquest, losing sight of al!
Which they had struggled for now mounted up,
Openly in the eye of earth and heaven,   *210*
The scale of liberty. I read her doom,
With anger vexed, with disappointment sore,
But not dismayed, nor taking to the shame
Of a false prophet. While resentment rose,
Striving to hide, what nought could heal, the wounds *215*
Of mortified presumption, I adhered
More firmly to old tenets, and, to prove
Their temper, strained them more; and thus, in heat
Of contest, did opinions every day
Grow into consequence, till round my mind   *220*
They clung, as if they were its life, nay more,
The very being of the immortal soul.

This was the time, when, all things tending fast
To depravation, speculative schemes—
That promised to abstract the hopes of Man   *225*
Out of his feelings, to be fixed thenceforth
For ever in a purer element—

206 **oppressors** The French had invaded Holland, Spain, Italy, and
Germany.

Found ready welcome. Tempting region *that*
For Zeal to enter and refresh herself,
230   Where passions had the privilege to work,
And never hear the sound of their own names.
But, speaking more in charity, the dream
Flattered the young, pleased with extremes, nor least
With that which makes our Reason's naked self
235   The object of its fervour. What delight!
How glorious! in self-knowledge and self-rule,
To look through all the frailties of the world,
And, with a resolute mastery shaking off
Infirmities of nature, time, and place,
240   Build social upon personal Liberty,
Which, to the blind restraints of general laws
Superior, magisterially adopts
One guide, the light of circumstances, flashed
Upon an independent intellect.
245   Thus expectation rose again; thus hope,
From her first ground expelled, grew proud once more.
Oft, as my thoughts were turned to human kind,
I scorned indifference; but, inflamed with thirst
Of a secure intelligence, and sick
250   Of other longing, I pursued what seemed
A more exalted nature; wished that Man
Should start out of his earthy, worm-like state,
And spread abroad the wings of Liberty,
Lord of himself, in undisturbed delight—
255   A noble aspiration! *yet* I feel
(Sustained by worthier as by wiser thoughts)
The aspiration, nor shall ever cease
To feel it;—but return we to our course.

Enough, 'tis true—could such a plea excuse
260   Those aberrations—had the clamorous friends
Of ancient Institutions said and done
To bring disgrace upon their very names;
Disgrace, of which, custom and written law,
And sundry moral sentiments as props
265   Or emanations of those institutes,
Too justly bore a part. A veil had been
Uplifted; why deceive ourselves? in sooth,

'Twas even so; and sorrow for the man
Who either had not eyes wherewith to see,
Or, seeing, had forgotten! A strong shock   *270*
Was given to old opinions; all men's minds
Had felt its power, and mine was both let loose,
Let loose and goaded. After what hath been
Already said of patriotic love,
Suffice it here to add, that, somewhat stern   *275*
In temperament, withal a happy man,
And therefore bold to look on painful things,
Free likewise of the world, and thence more bold,
I summoned my best skill, and toiled, intent
To anatomise the frame of social life,   *280*
Yea, the whole body of society
Searched to its heart. Share with me, Friend! the wish
That some dramatic tale,° endued with shapes
Livelier, and flinging out less guarded words
Than suit the work we fashion, might set forth   *285*
What then I learned, or think I learned, of truth,
And the errors into which I fell, betrayed
By present objects, and by reasonings false
From their beginnings, inasmuch as drawn
Out of a heart that had been turned aside   *290*
From Nature's way by outward accidents,
And which was thus confounded, more and more
Misguided, and misguiding. So I fared,
Dragging all precepts, judgments, maxims, creeds,
Like culprits to the bar; calling the mind,   *295*
Suspiciously, to establish in plain day
Her titles and her honours; now believing,
Now disbelieving; endlessly perplexed
With impulse, motive, right and wrong, the ground
Of obligation, what the rule and whence   *300*
The sanction; till, demanding formal *proof*,
And seeking it in every thing, I lost
All feeling of conviction, and, in fine,
Sick, wearied out with contrarieties,
Yielded up moral questions in despair.   *305*

283 **some dramatic tale** *The Borderers* (1842), a first version of
which dates from 1796–97.

This was the crisis of that strong disease,
This the soul's last and lowest ebb; I drooped,
Deeming our blessèd reason of least use
Where wanted most: "The lordly attributes
810 Of will and choice," I bitterly exclaimed,
"What are they but a mockery of a Being
Who hath in no concerns of his a test
Of good and evil; knows not what to fear
Or hope for, what to covet or to shun;
815 And who, if those could be discerned, would yet
Be little profited, would see, and ask
Where is the obligation to enforce?
And, to acknowledged law rebellious, still,
As selfish passion urged, would act amiss;
820 The dupe of folly, or the slave of crime."

Depressed, bewildered thus, I did not walk
With scoffers, seeking light and gay revenge
From indiscriminate laughter, nor sate down
In reconcilement with an utter waste
825 Of intellect; such sloth I could not brook,
(Too well I loved, in that my spring of life,
Pains-taking thoughts, and truth, their dear reward)
But turned to abstract science, and there sought
Work for the reasoning faculty enthroned
830 Where the disturbances of space and time—
Whether in matters various properties
Inherent, or from human will and power
Derived—find no admission. Then it was—
Thanks to the bounteous Giver of all good!—
835 That the belovèd Sister° in whose sight
Those days were passed, now speaking in a voice
Of sudden admonition—like a brook
That did but *cross* a lonely road, and now
Is seen, heard, felt, and caught at every turn,
840 Companion never lost through many a league—
Maintained for me a saving intercourse
With my true self; for, though bedimmed and changed
Much, as it seemed, I was no further changed
Than as a clouded and a waning moon:

335 **Sister** Dorothy.

She whispered still that brightness would return, 345
She, in the midst of all, preserved me still
A Poet, made me seek beneath that name,
And that alone, my office upon earth;
And, lastly, as hereafter will be shown,
If willing audience fail not, Nature's self, 350
By all varieties of human love
Assisted, led me back through opening day
To those sweet counsels between head and heart
Whence grew that genuine knowledge, fraught with
     peace,
Which, through the later sinking of this cause, 355
Hath still upheld me, and upholds me now
In the catastrophe (for so they dream,
And nothing less), when, finally to close
And rivet down the gains of France, a Pope
Is summoned in, to crown° an Emperor— 360
This last opprobrium, when we see a people
That once looked up in faith, as if to Heaven
For manna, take a lesson from the dog
Returning to his vomit; when the sun
That rose in splendour, was alive, and moved 365
In exultation with a living pomp
Of clouds—his glory's natural retinue—
Hath dropped all functions by the gods bestowed,
And, turned into a gewgaw, a machine,
Sets like an Opera phantom.

              Thus, O Friend! 370
Through times of honour and through times of shame
Descending, have I faithfully retraced
The perturbations of a youthful mind
Under a long-lived storm of great events—
A story destined for thy ear, who now, 375
Among the fallen of nations, dost abide
Where Etna, over hill and valley, casts
His shadow stretching towards Syracuse,
The city of Timoleon!° Righteous Heaven!
How are the mighty prostrated! They first, 380

360 **crown** Napoleon became Emperor on December 2, 1804. 379
Timoleon who, in 343 B.C., liberated Syracuse from Dionysius the
younger.

They first of all that breathe should have awaked
When the great voice was heard from out the tombs
Of ancient heroes. If I suffered grief
For ill-requited France, by many deemed
385 A trifler only in her proudest day;
Have been distressed to think of what she once
Promised, now is; a far more sober cause
Thine eyes must see of sorrow in a land,
Though with the wreck of loftier years bestrewn
390 To the reanimating influence lost
Of memory, to virtue lost and hope.

But indignation works where hope is not,
And thou, O Friend! wilt be refreshed. There is
One great society alone on earth:
395 The noble Living and the noble Dead.

Thine be such converse strong and sanative,
A ladder for thy spirit to reascend
To health and joy and pure contentedness;
To me the grief confined, that thou art gone
400 From this last spot of earth, where Freedom now
Stands single in her only sanctuary;
A lonely wanderer art gone, by pain
Compelled and sickness, at this latter day,
This sorrowful reverse for all mankind.
405 I feel for thee, must utter what I feel:
The sympathies erewhile in part discharged,
Gather afresh, and will have vent again:
My own delights do scarcely seem to me
My own delights; the lordly Alps themselves,
410 Those rosy peaks, from which the Morning looks
Abroad on many nations, are no more
For me that image of pure gladsomeness
Which they were wont to be. Through kindred scenes,
For purpose, at a time, how different!
415 Thou tak'st thy way, carrying the heart and soul
That Nature gives to Poets, now by thought
Matured, and in the summer of their strength.
Oh! wrap him in your shades, ye giant woods,
On Etna's side; and thou, O flowery field

Of Enna!° is there not some nook of thine,   *420*
From the first play-time of the infant world
Kept sacred to restorative delight,
When from afar invoked by anxious love?

*   *   *   *

Book Twelfth

Imagination and Taste, How Impaired and Restored

Long time have human ignorance and guilt
Detained us, on what spectacles of woe
Compelled to look, and inwardly oppressed
With sorrow, disappointment, vexing thoughts,
Confusion of the judgment, zeal decayed,   *5*
And, lastly, utter loss of hope itself
And things to hope for! Not with these began
Our song, and not with these our song must end.
Ye motions of delight, that haunt the sides
Of the green hills; ye breezes and soft airs,   *10*
Whose subtle intercourse with breathing flowers,
Feelingly watched, might teach Man's haughty race
How without injury to take, to give
Without offence; ye who, as if to show
The wondrous influence of power gently used,   *15*
Bend the complying heads of lordly pines,
And, with a touch, shift the stupendous clouds
Through the whole compass of the sky; ye brooks,
Muttering along the stones, a busy noise
By day, a quiet sound in silent night;   *20*
Ye waves, that out of the great deep steal forth
In a calm hour to kiss the pebbly shore,
Not mute, and then retire, fearing no storm;
And you, ye groves, whose ministry it is
To interpose the covert of your shades,   *25*
Even as a sleep, between the heart of man
And outward troubles, between man himself,

420 **Enna** in pastoral Sicily, "that fair field / Of Enna, where
Proserpin gath'ring flow'rs / Herself a fairer Flow'r by gloomy *Dis*
/ Was gather'd . . ." (*Paradise Lost* IV. 268–71). Coleridge (the
Friend" of line 393) spent August–September 1804 in Sicily.

Not seldom, and his own uneasy heart:
Oh! that I had a music and a voice
30 Harmonious as your own, that I might tell
What ye have done for me. The morning shines,
Nor heedeth Man's perverseness; Spring returns,—
I saw the Spring return, and could rejoice,
In common with the children of her love,
35 Piping on boughs, or sporting on fresh fields,
Or boldly seeking pleasure nearer heaven
On wings that navigate cerulean skies.
So neither were complacency, nor peace,
Nor tender yearnings, wanting for my good
40 Through these distracted times; in Nature still
Glorying, I found a counterpoise in her,
Which, when the spirit of evil reached its height,
Maintained for me a secret happiness.

This narrative, my Friend! hath chiefly told
45 Of intellectual power, fostering love,
Dispensing truth, and, over men and things,
Where reason yet might hesitate, diffusing
Prophetic sympathies of genial faith:
So was I favoured—such my happy lot—
50 Until that natural graciousness of mind
Gave way to overpressure from the times
And their disastrous issues. What availed,
When spells forbade the voyager to land,
That fragrant notice of a pleasant shore
55 Wafted, at intervals, from many a bower
Of blissful gratitude and fearless love?
Dare I avow that wish was mine to see,
And hope that future times *would* surely see,
The man to come, parted, as by a gulph,
60 From him who had been; that I could no more
Trust the elevation which had made me one
With the great family that still survives
To illuminate the abyss of ages past,
Sage, warrior, patriot, hero; for it seemed
65 That their best virtues were not free from taint
Of something false and weak, that could not stand
The open eye of Reason. Then I said,

"Go to the Poets, they will speak to thee
More perfectly of purer creatures;—yet
If reason be nobility in man,   *70*
Can aught be more ignoble than the man
Whom they delight in, blinded as he is
By prejudice, the miserable slave
Of low ambition or distempered love?"

In such strange passion, if I may once more   *75*
Review the past, I warred against myself—
A bigot to a new idolatry—
Like a cowled monk who hath forsworn the world,
Zealously laboured to cut off my heart
From all the sources of her former strength;   *80*
And as, by simple waving of a wand,
The wizard instantaneously dissolves
Palace or grove, even so could I unsoul
As readily by syllogistic words
Those mysteries of being which have made,   *85*
And shall continue evermore to make,
Of the whole human race one brotherhood.

What wonder, then, if, to a mind so far
Perverted, even the visible Universe
Fell under the dominion of a taste   *90*
Less spiritual, with microscopic view
Was scanned, as I had scanned the moral world?

O Soul of Nature! excellent and fair!
That didst rejoice with me, with whom I, too,
Rejoiced through early youth, before the winds   *95*
And roaring waters, and in lights and shades
That marched and countermarched about the hills
In glorious apparition, Powers on whom
I daily waited, now all eye and now
All ear; but never long without the heart   *100*
Employed, and man's unfolding intellect:
O Soul of Nature! that, by laws divine
Sustained and governed, still dost overflow
With an impassioned life, what feeble ones
Walk on this earth! how feeble have I been   *105*

When thou wert in thy strength! Nor this through
    stroke
Of human suffering, such as justifies
Remissness and inaptitude of mind,
But through presumption; even in pleasure pleased
110 Unworthily, disliking here, and there
Liking; by rules of mimic art transferred
To things above all art; but more,—for this,
Although a strong infection of the age,
Was never much my habit—giving way
115 To a comparison of scene with scene,
Bent overmuch on superficial things,
Pampering myself with meagre novelties
Of colour and proportion; to the moods
Of time and season, to the moral power,
120 The affections and the spirit of the place,
Insensible. Nor only did the love
Of sitting thus in judgment interrupt
My deeper feelings, but another cause,
More subtle and less easily explained,
125 That almost seems inherent in the creature,
A twofold frame of body and of mind.
I speak in recollection of a time
When the bodily eye, in every stage of life
The most despotic of our senses, gained
130 Such strength in *me* as often held my mind
In absolute dominion. Gladly here,
Entering upon abstruser argument,
Could I endeavour to unfold the means
Which Nature studiously employs to thwart
135 This tyranny, summons all the senses each
To counteract the other, and themselves,
And makes them all, and the objects with which all
Are conversant, subservient in their turn
To the great ends of Liberty and Power.
140 But leave we this: enough that my delights
(Such as they were) were sought insatiably.
Vivid the transport, vivid though not profound;
I roamed from hill to hill, from rock to rock,
Still craving combinations of new forms,
145 New pleasure, wider empire for the sight,

Proud of her own endowments, and rejoiced
To lay the inner faculties asleep.
Amid the turns and counterturns, the strife
And various trials of our complex being,
As we grow up, such thraldom of that sense   *150*
Seems hard to shun. And yet I knew a maid,°
A young enthusiast, who escaped these bonds;
Her eye was not the mistress of her heart;
Far less did rules prescribed by passive taste,
Or barren intermeddling subtleties,   *155*
Perplex her mind; but, wise as women are
When genial circumstance hath favoured them,
She welcomed what was given, and craved no more;
Whate'er the scene presented to her view,
That was the best, to that she was attuned   *160*
By her benign simplicity of life,
And through a perfect happiness of soul,
Whose variegated feelings were in this
Sisters, that they were each some new delight.
Birds in the bower, and lambs in the green field,   *165*
Could they have known her, would have loved;
        methought
Her very presence such a sweetness breathed,
That flowers, and trees, and even the silent hills,
And everything she looked on, should have had
An intimation how she bore herself   *170*
Towards them and to all creatures. God delights
In such a being; for, her common thoughts
Are piety, her life is gratitude.

Even like this maid, before I was called forth
From the retirement of my native hills,   *175*
I loved whate'er I saw: nor lightly loved,
But most intensely; never dreamt of aught
More grand, more fair, more exquisitely framed
Than those few nooks to which my happy feet
Were limited. I had not at that time   *180*
Lived long enough, nor in the least survived
The first diviner influence of this world,
As it appears to unaccustomed eyes.

151 **maid** Mary Hutchinson, who became his wife.

Worshipping then among the depth of things,
185 As piety ordained, could I submit
To measured admiration, or to aught
That should preclude humility and love?
I felt, observed, and pondered; did not judge,
Yea, never though of judging; with the gift
190 Of all this glory filled and satisfied.
And afterwards, when through the gorgeous Alps
Roaming, I carried with me the same heart:
In truth, the degradation—howsoe'er
Induced, effect, in whatsoe'er degree,
195 Of custom that prepares a partial scale
In which the little oft outweighs the great;
Or any other cause that hath been named;
Or lastly, aggravated by the times
And their impassioned sounds, which well might make
200 The milder minstrelsies of rural scenes
Inaudible—was transient; I had known
Too forcibly, too early in my life,
Visitings of imaginative power
For this to last: I shook the habit off
205 Entirely and for ever, and again
In Nature's presence stood, as now I stand,
A sensitive being, a *creative* soul.

There are in our existence spots of time,°
That with distinct pre-eminence retain
210 A renovating virtue, whence, depressed
By false opinion and contentious thought,
Or aught of heavier or more deadly weight,
In trivial occupations, and the round
Of ordinary intercourse, our minds
215 Are nourished and invisibly repaired;
A virtue, by which pleasure is enhanced,
That penetrates, enables us to mount,
When high, more high, and lifts us up when fallen.
This efficacious spirit chiefly lurks
220 Among those passages of life that give

208 **spots of time** childhood memories that have survived and renew
("renovate") the poet. An early manuscript calls them "islands in
the unnavigable depth / Of our departed time."

Profoundest knowledge to what point, and how,
The mind is lord and master—outward sense
The obedient servant of her will. Such moments
Are scattered everywhere, taking their date
From our first childhood. I remember well,   225
That once, while yet my inexperienced hand
Could scarcely hold a bridle, with proud hopes
I mounted, and we journeyed towards the hills:
An ancient servant of my father's house
Was with me, my encourager and guide: 230
We had not travelled long, ere some mischance
Disjoined me from my comrade; and, through fear
Dismounting, down the rough and stony moor
I led my horse, and, stumbling on, at length
Came to a bottom, where in former times   235
A murderer had been hung in iron chains.
The gibbet-mast had mouldered down, the bones
And iron case were gone; but on the turf,
Hard by, soon after that fell deed was wrought,
Some unknown hand had carved the murderer's name.   240
The monumental letters were inscribed
In times long past; but still, from year to year
By superstition of the neighbourhood,
The grass is cleared away, and to this hour
The characters are fresh and visible: 245
A casual glance had shown them, and I fled,
Faltering and faint, and ignorant of the road:
Then, reascending the bare common, saw
A naked pool that lay beneath the hills,
The beacon on the summit, and, more near,   250
A girl, who bore a pitcher on her head,
And seemed with difficult steps to force her way
Against the blowing wind. It was, in truth,
An ordinary sight; but I should need
Colours and words that are unknown to man,   255
To paint the visionary dreariness
Which, while I looked all round for my lost guide,
Invested moorland waste and naked pool,
The beacon crowning the lone eminence,
The female and her garments vexed and tossed   260
By the strong wind. When, in the blessèd hours

Of early love, the loved one at my side,
I roamed, in daily presence of this scene,
Upon the naked pool and dreary crags,
265 And on the melancholy beacon fell
A spirit of pleasure and youth's golden gleam;
And think ye not with radiance more sublime
For these remembrances, and for the power
They had left behind? So feeling comes in aid
270 Of feeling, and diversity of strength
Attends us, if but once we have been strong.
Oh! mystery of man, from what a depth
Proceed thy honours. I am lost, but see
In simple childhood something of the base
275 On which thy greatness stands; but this I feel,
That from thyself it comes, that thou must give,
Else never canst receive. The days gone by
Return upon me almost from the dawn
Of life: the hiding-places of man's power
280 Open; I would approach them, but they close.
I see by glimpses now; when age comes on,
May scarcely see at all; and I would give,
While yet we may, as far as words can give,
Substance and life to what I feel, enshrining,
285 Such is my hope, the spirit of the Past
For future restoration.——Yet another
Of these memorials:——
　　　　　　　　　　One Christmas-time,
On the glad eve of its dear holidays,
Feverish, and tired, and restless, I went forth
290 Into the fields, impatient for the sight
Of those led palfreys that should bear us home;
My brothers and myself. There rose a crag,
That, from the meeting-point of two highways
Ascending, overlooked them both, far stretched;
295 Thither, uncertain on which road to fix
My expectation, thither I repaired,
Scout-like, and gained the summit; 'twas a day
Tempestuous, dark, and wild, and on the grass
I sate half-sheltered by a naked wall;
300 Upon my right hand couched a single sheep,
Upon my left a blasted hawthorn stood;

With those companions at my side, I watched,
Straining my eyes intensely, as the mist
Gave intermitting prospect of the copse
And plain beneath. Ere we to school returned,— 305
That dreary time,—ere we had been ten days
Sojourners in my father's house, he died;
And I and my three brothers, orphans then,
Followed his body to the grave. The event,
With all the sorrow that it brought, appeared 310
A chastisement; and when I called to mind
That day so lately past, when from the crag
I looked in such anxiety of hope;
With trite reflections of morality,
Yet in the deepest passion, I bowed low 315
To God, Who thus corrected my desires;
And, afterwards, the wind and sleety rain,
And all the business of the elements,
The single sheep, and the one blasted tree,
And the bleak music from that old stone wall, 320
The noise of wood and water, and the mist
That on the line of each of those two roads
Advanced in such indisputable shapes;
All these were kindred spectacles and sounds
To which I oft repaired, and thence would drink, 325
As at a fountain; and on winter nights,
Down to this very time, when storm and rain
Beat on my roof, or, haply, at noon-day,
While in a grove I walk, whose lofty trees,
Laden with summer's thickest foliage, rock 330
In a strong wind, some working of the spirit,
Some inward agitations thence are brought,
Whate'er their office, whether to beguile
Thoughts over busy in the course they took,
Or animate an hour of vacant ease. 335

Book Thirteenth

Imagination and Taste, How Impaired and Restored
(Concluded)

From Nature doth emotion come, and moods
Of calmness equally are Nature's gift:

This is her glory; these two attributes
Are sister horns that constitute her strength.
5 Hence Genius, born to thrive by interchange
Of peace and excitation, finds in her
His best and purest friend; from her receives
That energy by which he seeks the truth,
From her that happy stillness of the mind
10 Which fits him to receive it when unsought.

*   *   *   *

Here, calling up to mind what then I saw,
A youthful traveller, and see daily now
In the familiar circuit of my home,
Here might I pause, and bend in reverence
225 To Nature, and the power of human minds,
To men as they are men within themselves.
How oft high service is performed within,
When all the external man is rude in show,—
Not like a temple rich with pomp and gold,
230 But a mere mountain chapel, that protects
Its simple worshippers from sun and shower.
Of these, said I, shall be my song; of these,
If future years mature me for the task,
Will I record the praises, making verse
235 Deal boldly with substantial things; in truth
And sanctity of passion, speak of these,
That justice may be done, obeisance paid
Where it is due: thus haply shall I teach,
Inspire, through unadulterated ears
240 Pour rapture, tenderness, and hope,—my theme
No other than the very heart of man,
As found among the best of those who live,
Not unexalted by religious faith,
Nor uninformed by books, good books, though few,
245 In Nature's presence. . . .

*   *   *   *

Also, about this time did I receive
280 Convictions still more strong than heretofore,
Not only that the inner frame is good,
And graciously composed, but that, no less,

Nature for all conditions wants not power
To consecrate, if we have eyes to see,
The outside of her creatures, and to breathe   *285*
Grandeur upon the very humblest face
Of human life. I felt that the array
Of act and circumstance, and visible form,
Is mainly to the pleasure of the mind
What passion makes them; that meanwhile the forms   *290*
Of Nature have a passion in themselves,
That intermingles with those works of man
To which she summons him; although the works
Be mean, have nothing lofty of their own;
And that the Genius of the Poet hence   *295*
May boldly take his way among mankind
Wherever Nature leads; that he hath stood
By Nature's side among the men of old,
And so shall stand for ever. Dearest Friend!
If thou partake the animating faith   *300*
That Poets, even as Prophets, each with each
Connected in a mighty scheme of truth,
Have each his own peculiar faculty,
Heaven's gift, a sense that fits him to perceive
Objects unseen before, thou wilt not blame   *305*
The humblest of this band who dares to hope
That unto him hath also been vouchsafed
An insight that in some sort he possesses,
A privilege whereby a work of his,
Proceeding from a source of untaught things,   *310*
Creative and enduring, may become
A power like one of Nature's. To a hope
Not less ambitious once among the wilds
Of Sarum's Plain,° my youthful spirit was raised;
There, as I ranged at will the pastoral downs   *315*
Trackless and smooth, or paced the bare white roads
Lengthening in solitude their dreary line,
Time with his retinue of ages fled
Backwards, nor checked his flight until I saw
Our dim ancestral Past in vision clear;   *320*
Saw multitudes of men, and, here and there,
A single Briton clothed in wolf-skin vest,

314 **Sarum's Plain** Salisbury Plain.

With shield and stone-axe, stride across the wold;°
The voice of spears was heard, the rattling spear
325 Shaken by arms of mighty bone, in strength,
Long mouldered, of barbaric majesty.
I called on Darkness—but before the word
Was uttered, midnight darkness seemed to take
All objects from my sight; and lo! again
330 The Desert visible by dismal flames;
It is the sacrificial altar, fed
With living men—how deep the groans! the voice
Of those that crowd the giant wicker thrills
The monumental hillocks, and the pomp
335 Is for both worlds, the living and the dead.
At other moments (for through that wide waste
Three summer days I roamed) where'er the Plain
Was figured o'er with circles, lines, or mounds,
That yet survive, a work, as some divine,
340 Shaped by the Druids,° so to represent
Their knowledge of the heavens, and image forth
The constellations; gently was I charmed
Into a waking dream, a reverie
That, with believing eyes, where'er I turned,
345 Beheld long-bearded teachers, with white wands
Uplifted, pointing to the starry sky,
Alternately, and plain below, while breath
Of music swayed their motions, and the waste
Rejoiced with them and me in those sweet sounds.

350   This for the past, and things that may be viewed
Or fancied in the obscurity of years
From monumental hints: and thou, O Friend!
Pleased with some unpremeditated strains
That served those wanderings to beguile, hast said
355 That then and there my mind had exercised
Upon the vulgar forms of present things,
The actual world of our familiar days,
Yet higher power; had caught from them a tone,
An image, and a character, by books
360 Not hitherto reflected. Call we this

323 **wold** hilly tract.   340 **Druids** believed to have been the builders
of Stonehenge.

A partial judgment—and yet why? for *then*
We were as strangers; and I may not speak
Thus wrongfully of verse, however rude,
Which on thy young imagination, trained
In the great City, broke like light from far.   365
Moreover, each man's Mind is to herself
Witness and judge; and I remember well
That in life's every-day appearances
I seemed about this time to gain clear sight
Of a new world—a world, too, that was fit   370
To be transmitted, and to other eyes
Made visible; as ruled by those fixed laws
Whence spiritual dignity originates,
Which do both give it being and maintain
A balance, an ennobling interchange   375
Of action from without and from within;
The excellence, pure function, and best power
Both of the object seen, and eye that sees.

Book Fourteenth

Conclusion

In one of those excursions (may they ne'er
Fade from remembrance!) through the Northern tracts
Of Cambria° ranging with a youthful friend,
I left Bethgelert's huts at couching-time,
And westward took my way, to see the sun   5
Rise from the top of Snowdon. To the door
Of a rude cottage at the mountain's base
We came, and roused the shepherd who attends
The adventurous stranger's steps, a trusty guide;
Then, cheered by short refreshment, sallied forth.   10

    It was a close, warm, breezeless summer night,
Wan, dull, and glaring, with a dripping fog
Low-hung and thick that covered all the sky;
But, undiscouraged, we began to climb
The mountain-side. The mist soon girt us round,   15
And, after ordinary travellers' talk

3 **Cambria** Wales.

With our conductor, pensively we sank
Each into commerce with his private thoughts:
Thus did we breast the ascent, and by myself
20 Was nothing either seen or heard that checked
Those musings or diverted, save that once
The shepherd's lurcher, who, among the crags,
Had to his joy unearthed a hedgehog, teased
His coiled-up prey with barkings turbulent.
25 This small adventure, for even such it seemed
In that wild place and at the dead of night,
Being over and forgotten, on we wound
In silence as before. With forehead bent
Earthward, as if in opposition set
30 Against an enemy, I panted up
With eager pace, and no less eager thoughts.
Thus might we wear a midnight hour away,
Ascending at loose distance each from each,
And I, as chanced, the foremost of the band;
35 When at my feet the ground appeared to brighten,
And with a step or two seemed brighter still;
Nor was time given to ask or learn the cause,
For instantly a light upon the turf
Fell like a flash, and lo! as I looked up
40 The Moon hung naked in a firmament
Of azure without cloud, and at my feet
Rested a silent sea of hoary mist.
A hundred hills their dusky backs upheaved
All over this still ocean; and beyond,
45 Far, far beyond, the solid vapours stretched,
In headlands, tongues, and promontory shapes,
Into the main Atlantic, that appeared
To dwindle, and give up his majesty,
Usurped upon far as the sight could reach.
50 Not so the ethereal vault; encroachment none
Was there, nor loss; only the inferior stars
Had disappeared, or shed a fainter light
In the clear presence of the full-orbed Moon,
Who, from her sovereign elevation, gazed
55 Upon the billowy ocean, as it lay
All meek and silent, save that through a rift—
Not distant from the shore whereon we stood,

A fixed, abysmal, gloomy, breathing-place—
Mounted the roar of waters, torrents, streams
Innumerable, roaring with one voice!   *60*
Heard over earth and sea, and, in that hour,
For so it seemed, felt by the starry heavens.

When into air had partially dissolved
That vision, given to spirits of the night
And three chance human wanderers, in calm thought   *65*
Reflected, it appeared to me the type
Of a majestic intellect, its acts
And its possessions, what it has and craves,
What in itself it is, and would become.
There I beheld the emblem of a mind   *70*
That feeds upon infinity, that broods
Over the dark abyss,° intent to hear
Its voices issuing forth to silent light
In one continuous stream; a mind sustained
By recognitions of transcendent power,   *75*
In sense conducting to ideal form,
In soul of more than mortal privilege.
One function, above all, of such a mind
Had Nature shadowed there, by putting forth,
'Mid circumstances awful and sublime,   *80*
That mutual domination° which she loves
To exert upon the face of outward things,
So moulded, joined, abstracted, so endowed
With interchangeable supremacy,
That men, least sensitive, see, hear, perceive,   *85*
And cannot choose but feel. The power, which all
Acknowledge when thus moved, which Nature thus
To bodily sense exhibits, is the express
Resemblance of that glorious faculty°
That higher minds bear with them as their own.   *90*
This is the very spirit in which they deal
With the whole compass of the universe:
They from their native selves can send abroad

70–72 **a mind . . . abyss** Cf. *Paradise Lost* I. 21.   81 **mutual domi-
nation** In the visionary landscape just described, the mutually domi-
nating images are the naked moon and roaring waters.   89 **faculty**
Imagination.

Kindred mutations; for themselves create
95 A like existence; and, whene'er it dawns
Created for them, catch it, or are caught
By its inevitable mastery,
Like angels stopped upon the wing by sound
Of harmony from Heaven's remotest spheres.
100 Them the enduring and the transient both
Serve to exalt; they build up greatest things
From least suggestions; ever on the watch,
Willing to work and to be wrought upon,
They need not extraordinary calls
105 To rouse them; in a world of life they live,
By sensible impressions not enthralled,
But by their quickening impulse made more prompt
To hold fit converse with the spiritual world,
And with the generations of mankind
110 Spread over time, past, present, and to come,
Age after age, till Time shall be no more.
Such minds are truly from the Deity,
For they are Powers; and hence the highest bliss
That flesh can know is theirs—the consciousness
115 Of Whom they are, habitually infused
Through every image and through every thought,
And all affections by communion raised
From earth to heaven, from human to divine;
Hence endless occupation for the Soul,
120 Whether discursive or intuitive;
Hence cheerfulness for acts of daily life,
Emotions which best foresight need not fear,
Most worthy then of trust when most intense.
Hence, amid ills that vex and wrongs that crush
125 Our hearts—if here the words of Holy Writ
May with fit reverence be applied—that peace
Which passeth understanding,° that repose
In moral judgments which from this pure source
Must come, or will by man be sought in vain.

130   Oh! who is he that hath his whole life long
Preserved, enlarged, this freedom in himself?
For this alone is genuine liberty:

126–27 **peace . . . understanding** Philippians 4:7.

Where is the favoured being who hath held
That course unchecked, unerring, and untired,
In one perpetual progress smooth and bright?—   *135*
A humbler destiny have we retraced,
And told of lapse and hesitating choice,
And backward wanderings along thorny ways:
Yet—compassed round by mountain solitudes,
Within whose solemn temple I received   *140*
My earliest visitations, careless then
Of what was given me; and which now I range,
A meditative, oft a suffering, man—
Do I declare—in accents which, from truth
Deriving cheerful confidence, shall blend   *145*
Their modulation with these vocal streams—
That, whatsoever falls my better mind,
Revolving with the accidents of life,
May have sustained, that, howsoe'er misled,
Never did I, in quest of right and wrong,   *150*
Tamper with conscience from a private aim;
Nor was in any public hope the dupe
Of selfish passions; nor did ever yield
Wilfully to mean cares or low pursuits,
But shrunk with apprehensive jealousy   *155*
From every combination which might aid
The tendency, too potent in itself,
Of use and custom to bow down the soul
Under a growing weight of vulgar sense,
And substitute a universe of death   *160*
For that which moves with light and life informed,
Actual, divine, and true. To fear and love,
To love as prime and chief, for there fear ends,
Be this ascribed; to early intercourse,
In presence of sublime or beautiful forms,   *165*
With the adverse principles of pain and joy—
Evil as one is rashly named by men
Who know not what they speak. By love subsists
All lasting grandeur, by pervading love;
That gone, we are as dust.—Behold the fields   *170*
In balmy spring-time full of rising flowers
And joyous creatures; see that pair, the lamb
And the lamb's mother, and their tender ways

Shall touch thee to the heart; thou callest this love,
175 And not inaptly so, for love it is,
Far as it carries thee. In some green bower
Rest, and be not alone, but have thou there
The One who is thy choice of all the world:
There linger, listening, gazing, with delight
180 Impassioned, but delight how pitiable!
Unless this love by a still higher love
Be hallowed, love that breathes not without awe;
Love that adores, but on the knees of prayer,
By heaven inspired; that frees from chains the soul,
185 Lifted, in union with the purest best,
Of earth-born passions, on the wings of praise
A mutual tribute to the Almighty's Throne.

This spiritual Love acts not nor can exist
Without Imagination, which, in truth,
190 Is but another name for absolute power
And clearest insight, amplitude of mind,
And Reason in her most exalted mood.
This faculty hath been the feeding source
Of our long labour: we have traced the stream
195 From the blind cavern whence is faintly heard
Its natal murmur; followed it to light
And open day; accompanied its course
Among the ways of Nature, for a time
Lost sight of it bewildered and engulphed:
200 Then given it greeting as it rose once more
In strength, reflecting from its placid breast
The works of man and face of human life;
And lastly, from its progress have we drawn
Faith in life endless, the sustaining thought
205 Of human Being, Eternity, and God.

Imagination having been our theme,
So also hath that intellectual Love,
For they are each in each, and cannot stand
Dividually.—Here must thou be, O Man!
210 Power to thyself; no Helper hast thou here;
Here keepest thou in singleness thy state:
No other can divide with thee this work:

No secondary hand can intervene
To fashion this ability; 'tis thine,
The prime and vital principle is thine   215
In the recesses of thy nature, far
From any reach of outward fellowship,
Else is not thine at all. But joy to him,
Oh, joy to him who here hath sown, hath laid
Here, the foundation of his future years!   220
For all that friendship, all that love can do,
All that a darling countenance can look
Or dear voice utter, to complete the man,
Perfect him, made imperfect in himself,
All shall be his: and he whose soul hath risen   225
Up to the height of feeling intellect
Shall want no humbler tenderness; his heart
Be tender as a nursing mother's heart;
Of female softness shall his life be full,
Of humble cares and delicate desires,   230
Mild interests and gentlest sympathies.

Child of my parents! Sister of my soul!
Thanks in sincerest verse have been elsewhere
Poured out for all the early tenderness
Which I from thee imbibed: and 'tis most true   235
That later seasons owed to thee no less;
For, spite of thy sweet influence and the touch
Of kindred hands that opened out the springs
Of genial thought in childhood, and in spite
Of all that unassisted I had marked   240
In life or nature of those charms minute
That win their way into the heart by stealth,
Still to the very going-out of youth
I too exclusively esteemed *that* love,
And sought *that* beauty, which, as Milton sings,°   245
Hath terror in it. Thou didst soften down
This over-sternness; but for thee, dear Friend!
My soul, too reckless of mild grace, had stood
In her original self too confident,
Retained too long a countenance severe;   250

245 Milton sings in *Paradise Lost* IX. 489-91.

A rock with torrents roaring, with the clouds
Familiar, and a favourite of the stars:
But thou didst plant its crevices with flowers,
Hang it with shrubs that twinkle in the breeze,
255 And teach the little birds to build their nests
And warble in its chambers. At a time
When Nature, destined to remain so long
Foremost in my affections, had fallen back
Into a second place, pleased to become
260 A handmaid to a nobler than herself,
When every day brought with it some new sense
Of exquisite regard for common things,
And all the earth was budding with these gifts
Of more refined humanity, thy breath,
265 Dear Sister! was a kind of gentler spring
That went before my steps. Thereafter came
One° whom with thee friendship had early paired;
She came, no more a phantom to adorn
A moment, but an inmate of the heart,
270 And yet a spirit, there for me enshrined
To penetrate the lofty and the low;
Even as one essence of pervading light
Shines, in the brightest of ten thousand stars,
And the meek worm that feeds her lonely lamp
Couched in the dewy grass.
275   With such a theme,
Coleridge! with this my argument, of thee
Shall I be silent? O capacious Soul!
Placed on this earth to love and understand,
And from thy presence shed the light of love,
280 Shall I be mute, ere thou be spoken of?
Thy kindred influence to my heart of hearts
Did also find its way. Thus fear relaxed
Her overweening grasp; thus thoughts and things
In the self-haunting spirit learned to take
285 More rational proportions; mystery,
The incumbent mystery of sense and soul,
Of life and death, time and eternity,
Admitted more habitually a mild

267 **One** his wife.

Interposition—a serene delight
In closelier gathering cares, such as become   290
A human creature, howsoe'er endowed,
Poet, or destined for a humbler name;
And so the deep enthusiastic joy,
The rapture of the hallelujah sent
From all that breathes and is, was chastened, stemmed   295
And balanced by pathetic° truth, by trust
In hopeful reason, leaning on the stay
Of Providence; and in reverence for duty,
Here, if need be, struggling with storms, and there
Strewing in peace life's humblest ground with herbs,   300
At every season green, sweet at all hours.

    And now, O Friend! this history is brought
To its appointed close: the discipline
And consummation of a Poet's mind,
In everything that stood most prominent,   305
Have faithfully been pictured; we have reached
The time (our guiding object from the first)
When we may, not presumptuously, I hope,
Suppose my powers so far confirmed, and such
My knowledge, as to make me capable   310
Of building up a Work° that shall endure.
Yet much hath been omitted, as need was;
Of books how much! and even of the other wealth
That is collected among woods and fields,
Far more: for Nature's secondary grace   315
Hath hitherto been barely touched upon,
The charm more superficial that attends
Her works, as they present to Fancy's choice
Apt illustrations of the moral world,
Caught at a glance, or traced with curious pains.   320

    Finally, and above all, O Friend! (I speak
With due regret) how much is overlooked
In human nature and her subtle ways,
As studied first in our own hearts, and then
In life among the passions of mankind,   325

---

296 **pathetic** sympathetic.   311 **Work** *The Recluse.*

Varying their composition and their hue,
Where'er we move, under the diverse shapes
That individual character presents
To an attentive eye. For progress meet,
330 Along this intricate and difficult path,
Whate'er was wanting, something had I gained,
As one of many schoolfellows compelled,
In hardy independence, to stand up
Amid conflicting interests, and the shock
335 Of various tempers; to endure and note
What was not understood, though known to be;
Among the mysteries of love and hate,
Honour and shame, looking to right and left,
Unchecked by innocence too delicate,
340 And moral notions too intolerant,
Sympathies too contracted. Hence, when called
To take a station among men, the step
Was easier, the transition more secure,
More profitable also; for, the mind
345 Learns from such timely exercise to keep
In wholesome separation the two natures,
The one that feels, the other that observes.

    Yet one word more of personal concern—
Since I withdrew unwillingly from France,
350 I led an undomestic wanderer's life,
In London chiefly harboured, whence I roamed,
Tarrying at will in many a pleasant spot
Of rural England's cultivated vales
Or Cambrian solitudes. A youth—(he bore
355 The name of Calvert°—it shall live, if words
Of mine can give it life,) in firm belief
That by endowments not from me withheld
Good might be furthered—in his last decay
By a bequest sufficient for my needs
360 Enabled me to pause for choice, and walk
At large and unrestrained, nor damped too soon
By mortal cares. Himself no Poet, yet

355 **Calvert** a friend who bequeathed to Wordsworth money to pursue his career as poet.

Far less a common follower of the world,
He deemed that my pursuits and labours lay
Apart from all that leads to wealth, or even 365
A necessary maintenance insures,
Without some hazard to the finer sense;
He cleared a passage for me, and the stream
Flowed in the bent of Nature.

       Having now
Told what best merits mention, further pains 370
Our present purpose seems not to require,
And I have other tasks. Recall to mind
The mood in which this labour was begun,
O Friend! The termination of my course
Is nearer now, much nearer; yet even then, 375
In that distraction and intense desire,
I said unto the life which I had lived,
Where art thou? Hear I not a voice from thee
Which 'tis reproach to hear? Anon I rose
As if on wings, and saw beneath me stretched 380
Vast prospect of the world which I had been
And was; and hence this Song, which like a lark
I have protracted, in the unwearied heavens
Singing, and often with more plaintive voice
To earth attempered and her deep-drawn sighs, 385
Yet centring all in love, and in the end
All gratulant, if rightly understood.

 Whether to me shall be allotted life,
And, with life, power to accomplish aught of worth,
That will be deemed no insufficient plea 390
For having given the story of myself,
Is all uncertain: but, belovèd Friend!
When, looking back, thou seest, in clearer view
Than any liveliest sight of yesterday,
That summer,° under whose indulgent skies, 395
Upon smooth Quantock's airy ridge we roved
Unchecked, or loitered 'mid her sylvan combs,
Thou in bewitching words, with happy heart,

395 **That summer** of 1797.

Didst chaunt the vision of that Ancient Man,
400 The bright-eyed Mariner, and rueful woes
Didst utter of the Lady Christabel;
And I, associate with such labour, steeped
In soft forgetfulness the livelong hours,
Murmuring of him° who, joyous hap, was found,
405 After the perils of his moonlight ride,
Near the loud waterfall; or who sate
In misery near the miserable Thorn;°
When thou dost to that summer turn thy thoughts,
And hast before thee all which then we were,
410 To thee, in memory of that happiness,
It will be known, by thee at least, my Friend!
Felt, that the history of a Poet's mind
Is labour not unworthy of regard:
To thee the work shall justify itself.

415   The last and later portions of this gift
Have been prepared, not with the buoyant spirits
That were our daily portion when we first
Together wantoned in wild Poesy,
But, under pressure of a private grief,°
420 Keen and enduring, which the mind and heart,
That in this meditative history
Have been laid open, needs must make me feel
More deeply, yet enable me to bear
More firmly; and a comfort now hath risen
425 From hope that thou art near, and wilt be soon
Restored to us in renovated health;
When, after the first mingling of our tears,
'Mong other consolations, we may draw
Some pleasure from this offering of my love.

430   Oh! yet a few short years of useful life,
And all will be complete, thy race be run,

---

404 **him** Johnny in Wordsworth's poem "The Idiot Boy."   399–407
Ancient Man . . . Thorn alluding to the most characteristic poems
written by Wordsworth and Coleridge in the long poetical summer
of 1797–98 and published in *Lyrical Ballads.*   419 **grief** the death
of Wordsworth's brother John in February, 1805.

Thy monument of glory will be raised;
Then, though (too weak to tread the ways of truth)
This age fall back to old idolatry,
Though men return to servitude as fast   *435*
As the tide ebbs, to ignominy and shame
By nations sink together, we shall still
Find solace—knowing what we have learnt to know,
Rich in true happiness if allowed to be
Faithful alike in forwarding a day   *440*
Of firmer trust, joint labourers in the work
(Should Providence such grace to us vouchsafe)
Of their deliverance, surely yet to come.
Prophets of Nature, we to them will speak
A lasting inspiration, sanctified   *445*
By reason, blest by faith: what we have loved,
Others will love, and we will teach them how;
Instruct them how the mind of man becomes
A thousand times more beautiful than the earth
On which he dwells, above this frame of things   *450*
(Which, 'mid all revolution in the hopes
And fears of men, doth still remain unchanged)
In beauty exalted, as it is itself
Of quality and fabric more divine.

NATURE'S MINISTRY°

It was a day
Upon the edge of Autumn, fierce with storm
The wind blew through the hills of Coniston
Compressed as in a tunnel, from the lake
Bodies of foam took flight, and the whole vale   *5*

0 **Nature's Ministry** In a manuscript of *The Prelude*, from 1804, these lines follow the famous passage concerning Mount Snowdon in Book XIV and further trace the "analogy betwixt / The mind of man and nature." The text is established from the *Oxford Prelude*, pp. 623–26, and the original manuscript.

Was wrought into commotion high and low
A mist flying up and down and bewildered showers
Ten thousand thousand waves mountains and crags,
And darkness, and the sun's tumultuous light
10 Green leaves were rent in handfuls from the trees
    [All distant things seemed silent]
The mountains all seemed silent, din so near
    [Blocked up the listener]
Pealed in the traveller's ear the clouds
The horse and rider staggered in the blast
And he who looked upon the stormy lake
15 Had fear for boat or vessel where none was
Meanwhile by what strange chance I cannot tell
What combination of the wind, and clouds
A large unmutilated rainbow stood
Immoveable in heav'n kept standing there
20 With a colossal stride bridging the vale
The substance thin as dreams lovelier than day.
Amid the deafening uproar stood unmoved
                [A [?] time untold]
Sustained itself through many minutes space
As if it were pinned down by adamant.
25   One Evening, walking in the public way,
A Peasant of the valley where I dwelt
Being my chance Companion, he stopped short
And pointed to an object full in view
At a small distance. 'Twas a horse, that stood
30 Alone upon a little breast of ground
With a clear silver moonlight sky behind.
With one leg from the ground the Creature stood
Insensible and still, breath motion gone
Hairs colour all but shape and substance gone,
35 Mane ears and tail as lifeless as the trunk
That had no stir of breath, we paused awhile
In pleasure of the sight and left him there
With all his functions silently sealed up
Like an amphibious work of Nature's hand
40 A Borderer dwelling betwixt life and death
A Living Statue or a Statued Life.
   To these appearances which Nature thrusts,

Upon our notice, her own naked work
Self-wrought unaided by the human mind,
Add others more imperious, those I mean   *45*
Which on the sight forces the man
To give new grandeur to her ministry
Man suffering or enjoying: meanest minds
Want not these monuments though overlooked
Or little prized, and books are full of them   *50*
Such power to pass at once from daily life
And our inevitable sympathy
With passions mingled up before our eyes,
Such presence is acknowledged when we trace
The history of Columbus think of him   *55*
And of his followers when in unknown seas
Far travelled first they saw the needle take
Another course, and faltering in its office
Turn from the Pole. Such object doth present
To those who read the story at their ease   *60*
Sir Humphrey Gilbert that bold voyager
When after one disastrous wreck he took
His station in the pinnace for the sake
Of honour and his Crew's encouragement
And they who followed in the second ship   *65*
The larger Brigantine which he had left,
Beheld him while amid the storm he sate
Upon the open deck of his small bark
In calmness with a book upon his knee
To use the language of the Chronicle   *70*
A soldier of Christ Jesus undismayed
The ship and he a moment afterwards
Engulphed and seen no more. Like spectacle
Doth that Land Traveller living yet appear
To the mind's eye when, from the Moors escaped   *75*
Alone and in the heart of Africa,
And having sunk to earth worn out with pain
And weariness that took at length away
The sense of Life, he found when he awaked
His horse in quiet standing at his side   *80*
His arm within the bridle and the Sun
Setting upon the desert. . . .

HOME AT GRASMERE°

Bleak season was it, turbulent and bleak
When hitherward we journeyed side by side
Through burst of sunshine and through flying showers,
155 Paced the long Vales how long they were, and yet
How fast that length of way was left behind,
Wensley's rich Vale and Sedbergh's naked heights.
The frosty wind, as if to make amends
For its keen breath, was aiding to our steps
160 And drove us onward like two ships at sea,
Or like two Birds companions in mid air
Parted and reunited by the blast.
Stern was the face of Nature, we rejoiced
In that stern countenance for our Souls thence drew
165 A feeling of their strength. The naked Trees,
The icy brooks, as on we passed, appeared
To question us. "Whence come ye, to what end?"
They seemed to say; "What would ye," said the shower,
"Wild Wanderers, whither through my dark domain?"
170 The sunbeam said, "be happy." When this Vale°
We entered, bright and solemn was the sky
That faced us with a passionate welcoming,
And led us to our threshold. Daylight failed
Insensibly, and round us gently fell
175 Composing darkness, with a quiet load
Of full contentment, in a little Shed
Disturbed, uneasy in itself as seemed,
And wondering at its new inhabitants.
It loves us now, this Vale so beautiful
180 Begins to love us! by a sullen storm,

0 **Home at Grasmere** Wordsworth settled with his sister at Grasmere
in late 1799, and in the following year he began this poem as Book I
of the first part of *The Recluse*. Completed, probably, in 1806, it
was not published till long after the poet's death; but when Words-
worth in 1814 issued *The Excursion* as the second part of *The
Recluse*, he indicated the scope of his project by quoting lines
754–860 ("On Man, on Nature, and on Human Life") from the
present poem. The text of these selections is established from the
Oxford Wordsworth (V, Appendix A) and the earliest manuscript.
170 **this Vale** Grasmere.

Two months unwearied of severest storm,
It put the temper of our minds to proof,
And found us faithful through the gloom, and heard
The Poet mutter his prelusive songs
With cheerful heart, an unknown voice of joy   *185*
Among the silence of the woods and hills;
Silent to any gladsomeness of sound
With all their Shepherds.

                    *   *   *   *

   But not betrayed by tenderness of mind
That feared, or wholly overlook'd the truth   *310*
Did we come hither, with romantic hope
To find in midst of so much loveliness,
Love, perfect love; of so much majesty
A like majestic frame of mind in those
Who here abide, the persons like the place.   *315*
Not from such hope, or aught of such belief
Hath issued any portion of the joy
Which I have felt this day.

                    *   *   *   *

I came not dreaming of unruffled life
Untainted manners; born among the hills
Bred also there, I wanted not a scale
To regulate my hopes; pleased with the good   *350*
I shrink not from the evil with disgust,
Or with immoderate pain. I look for Man
The common Creature of the brotherhood
Differing but little from the Man elsewhere,
For selfishness and envy, and revenge   *355*
Ill neighbourhood—pity that this should be,
Flattery and double-dealing, strife and wrong.

   Yet is it something gained, it is in truth
A mighty gain, that Labour here preserves
His rosy face, a Servant only here   *360*
Of the fire-side or of the open field,
A Freeman therefore sound and unimpaired;
That extreme penury is here unknown
And cold and hunger's abject wretchedness
Mortal to body and the heaven-born mind;   *365*

That they who want, are not too great a weight
For those who can relieve. Here may the heart
Breathe in the air of fellow-suffering
Dreadless, as in a kind of fresher breeze
370 Of her own native element, the hand
Be ready and unwearied without plea
From tasks too frequent, or beyond its power
For languor or indifference or despair.
And as these lofty barriers break the force
375 Of winds—this deep Vale, as it doth in part
Conceal us from the Storm,—so here abides
A Power and a protection for the mind
Dispensed indeed to other solitudes
Favored by noble privilege like this
380 Where kindred independence of estate
Is prevalent, where he who tills the field,
He, happy Man! is Master of the field
And treads the mountains which his Fathers trod.

*   *   *   *

No, we are not alone, we do not stand,
My Sister, here misplaced and desolate
Loving what no one cares for but ourselves;
430 We shall not scatter through the plains and rocks
Of this fair Vale, and o'er its spacious heights
Unprofitable kindliness, bestowed
On objects unaccustomed to the gifts
Of feeling, which were cheerless and forlorn
435 But few weeks past, and would be so again
Were we not here; we do not tend a lamp
Whose lustre we alone participate
Which shines dependent upon us alone
Mortal though bright, a dying, dying flame.
440 Look where we will, some human hand has been
Before us with its offering; not a tree
Sprinkles these little pastures but the same
Hath furnished matter for a thought; perchance
For some one serves as a familiar friend.
445 Joy spreads and sorrow spreads; and this whole vale
Home of untutored Shepherds as it is
Swarms with sensation, as with gleams of sunshine,

Shadows or breezes, scents or sounds. Nor deem
These feelings though subservient more than ours
To every day's demand for daily bread, 450
And borrowing more their spirit, and their shape
From self-respecting interests; deem them not
Unworthy therefore, and unhallowed: no,
They lift the animal being, do themselves
By nature's kind and ever-present aid 455
Refine the selfishness from which they spring
Redeem by love the individual sense
Of anxiousness with which they are combined.
And thus it is that fitly they become
Associates in the joy of purest minds 460
They blend therewith congenially: meanwhile
Calmly they breathe their own undying life
Through this their mountain sanctuary; long
Oh long may it remain inviolate,
Diffusing health and sober cheerfulness 465
And giving to the moments as they pass
Their little boons of animating thought
That sweeten labour, make it seen and felt
To be no arbitrary weight imposed
But a glad function natural to Man. 470

    Fair proof of this, Newcomer though I be,
Already have I gained; the inward frame
Though slowly opening, opens every day
With process not unlike to that which cheers
A pensive Stranger, journeying at his leisure 475
Through some Helvetian Dell, when low-hung mists
Break up, and are beginning to recede;
How pleased he is where thin and thinner grows
The veil, or where it parts at once, to spy
The dark pines thrusting forth their spiky heads; 480
To watch the spreading lawns with cattle grazed,
Then to be greeted by the scattered huts,
As they shine out; and *see* the streams whose murmur
Had soothed his ear while they were hidden: how
    pleased
To have about him which way e'er he goes 485
Something on every side concealed from view

In every quarter something visible
Half-seen or wholly, lost and found again
Alternate progress and impediment
490 And yet a growing prospect in the main.

*   *   *   *

                What sighs more deep than his,
Whose nobler will hath long been sacrificed;
Who must inhabit, under a black sky,
A City where, if indifference to disgust
605 Yield not, to scorn, or sorrow, living Men
Are ofttimes to their fellow-men no more
Than to the Forest Hermit are the leaves
That hang aloft in myriads, nay far less,
For they protect his walk from sun and shower
610 Swell his devotion with their voice in storms
And whisper while the stars twinkle among them
His lullaby. From crowded streets remote
Far from the living and dead wilderness
Of the thronged World, Society is here
615 A true Community, a genuine frame
Of many into one incorporate.

*   *   *   *

625   Dismissing therefore all Arcadian dreams
All golden fancies of the golden Age
The bright array of shadowy thoughts from times
That were before all time, or are to be
Ere time expire, the pageantry that stirs
630 And will be stirring when our eyes are fixed
On lovely objects and we wish to part
With all remembrance of a jarring world,
    —Take we at once this one sufficient hope,
What need of more? that we shall neither droop
635 Nor pine for want of pleasure in the life
Scattered about us, nor through dearth of aught
That keeps in health the insatiable mind,
    —That we shall have for knowledge and for love
Abundance, and that, feeling as we do
640 How goodly, how exceeding fair, how pure
From all reproach is yon ethereal vault,

And this deep Vale its earthly counterpart. . . .

*   *   *   *

Then farewell to the Warrior's schemes,° farewell   *745*
The forwardness of Soul which looks that way
Upon a less incitement than the cause
Of Liberty endangered, and farewell
That other hope, long mine, the hope to fill
The heroic trumpet° with the Muse's breath!   *750*
Yet in this peaceful Vale we will not spend
Unheard-of days, though loving peaceful thoughts.
A voice shall speak, and what will be the Theme?°
    "On Man, on Nature, and on Human Life
Musing in Solitude, I oft perceive   *755*
Fair trains of imagery before me rise,
Accompanied by feelings of delight
Pure, or with no unpleasing sadness mixed:
And I am conscious of affecting thoughts
And dear remembrances, whose presence soothes   *760*
Or elevates the Mind, intent to weigh
The good and evil of our mortal state.
—To these emotions, whencesoe'er they come,
Whether from breath of outward circumstance,
Or from the Soul—an impulse to herself,   *765*
I would give utterance in numerous Verse.
—Of Truth, of Grandeur, Beauty, Love, and Hope—
And melancholy Fear subdued by Faith;
Of blessèd consolations in distress;
Of moral strength, and intellectual power;   *770*
Of joy in widest commonalty spread;
Of the individual Mind that keeps her own
Inviolate retirement, subject there
To Conscience only, and the law supreme
Of that Intelligence which governs all;   *775*
I sing:—"fit audience let me find though few!"°
    So prayed, more gaining than he asked, the Bard,

745 **Warrior's schemes** heroic (war) poetry.   750 **heroic trumpet**
Cf. *The Prelude* I. 166–220.   753 The extant manuscript stops here.
The remainder is printed as in the "Prospectus" to the 1814 *Excursion.*   776 "**fit . . . few**" *Paradise Lost* VIII. 31. From Milton's
invocation of Urania (778), who is associated with knowledge of
Creation.

Holiest of Men.—Urania, I shall need
Thy guidance, or a greater Muse, if such
780 Descend to earth or dwell in highest heaven!
For I must tread on shadowy ground, must sink
Deep—and, aloft ascending, breathe in worlds
To which the heaven of heavens is but a veil.
All strength—all terror, single or in bands,
785 That ever was put forth in personal form;
Jehovah—with his thunder, and the choir
Of shouting Angels, and the empyreal thrones,
I pass them, unalarmed. Not Chaos, not
The darkest pit of lowest Erebus,
790 Nor aught of blinder vacancy—scooped out
By help of dreams, can breed such fear and awe
As fall upon us often when we look
Into our Minds, into the Mind of Man,
My haunt, and the main region of my Song.
795 —Beauty—a living Presence of the earth,
Surpassing the most fair ideal Forms
Which craft of delicate Spirits hath composed
From earth's materials—waits upon my steps;
Pitches her tents before me as I move,
800 An hourly neighbour. Paradise, and groves
Elysian, Fortunate Fields—like those of old
Sought in the Atlantic Main, why should they be
A history only of departed things,
Or a mere fiction of what never was?
805 For the discerning intellect of Man,
When wedded to this goodly universe
In love and holy passion, shall find these
A simple produce of the common day.
—I, long before the blissful hour arrives,
810 Would chaunt, in lonely peace, the spousal verse
Of this great consummation:—and, by words
Which speak of nothing more than what we are,
Would I arouse the sensual from their sleep
Of Death, and win the vacant and the vain
815 To noble raptures; while my voice proclaims
How exquisitely the individual Mind
(And the progressive powers perhaps no less
Of the whole species) to the external World

Is fitted:—and how exquisitely, too,
Theme this but little heard of among Men,   820
The external World is fitted to the Mind;
And the creation (by no lower name
Can it be called) which they with blended might
Accomplish:—this is our high argument.
—Such grateful haunts foregoing, if I oft   825
Must turn elsewhere—to travel near the tribes
And fellowships of men, and see ill sights
Of madding passions mutually inflamed;
Must hear Humanity in fields and groves
Pipe solitary anguish; or must hang   830
Brooding above the fierce confederate storm
Of sorrow, barricadoed evermore
Within the walls of Cities; may these sounds
Have their authentic comment,—that, even these
Hearing, I be not downcast or forlorn!   835
—Come thou prophetic Spirit, that inspir'st
The human Soul of universal earth,
Dreaming on things to come; and dost possess
A metropolitan° Temple in the hearts
Of mighty Poets; upon me bestow   840
A gift of genuine insight; that my Song
With star-like virtue in its place may shine;
Shedding benignant influence,—and secure,
Itself, from all malevolent effect
Of those mutations that extend their sway   845
Throughout the nether sphere!—And if with this
I mix more lowly matter; with the thing
Contemplated, describe the Mind and Man
Contemplating; and who, and what he was,
The transitory Being that beheld   850
This Vision,—when and where, and how he lived;—
Be not this labour useless. If such theme
May sort with highest objects, then, dread Power,
Whose gracious favour is the primal source
Of all illumination, may my Life   855
Express the image of a better time,
More wise desires, and simpler manners;—nurse

839 **metropolitan** from the Greek for "mother-city."

My heart in genuine freedom:—all pure thoughts
Be with me;—so shall thy unfailing love
860 Guide, and support, and cheer me to the end!

1800–1806

THE EXCURSION°

Ancient Myth

—Truth has her pleasure-grounds, her haunts of ease
And easy contemplation; gay parterres,
590 And labyrinthine walks, her sunny glades
And shady groves in studied contrast—each,
For recreation, leading into each:
These may he range, if willing to partake
Their soft indulgences, and in due time
595 May issue thence, recruited for the tasks
And course of service Truth requires from those
Who tend her altars, wait upon her throne,
And guard her fortresses. Who thinks, and feels,
And recognizes ever and anon
600 The breeze of nature stirring in his soul,
Why need such man go desperately astray,
And nurse "the dreadful appetite of death?"
If tired with systems, each in its degree
Substantial, and all crumbling in their turn,
605 Let him build systems of his own, and smile
At the fond work, demolished with a touch;
If unreligious, let him be at once,
Among ten thousand innocents, enrolled

0 **The Excursion** The second part of *The Recluse* and the only one published in the poet's lifetime. It is in the form of a philosophical conversation between four persons (Poet, Wanderer, Solitary, and Pastor) in the English countryside. The conversation lasts for nine books and is inconclusive in dispelling the Solitary's melancholy. This excerpt (from Book IV), spoken by the Wanderer, is a defense of the imaginative truth of ancient mythology and widely influenced the younger Romantics upon its publication in 1814.

A pupil in the many-chambered school,
Where superstition weaves her airy dreams.   610

Life's autumn past, I stand on winter's verge;
And daily lose what I desire to keep:
Yet rather would I instantly decline
To the traditionary sympathies°
Of a most rustic ignorance and take   615
A fearful apprehension from the owl
Or death-watch: and as readily rejoice,
If two auspicious magpies crossed my way;—
To this would rather bend than see and hear
The repetitions wearisome of sense,   620
Where soul is dead, and feeling hath no place;
Where knowledge, ill begun in cold remark
On outward things, with formal inference ends;
Or, if the mind turn inward, she recoils
At once—or, not recoiling, is perplexed—   625
Lost in a gloom of uninspired research;
Meanwhile, the heart within the heart, the seat
Where peace and happy consciousness should dwell,
On its own axis restlessly revolving,
Seeks, yet can nowhere find, the light of truth.   630

Upon the breast of new-created earth
Man walked; and when and wheresoe'er he moved,
Alone or mated, solitude was not.
He heard, borne on the wind, the articulate voice
Of God; and Angels to his sight appeared   635
Crowning the glorious hills of paradise;
Or through the groves gliding like morning mist
Enkindled by the sun. He sate—and talked
With wingèd Messengers; who daily brought
To his small island in the ethereal deep   640
Tidings of joy and love.—From those pure heights
(Whether of actual vision, sensible
To sight and feeling, or that in this sort
Have condescendingly been shadowed forth°

614 **traditionary sympathies** legends and superstitions, especially those representing Nature as having intelligence and feeling ("sympathies"). 644 **condescendingly . . . forth** adjusted to the human understanding.

645 Communications spiritually maintained,
And intuitions moral and divine)
Fell Human-kind—to banishment condemned
That flowing years repealed not: and distress
And grief spread wide; but Man escaped the doom
650 Of destitution;—solitude was not.
—Jehovah—shapeless Power above all Powers,
Single and one, the omnipresent God,
By vocal utterance, or blaze of light,
Or cloud of darkness, localised in heaven;
655 On earth, enshrined within the wandering ark;
Or, out of Sion, thundering from his throne
Between the Cherubim—on the chosen Race
Showered miracles, and ceased not to dispense
Judgments, that filled the land from age to age
660 With hope, and love, and gratitude, and fear;
And with amazement smote;—thereby to assert
His scorned, or unacknowledged, sovereignty.
And when the One, ineffable of name,
Of nature indivisible, withdrew
665 From mortal adoration or regard,
Not then was Deity engulfed; nor Man,
The rational creature, left, to feel the weight
Of his own reason, without sense or thought
Of higher reason and a purer will,
670 To benefit and bless, through mightier power:—
Whether the Persian—zealous to reject
Altar and image, and the inclusive walls
And roofs of temples built by human hands—
To loftiest heights ascending, from their tops,
675 With myrtle-wreathed tiara on his brow,
Presented sacrifice to moon and stars,
And to the winds and mother elements,
And the whole circle of the heavens, for him
A sensitive existence, and a God,
680 With lifted hands invoked, and songs of praise:
Or, less reluctantly to bonds of sense
Yielding his soul, the Babylonian framed
For influence undefined a personal shape;
And, from the plain, with toil immense, upreared
685 Tower eight times planted on the top of tower,

That Belus,° nightly to his splendid couch
Descending, there might rest; upon that height
Pure and serene, diffused—to overlook
Winding Euphrates, and the city vast
Of his devoted worshippers, far-stretched,   690
With grove and field and garden interspersed;
Their town, and foodful region for support
Against the pressure of beleaguering war.

    Chaldean Shepherds, ranging trackless fields,
Beneath the concave of unclouded skies   695
Spread like a sea, in boundless solitude,
Looked on the polar star, as on a guide
And guardian of their course, that never closed
His stedfast eye. The planetary Five
With a submissive reverence they beheld;   700
Watched, from the centre of their sleeping flocks,
Those radiant Mercuries, that seemed to move
Carrying through ether, in perpetual round,
Decrees and resolutions of the Gods;
And, by their aspects, signifying works   705
Of dim futurity, to Man revealed.
—The imaginative faculty was lord
Of observations natural; and, thus
Led on, those shepherds made report of stars
In set rotation passing to and fro,   710
Between the orbs of our apparent sphere
And its invisible counterpart, adorned
With answering constellations, under earth,
Removed from all approach of living sight
But present to the dead; who, so they deemed,   715
Like those celestial messengers beheld
All accidents, and judges were of all.

    The lively Grecian, in a land of hills,
Rivers and fertile plains, and sounding shores,—
Under a cope of sky more variable,   720
Could find commodious place for every God,
Promptly received, as prodigally brought,

686 **Belus** a Chaldean deity, believed to have made nocturnal visits
to his temple.

From the surrounding countries, at the choice
Of all adventurers. With unrivalled skill,
725 As nicest observation furnished hints
For studious fancy, his quick hand bestowed
On fluent operations a fixed shape;
Metal or stone, idolatrously served.
And yet—triumphant o'er this pompous show
730 Of art, this palpable array of sense,
On every side encountered; in despite
Of the gross fictions chanted in the streets
By wandering Rhapsodists; and in contempt
Of doubt and bold denial hourly urged
735 Amid the wrangling schools—a SPIRIT hung,
Beautiful region! o'er thy towns and farms,
Statues and temples, and memorial tombs;
And emanations were perceived; and acts
Of immortality, in Nature's course,
740 Exemplified by mysteries, that were felt
As bonds, on grave philosopher imposed
And armèd warrior; and in every grove
A gay or pensive tenderness prevailed,
When piety more awful had relaxed.
745 —"Take, running river, take these locks of mine"—
Thus would the Votary say—"this severed hair,
My vow fulfilling, do I here present,
Thankful for my belovèd child's return.
Thy banks, Cephisus, he again hath trod,
750 Thy murmurs heard; and drunk the crystal lymph
With which thou dost refresh the thirsty lip,
And, all day long, moisten these flowery fields!"
And, doubtless, sometimes, when the hair was shed
Upon the flowing stream, a thought arose
755 Of Life continuous, Being unimpaired;
That hath been, is, and where it was and is
There shall endure,—existence unexposed
To the blind walk of mortal accident;
From diminution safe and weakening age;
760 While man grows old, and dwindles, and decays;
And countless generations of mankind
Depart; and leave no vestige where they trod.

(?)   1814

THE WHITE DOE OF RYLSTONE;°
or,
The Fate of the Nortons

During the Summer of 1807 I visited, for the first time,
the beautiful country that surrounds Bolton Priory in York-
shire; and the Poem of the WHITE DOE, founded upon a Tra-
dition connected with that place, was composed at the close
of the same year.

Dedication

In trellised shed with clustering roses gay,
And, MARY! oft beside our blazing fire,
When years of wedded life were as a day
Whose current answers to the heart's desire,
Did we together read in Spenser's Lay°   5
How Una, sad of soul—in sad attire,
The gentle Una, of celestial birth,
To seek her Knight went wandering o'er the earth.

Ah, then, Belovèd! pleasing was the smart,
And the tear precious in compassion shed   10
For Her, who, pierced by sorrow's thrilling dart,
Did meekly bear the pang unmerited;
Meek as that emblem of her lowly heart
The milk-white Lamb which in a line she led,—
And faithful, loyal in her innocence,   15
Like the brave Lion slain in her defence.

0 **The White Doe of Rylstone** This poem, set in "Eliza's golden
time," blends two stories: that of Richard Norton and his eight
sons, all killed in the Catholic revolt of 1569; and that of an
"animal form divine," the white doe, who is said to have made,
every Sunday, a pilgrimage from Rylstone (seat of the Nortons)
to Bolton Abbey Churchyard. The cantos omitted deal chiefly with
the story of the revolt. Wordsworth makes the doe's appearance and
its consolation of Emily Norton (the only family survivor) the
poem's imaginative center. It is a late "lyrical ballad," in which our
interest remains focused on states of mind rather than on dramatic
incidents. 5 **Spenser's Lay** See *The Fairie Queene*, Book I.

Notes could we hear as of a faery shell
Attuned to words with sacred wisdom fraught;
Free Fancy prized each specious miracle,
20 And all its finer inspiration caught;
Till in the bosom of our rustic Cell,
We by a lamentable change° were taught
That "bliss with mortal Man may not abide:"
How nearly joy and sorrow are allied!

25 For us the stream of fiction ceased to flow,
For us the voice of melody was mute.
—But, as soft gales dissolve the dreary snow,
And give the timid herbage leave to shoot,
Heaven's breathing influence failed not to bestow
30 A timely promise of unlooked-for fruit,
Fair fruit of pleasure and serene content
From blossoms wild of fancies innocent.

It soothed us—it beguiled us—then, to hear
Once more of troubles wrought by magic spell;
35 And griefs whose aery motion comes not near
The pangs that tempt the Spirit to rebel:
Then, with mild Una in her sober cheer,
High over hill and low adown the dell
Again we wandered, willing to partake
40 All that she suffered for her dear Lord's sake.

Then, too, this Song *of mine* once more could please,
Where anguish, strange as dreams of restless sleep,
Is tempered and allayed by sympathies
Aloft ascending, and descending deep,
45 Even to the inferior Kinds; whom forest-trees
Protect from beating sunbeams, and the sweep
Of the sharp winds;—fair Creatures!—to whom Heaven
A calm and sinless life, with love, hath given.

This tragic Story cheered us; for it speaks
50 Of female patience winning firm repose;
And, of the recompense that conscience seeks,

22 **change** the death of Wordsworth's brother in 1805 or the loss
of his children, Catherine and Thomas, in 1812.

A bright, encouraging, example shows;
Needful when o'er wide realms the tempest breaks,
Needful amid life's ordinary woes;—
Hence, not for them unfitted who would bless   55
A happy hour with holier happiness.

He serves the Muses erringly and ill,
Whose aim is pleasure light and fugitive:
O, that my mind were equal to fulfil
The comprehensive mandate which they give—   60
Vain aspiration of an earnest will!
Yet in this moral Strain a power may live,
Belovèd Wife! such solace to impart
As it hath yielded to thy tender heart.

1815   1815

Canto First

*   *   *   *

Fast the church-yard fills;—anon
Look again, and they all are gone;
The cluster round the porch, and the folk
Who sate in the shade of the Prior's Oak!
And scarcely have they disappeared   35
Ere the prelusive hymn is heard:—
With one consent the people rejoice,
Filling the church with a lofty voice!
They sing a service which they feel:
For 'tis the sunrise now of zeal;   40
Of a pure faith the vernal prime—
In great Eliza's golden time.

A moment ends the fervent din,
And all is hushed, without and within;
For though the priest, more tranquilly,   45
Recites the holy liturgy,
The only voice which you can hear
Is the river murmuring near.
—When soft!—the dusky trees between,
And down the path through the open green,   50
Where is no living thing to be seen;

And through yon gateway, where is found,
Beneath the arch with ivy bound,
Free entrance to the church-yard ground—
55 Comes gliding in with lovely gleam,
Comes gliding in serene and slow,
Soft and silent as a dream,
A solitary Doe!
White she is as lily of June,
60 And beauteous as the silver moon
When out of sight the clouds are driven
And she is left alone in heaven;
Or like a ship some gentle day
In sunshine sailing far away,
65 A glittering ship, that hath the plain
Of ocean for her own domain.

Lie silent in your graves, ye dead!
Lie quiet in your church-yard bed!
Ye living, tend your holy cares;
70 Ye multitude, pursue your prayers;
And blame not me if my heart and sight
Are occupied with one delight!
'Tis a work for sabbath hours
If I with this bright Creature go:
75 Whether she be of forest bowers,
From the bowers of earth below;
Or a Spirit for one day given,
A pledge of grace from purest heaven.

What harmonious pensive changes
80 Wait upon her as she ranges
Round and through this Pile of state
Overthrown and desolate!
Now a step or two her way
Leads through space of open day,
85 Where the enamoured sunny light
Brightens her that was so bright;
Now doth a delicate shadow fall,
Falls upon her like a breath,
From some lofty arch or wall,
90 As she passes underneath:

Now some gloomy nook partakes
Of the glory that she makes,—
High-ribbed vault of stone, or cell,
With perfect cunning framed as well
Of stone, and ivy, and the spread   95
Of the elder's bushy head;
Some jealous and forbidding cell,
That doth the living stars repel,
And where no flower hath leave to dwell.

    The presence of this wandering Doe   100
Fills many a damp obscure recess
With lustre of a saintly show;
And, reappearing, she no less
Sheds on the flowers that round her blow
A more than sunny liveliness.   105
But say, among these holy places,
Which thus assiduously she paces,
Comes she with a votary's task,
Rite to perform, or boon to ask?
Fair Pilgrim! harbours she a sense   110
Of sorrow, or of reverence?
Can she be grieved for quire or shrine,
Crushed as if by wrath divine?
For what survives of house where God
Was worshipped, or where Man abode;   115
For old magnificence undone;
Or for the gentler work begun
By Nature, softening and concealing,
And busy with a hand of healing?
Mourns she for lordly chamber's hearth   120
That to the sapling ash gives birth;
For dormitory's length laid bare
Where the wild rose blossoms fair;
Or altar, whence the cross was rent,
Now rich with mossy ornament?   125
—She sees a warrior carved in stone,
Among the thick weeds, stretched alone;
A warrior, with his shield of pride
Cleaving humbly to his side,
And hands in resignation prest,   130

Palm to palm, on his tranquil breast;
As little she regards the sight
As a common creature might:
If she be doomed to inward care,
135 Or service, it must lie elsewhere.
—But hers are eyes serenely bright,
And on she moves—with pace how light!
Nor spares to stoop her head, and taste
The dewy turf with flowers bestrown;
140 And thus she fares, until at last
Beside the ridge of a grassy grave
In quietness she lays her down;
Gentle as a weary wave
Sinks, when the summer breeze hath died,
145 Against an anchored vessel's side;
Even so, without distress, doth she
Lie down in peace, and lovingly.

The day is placid in its going,
To a lingering motion bound,
150 Like the crystal stream now flowing
With its softest summer sound:
So the balmy minutes pass,
While this radiant Creature lies
Couched upon the dewy grass,
155 Pensively with downcast eyes.
—But now again the people raise
With awful cheer a voice of praise;
It is the last, the parting song;
And from the temple forth they throng,
160 And quickly spread themselves abroad,
While each pursues his several road.
But some—a variegated band
Of middle-aged, and old, and young,
And little children by the hand
165 Upon their leading mothers hung—
With mute obeisance gladly paid
Turn towards the spot where, full in view,
The white Doe, to her service true,
Her sabbath couch has made.

It was a solitary mound;   *170*
Which two spears' length of level ground
Did from all other graves divide:
As if in some respect of pride;
Or melancholy's sickly mood,
Still shy of human neighbourhood;   *175*
Or guilt, that humbly would express
A penitential loneliness.

   "Look, there she is, my Child! draw near;
She fears not, wherefore should we fear?
She means no harm;"—but still the Boy,   *180*
To whom the words were softly said,
Hung back, and smiled, and blushed for joy,
A shame-faced blush of glowing red!
Again the Mother whispered low,
"Now you have seen the famous Doe;   *185*
From Rylstone she hath found her way
Over the hills this sabbath day;
Her work, whate'er it be, is done,
And she will depart when we are gone;
Thus doth she keep, from year to year,   *190*
Her sabbath morning, foul or fair."

   Bright was the Creature, as in dreams
The Boy had seen her, yea, more bright;
But is she truly what she seems?
He asks with insecure delight,   *195*
Asks of himself, and doubts,—and still
The doubt returns against his will:
Though he, and all the standers-by,
Could tell a tragic history
Of facts divulged, wherein appear   *200*
Substantial motive, reason clear,
Why thus the milk-white Doe is found
Couchant beside that lonely mound;
And why she duly loves to pace
The circuit of this hallowed place.   *205*
Nor to the Child's enquiring mind
Is such perplexity confined:

For, spite of sober Truth that sees
A world of fixed remembrances
210 Which to this mystery belong,
If, undeceived, my skill can trace
The characters of every face,
There lack not strange delusion here,
Conjecture vague, and idle fear,
215 And superstitious fancies strong,
Which do the gentle Creature wrong.

     That bearded, staff-supported Sire—
Who in his boyhood often fed
Full cheerily on convent-bread
220 And heard old tales by the convent-fire,
And to his grave will go with scars,
Relics of long and distant wars—
That Old Man, studious to expound
The spectacle, is mounting high
225 To days of dim antiquity;
When Lady Aäliza mourned
Her Son, and felt in her despair
The pang of unavailing prayer;
Her Son in Wharf's abysses drowned,
230 The noble Boy of Egremound.°
From which affliction—when the grace
Of God had in her heart found place—
A pious structure, fair to see,
Rose up, this stately Priory!
235 The Lady's work;—but now laid low;
To the grief of her soul that doth come and go,
In the beautiful form of this innocent Doe;
Which, though seemingly doomed in its breast to
          sustain
A softened remembrance of sorrow and pain,
240 Is spotless, and holy, and gentle, and bright;
And glides o'er the earth like an angel of light.

226–30 Lady Aäliza . . . Boy of Egremound. Tradition held that the
"Boy of Egremound" drowned attempting to leap across a chasm
through which the Wharf flowed. His mother then built Bolton
Abbey by the river's side.

Pass, pass who will, yon chantry door;
And, through the chink in the fractured floor
Look down, and see a griesly sight;
A vault where the bodies are buried upright!   245
There, face by face, and hand by hand,
The Claphams and Mauleverers stand;
And, in his place, among son and sire,
Is John de Clapham, that fierce Esquire,
A valiant man, and a name of dread   250
In the ruthless wars of the White and Red;
Who dragged Earl Pembroke from Banbury church
And smote off his head on the stones of the porch!
Look down among them, if you dare;
Oft does the White Doe loiter there,   255
Prying into the darksome rent;
Nor can it be with good intent:
So thinks that Dame of haughty air,
Who hath a Page her book to hold,
And wears a frontlet edged with gold.   260
Harsh thoughts with her high mood agree—
Who counts among her ancestry
Earl Pembroke, slain so impiously!

That slender Youth, a scholar pale,
From Oxford come to his native vale,   265
He also hath his own conceit.°
It is, thinks he, the gracious Fairy,
Who loved the Shepherd-lord° to meet
In his wanderings solitary:
Wild notes she in his hearing sang,   270
A song of Nature's hidden powers;
That whistled like the wind, and rang
Among the rocks and holly bowers.
'Twas said that She all shapes could wear;
And oftentimes before him stood,   275
Amid the trees of some thick wood,
In semblance of a lady fair;

266 **conceit** fanciful thought. 267–68 **Fairy . . . Shepherd-lord**
Wordsworth draws upon a local story concerning Henry de Clifford
(1455[?]–1523), tenth Baron of Westmorland. Pursued by Yorkists,
he disguised himself as a shepherd and was eventually restored to
his estate and honors.

And taught him signs, and showed him sights,
In Craven's dens, on Cumbrian heights;
280 When under cloud of fear he lay,
A shepherd clad in homely grey;
Nor left him at his later day.
And hence, when he, with spear and shield,
Rode full of years to Flodden-field,
285 His eye could see the hidden spring,
And how the current was to flow;
The fatal end of Scotland's King,
And all that hopeless overthrow.
But not in wars did he delight,
290 *This* Clifford wished for worthier might;
Nor in broad pomp, or courtly state;
Him his own thoughts did elevate,—
Most happy in the shy recess
Of Barden's lowly quietness.
295 And choice of studious friends had he
Of Bolton's dear fraternity;
Who, standing on this old church tower,
In many a calm propitious hour,
Perused, with him, the starry sky;
300 Or, in their cells, with him did pry
For other lore,—by keen desire
Urged to close toil with chemic fire;
In quest belike of transmutations
Rich as the mine's most bright creations.
305 But they and their good works are fled,
And all is now disquieted—
And peace is none, for living or dead!

Ah, pensive Scholar, think not so,
But look again at the radiant Doe!
310 What quiet watch she seems to keep,
Alone, beside that grassy heap!
Why mention other thoughts unmeet
For vision so composed and sweet?
While stand the people in a ring,
315 Gazing, doubting, questioning;
Yea, many overcome in spite
Of recollections clear and bright;

Which yet do unto some impart
An undisturbed repose of heart.
And all the assembly own a law   820
Of orderly respect and awe;
But see—they vanish one by one,
And last, the Doe herself is gone.

*   *   *   *

Canto Seventh

*   *   *   *

'Tis done;°—despoil and desolation
O'er Rylstone's fair domain have blown;
Pools, terraces, and walks are sown   1570
With weeds; the bowers are overthrown,
Or have given way to slow mutation,
While, in their ancient habitation
The Norton name hath been unknown.
The lordly Mansion of its pride   1575
Is stripped; the ravage hath spread wide
Through park and field, a perishing
That mocks the gladness of the Spring!
And, with this silent gloom agreeing,
Appears a joyless human Being,   1580
Of aspect such as if the waste
Were under her dominion placed.
Upon a primrose bank, her throne
Of quietness, she sits alone;
Among the ruins of a wood,   1585
Erewhile a covert bright and green,
And where full many a brave tree stood,
That used to spread its boughs, and ring
With the sweet birds' carolling.
Behold her, like a virgin Queen,   1590
Neglecting in imperial state
These outward images of fate,
And carrying inward a serene
And perfect sway, through many a thought
Of chance and change, that hath been brought   1595

1568 **'Tis done** referring to the fall of the Nortons.

To the subjection of a holy,
Though stern and rigorous, melancholy!
The like authority, with grace
Of awfulness, is in her face,—
1600 There hath she fixed it; yet it seems
To o'ershadow by no native right
That face, which cannot lose the gleams,
Lose utterly the tender gleams,
Of gentleness and meek delight,
1605 And loving-kindness ever bright:
Such is her sovereign mien:—her dress
(A vest with woolen cincture tied,
A hood of mountain-wool undyed)
Is homely,—fashioned to express
1610 A wandering Pilgrim's humbleness.

And she *hath* wandered, long and far,
Beneath the light of sun and star;
Hath roamed in trouble and in grief,
Driven forward like a withered leaf,
1615 Yea, like a ship at random blown
To distant places and unknown.
But now she dares to seek a haven
Among her native wilds of Craven;
Hath seen again her Father's roof,
1620 And put her fortitude to proof;
The mighty sorrow hath been borne,
And she is thoroughly forlorn:
Her soul doth in itself stand fast,
Sustained by memory of the past
1625 And strength of Reason; held above
The infirmities of mortal love;
Undaunted, lofty, calm, and stable,
And awfully impenetrable.

And so—beneath a mouldered tree,
1630 A self-surviving leafless oak
By unregarded age from stroke
Of ravage saved—sate Emily.
There did she rest, with head reclined,
Herself most like a stately flower,

(Such have I seen) whom chance of birth 1635
Hath separated from its kind,
To live and die in a shady bower,
Single on the gladsome earth.

When, with a noise like distant thunder,
A troop of deer came sweeping by; 1640
And, suddenly, behold a wonder!
For One, among those rushing deer,
A single One, in mid career
Hath stopped, and fixed her large full eye
Upon the Lady Emily; 1645
A Doe most beautiful, clear-white,
A radiant creature, silver-bright!

Thus checked, a little while it stayed;
A little thoughtful pause it made;
And then advanced with stealth-like pace, 1650
Drew softly near her, and more near—
Looked round—but saw no cause for fear;
So to her feet the Creature came,
And laid its head upon her knee,
And looked into the Lady's face, 1655
A look of pure benignity,
And fond unclouded memory.
It is, thought Emily, the same,
The very Doe of other years!—
The pleading look the Lady viewed, 1660
And, by her gushing thoughts subdued,
She melted into tears—
A flood of tears that flowed apace
Upon the happy Creature's face.

Oh, moment ever blest! O Pair 1665
Beloved of Heaven, Heaven's chosen care,
This was for you a precious greeting;
And may it prove a fruitful meeting!
Joined are they, and the sylvan Doe
Can she depart? can she forego 1670
The Lady, once her playful peer,
And now her sainted Mistress dear?

And will not Emily receive
This lovely chronicler of things
1675 Long past, delights and sorrowings?
Lone Sufferer! will not she believe
The promise in that speaking face;
And welcome, as a gift of grace,
The saddest thought the Creature brings?

1680   That day, the first of a re-union
Which was to teem with high communion,
That day of balmy April weather,
They tarried in the wood together.
And when, ere fall of evening dew,
1685 She from her sylvan haunt withdrew,
The White Doe tracked with faithful pace
The Lady to her dwelling-place;
That nook where, on paternal ground,
A habitation she had found,
1690 The Master of whose humble board
Once owned her Father for his Lord;
A hut, by tufted trees defended,
Where Rylstone brook with Wharf is blended.

    When Emily by morning light
1695 Went forth, the Doe stood there in sight.
She shrunk:—with one frail shock of pain
Received and followed by a prayer,
She saw the Creature once again;
Shun will she not, she feels, will bear;—
1700 But, wheresoever she looked round,
All now was trouble-haunted ground;
And therefore now she deems it good
Once more this restless neighbourhood
To leave.—Unwooed, yet unforbidden,
1705 The White Doe followed up the vale,
Up to another cottage, hidden
In the deep fork of Amerdale;
And there may Emily restore
Herself, in spots unseen before.
1710 —Why tell of mossy rock, or tree,
By lurking Dernbrook's pathless side,

Haunts of a strengthening amity
That calmed her, cheered, and fortified?
For she hath ventured now to read
Of time, and place, and thought, and deed—   *1715*
Endless history that lies
In her silent Follower's eyes;
Who with a power like human reason
Discerns the favourable season,
Skilled to approach or to retire,—   *1720*
From looks conceiving her desire;
From look, deportment, voice, or mien,
That vary to the heart within.
If she too passionately wreathed
Her arms, or over-deeply breathed,   *1725*
Walked quick or slowly, every mood
In its degree was understood;
Then well may their accord be true,
And kindliest intercourse° ensue.
—Oh! surely 'twas a gentle rousing   *1730*
When she by sudden glimpse espied
The White Doe on the mountain browsing,
Or in the meadow wandered wide!
How pleased, when down the Straggler sank
Beside her, on some sunny bank!   *1735*
How soothed, when in thick bower enclosed,
They, like a nested pair, reposed!
Fair Vision! when it crossed the Maid
Within some rocky cavern laid,
The dark cave's portal gliding by,   *1740*
White as whitest cloud on high
Floating through the azure sky.
—What now is left for pain or fear?
That Presence, dearer and more dear,
While they, side by side, were straying,   *1745*
And the shepherd's pipe was playing,
Did now a very gladness yield
At morning to the dewy field,
And with a deeper peace endued
The hour of moonlight solitude.   *1750*

1729 **intercourse** sociability.

With her Companion, in such frame
Of mind, to Rylstone back she came;
And, ranging through the wasted groves,
Received the memory of old loves,
1755 Undisturbed and undistrest,
Into a soul which now was blest
With a soft spring-day of holy,
Mild, and grateful, melancholy:
Not sunless gloom or unenlightened,
1760 But by tender fancies brightened.

*   *   *   *

But most to Bolton's sacred Pile,
On favouring nights, she loved to go;
There ranged through cloister, court, and aisle,
Attended by the soft-paced Doe;
1815 Nor feared she in the still moonshine
To look upon Saint Mary's shrine;
Nor on the lonely turf that showed
Where Francis° slept in his last abode.
For that she came; there oft she sate
1820 Forlorn, but not disconsolate:
And, when she from the abyss returned
Of thought, she neither shrunk nor mourned;
Was happy that she lived to greet
Her mute Companion as it lay
1825 In love and pity at her feet;
How happy in its turn to meet
The recognition! the mild glance
Beamed from that gracious countenance;
Communication, like the ray
1830 Of a new morning, to the nature
And prospects of the inferior Creature!

A mortal Song we sing, by dower
Encouraged of celestial power;
Power which the viewless Spirit shed
1835 By whom we were first visited;
Whose voice we heard, whose hand and wings
Swept like a breeze the conscious strings,

1818 **Francis** Emily's eldest brother.

When, left in solitude, erewhile
We stood before this ruined Pile,
And, quitting unsubstantial dreams, 1840
Sang in this Presence kindred themes;
Distress and desolation spread
Through human hearts, and pleasure dead,—
Dead—but to live again on earth,
A second and yet nobler birth; 1845
Dire overthrow, and yet how high
The re-ascent in sanctity!
From fair to fairer; day by day
A more divine and loftier way!
Even such this blessèd Pilgrim trod, 1850
By sorrow lifted towards her God;
Uplifted to the purest sky
Of undisturbed mortality.
Her own thoughts loved she; and could bend
A dear look to her lowly Friend; 1855
There stopped; her thirst was satisfied
With what this innocent spring supplied:
Her sanction inwardly she bore,
And stood apart from human cares:
But to the world returned no more, 1860
Although with no unwilling mind
Help did she give at need, and joined
The Wharfdale peasants in their prayers.
At length, thus faintly, faintly tied
To earth, she was set free, and died. 1865
Thy soul, exalted Emily,
Maid of the blasted family,
Rose to the God from whom it came!
—In Rylstone Church her mortal frame
Was buried by her Mother's side. 1870

Most glorious sunset! and a ray
Survives—the twilight of this day—
In that fair Creature whom the fields
Support, and whom the forest shields;
Who, having filled a holy place, 1875
Partakes, in her degree, Heaven's grace;
And bears a memory and a mind

Raised far above the law of kind;
Haunting the spots with lonely cheer
1880 Which her dear Mistress once held dear:
Loves most what Emily loved most—
The enclosure of this church-yard ground;
Here wanders like a gliding ghost,
And every sabbath here is found;
1885 Comes with the people when the bells
Are heard among the moorland dells,
Finds entrance through yon arch, where way
Lies open on the sabbath-day;
Here walks amid the mournful waste
1890 Of prostrate altars, shrines defaced,
And floors encumbered with rich show
Of fret-work imagery laid low;
Paces softly, or makes halt,
By fractured cell, or tomb, or vault;
1895 By plate of monumental brass
Dim-gleaming among weeds and grass,
And sculptured Forms of Warriors brave:
But chiefly by that single grave,
That one sequestered hillock green,
1900 The pensive visitant is seen.
There doth the gentle Creature lie
With those adversities unmoved;
Calm spectacle, by earth and sky
In their benignity approved!
1905 And aye, methinks, this hoary Pile,
Subdued by outrage and decay,
Looks down upon her with a smile,
A gracious smile, that seems to say—
"Thou, thou art not a Child of Time,
1910 But Daughter of the Eternal Prime!"

1807

1815

IV. Endings

No more: the end is sudden and abrupt,
Abrupt—as without preconceived design
Was the beginning, yet the several Lays
Have moved in order, to each other bound
By a continuous and acknowledged tie   5
Though unapparent. . . .

"Apology," *Yarrow Revisited* (1835)

EVENING VOLUNTARIES°

I

Calm is the fragrant air, and loth to lose
Day's grateful warmth, tho' moist with falling dews.
Look for the stars, you'll say that there are none;
Look up a second time, and, one by one,
You mark them twinkling out with silvery light,   5
And wonder how they could elude the sight!
The birds, of late so noisy in their bowers,
Warbled a while with faint and fainter powers,
But now are silent as the dim-seen flowers:
Nor does the village Church-clock's iron tone   10
The time's and season's influence disown;
Nine beats distinctly to each other bound
In drowsy sequence—how unlike the sound
That, in rough winter, oft inflicts a fear
On fireside listeners, doubting what they hear!   15
The shepherd, bent on rising with the sun,
Had closed his door before the day was done,
And now with thankful heart to bed doth creep,
And joins his little children in their sleep.
The bat, lured forth where trees the lane o'ershade,   20
Flits and reflits along the close arcade;
The busy dor-hawk chases the white moth
With burring note, which Industry and Sloth
Might both be pleased with, for it suits them both.
A stream is heard—I see it not, but know   25
By its soft music whence the waters flow:
Wheels and the tread of hoofs are heard no more;
One boat there was, but it will touch the shore
With the next dipping of its slackened oar;

0 **Evening Voluntaries** A "Voluntary" is a piece "thrown off as an impromptu" (Wordsworth's Note).

30 Faint sound, that, for the gayest of the gay,
    Might give to serious thought a moment's sway,
    As a last token of man's toilsome day!

1832   1835

COMPOSED UPON AN EVENING OF EXTRAORDINARY SPLENDOUR AND BEAUTY

I

    Had this effulgence disappeared
    With flying haste, I might have sent,
    Among the speechless clouds, a look
    Of blank astonishment;
5   But 'tis endued with power to stay,
    And sanctify one closing day,
    That frail Mortality may see—
    What is?—ah no, but what *can* be!
    Time was when field and watery cove
10 With modulated echoes rang,
    While choirs of fervent Angels sang
    Their vespers in the grove;
    Or, crowning, star-like, each some sovereign height,
    Warbled, for heaven above and earth below,
15 Strains suitable to both.—Such holy rite,
    Methinks, if audibly repeated now
    From hill or valley, could not move
    Sublimer transport, purer love,
    Than doth this silent spectacle—the gleam—
20 The shadow—and the peace supreme!

II

    No sound is uttered,—but a deep
    And solemn harmony pervades
    The hollow vale from steep to steep,
    And penetrates the glades.

Far-distant images draw nigh,   25
Called forth by wondrous potency
Of beamy radiance, that imbues,
Whate'er it strikes, with gem-like hues!
In vision exquisitely clear,
Herds range along the mountain side;   30
And glistering antlers are descried;
And gilded flocks appear.
Thine is the tranquil hour, purpureal Eve!
But long as god-like wish, or hope divine,
Informs my spirit, ne'er can I believe   35
That this magnificence is wholly thine!
—From worlds not quickened by the sun
A portion of the gift is won;
An intermingling of Heaven's pomp is spread
On ground which British shepherds tread!   40

III

And, if there be whom broken ties
Afflict, or injuries assail,
Yon hazy ridges to their eyes
Present a glorious scale,°
Climbing suffused with sunny air,   45
To stop—no record hath told where!
And tempting Fancy to ascend,
And with immortal Spirits blend!
—Wings at my shoulders seem to play;
But, rooted here, I stand and gaze   50
On those bright steps that heaven-ward raise
Their practicable way.
Come forth, ye drooping old men, look abroad,
And see to what fair countries ye are bound!
And if some traveller, weary of his road,   55
Hath slept since noon-tide on the grassy ground,
Ye Genii! to his covert speed;
And wake him with such gentle heed
As may attune his soul to meet the dower
Bestowed on this transcendent hour!   60

44 **glorious scale** There is an implicit reference in what follows to
Jacob's ladder (Genesis 28:12 ff.).

IV

Such hues from their celestial Urn
Were wont to stream before mine eye,
Where'er it wandered in the morn
Of blissful infancy.
65 This glimpse of glory, why renewed?
Nay, rather speak with gratitude;
For, if a vestige of those gleams
Survived, 'twas only in my dreams.
Dread Power! whom peace and calmness serve
70 No less than Nature's threatening voice,
If aught unworthy be my choice,
From THEE if I would swerve;
Oh, let thy grace remind me of the light
Full early lost, and fruitlessly deplored;
75 Which, at this moment, on my waking sight
Appears to shine, by miracle restored;
My soul, though yet confined to earth,
Rejoices in a second birth!
—'Tis past, the visionary splendour fades;
80 And night approaches with her shades.

1817   1820

YARROW REVISITED

The gallant Youth, who may have gained,
    Or seeks, a "winsome Marrow,"°
Was but an Infant in the lap
    When first I looked on Yarrow;
5 Once more, by Newark's Castle-gate
    Long left without a warder,

2 **"winsome Marrow"** Marrow means helpmate or spouse. The
phrase is from William Hamilton's "The Braes of Yarrow."

I stood, looked, listened, and with Thee,
   Great Minstrel of the Border!°

Grave thoughts ruled wide on that sweet day,
   Their dignity installing   *10*
In gentle bosoms, while sere leaves
   Were on the bough, or falling;
But breezes played, and sunshine gleamed—
   The forest to embolden;
Reddened the fiery hues, and shot   *15*
   Transparence through the golden.

For busy thoughts the Stream flowed on
   In foamy agitation;
And slept in many a crystal pool
   For quiet contemplation: *20*
No public and no private care
   The freeborn mind enthralling,
We made a day of happy hours,
   Our happy days recalling.

Brisk Youth appeared, the Morn of youth,   *25*
   With freaks of graceful folly,—
Life's temperate Noon, her sober Eve,
   Her Night not melancholy;
Past, present, future, all appeared
   In harmony united,   *30*
Like guests that meet, and some from far,
   By cordial love invited.

And if, as Yarrow, through the woods
   And down the meadow ranging,
Did meet us with unaltered face,   *35*
   Though we were changed and changing;
If, *then,* some natural shadows spread
   Our inward prospect over,
The soul's deep valley was not slow
   Its brightness to recover.   *40*

8 Great . . . Border "The following Stanzas are a memorial of a day passed with Sir Walter Scott, and other Friends visiting the Banks of the Yarrow under his guidance . . ." (Wordsworth's prefatory Note).

Eternal blessings on the Muse,
　　And her divine employment!
The blameless Muse, who trains her Sons
　　For hope and calm enjoyment;
45　Albeit sickness, lingering yet,
　　Has o'er their pillow brooded;
And Care waylays their steps—a Sprite
　　Not easily eluded.

For thee, O SCOTT! compelled to change
50　　Green Eildon-hill and Cheviot
For warm Vesuvio's vine-clad slopes;
　　And leave thy Tweed and Tiviot
For mild Sorento's breezy waves;
　　May classic Fancy, linking
55　With native Fancy her fresh aid,
　　Preserve thy heart from sinking!

O! while they minister to thee,
　　Each vying with the other,
May Health return to mellow Age,
60　　With Strength, her venturous brother;
And Tiber, and each brook and rill
　　Renowned in song and story,
With unimagined beauty shine,
　　Nor lose one ray of glory!

65　For Thou, upon a hundred streams,
　　By tales of love and sorrow,
Of faithful love, undaunted truth,
　　Hast shed the power of Yarrow;
And streams unknown, hills yet unseen,
70　　Wherever they invite Thee,
At parent Nature's grateful call,
　　With gladness must requite Thee.

A gracious welcome shall be thine,
　　Such looks of love and honour
75　As thy own Yarrow gave to me
　　When first I gazed upon her;

Beheld what I had feared to see,
 Unwilling to surrender
Dreams treasured up from early days,
 The holy and the tender.   80

And what, for this frail world, were all
 That mortals do or suffer,
Did no responsive harp, no pen,
 Memorial tribute offer?
Yea, what were mighty Nature's self?   85
 Her features, could they win us,
Unhelped by the poetic voice
 That hourly speaks within us?

Nor deem that localised Romance
 Plays false with our affections;   90
Unsanctifies our tears—made sport
 For fanciful dejections:
Ah, no! the visions of the past
 Sustain the heart in feeling
Life as she is—our changeful Life,   95
 With friends and kindred dealing.

Bear witness, Ye, whose thoughts that day
 In Yarrow's groves were centred;
Who through the silent portal arch
 Of mouldering Newark entered;   100
And clomb the winding stair that once
 Too timidly was mounted
By the "last Minstrel," (not the last!)
 Ere he his Tale recounted.

Flow on for ever, Yarrow Stream!   105
 Fulfil thy pensive duty,
Well pleased that future Bards should chant
 For simple hearts thy beauty;
To dream-light dear while yet unseen,
 Dear to the common sunshine,   110
And dearer still, as now I feel,
 To memory's shadowy moonshine!

1831   1835

PROCESSIONS

Suggested on a Sabbath Morning in the Vale of Chamouny

To appease the Gods; or public thanks to yield;
Or to solicit knowledge of events,
Which in her breast Futurity concealed;
And that the past might have its true intents
5 Feelingly told by living monuments—
Mankind of yore were prompted to devise
Rites such as yet Persepolis presents
Graven on her cankered walls, solemnities
That moved in long array before admiring eyes.

10 The Hebrews° thus, carrying in joyful state
Thick boughs of palm, and willows from the brook,
Marched round the altar—to commemorate
How, when their course they through the desert took,
Guided by signs which ne'er the sky forsook,
15 They lodged in leafy tents and cabins low;
Green boughs were borne, while, for the blast that
    shook
Down to the earth the walls of Jericho,
Shouts rise, and storms of sound from lifted trumpets
    blow!

And thus, in order, 'mid the sacred grove
20 Fed in the Libyan waste by gushing wells,
The priests and damsels of Ammonian Jove
Provoked responses with shrill canticles;
While, in a ship begirt with silver bells,
They round his altar bore the hornèd God,
25 Old Cham, the solar Deity, who dwells
Aloft, yet in a tilting vessel rode,
When universal sea the mountains overflowed.

10 Hebrews Leviticus 23:40–43.

Why speak of Roman Pomps? the haughty claims
Of Chiefs triumphant after ruthless wars;
The feast of Neptune—and the Cereal Games,°   *80*
With images, and crowns, and empty cars;
The dancing Salii—on the shields of Mars
Smiting with fury; and a deeper dread
Scattered on all sides by the hideous jars
Of Corybantian° cymbals, while the head   *85*
Of Cybelè was seen, sublimely turreted!°

At length a Spirit more subdued and soft
Appeared—to govern Christian pageantries:
The Cross, in calm procession, borne aloft
Moved to the chant of sober litanies.   *40*
Even such, this day, came wafted on the breeze
From a long train—in hooded vestments fair
Enwrapt—and winding, between Alpine trees
Spiry and dark, around their House of prayer,
Below the icy bed of bright ARGENTIERE.   *45*

Still in the vivid freshness of a dream,
The pageant haunts me as it met our eyes!
Still, with those white-robed Shapes—a living Stream,
The glacier Pillars join in solemn guise°
For the same service, by mysterious ties;   *50*
Numbers exceeding credible account
Of number, pure and silent Votaries
Issuing or issued from a wintry fount;
The impenetrable heart of that exalted Mount!

They, too, who send so far a holy gleam   *55*
While they the Church engird with motion slow,
A product of that awful Mountain seem,
Poured from his vaults of everlasting snow;

30 **Cereal Games** celebrations in honor of the Greek harvest god-
dess, Ceres.   32–35 **Salii . . . Corybantian** The Salii were priests of
Mars, and the Corybantes priests of Cybele, a Phrygian nature god-
dess. Wordsworth is using Ovid, *Fasti* iv.   36 **turreted** wearing a
turret-like crown.   49 **The . . . guise** In a note, Wordsworth men-
tions "the Glacier-columns, whose sisterly resemblance to the
moving Figures gave it a most beautiful and solemn peculiarity."

Not virgin lilies marshalled in bright row,
60 Not swans descending with the stealthy tide,
A livelier sisterly resemblance show
Than the fair Forms, that in long order glide,
Bear to the glacier band—those Shapes aloft descried.

Trembling, I look upon the secret springs
65 Of that licentious craving in the mind
To act the God among external things,
To bind, on apt suggestion, or unbind;
And marvel not that antique Faith° inclined
To crowd the world with metamorphosis,
70 Vouchsafed in pity or in wrath assigned;
Such insolent temptations wouldst thou miss,
Avoid these sights; nor brood o'er Fable's dark abyss!

1821   1822

ON THE POWER OF SOUND

Argument

The Ear addressed, as occupied by a spiritual functionary,
in communion with sounds, individual, or combined in
studied harmony.—Sources and effects of those sounds
(to the close of 6th Stanza).—The power of music, whence
proceeding, exemplified in the idiot.—Origin of music, and
its effect in early ages—how produced (to the middle of
10th Stanza).—The mind recalled to sounds acting casually
and severally.—Wish uttered (11th Stanza) that these could
be united into a scheme or system for moral interests and
intellectual contemplation.—(Stanza 12th.)—The Pytha-
gorean theory of numbers and music, with their supposed
power over the motions of the universe—imaginations con-
sonant with such a theory.—Wish expressed (in 11th
Stanza) realized, in some degree, by the representation of
all sounds under the form of thanksgiving to the Creator.

68 **antique Faith** faith of the ancients.

—(Last Stanza) the destruction of earth and the planetary system—the survival of audible harmony, and its support in the Divine Nature, as revealed in Holy Writ.

I

Thy functions are ethereal,
As if within thee dwelt a glancing mind,
Organ of vision! And a Spirit aërial
Informs the cell of Hearing, dark and blind;
Intricate labyrinth, more dread for thought   5
To enter than oracular cave;
Strict passage, through which sighs are brought,
And whispers for the heart, their slave;

And shrieks, that revel in abuse
Of shivering flesh; and warbled air,   10
Whose piercing sweetness can unloose
The chains of frenzy, or entice a smile
Into the ambush of despair;
Hosannas pealing down the long-drawn aisle,
And requiems answered by the pulse that beats   15
Devoutly, in life's last retreats!

II

The headlong streams and fountains
Serve Thee, invisible Spirit, with untired powers;
Cheering the wakeful tent on Syrian mountains,
They lull perchance ten thousand thousand flowers.   20
That roar, the prowling lion's *Here I am,*
How fearful to the desert wide!
That bleat, how tender! of the dam
Calling a straggler to her side.
Shout, cuckoo!—let the vernal soul   25
Go with thee to the frozen zone;
Toll from thy loftiest perch, lone bell-bird, toll
At the still hour to Mercy dear,
Mercy from her twilight throne
Listening to nun's faint throb of holy fear,   30
To sailor's prayer breathed from a darkening sea
Or widow's cottage-lullaby.

III

Ye Voices, and ye Shadows
And Images of voice—to hound and horn
85 From rocky steep and rock-bestudded meadows
Flung back, and, in the sky's blue caves, reborn—
On with your pastime! till the church-tower bells
A greeting give of measured glee;
And milder echoes from their cells
40 Repeat the bridal symphony.
Then, or far earlier, let us rove
Where mists are breaking up or gone,
And from aloft look down into a cove
Besprinkled with a careless quire,
45 Happy milk-maids, one by one
Scattering a ditty each to her desire,
A liquid concert matchless by nice Art,
A stream as if from one full heart.

IV

Blest be the song that brightens
50 The blind man's gloom, exalts the veteran's mirth;
Unscorned the peasant's whistling breath, that lightens
His duteous toil of furrowing the green earth.
For the tired slave, Song lifts the languid oar,
And bids it aptly fall, with chime
55 That beautifies the fairest shore,
And mitigates the harshest clime.
Yon pilgrims see—in lagging file
They move; but soon the appointed way
A choral *Ave Marie* shall beguile,
60 And to their hope the distant shrine
Glisten with a livelier ray:
Nor friendless he, the prisoner of the mine,
Who from the well-spring of his own clear breast
Can draw, and sing his griefs to rest.

V

65 When civic renovation
Dawns on a kingdom, and for needful haste
Best eloquence avails not, Inspiration

Mounts with a tune, that travels like a blast
Piping through cave and battlemented tower;
Then starts the sluggard, pleased to meet   70
That voice of Freedom, in its power
Of promises, shrill, wild, and sweet!
Who, from a martial *pageant,* spreads
Incitements of a battle-day,
Thrilling the unweaponed crowd with plumeless
        heads?—   75
Even She whose Lydian airs inspire
Peaceful striving, gentle play
Of timid hope and innocent desire
Shot from the dancing Graces, as they move
Fanned by the plausive wings of Love.   80

VI

How oft along thy mazes,
Regent of sound, have dangerous Passions trod!
O Thou, through whom the temple rings with praises,
And blackening clouds in thunder speak of God,
Betray not by the cozenage of sense   85
Thy votaries, wooingly resigned
To a voluptuous influence
That taints the purer, better, mind;
But lead sick Fancy to a harp
That hath in noble tasks been tried;   90
And, if the virtuous feel a pang too sharp,
Soothe it into patience—stay
The uplifted arm of Suicide;
And let some mood of thine in firm array
Knit every thought the impending issue needs,   95
Ere martyr burns, or patriot bleeds!

VII

As Conscience, to the centre
Of being, smites with irresistible pain,
So shall a solemn cadence, if it enter
The mouldy vaults of the dull idiot's brain,   100
Transmute him to a wretch from quiet hurled—
Convulsed as by a jarring din;

And then aghast, as at the world
Of reason partially let in
105 By concords winding with a sway
Terrible for sense and soul!
Or, awed he weeps, struggling to quell dismay.
Point not these mysteries to an Art
Lodged above the starry pole;
110 Pure modulations flowing from the heart
Of divine Love, where Wisdom, Beauty, Truth
With Order dwell, in endless youth?

VIII

Oblivion may not cover
All treasures hoarded by the miser, Time.
115 Orphean Insight! truth's undaunted lover,
To the first leagues of tutored passion climb,
When Music deigned within this grosser sphere°
Her subtle essence to enfold,
And voice and shell drew forth a tear
120 Softer than Nature's self could mould.
Yet *strenuous* was the infant Age:
Art, daring because souls could feel,
Stirred nowhere but an urgent equipage
Of rapt imagination sped her march
125 Through the realms of woe and weal:
Hell to the lyre bowed low; the upper arch
Rejoiced that clamorous spell and magic verse
Her wan disasters could disperse.

IX

The GIFT to king Amphion
130 That walled a city with its melody
Was for belief no dream: °—thy skill, Arion!°
Could humanise the creatures of the sea,

117 **this grosser sphere** the earth as opposed to the heavens, which were thought to generate a subtle "music of the spheres." 129–31 **The Gift . . . dream** Amphion built the walls of Thebes by so charming the stones with his lute that they danced into place. 131 **Arion** a Greek poet, forced overboard by pirates, but like Orpheus saved by the effect of his song.

Where men were monsters. A last grace he craves,
Leave for one chant;—the dulcet sound
Steals from the deck o'er willing waves,   *135*
And listening dolphins gather round.
Self-cast, as with a desperate course,
'Mid that strange audience, he bestrides
A proud One docile as a managed horse;
And singing, while the accordant hand   *140*
Sweeps his harp, the Master rides;
So shall he touch at length a friendly strand,
And he, with his preserver, shine starbright
In memory, through silent night.

X

The pipe of Pan, to shepherds   *145*
Couched in the shadow of Maenalian pines,°
Was passing sweet; the eyeballs of the leopards,
That in high triumph drew the Lord of vines,
How did they sparkle to the cymbal's clang!
While Fauns and Satyrs beat the ground   *150*
In cadence,—and Silenus swang
This way and that, with wild-flowers crowned.
To life, to *life* give back thine ear:
Ye who are longing to be rid
Of fable, though to truth subservient, hear   *155*
The little sprinkling of cold earth that fell
Echoed from the coffin-lid;
The convict's summons in the steeple's knell;
"The vain distress-gun," from a leeward shore,
Repeated—heard, and heard no more!   *160*

XI

For terror, joy, or pity,
Vast is the compass and the swell of notes:
From the babe's first cry to voice of regal city,
Rolling a solemn sea-like bass, that floats
Far as the woodlands—with the trill to blend   *165*
Of that shy songstress, whose love-tale
Might tempt an angel to descend,

146 **Maenalian** Arcadian.

While hovering o'er the moonlight vale.
Ye wandering Utterances, has earth no scheme,
170 No scale of moral music—to unite
Powers that survive but in the faintest dream
Of memory?—O that ye might stoop to bear
Chains, such precious chains of sight
As laboured minstrelsies through ages wear!
175 O for a balance fit the truth to tell
Of the Unsubstantial, pondered well!

XII

By one pervading spirit
Of tones and numbers all things are controlled,
As sages taught, where faith was found to merit
180 Initiation in that mystery old.
The heavens, whose aspect makes our minds as still
As they themselves appear to be,
Innumerable voices fill
With everlasting harmony;
185 The towering headlands, crowned with mist,
Their feet among the billows, know
That Ocean is a mighty harmonist;
Thy pinions, universal Air,
Ever waving to and fro,
190 Are delegates of harmony, and bear
Strains that support the Seasons in their round;
Stern Winter loves a dirge-like sound.

XIII

Break forth into thanksgiving,
Ye banded instruments of wind and chords;
195 Unite, to magnify the Ever-living,
Your inarticulate notes with the voice of words!
Nor hushed be service from the lowing mead,
Nor mute the forest hum of noon;
Thou too be heard, lone eagle! freed
200 From snowy peak and cloud, attune
Thy hungry barkings to the hymn
Of joy, that from her utmost walls

The six-days' Work° by flaming Seraphim
Transmits to Heaven! As Deep to Deep
Shouting through one valley calls,   *205*
All worlds, all natures, mood and measure keep
For praise and ceaseless gratulation, poured
Into the ear of God, their Lord!

XIV

A Voice to Light gave Being;
To Time, and Man his earth-born chronicler;   *210*
A Voice shall finish doubt and dim foreseeing,
And sweep away life's visionary stir;°
The trumpet (we, intoxicate with pride,
Arm at its blast for deadly wars)
To archangelic lips applied,   *215*
The grave shall open, quench the stars.
O Silence! are Man's noisy years
No more than moments of thy life?
Is Harmony, blest queen of smiles and tears,
With her smooth tones and discords just,   *220*
Tempered into rapturous strife,
Thy destined bond-slave? No! though earth be dust
And vanish, though the heavens dissolve, her stay
Is in the WORD, that shall not pass away.

1828   1835

from LINES SUGGESTED BY A PORTRAIT FROM THE PENCIL OF F. STONE

*   *   *   *

I gaze upon a Portrait whose mild gleam
Of beauty never ceases to enrich
The common light; whose stillness charms the air,
Or seems to charm it, into like repose;
Whose silence, for the pleasure of the ear,   *10*
Surpasses sweetest music. There she sits
With emblematic purity attired

203 **six-days' Work** creation. The stanza imitates Psalm 150.   209–12
A Voice . . . stir Cf. Genesis 1:3 and Revelation 8:7–13.

In a white vest, white as her marble neck
Is, and the pillar of the throat would be
15 But for the shadow by the drooping chin
Cast into that recess—the tender shade,
The shade and light, both there and everywhere,
And through the very atmosphere she breathes,
Broad, clear, and toned harmoniously, with skill
20 That might from nature have been learnt in the hour
When the lone shepherd sees the morning spread
Upon the mountains. Look at her, whoe'er
Thou be that, kindling with a poet's soul,
Hast loved the painter's true Promethean craft
25 Intensely—from Imagination take
The treasure,—what mine eyes behold see thou,
Even though the Atlantic ocean roll between.

A silver line, that runs from brow to crown
And in the middle parts the braided hair,
30 Just serves to show how delicate a soil
The golden harvest grows in; and those eyes,
Soft and capacious as a cloudless sky
Whose azure depth their colour emulates,
Must needs be conversant with upward looks,
35 Prayer's voiceless service; but now, seeking nought
And shunning nought, their own peculiar life
Of motion they renounce, and with the head
Partake its inclination towards earth
In humble grace, and quiet pensiveness
40 Caught at the point where it stops short of sadness.

Offspring of soul-bewitching Art, make me
Thy confidant! say, whence derived that air
Of calm abstraction? Can the ruling thought
Be with some lover far away, or one
45 Crossed by misfortune, or of doubted faith?
Inapt conjecture! Childhood here, a moon
Crescent in simple loveliness serene,
Has but approached the gates of womanhood,
Not entered them; her heart is yet unpierced
50 By the blind Archer-god; her fancy free:
The fount of feeling, if unsought elsewhere,

Will not be found.
                    Her right hand, as it lies
Across the slender wrist of the left arm
Upon her lap reposing, holds—but mark
How slackly, for the absent mind permits   55
No firmer grasp—a little wild-flower, joined
As in a posy, with a few pale ears
Of yellowing corn, the same that overtopped
And in their common birthplace sheltered it
Till they were plucked together; a blue flower   60
Called by the thrifty husbandman a weed;
But Ceres, in her garland, might have worn
That ornament, unblamed. The floweret, held
In scarcely conscious fingers, was, she knows,
(Her Father told her so) in youth's gay dawn   65
Her Mother's favourite; and the orphan Girl,
In her own dawn—a dawn less gay and bright,
Loves it, while there in solitary peace
She sits, for that departed Mother's sake.

*   *   *   *

1834   1835

TO A PAINTER

Though I beheld at first with blank surprise
This Work, I now have gazed on it so long
I see its truth with unreluctant eyes;
O, my Belovèd! I have done thee wrong,
Conscious of blessedness, but, whence it sprung,   5
Ever too heedless, as I now perceive:
Morn into noon did pass, noon into eve,
And the old day was welcome as the young,
As welcome, and as beautiful—in sooth
More beautiful, as being a thing more holy: 10
Thanks to thy virtues, to the eternal youth
Of all thy goodness, never melancholy;
To thy large heart and humble mind, that cast
Into one vision, future, present, past.

1840   1842

SCORN NOT THE SONNET

Scorn not the Sonnet; Critic, you have frowned,
Mindless of its just honours; with this key
Shakespeare unlocked his heart; the melody
Of this small lute gave ease to Petrarch's wound;
5   A thousand times this pipe did Tasso sound;
With it Camöens soothed an exile's grief;
The Sonnet glittered a gay myrtle leaf
Amid the cypress with which Dante crowned
His visionary brow: a glow-worm lamp,
10   It cheered mild Spenser, called from Faery-land
To struggle through dark ways; and, when a damp
Fell round the path of Milton, in his hand
The Thing became a trumpet; whence he blew
Soul-animating strains—alas, too few!

1820–27   1827

WATER SONNETS°

Composed by the Side of Grasmere Lake

Clouds, lingering yet, extend in solid bars
Through the grey west; and lo! these waters, steeled
By breezeless air to smoothest polish, yield
A vivid repetition of the stars;
5   Jove, Venus, and the ruddy crest of Mars
Amid his fellows beauteously revealed
At happy distance from earth's groaning field,
Where ruthless mortals wage incessant wars.
Is it a mirror?—or the nether Sphere
10   Opening to view the abyss in which she feeds
Her own calm fires?—But list! a voice is near;
Great Pan himself low-whispering through the reeds,

0 **Water Sonnets** These are selected from the many water sonnets
printed by Wordsworth in his forties and fifties.

"Be thankful, thou; for, if unholy deeds
Ravage the world, tranquillity is here!"

1807   1819

Pure Element of Waters

Pure element of waters! wheresoe'er
Thou dost forsake thy subterranean haunts,
Green herbs, bright flowers, and berry-bearing plants,
Rise into life and in thy train appear:
And, through the sunny portion of the year,   5
Swift insects shine, thy hovering pursuivants:
And, if thy bounty fail, the forest pants;
And hart and hind and hunter with his spear
Languish and droop together. Nor unfelt
In man's perturbèd soul thy sway benign;   10
And, haply, far within the marble belt
Of central earth, where tortured Spirits pine
For grace and goodness lost, thy murmurs melt
Their anguish,—and they blend sweet songs with thine.

1818   ·   1819

Gordale

At early dawn, or rather when the air
Glimmers with fading light, and shadowy Eve
Is busiest to confer and to bereave;
Then, pensive Votary! let thy feet repair
To Gordale-chasm, terrific as the lair   5
Where the young lions couch; for so, by leave
Of the propitious hour, thou may'st perceive
The local Deity, with oozy hair
And mineral crown, beside his jagged urn,
Recumbent: Him thou may'st behold, who hides   10
His lineaments by day, yet there presides,
Teaching the docile waters how to turn,
Or (if need be) impediment to spurn,
And force their passage to the salt-sea tides!

1818   1819

To the Torrent at the Devil's Bridge, North Wales, 1824

How art thou named? In search of what strange land,
From what huge height, descending? Can such force
Of waters issue from a British source,
Or hath not Pindus° fed thee, where the band
5   Of Patriots scoop their freedom out, with hand
Desperate as thine? Or come the incessant shocks
From that young Stream, that smites the throbbing rocks,
Of Viamala? There I seem to stand,
  As in life's morn;° permitted to behold,
10 From the dread chasm, woods climbing above woods,
In pomp that fades not; everlasting snows;
And skies that ne'er relinquish their repose;
Such power possess the family of floods
Over the minds of Poets, young or old!

1824

1827

After-Thought

I thought of Thee,° my partner and my guide,
As being past away.—Vain sympathies!
For, backward, Duddon! as I cast my eyes,
I see what was, and is, and will abide;
5   Still glides the Stream, and shall for ever glide;
The Form remains, the Function never dies;
While we, the brave, the mighty, and the wise,
We Men, who in our morn of youth defied
The elements, must vanish;—be it so!
10 Enough, if something from our hands have power
To live, and act, and serve the future hour;
And if, as toward the silent tomb we go,

4 **Pindus** mountain range where, at this date, the Greek War of
Independence was being fought.   9 **As in life's morn** He had viewed
the scenic gorge of Viamala more than thirty years before during
his tour of the Alps (1790).

1 **Thee** the river. This poem concludes a sonnet sequence following
the Duddon from its source in the Lake District to the Irish Sea.

Through love, through hope, and faith's transcendent
    dower,
We feel that we are greater than we know.

1818–20   1820

ON THE PROJECTED KENDAL AND WINDERMERE RAILWAY

Is then no nook of English ground secure
From rash assault? Schemes of retirement sown
In youth, and 'mid the busy world kept pure
As when their earliest flowers of hope were blown,
Must perish;—how can they this blight endure?   *5*
And must he too the ruthless change bemoan
Who scorns a false utilitarian lure
'Mid his paternal fields at random thrown?
Baffle the threat, bright Scene, from Orrest-head
Given to the pausing traveller's rapturous glance: *10*
Plead for thy peace, thou beautiful romance
Of nature; and, if human hearts be dead,
Speak, passing winds; ye torrents, with your strong
And constant voice, protest against the wrong.

1844   1844

MUTABILITY

From low to high doth dissolution climb,
And sink from high to low, along a scale
Of awful notes, whose concord shall not fail;
A musical but melancholy chime,

5 Which they can hear who meddle not with crime,
   Nor avarice, nor over-anxious care.
   Truth fails not; but her outward forms that bear
   The longest date do melt like frosty rime,
   That in the morning whitened hill and plain
10 And is no more; drop like the tower sublime
   Of yesterday, which royally did wear
   His crown of weeds, but could not even sustain
   Some casual shout that broke the silent air,
   Or the unimaginable touch of Time.

1821   1822

I SAW THE FIGURE OF A LOVELY MAID°

   I saw the figure of a lovely Maid
   Seated alone beneath a darksome tree,
   Whose fondly-overhanging canopy
   Set off her brightness with a pleasing shade.
5 No Spirit was she; *that* my heart betrayed,
   For she was one I loved exceedingly;
   But while I gazed in tender reverie
   (Or was it sleep that with my Fancy played?)
   The bright corporeal presence—form and face—
10 Remaining still distinct grew thin and rare,
   Like sunny mist;—at length the golden hair,
   Shape, limbs, and heavenly features, keeping pace
   Each with the other in a lingering race
   Of dissolution, melted into air.

1821   1822

0 I Saw . . . Maid A poem on his daughter's death that came to
him while working on *Ecclesiastical Sonnets*. It introduces Part III
of that sequence.

EXTEMPORE EFFUSION UPON THE
DEATH OF JAMES HOGG°

When first, descending from the moorlands,
I saw the Stream of Yarrow glide
Along a bare and open valley,
The Ettrick Shepherd was my guide.

When last along its banks I wandered,   5
Through groves that had begun to shed
Their golden leaves upon the pathways,
My steps the Border-minstrel led.

The mighty Minstrel breathes no longer,
'Mid mouldering ruins low he lies;   10
And death upon the braes of Yarrow,
Has closed the Shepherd-poet's eyes:

Nor has the rolling year twice measured,
From sign to sign, its stedfast course,
Since every mortal power of Coleridge   15
Was frozen at its marvellous source;

The rapt One, of the godlike forehead,
The heaven-eyed creature sleeps in earth:
And Lamb, the frolic and the gentle,
Has vanished from his lonely hearth.   20

Like clouds that rake the mountain-summits,
Or waves that own no curbing hand,
How fast has brother followed brother,
From sunshine to the sunless land!

Yet I, whose lids from infant slumber   25
Were earlier raised, remain to hear
A timid voice, that asks in whispers,
"Who next will drop and disappear?"

0 **Extempore . . . James Hogg** Hogg, a shepherd-poet ("Ettrick
Shepherd," line 4), and here considered a guardian of rural poetry,
died in 1835. Wordsworth's author-friends, Sir Walter Scott (line 8),
S. T. Coleridge (15), Charles Lamb (19), George Crabbe (31),
and Felicia Hemans (39) had all died in the preceding three years.

Our haughty life is crowned with darkness,
30 Like London with its own black wreath,
On which with thee, O Crabbe! forth-looking,
I gazed from Hampstead's breezy heath.

As if but yesterday departed,
Thou too art gone before; but why,
35 O'er ripe fruit, seasonably gathered,
Should frail survivors heave a sigh?

Mourn rather for that holy Spirit,
Sweet as the spring, as ocean deep;
For Her who, ere her summer faded,
40 Has sunk into a breathless sleep.

No more of old romantic sorrows,
For slaughtered Youth or love-lorn Maid!
With sharper grief is Yarrow smitten,
And Ettrick mourns with her their Poet dead.

1835   1835

ADDRESS FROM THE SPIRIT OF COCKERMOUTH CASTLE°

"Thou look'st upon me, and dost fondly think,
Poet! that, stricken as both are by years,
We, differing once so much, are now Compeers,
Prepared, when each has stood his time, to sink
5 Into the dust. Erewhile a sterner link
United us; when thou, in boyish play,
Entering my dungeon, didst become a prey
To soul-appalling darkness. Not a blink
Of light was there;—and thus did I, thy Tutor,
10 Make thy young thoughts acquainted with the grave;
While thou wert chasing the winged butterfly
Through my green courts; or climbing, a bold suitor,
Up to the flowers whose golden progeny
Still round my shattered brow in beauty wave."

1833   1835

0 **Address from . . . Castle** Cockermouth was the poet's birthplace.

V.   Selected Prose

LETTER TO THE BISHOP OF LANDAFF[1]

* * * *

You say: "I fly with terror and abhorrence even from the altar of Liberty, when I see it stained with the blood of the aged, of the innocent, of the defenceless sex, of the ministers of religion, and of the faithful adherents of a fallen monarch." What! have you so little knowledge of the nature of man as to be ignorant that a time of revolution is not the season of true Liberty? Alas, the obstinacy and perversion of man is such that she is too often obliged to borrow the very arms of Despotism to overthrow him, and, in order to reign in peace, must establish herself by violence. She deplores such stern necessity, but the safety of the people, her supreme law, is her consolation. This apparent contradiction between the principles of liberty and the march of revolutions; this spirit of jealousy, of severity, of disquietude, of vexation, indispensable from a state of war between the oppressors and oppressed, must of necessity confuse the ideas of morality, and contract the benign exertion of the best affections of the human heart. Political virtues are developed at the expense of moral ones; and the sweet emotions of compassion, evidently dangerous when traitors are to be punished, are too often altogether smothered. But is this a sufficient reason to reprobate a convulsion from which is to spring a fairer order of things? It is the province of education to rectify the erroneous notions which a habit of oppression, and even of resistance, may

[1] **Letter to the Bishop of Landaff** Incidents like the September massacres and the execution of Louis XVI turned such once-sympathetic Englishmen as Richard Watson, Bishop of Landaff (Wales), against the French Revolution. As France was declaring war upon England, the Bishop published his "Strictures on the French Revolution" in which he castigated the Republic and eulogized Britain's Monarchy. Wordsworth, twenty-three and fresh from his travels in France, composed this reply but did not publish it. It was eventually printed in 1876 by A. Grosart.

have created, and to soften this ferocity of character, proceeding from a necessary suspension of the mild and social virtues; it belongs to her to create a race of men who, truly free, will look upon their fathers as only enfranchised.

*   *   *   *

Perhaps in the very outset of this inquiry the principle on which I proceed will be questioned, and I shall be told that the people are not the proper judges of their own welfare. But because under every government of modern times, till the foundation of the American Republic, the bulk of mankind have appeared incapable of discerning their true interests, no conclusion can be drawn against my principle. At this moment have we not daily the strongest proofs of the success with which, in what you call the best of all monarchical governments, the popular mind may be debauched?

*   *   *   *

You ask with triumphant confidence, to what other law are the people of England subject than the general will of the society to which they belong? Is your Lordship to be told that acquiescence is not choice, and that obedience is not freedom? If there is a single man in Great Britain who has no suffrage in the election of a representative, the will of the society of which he is a member is not generally expressed.

*   *   *   *

"The greatest freedom that can be enjoyed by man in a state of civil society, the greatest security that can be given with respect to the protection of his character, property, personal liberty, limb, and life, is afforded to every individual by our present constitution.

"Let it never be forgotten by ourselves, and let us impress the observation upon the hearts of our children, that we are in possession of both (liberty and equality), of as much of both as can be consistent with the end for which civil society was introduced among mankind."

Many of my readers will hardly believe me when I inform them that these passages are copied verbatim from your Appendix.[2] Mr. Burke roused the indignation of all ranks of men when, by a refinement in cruelty superior to

[2] **Appendix** The Bishop's "Strictures" formed an Appendix to an earlier Sermon.

that which in the East yokes the living to the dead, he strove to persuade us[3] that we and our posterity to the end of time were riveted to a constitution by the indissoluble compact of—a dead parchment, and were bound to cherish a corse at the bosom when reason might call aloud that it should be entombed. Your Lordship aims at the same detestable object by means more criminal, because more dangerous and insidious. Attempting to lull the people of England into a belief that any inquiries directed towards the nature of liberty and equality can in no other way lead to their happiness than by convincing them that they have already arrived at perfection in the science of government, what is your object but to exclude them for ever from the most fruitful field of human knowledge? Besides, it is another cause to execrate this doctrine that the consequence of such fatal delusion would be that they must entirely draw off their attention, not only from the government, but from their governors; that the stream of public vigilance, far from clearing and enriching the prospect of society, would by its stagnation consign it to barrenness, and by its putrefaction infect it with death. You have aimed an arrow at liberty and philosophy, the eyes of the human race. . . .

* * * *

1793

GROWTH OF A CRIMINAL MIND[1]

Let us suppose a young man of great intellectual powers yet without any solid principles of genuine benevolence. His master passions are pride and the love of distinction. He has deeply imbibed a spirit of enterprise in a tumultuous age. He goes into the world and is betrayed into a great crime.—That influence on which all his happiness is built immediately deserts him. His talents are robbed of their

[3] **Mr. Burke . . . persuade us** in *Reflections on the French Revolution* (1790).

[1] **Growth of a Criminal Mind** is from Wordsworth's essay on the character of Oswald (Rivers) in *The Borderers.*

weight, his exertions are unavailing, and he quits the world in disgust, with strong misanthropic feelings. In his retirement, he is impelled to examine the unreasonableness of established opinions; and the force of his mind exhausts itself in constant efforts to separate the elements of virtue and vice. It is his pleasure and his consolation to hunt out whatever is bad in actions usually esteemed virtuous, and to detect the good in actions which the universal sense of mankind teaches us to reprobate. While the general exertion of his intellect seduces him from the remembrance of his own crime, the particular conclusions to which he is led have a tendency to reconcile him to himself. His feelings are interested in making him a moral sceptic, and as his scepticism increases he is raised in his own esteem. After this process has been continued some time his natural energy and restlessness impel him again into the world. In this state, pressed by the recollection of his guilt he seeks relief from two sources, action and meditation. Of actions those are most attractive which best exhibit his own powers, partly from the original pride of his own character, and still more because the loss of authority and influence which followed upon his crime was the first circumstance which impressed him with the magnitude of that crime, and brought along with it those tormenting sensations by which he is assailed. The recovery of his original importance and the exhibition of his own powers are therefore in his mind almost identified with the extinction of those powerful feelings which attend the recollection of his guilt. Perhaps there is no cause which has greater weight in preventing the return of bad men to virtue than that good actions being for the most part in their nature silent and regularly progressive, they do not present those sudden results which can afford a sufficient stimulus to a troubled mind. In processes of vice the effects are more frequently immediate, palpable and extensive. Power is much more easily manifested in destroying than in creating. A child, Rousseau has observed, will tear in pieces fifty toys before he will think of making one. From these causes, assisted by disgust and misanthropic feeling, the character we are now contemplating will have a strong tendency to vice. His energies are most impressively manifest in works of devastation. He is the Orlando of Ariosto, the Cardenio of Cervantes, who lays waste the groves that should shelter him. He has rebelled against the world and the laws of the world, and he regards them as tyrannical masters; convinced that he is right in some of his conclusions, he nourishes a contempt for mankind the more dangerous because he has been led to it by reflection. Being in the habit of considering the world as a body which is in some sort of war with him, he has a feeling borrowed from that habit which gives an additional zest to his hatred of those members of society whom he hates and to his own contempt of those whom he despises. Add to this, that a mind fond of nourishing sentiments of contempt will be prone to the admission of those feelings which are considered under any uncommon bond of relation (as must be the case with a man who has quarrelled with the world), and the feelings will mutually strengthen each other. In this morbid state of mind he cannot exist without occupation, he requires constant provocations, all his pleasures are prospective, he is perpetually chasing a phantom, he commits new crimes to drive away the memory of the past. But the lenitives[2] of his pain are twofold, meditation as well as action. Accordingly, his reason is almost exclusively employed in justifying his past enormities and in enabling him to commit new ones. He is perpetually imposing upon himself, he has a sophism for every crime. The *mild* effusions of thought, the milk of human reason are unknown to him. His imagination is powerful, being strengthened by the habit of picturing possible forms of society where his crimes would be no longer crimes, and he would enjoy that estimation to which, from his intellectual attainments, he deems himself entitled. The nicer shades of manners he disregards; but whenever upon looking back upon past ages, or in surveying the practices of different countries in the age in which he lives, he finds such contrarieties as seem to affect the principles of *morals,* he exults over his discovery, and applies it to his heart as the dearest of consolations. Such a mind cannot but discover some truths, but he is unable to profit by them, and in his hands they become instruments of evil.

[2] **lenitives** alleviations.

He presses truth and falsehood into the same service. He looks at society through an optical glass of a peculiar tint; something of the forms of objects he takes from objects, but their colour is exclusively what he gives them; it is one, and it is his own. Having indulged a habit, dangerous in a man who has fallen, of dallying with moral calculations, he becomes an empiric, and a daring and unfeeling empiric. He disguises from himself his own malignity by assuming the character of a speculator in morals, and one who has the hardihood to realize his speculations.

It will easily be perceived that to such a mind those enterprises which are most extraordinary will in time appear the most inviting. His appetite from being exhausted becomes unnatural. Accordingly he will struggle so to characterize and to exalt actions little and contemptible in themselves by a forced greatness of *manner*, and will chequer and degrade enterprises great in their atrocity by grotesque littleness of manner and fantastic obliquities. He is like a worn out voluptuary—he finds his temptation in strangeness, he is unable to suppress a low hankering after the double entendre in vice; yet his thirst after the extraordinary buoys him up, and supported by a habit of constant reflection he frequently breaks out into what has the appearance of greatness; and in sudden emergencies, when he is called upon by surprise and thrown out of the path of his regular habits, or when dormant associations are awakened tracing the revolutions through which his character has passed, in painting his former self he really *is* great.

Benefits conferred on a man like this will be the seeds of a worse feeling than ingratitude. They will give birth to positive hatred. Let him be deprived of power, though by means which he despises, and he will never forgive. It will scarcely be denied that such a mind, by very slight external motives, may be led to the commission of the greatest enormities. Let its malignant feelings be fixed on a particular object, and the rest follows of itself.

Having shaken off the obligations of religion and morality in a dark and tempestuous age, it is probable that such a character will be infected with a tinge of superstition. The period in which he lives teems with great events which he feels he cannot control. That influence which his pride makes him unwilling to allow to his fellowmen he has no reluctance to ascribe to invisible agents: his pride impells him to superstition and shapes the nature of his belief: his creed is his own: it is made and not adopted.

A character like this, or some of its features at least, I have attempted to delineate in the following drama. I have introduced him deliberately prosecuting the destruction of an amiable young man by the most atrocious means, and with a pertinacity, as it should seem, not to be accounted for but on the supposition of the most malignant injuries. No such injuries however appear to have been sustained. What then are his motives? First it must be observed that to make the non-existence of a common motive itself a motive to action is a practice which we are never so prone to attribute exclusively to madmen as when we forget ourselves. Our love of the marvellous is not confined to external things. There is no object on which it settles with more delight than on our own minds. This habit is in the very essence of the habit which we are delineating.

But there are particles of that poisonous mineral of which Iago speaks gnawing his innards; his malevolent feelings are excited, and he hates the more deeply because he feels he ought not to hate.

We all know that the dissatisfaction accompanying the first impulses towards a criminal action, where the mind is familiar with guilt, acts as a stimulus to proceed in that action. Uneasiness must be driven away by fresh uneasiness, obstinacy, waywardness and wilful blindness are alternatives resorted to, till there is an universal insurrection of every depraved feeling of the heart.

Besides, in a course of criminal conduct every fresh step that we make appears a justification of the one which preceded it, it seems to bring again the moment of liberty and choice; it banishes the idea of repentance, and seems to set remorse at defiance. Every time we plan a fresh accumulation of our guilt we have restored to us something like that original state of mind, that perturbed pleasure, which first made the crime attractive.

*   *   *   *

1797   1926

PREFACE TO *LYRICAL BALLADS*[1]

. . . It is supposed, that by the act of writing in verse an Author makes a formal engagement that he will gratify certain known habits of association; that he not only thus apprises the Reader that certain classes of ideas and expressions will be found in his book, but that others will be carefully excluded. This exponent or symbol held forth by metrical language must in different eras of literature have excited very different expectations: for example, in the age of Catullus, Terence and Lucretius, and that of Statius or Claudian; and in our own country, in the age of Shakespeare and Beaumont and Fletcher, and that of Donne and Cowley, or Dryden, or Pope. I will not take upon me to determine the exact import of the promise which by the act of writing in verse an Author, in the present day, makes to his Reader; but I am certain, it will appear to many persons that I have not fulfilled the terms of an engagement thus voluntarily contracted. They who have been accustomed to the gaudiness and inane phraseology of many modern writers, if they persist in reading this book to its conclusion, will, no doubt, frequently have to struggle with feelings of strangeness and aukwardness: they will look round for poetry, and will be induced to inquire by what species of courtesy these attempts can be permitted to assume that title. I hope therefore the Reader will not censure me, if I attempt to state what I have proposed to myself to perform; and also, (as far as the limits of a preface will permit) to explain some of the chief reasons which have determined me in the choice of my purpose: that at least he may be spared any unpleasant feeling of disappointment, and that I myself may be protected from the most dishonourable accusation which can be brought against an Author, namely, that of an indolence which prevents him from endeavouring to ascertain what is his duty, or, when his duty is ascertained, prevents him from performing it.

The principal object, then, which I proposed to myself in these Poems was to choose incidents and situations from

---

[1] **Lyrical Ballads** In January, 1801, Wordsworth published a second edition and added a Preface. Another edition appeared in 1802, and Wordsworth took the opportunity to expand the Preface. The following is from the expanded version.

common life, and to relate or describe them, throughout, as
far as was possible, in a selection of language really used
by men; and, at the same time, to throw over them a certain
colouring of imagination, whereby ordinary things should
be presented to the mind in an unusual way; and, further,
and above all, to make these incidents and situations inter-
esting by tracing in them, truly though not ostentatiously,
the primary laws of our nature: chiefly, as far as regards the
manner in which we associate ideas in a state of excitement.
Low and rustic life was generally chosen, because in that
condition, the essential passions of the heart find a better
soil in which they can attain their maturity, are less under
restraint, and speak a plainer and more emphatic language;
because in that condition of life our elementary feelings
co-exist in a state of greater simplicity, and, consequently,
may be more accurately contemplated, and more forcibly
communicated; because the manners of rural life germinate
from those elementary feelings; and, from the necessary
character of rural occupations, are more easily compre-
hended; and are more durable; and lastly, because in that
condition the passions of men are incorporated with the
beautiful and permanent forms of nature. The language,
too, of these men is adopted (purified indeed from what
appear to be its real defects, from all lasting and rational
causes of dislike or disgust) because such men hourly com-
municate with the best objects from which the best part of
language is originally derived; and because, from their rank
in society and the sameness and narrow circle of their inter-
course, being less under the influence of social vanity they
convey their feelings and notions in simple and unelabo-
rated expressions. Accordingly, such a language, arising out
of repeated experience and regular feelings, is a more per-
manent, and a far more philosophical language, than that
which is frequently substituted for it by Poets, who think
that they are conferring honour upon themselves and their
art, in proportion as they separate themselves from the
sympathies of men, and indulge in arbitrary and capricious
habits of expression, in order to furnish food for fickle
tastes, and fickle appetites, of their own creation.

I cannot, however, be insensible of the present outcry
against the triviality and meanness both of thought and lan-

guage, which some of my contemporaries have occasionally introduced into their metrical compositions; and I acknowledge that this defect, where it exists, is more dishonourable to the Writer's own character than false refinement or arbitrary innovation, though I should contend at the same time that it is far less pernicious in the sum of its consequences. From such verses the Poems in these volumes will be found distinguished at least by one mark of difference, that each of them has a worthy *purpose*. Not that I mean to say, that I always began to write with a distinct purpose formally conceived; but I believe that my habits of meditation have so formed my feelings, as that my descriptions of such objects as strongly excite those feelings, will be found to carry along with them a *purpose*. If in this opinion I am mistaken, I can have little right to the name of a Poet. For all good poetry is the spontaneous overflow of powerful feelings: but though this be true, Poems to which any value can be attached, were never produced on any variety of subjects but by a man, who being possessed of more than usual organic sensibility, had also thought long and deeply. For our continued influxes of feeling are modified and directed by our thoughts, which are indeed the representatives of all our past feelings; and, as by contemplating the relation of these general representatives to each other we discover what is really important to men, so, by the repetition and continuance of this act, our feelings will be connected with important subjects, till at length, if we be originally possessed of much sensibility, such habits of mind will be produced, that, by obeying blindly and mechanically the impulses of those habits, we shall describe objects, and utter sentiments, of such a nature and in such connection with each other, that the understanding of the being to whom we address ourselves, if he be in a healthful state of association, must necessarily be in some degree enlightened, and his affections ameliorated.

I have said that each of these poems has a purpose. I have also informed my Reader what this purpose will be found principally to be: namely, to illustrate the manner in which our feelings and ideas are associated in a state of excitement. But, speaking in language somewhat more appropriate, it is to follow the fluxes and refluxes of the mind when agitated by the great and simple affections of our nature. This object I have endeavoured in these short essays to attain by various means; by tracing the maternal passion through many of its more subtile windings, as in the poems of the IDIOT BOY and the MAD MOTHER; by accompanying the last struggles of a human being, at the approach of death, cleaving in solitude to life and society, as in the Poem of the FORSAKEN INDIAN; by showing, as in the Stanzas entitled WE ARE SEVEN, the perplexity and obscurity which in childhood attend our notion of death, or rather our utter inability to admit that notion; or by displaying the strength of fraternal, or to speak more philosophically, of moral attachment when early associated with the great and beautiful objects of nature, as in THE BROTHERS; or, as in the Incident of SIMON LEE, by placing my Reader in the way of receiving from ordinary moral sensations another and more salutary impression than we are accustomed to receive from them. It has also been part of my general purpose to attempt to sketch characters under the influence of less impassioned feelings, as in the TWO APRIL MORNINGS, THE FOUNTAIN, THE OLD MAN TRAVELLING, THE TWO THIEVES, &c. characters of which the elements are simple, belonging rather to nature than to manners, such as exist now, and will probably always exist, and which from their constitution may be distinctly and profitably contemplated. I will not abuse the indulgence of my Reader by dwelling longer upon this subject; but it is proper that I should mention one other circumstance which distinguishes these Poems from the popular Poetry of the day; it is this, that the feeling therein developed gives importance to the action and situation, and not the action and situation to the feeling. . . .

I will not suffer a sense of false modesty to prevent me from asserting, that I point my Reader's attention to this mark of distinction, far less for the sake of these particular Poems than from the general importance of the subject. The subject is indeed important! For the human mind is capable of being excited without the application of gross and violent stimulants; and he must have a very faint perception of its beauty and dignity who does not know this, and who does not further know, that one being is elevated above another, in proportion as he possesses this capability. It has therefore appeared to me, that to endeavour to produce or enlarge this capability is one of the best services in which, at any period, a Writer can be engaged; but this service, excellent at all times, is especially so at the present day. For a multitude of causes, unknown to former times, are now acting with a combined force to blunt the discriminating powers of the mind, and unfitting it for all voluntary exertion to reduce it to a state of almost savage torpor. The most effective of these causes are the great national events which are daily taking place, and the increasing accumulation of men in cities, where the uniformity of their occupations produces a craving for extraordinary incident, which the rapid communication of intelligence hourly gratifies. To this tendency of life and manners the literature and theatrical exhibitions of the country have conformed themselves. The invaluable works of our elder writers, I had almost said the works of Shakespeare and Milton, are driven into neglect by frantic novels, sickly and stupid German Tragedies, and deluges of idle and extravagant stories in verse.—When I think upon this degrading thirst after outrageous stimulation, I am almost ashamed to have spoken of the feeble effort with which I have endeavoured to counteract it; and, reflecting upon the magnitude of the general evil, I should be oppressed with no dishonorable melancholy, had I not a deep impression of certain inherent and indestructible qualities of the human mind, and likewise of certain powers in the great and permanent objects that act upon it, which are equally inherent and indestructible; and did I not further add to this impression a belief, that the time is approaching when the evil will be systematically opposed, by men of greater powers, and with far more distinguished success.

Having dwelt thus long on the subjects and aim of these Poems, I shall request the Reader's permission to apprize him of a few circumstances relating to their *style*, in order, among other reasons, that I may not be censured for not having performed what I never attempted. The Reader will find that personifications of abstract ideas rarely occur in these volumes; and, I hope, are utterly rejected as an ordinary device to elevate the style, and raise it above prose. I have proposed to myself to imitate, and, as far as is possible, to adopt the very language of men; and assuredly such

personifications do not make any natural or regular part of
that language. They are, indeed, a figure of speech occa-
sionally prompted by passion, and I have made use of them
as such; but I have endeavoured utterly to reject them as a
mechanical device of style, or as a family language which
Writers in metre seem to lay claim to by prescription. I
have wished to keep my Reader in the company of flesh and
blood, persuaded that by so doing I shall interest him. I am,
however, well aware that others who pursue a different
track may interest him likewise; I do not interfere with their
claim, I only wish to prefer a different claim of my own.
There will also be found in these volumes little of what is
usually called poetic diction; I have taken as much pains to
avoid it as others ordinarily take to produce it; this I have
done for the reason already alleged, to bring my language
near to the language of men, and further, because the plea-
sure which I have proposed to myself to impart is of a kind
very different from that which is supposed by many persons
to be the proper object of poetry. I do not know how, with-
out being culpably particular, I can give my Reader a more
exact notion of the style in which I wished these poems to
be written, than by informing him that I have at all times
endeavoured to look steadily at my subject; consequently,
I hope that there is in these Poems little falsehood of de-
scription, and that my ideas are expressed in language fitted
to their respective importance. Something I must have
gained by this practice, as it is friendly to one property of
all good poetry, namely good sense; but it has necessarily
cut me off from a large portion of phrases and figures of
speech which from father to son have long been regarded as
the common inheritance of Poets. I have also thought it
expedient to restrict myself still further, having abstained
from the use of many expressions, in themselves proper and
beautiful, but which have been foolishly repeated by bad
Poets, till such feelings of disgust are connected with them
as it is scarcely possible by any art of association to over-
power.

If in a poem there should be found a series of lines, or
even a single line, in which the language, though naturally
arranged, and according to the strict laws of metre, does
not differ from that of prose, there is a numerous class of

critics, who, when they stumble upon these prosaisms, as they call them, imagine that they have made a notable discovery, and exult over the Poet as over a man ignorant of his own profession. Now these men would establish a canon of criticism which the Reader will conclude he must utterly reject, if he wishes to be pleased with these volumes. And it would be a most easy task to prove to him, that not only the language of a large portion of every good poem, even of the most elevated character, must necessarily, except with reference to the metre, in no respect differ from that of good prose, but likewise that some of the most interesting parts of the best poems will be found to be strictly the language of prose, when prose is well written. The truth of this assertion might be demonstrated by innumerable passages from almost all the poetical writings, even of Milton himself. I have not space for much quotation; but, to illustrate the subject in a general manner, I will here adduce a short composition of Gray,[2] who was at the head of those who, by their reasonings, have attempted to widen the space of separation betwixt Prose and Metrical composition, and was more than any other man curiously elaborate in the structure of his own poetic diction.

> In vain to me the smiling mornings shine,
> And reddening Phoebus lifts his golden fire:
> The birds in vain their amorous descant join,
> Or cheerful fields resume their green attire.
> These ears, alas! for other notes repine;
> *A different object do these eyes require;*
> *My lonely anguish melts no heart but mine;*
> *And in my breast the imperfect joys expire;*
> Yet morning smiles the busy race to cheer,
> And new-born pleasure brings to happier men;
> The fields to all their wonted tribute bear;
> To warm their little loves the birds complain.
> *I fruitless mourn to him that cannot hear,*
> *And weep the more because I weep in vain.*

[2] **Gray** Thomas Gray (1716–71) once wrote to Richard West: "The language of the age is never the language of poetry. . . . Our poetry . . . has a language peculiar to itself; to which almost every one, that has written, has added something by enriching it with foreign idioms and derivatives: nay sometimes words of their own composition. . . ." (See also pp. 424–26 below.) Wordsworth goes on to criticize Gray's "Sonnet on the Death of Richard West."

It will easily be perceived that the only part of this Sonnet which is of any value is the lines printed in Italics: it is equally obvious, that, except in the rhyme, and in the use of the single word "fruitless" for fruitlessly, which is so far a defect, the language of these lines does in no respect differ from that of prose.

By the foregoing quotation I have shown that the language of Prose may yet be well adapted to Poetry; and I have previously asserted that a large portion of the language of every good poem can in no respect differ from that of good Prose. I will go further. I do not doubt that it may be safely affirmed, that there neither is, nor can be, any essential difference between the language of prose and metrical composition. We are fond of tracing the resemblance between Poetry and Painting, and, accordingly, we call them Sisters: but where shall we find bonds of connection sufficiently strict to typify the affinity betwixt metrical and prose composition? They both speak by and to the same organs; the bodies in which both of them are clothed may be said to be of the same substance, their affections are kindred, and almost identical, not necessarily different even in degree; Poetry sheds no tears "such as Angels weep," but natural and human tears; she can boast of no celestial Ichor that distinguishes her vital juices from those of prose; the same human blood circulates through the veins of them both.

If it be affirmed that rhyme and metrical arrangement of themselves constitute a distinction which overturns what I have been saying on the strict affinity of metrical language with that of prose, and paves the way for other artificial distinctions which the mind voluntarily admits, I answer that the language of such Poetry as I am recommending is, as far as is possible, a selection of the language really spoken by men; that this selection, wherever it is made with true taste and feeling, will of itself form a distinction far greater than would at first be imagined, and will entirely separate the composition from the vulgarity and meanness of ordinary life; and, if metre be superadded thereto, I believe that a dissimilitude will be produced altogether sufficient for the gratification of a rational mind. What other distinction would we have? Whence is it to come? And where is it to exist? Not, surely, where the Poet speaks through the mouths of his characters: it cannot be necessary here, either for elevation of style, or any of its supposed ornaments; for, if the Poet's subject be judiciously chosen, it will naturally, and upon fit occasion, lead him to passions the language of which, if selected truly and judiciously, must necessarily be dignified and variegated, and alive with metaphors and figures. I forbear to speak of an incongruity which would shock the intelligent Reader, should the Poet interweave any foreign splendour of his own with that which the passion naturally suggests: it is sufficient to say that such addition is unnecessary. And, surely, it is more probable that those passages, which with propriety abound with metaphors and figures, will have their due effect, if, upon other occasions where the passions are of a milder character, the style also be subdued and temperate.

But, as the pleasure which I hope to give by the Poems I now present to the Reader must depend entirely on just notions upon this subject, and, as it is in itself of the highest importance to our taste and moral feelings, I cannot content myself with these detached remarks. And if, in what I am about to say, it shall appear to some that my labour is unnecessary, and that I am like a man fighting a battle without enemies, I would remind such persons that, whatever may be the language outwardly holden by men, a practical faith in the opinions which I am wishing to establish is almost unknown. If my conclusions are admitted, and carried as far as they must be carried if admitted at all, our judgments concerning the works of the greatest Poets both ancient and modern will be far different from what they are at present, both when we praise, and when we censure: and our moral feelings influencing, and influenced by these judgments will, I believe, be corrected and purified.

Taking up the subject, then, upon general grounds, I ask what is meant by the word Poet? What is a Poet? To whom does he address himself? And what language is to be expected from him? He is a man speaking to men: a man, it is true, endued with more lively sensibility, more enthusiasm and tenderness, who has a greater knowledge of human nature, and a more comprehensive soul, than are supposed to be common among mankind; a man pleased with his own passions and volitions, and who rejoices more than other men in the spirit of life that is in him; delighting to contemplate similar volitions and passions as manifested in the goings-on of the Universe, and habitually impelled to create them where he does not find them. To these qualities he has added a disposition to be affected more than other men by absent things as if they were present, an ability of conjuring up in himself passions, which are indeed far from being the same as those produced by real events, yet (especially in those parts of the general sympathy which are pleasing and delightful) do more nearly resemble the passions produced by real events, than any thing which, from the motions of their own minds merely, other men are accustomed to feel in themselves; whence, and from practice, he has acquired a greater readiness and power in expressing what he thinks and feels, and especially those thoughts and feelings which, by his own choice, or from the structure of his own mind, arise in him without immediate external excitement.

But, whatever portion of this faculty we may suppose even the greatest Poet to possess, there cannot be a doubt but that the language which it will suggest to him, must, in liveliness and truth, fall far short of that which is uttered by men in real life, under the actual pressure of those passions, certain shadows of which the Poet thus produces, or feels to be produced, in himself. However exalted a notion we would wish to cherish of the character of a Poet, it is obvious, that, while he describes and imitates passions, his situation is altogether slavish and mechanical, compared with the freedom and power of real and substantial action and suffering. So that it will be the wish of the Poet to bring his feelings near to those of the persons whose feelings he describes, nay, for short spaces of time perhaps, to let himself slip into an entire delusion, and even confound and identify his own feelings with theirs; modifying only the language which is thus suggested to him, by a consideration that he describes for a particular purpose, that of giving pleasure. Here, then, he will apply the principle on which I have so much insisted, namely, that of selection; on this he will depend for removing what would otherwise be painful or disgusting in the passion; he will feel that there is no necessity to trick out or to elevate nature: and, the more industriously he applies this principle, the deeper will be his faith that no words, which his fancy or imagination can suggest, will be to be compared with those which are the emanations of reality and truth.

But it may be said by those who do not object to the general spirit of these remarks, that, as it is impossible for the Poet to produce upon all occasions language as exquisitely fitted for the passion as that which the real passion itself suggests, it is proper that he should consider himself as in the situation of a translator, who deems himself justified when he substitutes excellences of another kind for those which are unattainable by him; and endeavours occasionally to surpass his original, in order to make some amends for the general inferiority to which he feels that he must submit. But this would be to encourage idleness and unmanly despair. Further, it is the language of men who speak of what they do not understand; who talk of Poetry as of a matter of amusement and idle pleasure; who will converse with us as gravely about a *taste* for Poetry, as they express it, as if it were a thing as indifferent as a taste for Rope-dancing, or Frontiniac or Sherry. Aristotle, I have been told, hath said, that Poetry is the most philosophic of all writing: it is so: its object is truth, not individual and local, but general, and operative; not standing upon external testimony, but carried alive into the heart by passion; truth which is its own testimony, which gives strength and divinity to the tribunal to which it appeals, and receives them from the same tribunal. Poetry is the image of man and nature. The obstacles which stand in the way of the fidelity of the Biographer and Historian, and of their consequent utility, are incalculably greater than those which are to be encountered by the Poet who has an adequate notion of the dignity of his art. The Poet writes under one restriction only, namely, that of the necessity of giving immediate pleasure to a human Being possessed of that information which may be expected from him, not as a lawyer, a physician, a mariner, an astronomer or a natural philosopher, but as a Man. Except this one restriction, there is no object standing between the Poet and the image of things; between this, and the Biographer and Historian, there are a thousand.

Nor let this necessity of producing immediate pleasure be considered as a degradation of the Poet's art. It is far otherwise. It is an acknowledgment of the beauty of the universe, an acknowledgment the more sincere, because it is not formal, but indirect; it is a task light and easy to him who looks at the world in the spirit of love: further, it is a homage paid to the native and naked dignity of man, to the grand elementary principle of pleasure, by which he knows, and feels, and lives, and moves. We have no sympathy but what is propagated by pleasure: I would not be misunderstood; but wherever we sympathize with pain it will be found that the sympathy is produced and carried on by subtle combinations with pleasure. We have no knowledge, that is, no general principles drawn from the contemplation of particular facts, but what has been built up by pleasure, and exists in us by pleasure alone. The Man of Science, the Chemist and Mathematician, whatever difficulties and disgusts they may have had to struggle with, know and feel this. However painful may be the objects with which the Anatomist's knowledge is connected, he feels that his knowledge is pleasure; and where he has no pleasure he has no knowledge. What then does the Poet? He considers man and the objects that surround him as acting and re-acting upon each other, so as to produce an infinite complexity of pain and pleasure; he considers man in his own nature and in his ordinary life as contemplating this with a certain quantity of immediate knowledge, with certain convictions, intuitions, and deductions which by habit become of the nature of intuitions; he considers him as looking upon this complex scene of ideas and sensations, and finding everywhere objects that immediately excite in him sympathies which, from the necessities of his nature, are accompanied by an over-balance of enjoyment.

To this knowledge which all men carry about with them, and to these sympathies in which without any other discipline than that of our daily life we are fitted to take delight, the Poet principally directs his attention. He considers man and nature as essentially adapted to each other, and the mind of man as naturally the mirror of the fairest and most interesting qualities of nature. And thus the Poet, prompted by this feeling of pleasure which accompanies him through the whole course of his studies, converses with general nature, with affections akin to those, which, through labour and length of time, the Man of Science has raised up in himself, by conversing with those particular parts of nature which are the objects of his studies. The knowledge both of the Poet and the Man of Science is pleasure; but the knowledge of the one cleaves to us as a necessary part of our existence, our natural and unalienable inheritance; the other is a personal and individual acquisition, slow to come to us, and by no habitual and direct sympathy connecting us with our fellow-beings. The Man of Science seeks truth as a remote and unknown benefactor; he cherishes and loves it in his solitude: the Poet, singing a song in which all human beings join with him, rejoices in the presence of truth as our visible friend and hourly companion. Poetry is the breath and finer spirit of all knowledge; it is the impassioned expression which is in the countenance of all Science. Emphatically may it be said of the Poet, as Shakespeare hath said of man, "that he looks before and after." He is the rock of defence of human nature; an upholder and preserver, carrying everywhere with him relationship and love. In spite of difference of soil and climate, of language and manners, of laws and customs, in spite of things silently gone out of mind and things violently destroyed, the Poet binds together by passion and knowledge the vast empire of human society, as it is spread over the whole earth, and over all time. The objects of the Poet's thoughts are every where; though the eyes and senses of man are, it is true, his favourite guides, yet he will follow wheresoever he can find an atmosphere of sensation in which to move his wings. Poetry is the first and last of all knowledge—it is as immortal as the heart of man. If the labours of Men of Science should ever create any material revolution, direct or indirect, in our condition, and in the impressions which we habitually receive, the Poet will sleep then no more than at present, but he will be ready to follow the steps of the Man of Science, not only in those general indirect effects, but he will be at his side, carrying sensation into the midst of the objects of the Science itself. The remotest discoveries of the Chemist, the Botanist, or Mineralogist, will be as proper objects of the Poet's art as any upon which it can be employed, if the time should ever come when these things shall be familiar to us, and the relations under which they are contemplated by the followers of these respective Sciences shall be manifestly and palpably material to us as enjoying and suffering beings. If the time should ever come when what is now called Science, thus familiarised to men, shall be ready to put on, as it were, a form of flesh and blood, the Poet will lend his divine spirit to aid the transfiguration, and will welcome the Being thus produced, as a dear and genuine inmate of the household of man.

* * * *

I have said that Poetry is the spontaneous overflow of powerful feelings: it takes its origin from emotion recollected in tranquillity: the emotion is contemplated till by a species of reaction the tranquillity gradually disappears, and an emotion, kindred to that which was before the subject of contemplation, is gradually produced, and does itself actually exist in the mind. In this mood successful composition generally begins, and in a mood similar to this it is carried on; but the emotion, of whatever kind and in whatever degree, from various causes is qualified by various pleasures, so that in describing any passions whatsoever, which are voluntarily described, the mind will upon the whole be in a state of enjoyment. Now, if Nature be thus cautious in preserving in a state of enjoyment a being thus employed, the Poet ought to profit by the lesson thus held forth to him, and ought especially to take care, that, whatever passions he communicates to his Reader, those passions, if his Reader's mind be sound and vigorous, should always be accompanied with an overbalance of pleasure. Now the music of harmonious metrical language, the sense of difficulty overcome, and the blind association of pleasure which has been previously received from works of rhyme or metre of the same or similar construction, an indistinct perception perpetually renewed of language closely resembling that of real life, and yet, in the circumstance of metre, differing from it so widely—all these imperceptibly make up a complex feeling of delight, which is of the most important use in tempering the painful feeling which will always be found intermingled with powerful descriptions of the deeper passions. . . .

1800, 1802   1802

POETIC DICTION[1]

. . . I am . . . anxious to give an exact notion of the sense in which I use the phrase *poetic diction*; and for this purpose I will here add a few words concerning the origin of the phraseology which I have condemned under that name. —The earliest Poets of all nations generally wrote from passion excited by real events; they wrote naturally, and as men: feeling powerfully as they did, their language was daring, and figurative. In succeeding times, Poets, and men ambitious of the fame of Poets, perceiving the influence of such language, and desirous of producing the same effect, without having the same animating passion, set themselves to a mechanical adoption of those figures of speech, and made use of them, sometimes with propriety, but much more frequently applied them to feelings and ideas with which they had no natural connection whatsoever. A language was thus insensibly produced, differing materially from the real language of men in *any situation*. The Reader or Hearer of this distorted language found himself in a perturbed and unusual state of mind: when affected by the genuine language of passion he had been in a perturbed and unusual state of mind also; in both cases he was willing that his common judgment and understanding should be laid asleep, and he had no instinctive and infallible perception of the true to make him reject the false; the one served as a passport for the other. The agitation and confusion of mind were in both cases delightful, and no wonder if he confounded the one with the other, and believed them both to be produced by the same, or similar causes. Besides, the Poet spake to him in the character of a man to be looked up to, a man of genius and authority. Thus, and from a

[1] **Poetic Diction** In his Preface to *Lyrical Ballads* (1802) Wordsworth complained of the unnaturalness and caprice of "what is usually called poetic diction," and in an Appendix, from which the following is taken, he elaborated on this remark.

variety of other causes, this distorted language was received with admiration; and Poets, it is probable, who had before contented themselves for the most part with misapplying only expressions which at first had been dictated by real passion, carried the abuse still further, and introduced phrases composed apparently in the spirit of the original figurative language of passion, yet altogether of their own invention, and distinguished by various degrees of wanton deviation from good sense and nature.

It is indeed true that the language of the earliest Poets was felt to differ materially from ordinary language, because it was the language of extraordinary occasions; but it was really spoken by men, language which the Poet himself had uttered when he had been affected by the events which he described, or which he had heard uttered by those around him. To this language it is probable that metre of some sort or other was early superadded. This separated the genuine language of Poetry still further from common life, so that whoever read or heard the poems of these earliest Poets felt himself moved in a way in which he had not been accustomed to be moved in real life, and by causes manifestly different from those which acted upon him in real life. This was the great temptation to all the corruptions which have followed: under the protection of this feeling succeeding Poets constructed a phraseology which had one thing, it is true, in common with the genuine language of poetry, namely, that it was not heard in ordinary conversation; that it was unusual. But the first Poets, as I have said, spake a language which, though unusual, was still the language of men. This circumstance, however, was disregarded by their successors; they found that they could please by easier means: they became proud of a language which they themselves had invented, and which was uttered only by themselves as their own. In process of time metre became a symbol or promise of this unusual language, and whoever took upon him to write in metre, according as he possessed more or less of true poetic genius, introduced less or more of this adulterated phraseology into his compositions, and the true and the false became so inseparably interwoven that the taste of men was gradually perverted; and this language was received as a natural language; and at length, by the influence of books upon men, did to a certain degree really become so. Abuses of this kind were imported from one nation to another, and with the progress of refinement this diction became daily more and more corrupt, thrusting out of sight the plain humanities of nature by a motley masquerade of tricks, quaintnesses, hieroglyphics, and enigmas.

1802(?)   1802

A SHORT HISTORY OF POETRY[1]

. . . It is remarkable that, excepting the nocturnal *Reverie* of Lady Winchilsea, and a passage or two in the *Windsor Forest* of Pope, the poetry of the period intervening between the publication of the *Paradise Lost* and *The Seasons*[2] does not contain a single new image of external nature; and scarcely presents a familiar one from which it can be inferred that the eye of the Poet had been steadily fixed upon his object, much less that his feelings had urged him to work upon it in the spirit of genuine imagination. To what a low state knowledge of the most obvious and important phenomena had sunk, is evident from the style in which Dryden has executed a description of Night in one of his Tragedies, and Pope his translation of the celebrated moonlight scene in the Iliad [*viii.* 687 ff.]. A blind man, in the habit of attending accurately to descriptions casually dropped from the lips of those around him, might easily depict these appearances with more truth. Dryden's lines[3] are vague, bombastic, and senseless; those of Pope, though he had Homer to guide him, are throughout false and contradictory. The verses of Dryden, once highly celebrated,

[1] A Short History of Poetry In 1815 Wordsworth published a *Collected Poems.* The present extract is from an essay supplementary to the Preface.
[2] period . . . The Seasons that is, between 1667 and 1730.
[3] Dryden's lines
          CORTES ALONE IN A NIGHT-GOWN
    "All things are hush'd as Nature's self lay dead;
    The mountains seem to nod their drowsy head.
    The little Birds in dreams their songs repeat,
    And sleeping Flowers beneath the Night-dew sweat:
    Even Lust and Envy sleep; yet Love denies
    Rest to my soul, and slumber to my eyes."
                              DRYDEN'S *Indian Emperor.*

are forgotten; those of Pope still retain their hold upon pub-
lic estimation,—nay, there is not a passage of descriptive
poetry, which at this day finds so many and such ardent
admirers. Strange to think of an enthusiast, as may have
been the case with thousands, reciting those verses under
the cope of a moonlight sky, without having his raptures in
the least disturbed by a suspicion of their absurdity!—If
these two distinguished writers could habitually think that
the visible universe was of so little consequence to a poet,
that it was scarcely necessary for him to cast his eyes upon
it, we may be assured that those passages of the elder poets
which faithfully and poetically describe the phenomena of
nature, were not at that time holden in much estimation,
and that there was little accurate attention paid to those
appearances.

*   *   *   *

. . . Thomson was fortunate in the very title of his poem,
which seemed to bring it home to the prepared sympathies
of every one: in the next place, notwithstanding his high
powers, he writes a vicious style; and his false ornaments
are exactly of that kind which would be most likely to strike
the undiscerning. He likewise abounds with sentimental
common-places, that, from the manner in which they were
brought forward, bore an imposing air of novelty. In any
well-used copy of the Seasons the book generally opens of
itself with the rhapsody on love, or with one of the stories
(perhaps Damon and Musidora); these also are prominent
in our collections of Extracts, and are the parts of his Work
which, after all, were probably most efficient in first recom-
mending the author to general notice. Pope, repaying
praises which he had received, and wishing to extol him to
the highest, only styles him "an elegant and philosophical
Poet;" nor are we able to collect any unquestionable proofs
that the true characteristics of Thomson's genius as an
imaginative poet were perceived, till the elder Warton, al-
most forty years after the publication of the Seasons,
pointed them out by a note in his Essay on the Life and
Writings of Pope. In the Castle of Indolence (of which
Gray speaks so coldly) these characteristics were almost as
conspicuously displayed, and in verse more harmonious,
and diction more pure. Yet that fine poem was neglected on

its appearance, and is at this day the delight only of a few!

When Thomson died, Collins breathed forth his regrets in an Elegiac Poem, in which he pronounces a poetical curse upon *him* who should regard with insensibility the place where the Poet's remains were deposited. The Poems of the mourner himself have now passed through innumerable editions, and are universally known; but if, when Collins died, the same kind of imprecation had been pronounced by a surviving admirer, small is the number whom it would not have comprehended. The notice which his poems attained during his lifetime was so small, and of course the sale so insignificant, that not long before his death he deemed it right to repay the bookseller the sum which he had advanced for them, and threw the edition into the fire.

Next in importance to the Seasons of Thomson, though at considerable distance from that work in order of time, come the Reliques of Ancient English Poetry; collected, new-modelled, and in many instances (if such a contradiction in terms may be used) composed by the Editor, Dr. Percy. This work did not steal silently into the world, as is evident from the number of legendary tales, that appeared not long after its publication; and had been modelled, as the authors persuaded themselves, after the old Ballad. The Compilation was however ill suited to the then existing taste of city society; and Dr. Johnson, 'mid the little senate to which he gave laws, was not sparing in his exertions to make it an object of contempt. The critic triumphed, the legendary imitators were deservedly disregarded, and, as undeservedly, their ill-imitated models sank, in this country, into temporary neglect; while Bürger, and other able writers of Germany, were translating or imitating these Reliques, and composing, with the aid of inspiration thence derived, poems which are the delight of the German nation.

*   *   *   *

But from humble ballads we must ascend to heroics.

All hail, Macpherson! hail to thee, Sire of Ossian![4] The Phantom was begotten by the snug embrace of an impudent

---

[4] **Macpherson . . . Ossian** In 1760–63 James Macpherson published the purported works of a "Northern Homer," a legendary Gaelic poet named Ossian.

Highlander upon a cloud of tradition—it travelled southward, where it was greeted with acclamation, and the thin Consistence took its course through Europe, upon the breath of popular applause. The Editor of the Reliques had indirectly preferred a claim to the praise of invention, by not concealing that his supplementary labours were considerable! how selfish his conduct, contrasted with that of the disinterested Gael, who, like Lear, gives his kingdom away, and is content to become a pensioner upon his own issue for a beggarly pittance!—Open this far-famed Book! —I have done so at random, and the beginning of the "Epic Poem Temora," in eight Books, presents itself. "The blue waves of Ullin roll in light. The green hills are covered with day. Trees shake their dusky heads in the breeze. Grey torrents pour their noisy streams. Two green hills with aged oaks surround a narrow plain. The blue course of a stream is there. On its banks stood Cairbar of Atha. His spear supports the king; the red eyes of his fear are sad. Cormac rises on his soul with all his ghastly wounds." Precious memorandums from the pocket-book of the blind Ossian!

If it be unbecoming, as I acknowledge that for the most part it is, to speak disrespectfully of Works that have enjoyed for a length of time a widely-spread reputation, without at the same time producing irrefragable proofs of their unworthiness, let me be forgiven upon this occasion.—Having had the good fortune to be born and reared in a mountainous country, from my very childhood I have felt the falsehood that pervades the volumes imposed upon the world under the name of Ossian. From what I saw with my own eyes, I knew that the imagery was spurious. In nature everything is distinct, yet nothing defined into absolute independent singleness. In Macpherson's work, it is exactly the reverse; everything(that is not stolen) is in this manner defined, insulated, dislocated, deadened,—yet nothing distinct. It will always be so when words are substituted for things.

* * * *

Yet, much as those pretended treasures of antiquity have been admired, they have been wholly uninfluential upon the literature of the Country. No succeeding writer appears to have caught from them a ray of inspiration; no author, in

the least distinguished, has ventured formally to imitate
them—except the boy, Chatterton,[5] on their first appear-
ance. He had perceived, from the successful trials which he
himself had made in literary forgery, how few critics were
able to distinguish between a real ancient medal and a
counterfeit of modern manufacture; and he set himself to
the work of filling a magazine with *Saxon Poems,*—coun-
terparts of those of Ossian, as like his as one of his misty
stars is to another. This incapability to amalgamate with the
literature of the Island, is, in my estimation, a decisive proof
that the book is essentially unnatural; nor should I require
any other to demonstrate it to be a forgery, audacious as
worthless.—Contrast, in this respect, the effect of Mac-
pherson's publication with the Reliques of Percy, so unas-
suming, so modest in their pretensions!—I have already
stated how much Germany is indebted to this latter work;
and for our own country, its poetry has been absolutely
redeemed by it.

* * * *

1815(?)   1815

FANCY AND IMAGINATION[1]

Let us come now to the consideration of the words Fancy
and Imagination, as employed in the classification of the
following Poems. "A man," says an intelligent author, "has
imagination in proportion as he can distinctly copy in idea
the impressions of sense: it is the faculty which *images*
within the mind the phenomena of sensation. A man has

[5] **Chatterton** See "Resolution and Independence," line 43.

[1] **Fancy and Imagination** During the later eighteenth century the key
term in discussions of poetic genius changed from "wit" to "imagination."
In a Preface to the edition of his poems published in 1815, from which
the following is taken, Wordsworth sought to explain his division of cer-
tain poems into those of imagination and those of fancy, and so made
this analysis of the two faculties.

fancy in proportion as he can call up, connect, or associate, at pleasure, those internal images ($\phi\alpha\nu\tau\acute{\alpha}\zeta\epsilon\iota\nu$ is to cause to appear) so as to complete ideal representations of absent objects. Imagination is the power of depicting, and fancy of evoking and combining. The imagination is formed by patient observation; the fancy by a voluntary activity in shifting the scenery of the mind. The more accurate the imagination, the more safely may a painter, or a poet, undertake a delineation, or a description, without the presence of the objects to be characterised. The more versatile the fancy, the more original and striking will be the decorations produced."—*British Synonyms discriminated, by W. Taylor.*

Is not this as if a man should undertake to supply an account of a building, and be so intent upon what he had discovered of the foundation, as to conclude his task without once looking up at the superstructure? Here, as in other instances throughout the volume, the judicious Author's mind is enthralled by Etymology; he takes up the original word as his guide and escort, and too often does not perceive how soon he becomes its prisoner, without liberty to tread in any path but that to which it confines him. It is not easy to find out how imagination, thus explained, differs from distinct remembrance of images; or fancy from quick and vivid recollection of them: each is nothing more than a mode of memory. If the two words bear the above meaning, and no other, what term is left to designate that faculty of which the Poet is "all compact;" he whose eye glances from earth to heaven, whose spiritual attributes body forth what his pen is prompt in turning to shape; or what is left to characterise Fancy, as insinuating herself into the heart of objects with creative activity?—Imagination, in the sense of the word as giving title to a class of the following Poems, has no reference to images that are merely a faithful copy, existing in the mind, of absent external objects; but is a word of higher import, denoting operations of the mind upon those objects, and processes of creation or of composition, governed by certain fixed laws. I proceed to illustrate my meaning by instances. A parrot *hangs* from the wires of his cage by his beak or by his claws; or a monkey from the bough of a tree by his paws or his tail. Each creature does so literally and actually. In the first Eclogue of Virgil, the shepherd, thinking of the time when he is to take leave of his farm, thus addresses his goats:

> "Non ego vos posthac viridi projectus in antro
> Dumosa *pendere* procul de rupe videbo."[2]
> ──"half way down
> *Hangs* one who gathers samphire,"[3]

is the well-known expression of Shakespeare, delineating an ordinary image upon the cliffs of Dover. In these two instances is a slight exertion of the faculty which I denominate imagination, in the use of one word: neither the goats nor the samphire-gatherer do literally hang, as does the parrot or the monkey; but, presenting to the senses something of such an appearance, the mind in its activity, for its own gratification, contemplates them as hanging.

> "As when far off at sea a fleet descried
> *Hangs* in the clouds, by equinoctial winds
> Close sailing from Bengala, or the isles
> Of Ternate or Tidore, whence merchants bring
> Their spicy drugs; they on the trading flood
> Through the wide Ethiopian to the Cape
> Ply, stemming nightly toward the Pole: so seemed
> Far off the flying Fiend."[4]

Here is the full strength of the imagination involved in the word *hangs*, and exerted upon the whole image: First, the fleet, an aggregate of many ships, is represented as one mighty person, whose track, we know and feel, is upon the waters; but, taking advantage of its appearance to the senses, the Poet dares to represent it as *hanging in the clouds*, both for the gratification of the mind in contemplating the image itself, and in reference to the motion and appearance of the sublime objects to which it is compared.

From impressions of sight we will pass to those of sound; which, as they must necessarily be of a less definite character, shall be selected from these volumes:

---

[2] "Non . . . videbo" "Never hereafter will I, prone in some green hollow, see you hanging in the distance from a bushy cliff" (lines 75–76). [3] "half . . . samphire" *King Lear* IV. vi. 15–16. [4] "As when . . . Fiend" *Paradise Lost* II. 636–43.

"Over his own sweet voice the Stock-dove *broods*;"[5]
of the same bird,

> "His voice was *buried* among trees,
> Yet to be come at by the breeze;"[6]

> "O, Cuckoo! shall I call thee *Bird*,
> Or but a wandering *Voice?*"[7]

The stock-dove is said to *coo,* a sound well imitating the note of the bird; but, by the intervention of the metaphor *broods,* the affections are called in by the imagination to assist in marking the manner in which the bird reiterates and prolongs her soft note, as if herself delighting to listen to it, and participating of a still and quiet satisfaction, like that which may be supposed inseparable from the continuous process of incubation. "His voice was buried among trees," a metaphor expressing the love of *seclusion* by which this Bird is marked; and characterising its note as not partaking of the shrill and the piercing, and therefore more easily deadened by the intervening shade; yet a note so peculiar and withal so pleasing, that the breeze, gifted with that love of the sound which the poet feels, penetrates the shades in which it is entombed, and conveys it to the ear of the listener.

> "Shall I call thee Bird,
> Or but a wandering Voice?"

This concise interrogation characterises the seeming ubiquity of the voice of the cuckoo, and dispossesses the creature almost of a corporeal existence; the Imagination being tempted to this exertion of her power by a consciousness in the memory that the cuckoo is almost perpetually heard throughout the season of spring, but seldom becomes an object of sight.

Thus far of images independent of each other, and immediately endowed by the mind with properties that do not inhere in them, upon an incitement from properties and qualities the existence of which is inherent and obvious. These processes of imagination are carried on either by

[5] "Over . . . broods" "Resolution and Independence," line 5.   [6] His . . . breeze" "O Nightingale! Thou Surely Art," lines 13–14.   [7] "O . . . Voice?" "To the Cuckoo," lines 3–4.

conferring additional properties upon an object, or abstracting from it some of those which it actually possesses, and thus enabling it to re-act upon the mind which hath performed the process, like a new existence.

I pass from the Imagination acting upon an individual image to a consideration of the same faculty employed upon images in a conjunction by which they modify each other. The Reader has already had a fine instance before him in the passage quoted from Virgil, where the apparently perilous situation of the goat, hanging upon the shaggy precipice, is contrasted with that of the shepherd contemplating it from the seclusion of the cavern in which he lies stretched at ease and in security. Take these images separately, and how unaffecting the picture compared with that produced by their being thus connected with, and opposed to, each other!

> "As a huge stone is sometimes seen to lie
> Couched on the bald top of an eminence,
> Wonder to all who do the same espy
> By what means it could thither come, and whence,
> So that it seems a thing endued with sense,
> Like a sea-beast crawled forth, which on a shelf
> Of rock or sand reposeth, there to sun himself.
>
> Such seemed this Man; not all alive or dead
> Nor all asleep, in his extreme old age.
>
> . . . .
>
> Motionless as a cloud the old Man stood,
> That heareth not the loud winds when they call,
> And moveth altogether if it move at all."[8]

In these images, the conferring, the abstracting, and the modifying powers of the Imagination, immediately and mediately acting, are all brought into conjunction. The stone is endowed with something of the power of life to approximate it to the sea-beast; and the sea-beast stripped of some of its vital qualities to assimilate it to the stone; which intermediate image is thus treated for the purpose of bringing the original image, that of the stone, to a nearer resemblance to the figure and condition of the aged Man; who is divested of so much of the indications of life and motion

[8] "As . . . all." "Resolution and Independence," lines 57–65, 75–77.

as to bring him to the point where the two objects unite and coalesce in just comparison. After what has been said, the image of the cloud need not be commented upon.

Thus far of an endowing or modifying power: but the Imagination also shapes and *creates;* and how? By innumerable processes; and in none does it more delight than in that of consolidating numbers into unity, and dissolving and separating unity into number,—alternations proceeding from, and governed by, a sublime consciousness of the soul in her own mighty and almost divine powers. Recur to the passage already cited from Milton. When the compact Fleet, as one Person, has been introduced "sailing from Bengala," "They," *i.e.* the "merchants," representing the fleet resolved into a multitude of ships, "ply" their voyage towards the extremities of the earth: "So," (referring to the word "As" in the commencement) "seemed the flying Fiend;" the image of his Person acting to recombine the multitude of ships into one body,—the point from which the comparison set out. "So seemed," and to whom seemed? To the heavenly Muse who dictates the poem, to the eye of the Poet's mind, and to that of the Reader, present at one moment in the wide Ethiopian, and the next in the solitudes, then first broken in upon, of the infernal regions!

"Modo me Thebis, modo ponit Athenis."[9]

Hear again this mighty Poet,—speaking of the Messiah going forth to expel from heaven the rebellious angels,

> "Attended by ten thousand thousand Saints
> He onward came: far off his coming shone,"—[10]

the retinue of Saints, and the Person of the Messiah himself, lost almost and merged in the splendour of that indefinite abstraction "His coming!"

As I do not mean here to treat this subject further than to throw some light upon the present Volumes, and especially upon one division of them, I shall spare myself and the Reader the trouble of considering the Imagination as it deals with thoughts and sentiments, as it regulates the

[9] **Modo . . . Athenis** "He places me now in Thebes, now in Athens." Horace, *Epistles* II. i. 213. [10] **"Attended . . . shone"** *Paradise Lost* VI. 767–68.

composition of characters, and determines the course of
actions: I will not consider it (more than I have already
done by implication) as that power which, in the language
of one of my most esteemed Friends, "draws all things to
one; which makes things animate or inanimate, beings with
their attributes, subjects with their accessories, take one
colour and serve to one effect."[11] The grand store-houses
of enthusiastic and meditative Imagination, of political, as
contra-distinguished from human and dramatic Imagina-
tion, are the prophetic and lyrical parts of the Holy Scrip-
tures, and the works of Milton; to which I cannot forbear
to add those of Spenser. I select these writers in preference
to those of ancient Greece and Rome, because the anthro-
pomorphitism of the Pagan religion subjected the minds of
the greatest poets in those countries too much to the bond-
age of definite form; from which the Hebrews were pre-
served by their abhorrence of idolatry. This abhorrence was
almost as strong in our great epic Poet, both from circum-
stances of his life, and from the constitution of his mind.
However imbued the surface might be with classical litera-
ture, he was a Hebrew in soul; and all things tended in him
towards the sublime. Spenser, of a gentler nature, main-
tained his freedom by aid of his allegorical spirit, at one
time inciting him to create persons out of abstractions; and,
at another, by a superior effort of genius, to give the univer-
sality and permanence of abstractions to his human beings,
by means of attributes and emblems that belong to the
highest moral truths and the purest sensations,—of which
his character of Una is a glorious example. Of the human
and dramatic Imagination the works of Shakespeare are an
inexhaustible source.

"I tax not you, ye Elements, with unkindness,
I never gave you kingdoms, call'd you Daughters!"[12]

*   *   *   *

To the mode in which Fancy has already been character-
ised as the power of evoking and combining, or, as my
friend Mr. Coleridge has styled it, "the aggregative and

[11] "draws . . . effect" Charles Lamb, "On the Genius of Hogarth."
[12] "I . . . Daughters!" *King Lear* III. ii. 16–17.

associative power,"[13] my objection is only that the defini-
tion is too general. To aggregate and to associate, to evoke
and to combine, belong as well to the Imagination as to the
Fancy; but either the materials evoked and combined are
different; or they are brought together under a different
law, and for a different purpose. Fancy does not require
that the materials which she makes use of should be sus-
ceptible of change in their constitution, from her touch;
and, where they admit of modification, it is enough for her
purpose if it be slight, limited, and evanescent. Directly the
reverse of these, are the desires and demands of the Imagi-
nation. She recoils from everything but the plastic, the
pliant, and the indefinite. She leaves it to Fancy to describe
Queen Mab as coming,

> "In shape no bigger than an agate-stone
> On the fore-finger of an alderman."[14]

Having to speak of stature, she does not tell you that her
gigantic Angel was as tall as Pompey's Pillar; much less
that he was twelve cubits, or twelve hundred cubits high;
or that his dimensions equalled those of Teneriffe or Atlas;
—because these, and if they were a million times as high it
would be the same, are bounded: The expression is, "His
stature reached the sky!" the illimitable firmament!—When
the Imagination frames a comparison, if it does not strike
on the first presentation, a sense of the truth of the likeness,
from the moment that it is perceived, grows—and con-
tinues to grow—upon the mind; the resemblance depending
less upon outline of form and feature, than upon expression
and effect; less upon casual and outstanding, than upon
inherent and internal, properties: moreover, the images
invariably modify each other.—The law under which the
processes of Fancy are carried on is as capricious as the
accidents of things, and the effects are surprising, playful,
ludicrous, amusing, tender, or pathetic, as the objects
happen to be appositely produced or fortunately combined.
Fancy depends upon the rapidity and profusion with which

---

[13] "Coleridge . . . power" Coleridge so defined fancy in Southey's
Omniana (1812); he later compared Wordsworth's ideas to his own in
Biographia Literaria (1817), Chapters XII–XIV. [14] "In . . . alderman"
Romeo and Juliet I. iv. 56–57.

she scatters her thoughts and images; trusting that their
number, and the felicity with which they are linked to-
gether, will make amends for the want of individual value:
or she prides herself upon the curious subtilty and the suc-
cessful elaboration with which she can detect their lurking
affinities. If she can win you over to her purpose, and
impart to you her feelings, she cares not how unstable or
transitory may be her influence, knowing that it will not be
out of her power to resume it upon an apt occasion. But the
Imagination is conscious of an indestructible dominion;—
the Soul may fall away from it, not being able to sustain its
grandeur; but, if once felt and acknowledged, by no act of
any other faculty of the mind can it be relaxed, impaired,
or diminished.—Fancy is given to quicken and to beguile
the temporal part of our nature, Imagination to incite and
to support the eternal.—Yet is it not the less true that
Fancy, as she is an active, is also, under her own laws and
in her own spirit, a creative faculty. In what manner Fancy
ambitiously aims at a rivalship with Imagination, and
Imagination stoops to work with the materials of Fancy,
might be illustrated from the compositions of all eloquent
writers, whether in prose or verse; and chiefly from those
of our own Country. Scarcely a page of the impassioned
parts of Bishop Taylor's Works can be opened that shall
not afford examples.—Referring the Reader to those inesti-
mable volumes, I will content myself with placing a conceit
(ascribed to Lord Chesterfield) in contrast with a passage
from the Paradise Lost:—

> "The dews of the evening most carefully shun,
> They are the tears of the sky for the loss of the sun."

After the transgression of Adam, Milton, with other appear-
ances of sympathising Nature, thus marks the immediate
consequence,

> "Sky lowered, and, muttering thunder, some sad drops
> Wept at completion of the mortal sin."[15]

The associating link is the same in each instance: Dew and
rain, not distinguishable from the liquid substance of tears,

---

[15] "Sky . . . sin" *Paradise Lost* IX. 1002–1003 (slightly altered).

are employed as indications of sorrow. A flash of surprise is the effect in the former case; a flash of surprise, and nothing more; for the nature of things does not sustain the combination. In the latter, the effects from the act, of which there is this immediate consequence and visible sign, are so momentous, that the mind acknowledges the justice and reasonableness of the sympathy in nature so manifested; and the sky weeps drops of water as if with human eyes, as "Earth had before trembled from her entrails, and Nature given a second groan."[16]

*   *   *   *

1815   1815

THE DOMINION OF WORDS[1]

. . . In a bulky volume of Poetry entitled ELEGANT EXTRACTS IN VERSE,[2] which must be known to most of my Readers, as it is circulated everywhere and in fact constitutes at this day the poetical library of our Schools, I find a number of epitaphs in verse, of the last century; and there is scarcely one which is not thoroughly tainted by the artifices which have over-run our writings in metre since the days of Dryden and Pope. Energy, stillness, grandeur, tenderness, those feelings which are the pure emanations of Nature, those thoughts which have the infinitude of truth, and those expressions which are not what the garb is to the body but what the body is to the soul, themselves a constituent part and power or function in the thought—all these are abandoned for their opposites,—as if our countrymen, through successive generations, had lost the sense of solemnity and pensiveness (not to speak of deeper emotions) and resorted to the tombs of their forefathers and contemporaries, only to be tickled and surprised. Would

[16] **"Earth . . . groan."** Adapted from *Paradise Lost* IX. 1000 ff.

[1] **The Dominion of Words** from "Essay on Epitaphs—III," written in 1810. [2] **Elegant . . . Verse** an anthology for young people by Vicissimus Knox (1770, with many subsequent editions).

we not recoil from such gratification, in such a place, if the general literature of the country had not co-operated with other causes insidiously to weaken our sensibilities and deprave our judgments? Doubtless, there are shocks of event and circumstance, public and private, by which for all minds the truths of Nature will be elicited; but sorrow for that individual or people to whom these special interferences are necessary, to bring them into communion with the inner spirit of things! for such intercourse must be profitless in proportion as it is unfrequently irregular and transient. Words are too awful an instrument for good and evil, to be trifled with; they hold above all other external powers a dominion over thoughts. If words be not (recurring to a metaphor before used) an incarnation of the thought, but only a clothing for it, then surely will they prove an ill gift; such a one as those possessed vestments, read of in the stories of superstitious times, which had power to consume and to alienate from his right mind the victim who put them on. Language, if it do not uphold, and feed, and leave in quiet, like the power of gravitation or the air we breathe, is a counter-spirit, unremittingly and noiselessly at work, to subvert, to lay waste, to vitiate, and to dissolve. . . . the taste, intellectual power and morals of a country are inseparably linked in mutual dependence. . . .

1810   1876

A DEFENSE OF NATURE POETRY[1]

. . . A Soul that has been dwarfed by a course of bad culture cannot after a certain age, be expanded into one of even ordinary proportion.—Mere error of opinion, mere apprehension of ill consequences from supposed mistaken views on my part, could never have rendered your correspondent blind to the innumerable analogies and types of

[1] A Defense . . . Poetry From a letter of January, 1815, to Catherine Clarkson, a friend, in response to a letter received by her from a critic of *The Excursion.*

infinity, insensible to the countless awakenings to noble aspiration, which I have transfused into that Poem[2] from the Bible of the Universe as it speaks to the ear of the intelligent, as it lies open to the eyes of the humble-minded. I have alluded to the Lady's errors of opinion—she talks of my being a worshipper of Nature—a passionate expression uttered incautiously in the Poem upon the Wye[3] has led her into this mistake, she, reading in cold-heartedness and substituting the letter for the spirit. Unless I am greatly mistaken, there is nothing of this kind in the Excursion. There is indeed a passage towards the end of the 4th. Book where the Wanderer introduces the simile of the Boy and the Shell, and what follows,[4] that has something, ordinarily but absurdly called *Spinosistic*. But the intelligent reader will easily see the *dramatic* propriety of the Passage. The Wanderer in the beginning of the book had given vent to his own devotional feelings and announced in some degree his own creed; he is here preparing the way for more distinct conceptions of the Deity by reminding the Solitary of such religious feelings as cannot but exist in the minds of those who affect atheism. She condemns me for not distinguishing between nature as the work of God and God himself. But where does she find this doctrine inculcated? Where does she gather that the Author of the Excursion looks upon nature and God as the same? He does not indeed consider the Supreme Being as bearing the same relation to the universe as a watch-maker bears to a watch. In fact, there is nothing in the course of religious education adopted in this country and in the use made by us of the holy scriptures that appears to me so injurious as the perpetually talking about *making* by God!—Oh! that your Correspondent had heard a conversation which I had in bed with my sweet little Boy, four and a half years old, upon this subject the other morning. "How did God make me? Where is God? How does he speak? He never spoke to *me*." I told him that God was a spirit, that he was not like his flesh which he could touch; but more like his thoughts in his mind which he could not touch.—The wind was tossing the

[2] **Poem** *The Excursion.*   [3] **a passionate ... Wye** See "Tintern Abbey," lines 151–52.   [4] **what follows** "Even such a shell the universe itself / Is to the ear of Faith," lines 1141–42.

fir trees, and the sky and light were dancing about in their dark branches, as seen through the window—Noting these fluctuations he exclaimed eagerly—"There's a bit of him I see it there!" This is not meant entirely for Father's prattle; but, for Heaven's sake, in your religious talk with children say as little as possible about *making*. One of the main objects of the Recluse is, to reduce the calculating understanding to its proper level among the human faculties. . . .

1815

PUBLIC ASSISTANCE FOR THE UNEMPLOYED[1]

The point to which I wish to draw the reader's attention is, that *all* persons who cannot find employment, or procure wages sufficient to support the body in health and strength, are entitled to a maintenance by law.

*   *   *   *

There can be no greater error, in this department of legislation, than the belief that this principle does by necessity operate for the degradation of those who claim, or are so circumstanced as to make it likely they may claim, through laws founded upon it, relief or assistance. The direct contrary is the truth: it may be unanswerably maintained that its tendency is to raise, not to depress; by stamping a value upon life, which can belong to it only where the laws have placed men who are willing to work, and yet cannot find employment, above the necessity of looking for protection against hunger and other natural evils, either to individual and casual charity, to despair and death, or to the breach of law by theft, or violence.

*   *   *   *

There is a story told, by a traveller in Spain, of a female who, by a sudden shock of domestic calamity, was driven

---

[1] **Public . . . Unemployed** To the volume *Yarrow Revisited and Other Poems* (1835) Wordsworth appended a Postscript on religion and economics from which the following is taken.

out of her senses, and ever after looked up incessantly to the sky, feeling that her fellow-creatures could do nothing for her relief. Can there be Englishmen who, with a good end in view, would, upon system, expose their brother Englishmen to a like necessity of looking upwards only; or downwards to the earth, after it shall contain no spot where the destitute can demand, by civil right, what by right of nature they are entitled to?

Suppose the objects of our sympathy not sunk into this blank despair, but wandering about as strangers in streets and ways, with the hope of succour from casual charity; what have we gained by such a change of scene? Woeful is the condition of the famished Northern Indian, dependent, among winter snows, upon the chance-passage of a herd of deer, from which one, if brought down by his rifle-gun, may be made the means of keeping him and his companions alive. As miserable is that of some savage Islander, who, when the land has ceased to afford him sustenance, watches for food which the waves may cast up, or in vain endeavours to extract it from the inexplorable deep. But neither of these is in a state of wretchedness comparable to that, which is so often endured in civilised society: multitudes, in all ages, have known it, of whom may be said:—

"Homeless, near a thousand homes they stood,
And near a thousand tables pined, and wanted food."[2]

Justly might I be accused of wasting time in an uncalled-for attempt to excite the feelings of the reader, if systems of political economy, widely spread, did not impugn the principle, and if the safeguards against such extremities were left unimpaired. It is broadly asserted by many, that every man who endeavours to find work, *may* find it: were this assertion capable of being verified, there still would remain a question, what kind of work, and how far may the labourer be fit for it? For if sedentary work is to be exchanged for standing; and some light and nice exercise of the fingers, to which an artisan has been accustomed all his life, for severe labour of the arms; the best efforts would turn to little account, and occasion would be given for the unthinking and the unfeeling unwarrantably to reproach

2 **"Homeless . . . food"** Wordsworth adapts lines 368–69 from his early poem, "Guilt and Sorrow."

those who are put upon such employment, as idle, froward, and unworthy of relief, either by law or in any other way! Were this statement correct, there would indeed be an end of the argument, the principle here maintained would be superseded. But, alas! it is far otherwise. That principle, applicable to the benefit of all countries, is indispensable for England, upon whose coast families are perpetually deprived of their support by shipwreck, and where large masses of men are so liable to be thrown out of their ordinary means of gaining bread, by changes in commercial intercourse, subject mainly or solely to the will of foreign powers; by new discoveries in arts and manufactures; and by reckless laws, in conformity with theories of political economy, which, whether right or wrong in the abstract, have proved a scourge to tens of thousands, by the abruptness with which they have been carried into practice.

* * * *

Sights of abject misery, perpetually recurring, harden the heart of the community. In the perusal of history, and of works of fiction, we are not, indeed, unwilling to have our commiseration excited by such objects of distress as they present to us; but, in the concerns of real life, men know that such emotions are not given to be indulged for their own sakes: there, the conscience declares to them that sympathy must be followed by action; and if there exist a previous conviction that the power to relieve is utterly inadequate to the demand, the eye shrinks from communication with wretchedness, and pity and compassion languish, like any other qualities that are deprived of their natural aliment. Let these considerations be duly weighed by those who trust to the hope that an increase of private charity, with all its advantages of superior discrimination, would more than compensate for the abandonment of those principles, the wisdom of which has been here insisted upon. How discouraging also would be the sense of injustice, which could not fail to arise in the minds of the well-disposed, if the burden of supporting the poor, a burden of which the selfish have hitherto by compulsion borne a share, should now, or hereafter, be thrown exclusively upon the benevolent.

1835 (?)   1835

Appendix

APPENDIX
FROM DOROTHY WORDSWORTH'S
GRASMERE JOURNAL[1]

The Leech Gatherer

[October 3, 1800.] When Wm. and I returned from accompanying Jones, we met an old man almost double. He had on a coat, thrown over his shoulders, above his waistcoat and coat. Under this he carried a bundle, and had an apron on and a night-cap. His face was interesting. He had dark eyes and a long nose. John, who afterwards met him at Wythburn, took him for a Jew. He was of Scotch parents, but had been born in the army. He had had a wife, and 'a good woman, and it pleased God to bless us with ten children'. All these were dead but one, of whom he had not heard for many years, a sailor. His trade was to gather leeches, but now leeches are scarce, and he had not strength for it. He lived by begging, and was making his way to Carlisle, where he should buy a few godly books to sell. He said leeches were very scarce, partly owing to this dry season, but many years they have been scarce—he supposed it owing to their being much sought after, that they did not breed fast, and were of slow growth. Leeches were formerly 2s. 6d. [per] 100; they are now 30s. He had been hurt in driving a cart, his leg broke, his body driven over, his skull fractured. He felt no pain till he recovered from his first insensibility. It was then late in the evening, when the light was just going away.

*   *   *   *

May 4th, Tuesday [1802]. William had slept pretty well and though he went to bed nervous, and jaded in the extreme, he rose refreshed. I wrote *The Leech Gatherer*[2] for him, which he had begun the night before, and of which he wrote several stanzas in bed this morning. It was very hot; we called at Mr. Simpson's door as we passed, but did not go in. We rested several times by the way, read, and repeated *The Leech Gatherer*. We were almost melted before we were at the top of the hill. We saw Coleridge on

---

[1] **Grasmere Journal** Written by Wordsworth's sister Dorothy (1771–1855) during their stay at Dove Cottage, it was an invaluable aid to Wordsworth's poetic recollection and an independent work of art.   [2] **The Leech Gatherer** See "Resolution and Independence."

the Wytheburn side of the water; he crossed the Beck to
us. Mr. Simpson was fishing there. William and I ate a
luncheon, then went on towards the waterfall. It is a glori-
ous wild solitude under that lofty purple crag. It stood
upright by itself. Its own self, and its shadow below, one
mass—all else was sunshine. We went on further. A Bird
at the top of the crags was flying round and round, and
looked in thinness and transparency, shape and motion like
a moth. We climbed the hill, but looked in vain for a shade,
except at the foot of the great waterfall, and there we did
not like to stay on account of the loose stones above our
heads. We came down, and rested upon a moss-covered
rock, rising out of the bed of the river. There we lay, ate
our dinner, and stayed there till about 4 o'clock or later.
William and C. repeated and read verses. I drank a little
Brandy and water, and was in Heaven. The Stag's horn
is very beautiful and fresh, springing upon the fells. Moun-
tain ashes, green. We drank tea at a farm house. The
woman had not a pleasant countenance, but was civil
enough. She had a pretty Boy, a year old, whom she
suckled. We parted from Coleridge at Sara's crag,[3] after
having looked at the letters which C. carved in the morning.
I kissed them all. Wm. deepened the T with C.'s pen-knife.
We sate afterwards on the wall, seeing the sun go down,
and the reflections in the still water. C. looked well, and
parted from us cheerfully, hopping up upon the side stones.
On the Rays we met a woman with two little girls, one in
her arms, the other, about four years old, walking by her
side, a pretty little thing, but half-starved. She had on a pair
of slippers that had belonged to some gentleman's child,
down at the heels, but it was not easy to keep them on, but,
poor thing! young as she was, she walked carefully with
them; alas, too young for such cares and such travels. The
mother, when we accosted her, told us that her husband
had left her, and gone off with another woman, and how
she *'pursued'* them. Then her fury kindled, and her eyes
rolled about. She changed again to tears. She was a Cocker-
mouth woman, thirty years of age—a child at Cockermouth
when I was. I was moved, and gave her a shilling—I believe

[3] **Sara's crag** Extending an ancient tradition, the Wordsworths often
commemorated places by naming them after persons associated with them.

6*d*. more than I ought to have given. We had the crescent
moon with the 'auld moon in her arms'. We rested often,
always upon the Bridges. Reached home at about ten
o'clock. The Lloyds had been here in our absence. We went
soon to bed. I repeated verses to William while he was in
bed; he was soothed, and I left him.

Daffodils[4]

[*April*] *15th, Thursday* [1802]. It was a threatening,
misty morning, but mild. We set off after dinner from Euse-
mere. Mrs. Clarkson went a short way with us, but turned
back. The wind was furious, and we thought we must have
returned. We first rested in the large Boat-house, then un-
der a furze bush opposite Mr. Clarkson's. Saw the plough
going in the field. The wind seized our breath. The Lake
was rough. There was a Boat by itself floating in the middle
of the Bay below Water Millock. We rested again in the
Water Millock Lane. The hawthorns are black and green,
the birches here and there greenish, but there is yet more of
purple to be seen on the twigs. We got over into a field to
avoid some cows—people working. A few primroses by the
roadside—woodsorrel flower, the anemone, scentless vio-
lets, strawberries, and that starry, yellow flower which Mrs.
C[oleridge] calls pile wort. When we were in the woods
beyond Gowbarrow park we saw a few daffodils close to the
water-side. We fancied that the lake had floated the seeds
ashore, and that the little colony had so sprung up. But as
we went along there were more and yet more; and at last,
under the boughs of the trees, we saw that there was a long
belt of them along the shore, about the breadth of a country
turnpike road. I never saw daffodils so beautiful. They grew
among the mossy stones about and about them; some rested
their heads upon these stones as on a pillow for weariness;
and the rest tossed and reeled and danced, and seemed as
if they verily laughed with the wind, that blew upon them
over the lake; they looked so gay, ever glancing, ever
changing. This wind blew directly over the lake to them.
There was here and there a little knot, and a few stragglers
a few yards higher up; but they were so few as not to dis-
turb the simplicity, unity, and life of that one busy highway.

4 **Daffodils** See "I Wandered Lonely as a Cloud."